ADVANCE PRAISE FOR

Blood's Will

"*Blood's Will: Speculative Fiction, Existence, and Inquiry of Currere* is a significant contribution—and really, a remarkable piece of work—by one of the nation's most important scholar/authors in the curriculum studies, teacher education, educational policy, and research fields. This work isn't merely a novel that you can't put down, it is a window to so many salient themes that we think about in our work on a daily basis and have few innovative resources to address them in our work as individuals and with students. I believe this book will be read widely and should be taught in our courses."

—Tom Poetter, Professor and Chair of the Department of
Educational Leadership at Miami University

"The whole story is like this long ecstasy trip for women in my demographic."
—Darian Schiffman, Academic Advisor at the University of Maryland, Baltimore County

"As a professor of literacy, I understand the value of narrative and inquiry in shaping our lives and the world around us. Morna McDermott McNulty offers a groundbreaking work of feminist ficto-*currere* that asks its readers the deeper questions about how the stories we tell create identity and the power of the imagination to reshape our worlds. *Blood's Will* weaves together threads of memory, fiction, and existence to create a tapestry of transformative inquiry."
—Nancy Rankie Shelton, Professor at the University of Maryland, Baltimore County

"*Blood's Will* is a speculative fiction in the vampire subgenre that also functions as a philosophical meditation on curriculum inquiry (with particular reference to the autobiographical method now known as *currere*) and dramatizes ontological, epistemological, and axiological questions about human knowledges and understandings of living and dying. It is clearly informed by feminist, counter-heteronormative, and what I would call post-humanist positions. This book is a significant contribution to the literature of curriculum theorizing."
—Noel Gough, Professor Emeritus at La Trobe University

"Not since Madeleine Grumet's *Bitter Milk: Women and Teaching* have I fallen under the spell of a powerful and creative feminist text. Morna McDermott McNulty's *Blood's Will* makes this passage between the public and private worlds for our contemporary times. No doubt, you too will devour this compelling postmodern feminist novel conveying larger life themes through the vampire archetype!"
—Carol Mullen, Professor of Educational Leadership at Virginia Tech

Blood's Will

omplicated Conversation

A Book Series of Curriculum Studies

William F. Pinar
General Editor

Volume 53

The Complicated Conversation series is part of the Peter Lang Education list.
Every volume is peer reviewed and meets
the highest quality standards for content and production.

PETER LANG
New York • Bern • Berlin
Brussels • Vienna • Oxford • Warsaw

Morna McDermott McNulty

Blood's Will

Speculative Fiction, Existence, and Inquiry of *Currere*

PETER LANG

New York • Bern • Berlin
Brussels • Vienna • Oxford • Warsaw

Library of Congress Cataloging-in-Publication Control Number: 2018021041

Bibliographic information published by **Die Deutsche Nationalbibliothek**.
Die Deutsche Nationalbibliothek lists this publication in the "Deutsche
Nationalbibliografie"; detailed bibliographic data are available
on the Internet at http://dnb.d-nb.de/.

ISSN 1534-2816
ISBN 978-1-4331-5766-0 (hardcover)
ISBN 978-1-4331-5767-7 (paperback)
ISBN 978-1-4331-5570-3 (ebook pdf)
ISBN 978-1-4331-5571-0 (epub)
ISBN 978-1-4331-5572-7 (mobi)
DOI 10.3726/b14189

The paper in this book meets the guidelines for permanence and durability
of the Committee on Production Guidelines for Book Longevity
of the Council of Library Resources.

© 2018 Peter Lang Publishing, Inc., New York
29 Broadway, 18th floor, New York, NY 10006
www.peterlang.com

Printed in the United States of America

Dedication

Dedicated to my husband Leonard and my children Molly and Conor.

Written in loving memory of my father Jack McDermott.

This book is also for my friends who inspired me, and encouraged me to never give up: Sue Gilliam, Laura Lewis, Darian Shiffman, and Carmen Hawkins DeCecco.

Table of Contents

Acknowledgements

With a debt of love and gratitude to my dear friends and courageous editors Nancy Rankie Shelton and Tom Poetter. I also have a debt of gratitude to Bill Pinar for his faith in this project.

Introduction

My name is Campbell Cote Phillips. I am the subject writing herself. I am not an educator, nor a curriculum theorist. I am a scholar of Cultural and Women's Studies. I explore the uses of curriculum inquiry as autobiography and narrative as they relate to various curricula in my field which is gender and cultural studies. More importantly, I share the idea that there is a curriculum to each of our lives. What you will be reading in this novel is the curriculum of my life, or, my *currere* (my life journey recalled and examined). As a close friend of mine once said, it is my, "theory for living, my theory for dying" (Daspit, 1999). I have done both, as you will see.

Charting complex and critical associations between the worlds of narrative and memory, the method of *currere* allows one to become more:

> (S)elf conscious about the "strokes" and "lines" etched into the personality by curricular experience...the process in which Pollack was engaged, processes that begin with relinquishing of so-called realism...allow us to see anew and understand anew. (Pinar, 1991, p. 246)

There are four different "stages" when engaged in the journey of *currere*: Recalling the past (regressive), being free of the present (analytical), being able to re-enter the present (synthetical), and gesturing towards what is not yet present (progressive). It is important to note however, that these stages are not considered linear or progressive. Rather, they should be understood as a set of interconnected, rhizomatic (Deleuze & Guattari, 1980) moments that "frame" the complex process of conscious self-actualization.

To be certain, my life has taken some spectacular turns, as you will see in reading my story. You may believe this book to be a work of fiction. It is, in as much as fiction signifies possibility. But what I have written is also true. And truth relies on limitations and finitudes. Which will you, the reader, choose? You shall read more on this subject in the Afterword to my story. But I am getting ahead of myself.

This is a work of autofiction (Doubrovsky, 1977), or fictionalized autobiography—an effort which engages with the *currere* process; what I will refer to here as ficto-*currere*. My narrative blends and blurs the lines between that which is true (or real) with that which is imaginatively constructed. It is a story that belongs to "a new class of memoiristic, autobiographical, and metafictional novels—we can call them autofictions—that jettison the logic of postmodernism in favor of a new position" (Sturgeon, 2014, para. 2). My ficto-*currere* involves themes of death and immortality. I am always thinking of those topics:

> For Daignault, "thinking happens only between suicide and murder … between nihilism and terrorism … to know is to commit murder, to terrorize". Nihilism refers to the abandonment of any attempt to know. It is the attitude which says anything goes or things are what they are. It is to give up, to turn ones ideals into empty fictions or memories, to have no hope. Daignault (1983) calls for us to live in the middle, in spaces that are neither terroristic or nihilistic. (in Pinar, et al, 1995, p. 76)

I have discovered a way to "live in the middle," as you shall see. Sturgeon agrees that, "fiction includes the narratives we tell ourselves, and the stories we're told, on the path between birth and death" (2014, para. 8). Fiction can represent "truth," or fact, in the form of experience. Just as often, as Truth (as hegemonic discourse) has oftentimes (in light of dominant Western history) been exposed to be little more than fiction (Rorty, 1989). I have chosen to write my autobiography as fiction in the 3rd person because the story is more believable as a 3rd person; written as a cool "objectivity." I write about Campbell as if she were someone other than myself. Maybe, she is.

The fiction and the *currere* in my story are re-assembled as a "décollage"; cutting and tearing identities and "truths" to reveal other interpretations. Artist Annette Kunow (2012) describes décollage in language that mirrors the ficto-*currere* writing process: "This wrenching, shredding is pricking under the 'skin'. It destroys leaving wounds. Parts of the hidden painting are diving on the scene with vehemence and make visible these repressed fears and desires" (p.4). This (re) assemblage between self and inquiry in *currere* is "phenomenologically related"

(Pinar, et. al., 1995, p. 414), a form of reflective autobiography that emphasizes, "reciprocity between subjectivity and objectivity in the constitution of experience and meanings" (p. 414).

The lived experience itself is not the story. My journey is incomplete without the retelling of it in the form of this narrative and a four-step process that "includes retelling the story of one's experiences, imagining future possibilities for self-understanding," and "an analysis of the relationships between past, present, and future life history and practice …" (Pinar, 2004, p. 35)

Retelling requires memory. Yet, recollection is incorporeal. Therefore, how might I separate memory from fiction? Or rather, why should I try? When crafted from memory, each of our stories are always part-fiction (Barone, 2007). Here it is then—a *currere* of possibility for life and death, written in my story. Each of us has our own. We also share in one another's as well. In the "Postscript for the next generation" Pinar, et al (1995) write, "Curriculum is an extraordinarily complicated conversation" (p. 848). As such, our lives, as curriculum, are a series of "open-ended, highly personal, and interest-driven events in which persons encounter each other" (p. 848). As a form of self-inquiry, the spiral narrative of *currere* (and four intertwined rhizomatic stages of the journey): what is "not yet," is equal to that "which was," and what "can be" blurs with what "has been." That was my final discovery.

I am not the first to take such a journey. Scholar of speculative fiction and curriculum inquiry, Noel Gough (2010) identifies fiction (and more particularly, speculative fiction) as a form of *currere* and a method of inquiry. I decided to transform my autobiography into autofiction, and then into a 3rd person narrative of speculative fiction; making my own history thus a speculative one, revealing the indeterminacy of my existence. Speculative fiction is fiction that includes themes of fantasy, science fiction, and horror. What some consider to be speculative fiction is quite real in the future to others. We live everyday surrounded by instances of both horror and fantasy, of fear and desire. I mean, whose life doesn't have just a little bit of each of those?

Gough examines the uses of writing-as-process (storytelling as an act of scholarship) by Bram Stoker as he wrote *Dracula* (1897). Naturally, I have some interest in the matter of vampires. Stoker, according to Gough (1996), "privileged writing to such an extent that many characters come to see the production of a manuscript as necessary for their own survival" (p. 260). There is a relationship in Stoker's vampire novel (as well as my own) between inquiry (the search for facts or truth, or at least answers that satisfy a compelling question) and storytelling.

Stoker's relationship to Jon Harker in the story of *Dracula* was one of a writer writing about a character who is writing about himself. We write ourselves into, and out, of existence. Fictional mortality. Those of us in academia know that the phrase "publish or perish" means everything. Some of us perhaps have done both. The (seeming) inevitability of death is nothing new for millions of people every day, people facing old age, terminal illness, or living in hostile war torn environments where death is possible every day. But I have lived most of my existence among the slumbering, comfortable, and seemingly healthy middle-aged, middle-class world. The illusion of immortality leads many of us to take for granted what we have, and to magnify the small problems, until they fog our perception of what matters to begin with. And then, what awaits us after death? I cannot answer that for you, just yet. I may ruin the story.

We might consider this theory for living and for dying—a process for knowledge-creation and meaning-making. What might you see in yourself through my story? Some of you may identify with me, and the journey I have undertaken. As they say in 12-step recovery meetings (Finn has taught me much), "Identify, don't compare, with what you hear."

Gough says, "As the story unfolds, acts of writing are increasingly seen to be essential for the self-preservation of particular individuals, but they eventually assume even greater significance" (1996, p. 260). He continues that, "(O)ur purposes often may be better served by (re)presenting the texts we produce as deliberate fictions rather than as 'factual' narratives 'reflecting all without distortion'" (p. 260).

Fiction is not the opposite of fact, it is the opposite of finitude. But while it is defensible to assert that reality exists beyond texts, much of what we think of as "real" is—and can only be—apprehended through fictional texts. Just as light can be wave and particle, we can acknowledge narrative (as a particle, i.e. a "fact"), but facts in themselves mean little until they are situated, and thus also like light wave, hence the elements of subjectivity. Barone (2000) too, reminds us that in "this reordering, elements of experience are recast into a form that is analogous but does not replicate an actual experience" (p. 138). Memories reflect the past, but as instruments of the present, they are also catalysts for future action.

By now, while reading this Introduction, you may have realized (or have known all along) that I too, am one of the fictional characters of this book, as much as I am (here) an author. This Introduction has become a "true" account of a fictional character (myself-depicted as real) writing her autobiography (as auto-fiction), and re-manufacturing it as speculative fiction. But this Introduction too, is fiction, written by someone else, other than me, Campbell Cote.

The purpose of an Introduction written by a character in the fictional book for which the Introduction is written, to be written as a real author, about an account she claims as non-fiction but has written as a third-person, is to invite the reader to an intertextual engagement with this book. It is, as Gough (2011) puts it, "a narrative experiment" (p. 4), a process by which I might:

Question whether it is possible, at least in principle, to establish inter subjectively reliable distinctions between "fiction" on the one hand and particular constructions of "reality" that we can call "factual" or "truthful" on the other. (p. 4)

I suggest no distinctions are possible expect those forcibly manufactured. As a form of decollage, I attempt the opposite: To scrape away at the veneer, and tear apart these distinctions, to re-assemble my "I" through multiple "eyes" (McDermott, 2011).

I wanted to raise the question: who is the authentic, or essential, author? Therein lies a contingency (and irony—as I am fully aware of my fictionalized existence), which allows for a pragmatic interpretation of the story (Rorty, 1989). I claimed earlier that this novel is a work of auto-fiction, which would suggest that I first would have to be "real," and thus fictionalizing what I called the "real" autobiographical account of my life events (before and after my relationship with Finn). I might argue that this Introduction itself is also the fictional account of an auto-biographical depiction of the other author (McDermott). A fictional auto-fiction. I invite you to read this novel as an act of ficto-*currere*, and enter it as a tesseract. The two share interchangeable qualities: A tesseract is a three-dimensional object. A tesseract is also a four dimensional object—a hyper-cube, unraveled. A hyper cube unravels to a tesseract. Four dimensions unravel to three. A hyper cube is a thing you are not equipped to understand only the tesseract. "We can see the thing unraveled, but not the thing itself" (Garland, 1999, p. 2).

Blood's Will is followed by an academic analysis (see *Afterword*), which further explores intersections between *currere*, inquiry, and speculative fiction. The point is that the novel retains the idea that, "the self is considered a living thing composed of fictions" (Sturgeon, 2014, para. 8). Yet, the analysis involves many plot spoilers, so it must be included in an Afterword, and not before. As a sample of ficto-*currere* based inquiry, like works of auto-fictional research, my story should trouble the "reader's expectation of outcomes" (Leavy, 2017, p. 198); outcomes that accompany fiction by following an anticipated narrative course and "attempt to neatly resolve the troubles in the text" (Watson, in Leavy, 2017, p. 198).

Instead, *currere* explores the rhizomatic and emergent nodal interstices of life—and life creates the fiction, cracking open new intersection of possibilities seeking to trouble expectations. This work of ficto-*currere* breaks the preconceived ideas we hold about reality, and the "master plot" (p. 197) we commonly anticipate in a fictional story. Instead, like Watson (in Leavy, 2017), "I keep the ending open, in order to mirror real life" (p. 197), events as they happened—blurred with my memory of them, and re-created through the writing process. Read. And then, I'll see you, my reader, on the other side.

References

Barone, T. (2000). *Aesthetics, politics, and educational inquiry: Essays and examples.* New York, NY: Peter Lang.

Barone, T. (2007). A return to the gold standard? Questioning the future of narrative construction as educational research. *Qualitative Inquiry, 13*(4), 454–470.

Daignault, J. (1983). Curriculum and action research: An artistic activity in a perverse way. *Journal of Curriculum Theorizing, 5*(3), 4–18.

Daspit, T. (1999). "Nothing died; it just got buried": Theory as exhumation, as duty dance. In M. Morris, M. Doll, & W.F. Pinar (Eds.), *How we work* (pp. 71–78). New York, NY: Peter Lang.

Deleuze, G., & Guattari, F. (1980). *A thousand plateaus.* Minneapolis, MN: University of Minnesota Press.

Doubrovsky, S. (1977). *Fils.* Collection folio. Paris: Gallimard.

Garland, A. (1999). *The tesseract.* New York, NY: Riverhead Books.

Gough, N. (1996). Textual authority in Bram Stoker's *Dracula*; or, what's really at stake in action research? *Educational Action Research, 4*, 257–265.

Gough, N. (1998). Reflections and diffractions: Functions of fiction in curriculum inquiry. In W. F. Pinar (Ed.), *Curriculum: Toward new identities* (pp. 93–128). New York, NY: Routledge.

Gough, N. (2010). Performing imaginative inquiry: Narrative experiments and rhizosemiotic play. In T. W. Nielsen, R. Fitzgerald, & M. Fettes (Eds.), *Imagination in educational theory and practice: A many-sided vision* (pp. 42–60). Newcastle upon Tyne: Cambridge Scholars Publishing.

Kunow, A. (2012). *Décollages.* Retrieved from https://esdsec.co.uk/decollage

Leavy, P. (2017). Fiction-based research. In P. Leavy (Ed.), *Handbook of arts-based research* (pp. 190–202). New York, NY: The Guildford Press.

McDermott, M. (2011). Curriculum of the eye/I. *Journal of Curriculum Theorizing, 27*(2), 130–144.

Pinar, W. F. (1991). The white cockatoo: Images of abstract expressionism in curriculum theory. In G. Willis & W. H. Schubert (Eds.), *Reflections from the heart of educational inquiry: Understanding curriculum and teaching through the arts* (pp. 245–249). Albany, NY: State University of New York Press.

Pinar, W. F., Reynolds, P.M., Slattery, P. & Taubman, P.M. (1995). Understanding curriculum: A post script for a new generation. In W. F. Pinar, W. M. Reynolds, P. Slattery, & P. M. Taubman (Eds.), *Understanding curriculum: An introduction to the study of historical and contemporary curriculum discourses* (pp. 847–868). New York, NY: Peter Lang.

Pinar, W. F. (2004). *What is curriculum theory?* New York, NY: Routledge.

Rorty, R. (1989). *Contingency, irony, and solidarity.* Cambridge, MA: Cambridge University Press.

Sturgeon, J. (2014). The death of the postmodern novel and the rise of autofiction. Retrieved from http://flavorwire.com/496570/2014-the-death-of-the-postmodern-novel-and-therise-of autofiction

CHAPTER ONE

Baltimore, 2011

Plowing her way through the maze of barren trees, stumps, and the occasional sign posts, Campbell Cote Phillips thought, *It isn't in having everything that I achieve happiness. It isn't in gaining possible immortality that I might feel free.* She listened to the wheels whisper quietly over the thick snow. Looking at the dark sky that glittered with a waterfall of snowflakes she decided, *It's in finding that one other person, whether a friend or a lover, it does not matter, to whom we feel bound. Some people spend their whole lives actively moving from person to person, looking for that feeling, sometimes leaving behind a wake of dead and broken families and relationships. However, if you're patient enough, those opportunities will find you. The most we can do is choose how to respond to these situations as they appear.*

Craning her head backward toward Ellis' car seat, she wondered if she could imagine her life any other way than the path she had chosen. It was then that the car began to slide. Through the darkness and the snow, Campbell could make out the image of a large oak tree looming in front of them and getting closer. There would be no avoiding it. Worse yet, at the angle the car was sliding, it seemed as if the side of the back seat holding her son Ellis would have the first impact. Without thinking, Campbell unclutched the steering wheel and unlocked her seat belt. Arching her body toward the back seat, she reached wildly to protect Ellis' body. Her legs and knees were lodged beneath the steering column. She braced for impact.

The impact of what Campbell's mind sensed would be an impending car crash in her dream woke her with a great force. The house was still and silent, blue morning light creeping in through the window. The familiar surroundings of her daffodil yellow bedroom, and her worn blue duvet soothed her nerves and slowed her heart to a regular rhythm. *Jesus, that felt real*, she thought. But there was no time to examine the dream any further. Real life was again settling in at 6:30 a.m., as it did every morning. And reality has no time for other possibilities. Unless, sometimes, it does.

Even after a hot shower, the memory of her early morning dream haunted her. There was a residue of panic pulsing in her brain. Campbell lifted her head from the bathroom sink and gazed at the reflection of her tired blue eyes. She mused, *There is no greater frustration than knowing you have a destiny, but not knowing what that destiny is*. This musing caused her to pause and look, but only for a moment. Her thought was interrupted by the faint call from her son Ellis, "Mom, I'm thirsty." This was not as much a demand as it was a reminder, a part of their morning routine. *It is my destiny to get milk, in the blue dinosaur cup*, she laughed to herself.

Campbell often found that these riddle-like musings broke into her daily consciousness. They would bounce around inside her mind in the same way that commercial jingles bounce around other people's heads. But for Campbell such philosophical considerations were not an intrusion. They were a welcome juxtaposition to the blunt reminders of her life as a middle aged, married working mother of two.

Somehow, unanswerable, profound questions softened the edges of the noise of reality. There was a time, it seemed so long ago, another lifetime really, when such thoughts were of the utmost importance; back when she had come out of her Ph.D. program like a rock star, ready to shake the academic world with groundbreaking ways of seeing and thinking about Cultural Studies. But soon after, she jumped track to get married and have children. She wanted a family as much as she had wanted a life of the philosopher king. Since she could not live two lives simultaneously, she had to choose. And so the former gave way to the latter. *At least for now*, she often reminded herself. *In time, the pendulum will swing back*. There were regrets for having settled for a position as Assistant (now Associate) Professor of Cultural Studies at Eastern University where she could teach, conduct the bare minimum of publishing, and focus on raising her children.

The TV was playing some hypnotic, annoying theme-song of Ellis's favorite cartoon. This meant Campbell had 15 minutes before the remainder of the morning frenzy began: making breakfast, loading the dishes, dressing the kids for school, packing her work materials, dropping the kids at school, and making the race before traffic hit the Baltimore beltway. If she was lucky she might get to work early enough to catch up with yesterday's emails about the meeting she had missed. As usual, her husband Brent had gotten up at 5:30 a.m. and was showered and out of the house before anyone else was awake. The morning battle was hers to fight.

When Campbell was a teenager, defined by black berets, poetry, punk, and angst, she believed that she had something important to do. But today, the most important thing was to remember to bring a snack in for Ellis' kindergarten: orange slices and pretzels. She didn't want the other mothers to judge her by the quality of the snack she brought in for their children. This was how her self-worth had come to be measured.

The children were rushed through the motions of picking out clothes, making sure teeth were brushed, and hair was combed. The 1950s brick rancher had received few improvements over the years since she and Brent had purchased it, and it couldn't hide the wear and tear of small children. Socks were strewn in corners, magic markers, and soiled fingerprints streaked the dining room wall, door trims were dented and scratched, and breakfast plates were scattered on the kitchen table. Campbell situated herself on the stair with Caroline. She began wondering, *Free will ... is that really a matter of fate disguised as choice?* She pulled Caroline's hair back, too tight apparently. Caroline jerked her head with a yowl of complaint. Campbell sighed apologetically. "Sorry, sweet pea." Caroline recoiled from the grooming, and slunk upstairs for her sweater. Drawn back to full consciousness, Campbell added, "Caroline, don't forget your book on Ancient Egypt today! It's on the bottom step!"

Campbell slipped back into musing. *Shoes, she thought. It's raining so I don't want the pumps. Cowboy boots are always good. They command respect in the classroom.* Then aloud she said, "Caroline, did you get that book? Third grade is a time to act responsibly you know!"

Campbell did one last glance in the mirror, reminded of how age had slowly and perceptibly crept up on her once cute (but never beautiful) looks, and how it had drained them into middle-aged attractiveness. "I need my roots done," she whispered, gingerly touching the mid-section of her scalp. Today, like the divide between hair roots and ends, a line which had been growing in Campbell's life, would finally rise to the surface, and that nagging sense of destiny would begin to reveal itself. Campbell snapped off the light. The messy house appeared worse in the dimness of the rainy day. Amazing how light makes everything better, she reflected. *I'll get to all this tonight when I get home,* she promised herself, as if to assure herself that her life wasn't slipping through her fingers. After a battle with Ellis over whether or not he should wear his raincoat, Campbell got both children in the car, started the engine, and turned on the wipers. She looked in the rearview mirror. Destiny rang in her consciousness with reverence.

CHAPTER TWO

Baltimore, 1976

The late November sky over Baltimore city was a steel grey as the winds quickened and tiny snowflakes flurried one by one, randomly coasting on the sharp breeze. Finn knew the snow would become heavier within the hour, and he would have to move fast if he was going to get a bed at the shelter tonight. Even on warmer days when park benches and building alcoves were suitable for sleep, the shelter on Greenmount Avenue always had a line around the corner. His migration to Baltimore from Kentucky had been a culture shock, even for someone in a perpetual haze of alcohol-induced hallucinations and paranoia. But over the years he had developed a pattern of survival, much of it learned from his homeless peers, which enabled him to move in the transitory fashion that suited him. The sidewalks of North Avenue had grown empty, except for a few holiday shoppers, and there were business people rushing home early. Finn realized only now that today was Thanksgiving.

Finn noticed a familiar figure standing on the corner. "Hey, Jesse," he called out. A trail of steam from his breath was followed by the odor of stale beer. Jesse looked over his shoulder, nodded at Finn, and gestured with his head that Finn should follow him. Pushing his hands into the pockets of his over-sized jacket, Finn trotted to catch up.

"Hey, man it is friggin' freezing out here. Let's roll. The Greenmount center is gonna be full before we get there."

Jesse pulled on a half lit cigarette, and thought before responding. "Nah. Man, I ain't goin' there. Forget that. There's a new place opened like a week ago. I hear it's clean with some good food."

"Oh yeah?" Finn paused. "They got room for me, ya think?" He hid the anxiousness in his voice. Knowing where he would sleep tonight would be a relief.

"Yeah," Jesse mouthed, expressionless. His weathered complexion was dotted with scars and facial hair. It was hard to believe he was only 30 years old, almost the same age as Finn. Years of alcoholism and homelessness made a man of thirty appear to be 50, inside and out.

That'll be me soon, Finn thought. They walked in silence for about three blocks.

Finn had known Jesse for about a year. Despite what Finn used to assume to be the nature of homeless people, it seemed that most of the "bums" he had met since he stepped off the bus in Penn Station tended to stay in one place. This was true, he believed, at least for the ones who were on the street due to a life of drugs or alcohol, like himself. But the older men, the ones who were sick or disabled, or the young mothers—they were like salmon swimming upstream, trying desperately to move up or out in any direction. Whereas guys like himself were the street "rats"—homeless youth who, if they didn't die first, simply grew into homeless adults with addiction problems. They didn't seem to want to go anywhere, or know how.

As they reached the intersection of St. Paul and Lafayette Street, Jesse took another cigarette out of his pocket. "Smoke?" he asked, offering the crumpled Newport to Finn. *They are also more generous than one would assume*, Finn thought.

"Yeah, thanks."

He placed the bent cigarette into the corner of his mouth. A young man wearing a thick woven hat with ear flaps and thick rimmed glasses strode by pushing a red bicycle.

"Yo, 'scuse me dude, you gotta light?" Finn reached his thumb and finger out with the cigarette between them. The young man deftly maneuvered an inch beyond Finn's outstretched arm, grazed the sidewalk curb, wobbled for a moment, and then moved swiftly past them as if he were avoiding a large stone or garbage can blocking the way. Jesse's gaze followed the man for a few moments, and then he muttered, "Shit, man, we're invisible, you know that."

"Hold on," Finn prompted. "I think I got matches here in my pocket." He drew up a small fist full of jumbled items including two pennies, a dime, a lint ball, a gum wrapper, a small gold charm, and a pack of matches that read Blue Moon on the cover with two dry matches left snuggled under the flap. Hoping to find a dryer place, they stepped into the under hang of a closed art gallery called Glassblowers International. Finn struck the first match, which emitted a quick bright flame and then immediately went out.

"Damn" he muttered and pulled out the last match.

"Hey, what was that gold thing in your pocket?" Jesse asked, watching as Finn lit the remaining match. The sky was now a pervasive grey that made it seem later in the day than it really was. Jesse could see the soft glow of Finn's brown eyes looking up at him warily as he brought the match to the cigarette pursed between his lips. After pulling enough air through the cigarette to create the warm orange glow at its tip, he took it from his mouth.

"It's a charm," Finn replied finally. He blew a swirl of smoke between his cracked lips. He reminded Jesse, "Let's go, man. What the hell. Where are we goin' anyway? Where is this place?" Then he started walking with Jesse following a step behind.

"Just a few blocks west, and then a right turn on Brentwood Avenue. It ain't far." Jesse asked again looking toward Finn's pocket, "So what was that shiny thing? Is it worth anything? You know, could you sell it for a fifth or somethin'?"

Finn knew where this conversation was leading. Where all things led: the next drink.

"No, it ain't for sale."

Resigned to giving Jesse an explanation, Finn pulled the charm back out. The gold glimmered in the lamp-light. Finn said, "It's a charm of St. Jude. It was my sister's. She used to have a charm necklace, you know, like when she was eight, for her First Communion. Before I left home she gave it to me."

Knowing he was perhaps sharing too much, he added, "St. Jude is the patron saint of lost causes. I guess Jenna knew that eventually I would end up like this and would need all the help I could get."

After gazing at the charm for another few moments he shoved it back into his jeans pocket.

"Huh," Jesse said. "Sentimental, I get it. I used to have a watch that belonged to my old man. I stole it from him actually." He laughed, but Finn's face didn't change. Uncomfortable silences were something Jesse did not like.

"Then I lost it in a poker game like two years ago. Shit, that sucked." He chuckled a little. "Thought I had that hand, a full house. But the other guy had a royal flush. I tried to grab the watch and run, but these big ass boys caught me and beat the shit out of me. Took the watch out of my hand and threw me out of the club."

"Tough luck," Finn replied.

"Yeah. Hard times in Pig Town. But those were some good times, too. Growing up. Before my old man died."

They walked in silence past another few row houses. "You originally from around here?" Jesse inquired.

"Been here 'bout seven years now I guess. Wandered around the East Coast for a year before that." The truth was that Finn had no real sense of how much time had passed. It was all a blurry nightmare. He added, "I'm from Kentucky coal country originally. Born and raised. 'Til I took off, that is." This genuine interest gave Finn an ill sort of feeling in his head. Jesse pressed further.

"So you talk to your sister at all?"

"No," Finn said, getting annoyed by the intimacy of Jesse's questions. Jesse was a friend, but Finn didn't reveal much of anything about himself to anyone. It was just easier that way.

Finn was grateful when they turned the corner at Brentwood Avenue and saw a sign with white and gold lettering hanging over a mid-century grey stone row house that read New Beginnings. They had to wait behind a group of old men, one with a shopping cart. A tall imposing man with dark almond skin and silver framed spectacles stood at the front of the line wielding a clipboard and pen. He looked up over his half rim glasses and made a mental count of how many men were standing in line. His eyes rested on Finn and Jesse for a length of time that made Finn uncomfortable. He turned back to the clipboard and scribbled something down. *What the hell is he so curious about?* Finn wondered. Knowing there would be a wait before they could get inside, Finn made a cup with his hands and blew warm air into them. He wanted to avoid any further conversation with Jesse. Finn turned toward the plate glass window in front of the shelter. He was immediately taken aback and braced himself to keep from toppling over. He caught sight of his own reflection.

"Holy crap," he murmured.

The reflection of Finn in this slightly warped window revealed a man about six feet tall, with honey-red dark blond hair so matted and dirty it dangled in chunks across his shoulders. His nose, mouth, and chin were almost completely invisible, buried underneath a moss of dark blond stubble that stretched down his throat and disappeared into a once white (now greyish) fisherman's knit sweater unthreaded around the neck. A few battle scars noted where the side of his face should be. Finn hadn't looked at himself in weeks. His grooming consisted mostly of sneaking into gas station bathrooms, or washing his face and hands in the fountain on Cathedral Avenue. Even the shelter he had previously frequented lacked mirrors in the bathroom. A piece of plywood replaced the mirrors.

After regaining his composure, Finn looked more closely. Beneath the layers of sweaters, denim, and coats, he could tell that he had lost at least twenty pounds. Before his alcoholism had taken control, over 10 years ago when he was still living in Kentucky, Finn weighed in at a healthy 180 pounds, which, for his height he carried well. His once broad shoulders were now hunched over, not just from the cold, and his eyelids sunk heavy over his brown eyes. Back in his early teens he had been somewhat of a heartthrob among the local high school girls. His attractive and dynamic personality usually won over parents and teachers, too. All the accolades and reinforcements were never enough to fill the hole in his soul. But that was a lifetime ago. His focus was interrupted by a nudge on the shoulder from Jesse.

"Come on man, we're next. Let's roll."

Keeping attention on his own self-reflection, Finn concluded, *My god, I'm already dead.*

CHAPTER THREE

Baltimore, 1976

Just a few miles from where Finn was shuffling his way through the doors of New Beginnings, Mrs. Elizabeth Cote was locking the ornamental wooden door on her family's late Victorian style house in the fashionable neighborhood of Roland Park. Satisfied that it was securely locked, she briskly wet her thumb between her lips. She brought it down sharply on her 6 year-old daughter's right cheek to clear away smudges she might have missed.

"Stop fidgeting with your dress, Campbell," she snipped, and her daughter dutifully placed her hands by her side. Her woolen dress made Campbell feel hot and itchy. The Peter Pan lace collar gnawed at her neck, but she dreaded her mother's reprimands more than the discomfort of the dress. She looked down to admire the way her patent leather black shoes reflected the light. Mr. William Cote pulled the wood-paneled station wagon up to the curb.

"Come along, Campbell," said Elizabeth with less agitation in her voice. "We don't want to be late." William Cote got out of the driver's seat and strolled around to open the back door. Campbell climbed in.

"I don't know why you dressed her like that, Libby. For god's sake, we're going to help in a soup kitchen, not attend the Queen's ball."

Elizabeth's lips tensed into a rigid line as he spoke. She pulled the seat belt across Campbell's lap and glared at her husband.

"Bill, I think it's important we look our best, don't you? It is Thanksgiving after all."

She closed the door without saying a word to Campbell. From the side window, all Campbell could see was the side of her mother's black lamb's wool coat and floral scarf draped along the seam of dark blue buttons. *They were shiny,* she thought, *just like her shoes.* She could hear her parents speaking sharply to each other. But not understanding the nature of her parents' conversation, she moved her attention back to her shoes, the only aspect of her outfit she liked.

"She would be dressed appropriately if we were headed to my cousin's in Annapolis tonight instead of to this absurd project you volunteered us for!" her mother argued. "Without discussing it with me first, I might add!"

William sighed. "I told you, Libby. We agreed at the dental clinic that we would help out this year with the new shelter that was being opened. Charlie takes a few free dental patients every month as a form of service to the community. He put this together. What do you want me to do? Be the only dentist in the group to say no? Everyone else from that office will be bringing their families, too."

"All the more reason to have Campbell dressed appropriately," her mother retorted triumphantly. "We want her to look like she's there to volunteer, not like she lives there!"

Elizabeth always made sure her daughter looked her best, particularly after Campbell started kindergarten. Campbell went to her half day morning program at the local Catholic school in a freshly washed and pressed white shirt and kilt skirt. Every morning her long blond hair was braided, so much so it often gave Campbell a headache. She would always try to discreetly loosen the braids once she was inside the classroom and outside the purview of her mother's sight. Campbell wouldn't understand until 20 years later that much of Elizabeth's obsession with her appearance emanated from her own misdirected frustrations.

Elizabeth had met William Cote only a few weeks after she had crossed the stage graduating summa cum laude from Columbia Teacher's College. Even in the midst of the women's movement washing over the nation, in the social climate where Elizabeth was raised, most women (if they worked at all) sought traditional "women's work" such as teaching or nursing. Elizabeth went to school to become a teacher, bright-eyed and eager to change the world. But, being young and romantic, she became smitten with William. He was an aspiring dental student whom she had met at a college social. Somehow her dreams of changing the world were quietly displaced by wedding plans, gift registries at Bloomingdales, and "nesting" for her new home in Baltimore where she and William would soon start a family.

Elizabeth had come from an upper middle class family where once married, a woman's place was at home. She did not want her family to appear financially insecure by holding down her own job. Campbell came a mere 18 months after they were married. Having a baby brought relief to Elizabeth who could now whole-heartedly throw her mental and physical energies into something that demanded real effort. She found much to her surprise that she enjoyed the commitment and relentless energy of caring for a baby: breast-feeding, washing diapers, preparing nicely cooked meals to be ready by five, keeping up with laundry, taking Campbell to play in the park, and keeping a clean house. At the age of six Campbell didn't have the memory to recall her mother's former sense of well-being, though she half-consciously knew that her mother hadn't always been as sad and angry as she had been lately.

Campbell couldn't know that now that she was beginning school her mother's short-lived feelings of contentment were coming to an end. Campbell's absence for those three hours in kindergarten each morning were a sign of things to come for Elizabeth. Waves of fear and emptiness rushed through Elizabeth as she moved through the vacant spaces of the house. Her daughter would begin to occupy less and less of Elizabeth's life as she grew older. *What now?* Elizabeth would wonder. She and Bill tried for a second child but a second pregnancy never occurred. And working while raising her young daughter was not an option in her mind

The car crept through the snowy side streets wet with the sound of slosh-ing tires and crushing ice. They stopped frequently for red lights and pedestrians. Campbell looked with the awe that only a child can have at the grand decorations and twinkling lights marking the beginning of the holiday season. *I like the pink ones the best*, Campbell thought to herself, gazing at a brick row house lined at the eaves with tiny purple, red, blue, green, yellow and pink blinking lights.

"Charlie's going to meet us at the door," William remarked to Elizabeth with a tone of consolation. "I'll let you and Campbell out in front and go find parking so you don't have to walk."

"I wouldn't be surprised if our car gets stolen," Elizabeth huffed. "Leaving it over there, in that neighborhood. And where am I supposed to leave my purse?"

She pulled down the mirror and ran her pinky across her lower lip to correct any residual lipstick, then snapped the mirror up. Campbell wondered what her mother meant by "that neighborhood." She could tell from the way her mother said the word that "there" wasn't something good, but she couldn't figure out how "there" was different than any other "there" she had been to.

Still gazing out the window, assessing each home's holiday showcase, she asked, "Mommy? Where are we going?"

Before Elizabeth could answer her father interjected, "We're going to help people who don't have a home to celebrate Thanksgiving, honey." Campbell loved the sound of her father's voice. It was soothing and wavy compared to her mother's choppy way of speaking to her.

"Why don't they have a home?" Campbell asked in a distant sort of way. She was seeking out other pink Christmas lights as the houses and trees blurred past her window.

William sighed and paused. "It's hard to explain sweetie, but it's important that you learn the value of helping others."

Although he was a soft spoken and easy going father, William was also a remote person. When playing ball in their trim backyard, or having tea parties upstairs in her bedroom, he always seemed to be somewhere else at the same time. The car finally stopped and William shifted into park. He got out, smiled and said hello to someone Campbell didn't recognize and then reached to open Campbell's door. Elizabeth escorted Campbell through the entrance to a building that had a white sign with gold lettering.

The room smelled like smoke, musty books, and other odors Campbell couldn't identify but decided she really didn't like. The entrance was crammed with people. Campbell couldn't really see their faces but alerted her attention to their clothes which she could see from her short height. She observed that people here weren't wearing blue wool dresses or lace or anything else that was familiar to her. There was a lot of denim, worn and faded. She saw a man draped in a red sleeping bag that reminded her of when she and her friend George played Superman using the quilt from her bed. *Is it a game that they're playing?* she wondered. Elizabeth grasped her hand and pulled her into the next room where Campbell was relieved that she could see more faces.

In the corner of the main room, men were seated on a brown and green striped couch watching television. Only a few of them noticed as Elizabeth and Campbell passed by. Elizabeth averted her eyes, but Campbell looked directly at one older man with a long beard and watery grey eyes. She smiled and lifted her free hand to wave, bending her fingers in a secretive way that only he would notice. He winked and beamed a smile back at her. She giggled quietly under her breath, then noticed in amazement that he had no teeth. She looked up, tugged at her mother's coat, and said sadly, "Mommy. That man has no teeth!"

"Keep moving, Campbell," Elizabeth urged.

Campbell turned to the old man and smiled. To her relief, he was smiling back at her. She twisted the red bows at the ends of her braids to see if they were still tied, then turned to face forward. Right before her mother yanked her into the kitchen, Campbell saw Finn.

CHAPTER FOUR

Baltimore, 2011

Before heading into their monthly faculty meeting Campbell hurried to get another cup of coffee from the café. She wondered if it was possible to live on caffeine, nicotine, and Luna bars. She saw two colleagues waiting at the elevator and gave a weak smile.

"How are you?" Roger asked. It was the obligatory question.

"Oh, you know" she sighed, "Halfway through the semester and no end in sight." She feigned exhaustion.

This was all routine, from some imaginary script they knew by heart; no one ever talked about anything real. *I just want to scream*, she thought. *Really, you want to know how I am ... Roger? I am bored! I feel like I am at this dead end in my career. My students are idiots and whiners. I can't remember the last time I wrote or did anything that had genuine worth. And I do it all to jump through the tenure hoops like a trained seal just to keep my job so I can pay my mortgage.*

The doors to the elevator opened with a whoosh. Roger gestured politely so that Campbell could enter first. "Ladies first," he said and smiled. She smiled back. Wishing she could push the STOP button and pin Roger to an elevator wall, what she wanted to say was: "To hell with 'ladies first' you arrogant prick."

And another thing, Roger, she thought as they moved past the third and second floors, *We all know you flirt with your female students. Like we don't notice that? Men … What are you all? Just a bunch of children with size ten shoes? You should have dinner with my husband sometime; you would have a lot to talk about! You're all so polite and politically correct on the outside and perverse man-children on the inside. It's hard enough caring for my two real kids, but I'll bet your wife has to fold your laundry, too! And make sure food is in the refrigerator, and the house is cleaned, and the kids are vaccinated on time because you don't lift a finger to do it. Then late at night when all of your wife's work is finally done, and the kids are asleep, that is at least until 2:00 am when one of them wakes her up for a glass of water or something, you expect her to get into some frilly little pair of naughty panties and do a dance for you. And all she wants is a hot bath, tasty food, and a good book. She probably hates you for this and you're too self-absorbed to notice.*

She knew she was thinking about Brent, but Roger just seemed like all the rest of them, so the description applied to him as well. The elevator "ding" sounded on the first floor and the doors opened. Campbell smiled at Roger saying, "See you in a few minutes!" and hurried off.

By the time she had made it through the line at the café Campbell was a few minutes late for the faculty meeting. She tiptoed in as quietly as possible. But naturally all heads turned when the door clicked open and shut. Campbell had stopped caring about what people at work thought of her a long time ago. Pretending to have a modicum of regret for being late, she made eye contact with some people sitting closest to the door and rolled her eyes as if to say, "Couldn't be helped … what a hectic day I'm having." The dean was filling everyone in on recent updates about program changes.

"As you know, Mike Hughes is out again on emergency medical leave," Dean Robart said. He glanced at Campbell lest she think her tardiness had gone unnoticed. *Kiss my ass,* she thought.

He continued, "The cancer seems to have come back." Several faculty broke out in murmurs of concern. After a pause he added, "So we found a replacement for him until he's back on his feet. Since we're mid-semester we had to find someone quickly to take over his popular culture classes. It wasn't easy!"

"Mike's part of our panel presentation, which is coming up in a few weeks!" Campbell said to Sandy under her breath. She felt guilty about her selfish reaction to the news, but it was true. How would they complete their panel at the convention without Mike's work?

Jerry Bates, a senior scholar with thinning grey hair, spectacles, and a tweed jacket raised his hand and spoke out, "Where is he from? Is he qualified?" Now bored with the conversation Campbell considered what a total cliché Jerry Bates was.

"Yes," replied Dean Robarts in a flat tone. He was prepared for the challenge from Jerry who took it upon himself to monitor and challenge everything that happened in their department.

"Dr. Finn McGinnis is a local scholar. He did his Ph.D. at University of Baltimore. We're lucky to find him so last minute like this," Dean Robart said in a tone loud enough to regain everyone's focus. At hearing the name, Dr. Finn McGinnis, Campbell snapped back to attention.

"I've heard of him already!" she whispered emphatically to Sandy, who was trying hard not to pay attention to Campbell's distractions. Sandy was dressed impeccably regardless of the circumstance as always. With her glowing almond colored skin, short black hair, and deep brown eyes, no one would have guessed Sandy's age. Sandy and Campbell had become like sisters over the last decade, working together. Sandy had been on the search committee for Campbell's position and the two bonded immediately over feminist theory. In the absence of any sisters or a mother, Sandy was the closest thing to a maternal bond Campbell had.

Just an hour earlier, while wrapping up her freshman seminar, Campbell overheard several of her students in the front row murmuring about the "cool new professor who had a class on Vampires." She needed to make sure she heard them correctly. "Vampires?" she asked incredulously.

"Yes! It's a cultural studies course. His name is Dr. McGinnis. He's soooo amazing," crooned Suzanne, the girl with the long black hair. "And super sexy to boot!"

Campbell mocked them silently, shaking her head.

Campbell now turned to Sandy who was doing her best to feign attention to the dean. "Do you think he'll fill in for Mike at the conference?" Campbell asked.

"Shhh …" replied Sandy. "I don't know. Maybe. You'll have to meet him and find out." She adjusted the brightly colored silk scarf around her neck which caught itself on one of her long silver earrings and she yanked at it gingerly. More affectionately she asked, "Are you and Brent coming to our holiday party? You better bring the kids! Charles is making his famous oatmeal cookies. Did the kids have a fun Halloween?"

Trying her best to be compliant, Campbell simply nodded "yes."

The rest of the meeting continued in a drone for Campbell. She was pre-occupied with getting home to fix dinner, help the kids with their homework, and now this new information about Dr. McGinnis. Something about him rested heavy in her psyche but she couldn't imagine why.

Concerned with getting home before the traffic ramped up, Campbell scurried out without talking to anyone. She rounded the corner near the parking lot. The sun was setting and dusk had taken over. Most students and faculty were heading home so just a few people remained around campus for the evening classes. Directly in front of her, about twenty yards away, heading in her direction loomed a 6 foot figure of a man with broad shoulders in a Carhartt jacket, carrying a leather satchel across his shoulder. Feeling some strange compulsion, Campbell gazed into his face. He appeared to be thirty-something. Because of the washed out yellow of the street lighting, she tried but failed to discern his facial features very well. She could see his hair pulled back into a blunt shoulder-length ponytail. She tried, but she couldn't tell the color of his eyes. As she passed he stared at her and she felt this strange gravitational pull, like a swimmer in a rip tide, toward him. Something about the way he looked into her eyes made her feel light headed. He didn't smile, yet he wasn't cold. He seemed like an overpowering mirage to her.

I know you, she thought. But she couldn't understand how or why.

Then, just like that, he passed her by without saying a word. Campbell had to regain her breathing as it seemed to stop for a few seconds. *Who, or what, the hell was that?* she asked herself. On the drive she smoked her cigarette in silence, musing over the "incident" with this handsome stranger. She replayed the 20 second moment, and each time it felt more delicious.

Two hours later, after tucking her children into bed, Campbell padded down the stairs to find Brent watching a football game in the family room. As she walked in he glanced up then turned his head back to the television screen. In an attempt to get his attention, she asked, "Who's playing?"

"Ravens and the Steelers. Supposed to be a tight game."

Then he leaped off the couch and shouted at the TV, "Come on, what the hell was that?"

Campbell realized that engaging him in conversation right now was going to fail. The game was too intense, and Brent was too passionate about football to give up watching this game for a chat with his wife. She felt the slow death of something within her as she walked back upstairs to load dishes into the dishwasher. Campbell knew that some un-namable element was about to crack open and a vast chasm would emerge and perhaps swallow her up whole.

By 11:00 p.m. they were both in bed. Campbell rolled a sweet lilac smelling hand lotion across her dried fingers and knuckles, and pulled herself under the flowered duvet cover. Brent was reading papers for work. His mood seemed more available. He lowered the papers, and looked at Campbell and smiled with genuine affection. She liked the way his light brown hair was now, the way it grew out when he needed a haircut. Frazzled and sweet. He had kept his lean and lanky mass into middle age.

"What?" she asked smiling back. "Nothing," he replied sweetly. He was, after all, a pretty good guy. Not perfect, but then again what husband was?

"I need to begin getting ready for my trip to the Cultural Studies conference," she said. "I have to leave in three weeks. The worst part is that Mike won't be coming because he's on medical leave now and I have no idea who this guy is who's taking his place or if he's even coming to sit in on our panel presentation."

Brent tried to appear as if he was listening. The truth was he only half comprehended most of what Campbell was referring to when she talked about her work.

"Oh, and don't forget that I work late tomorrow," she continued, "Kim will be here when you get home and you'll have to do bedtime."

"That's fine. We're almost done with the Bergman job, so tomorrow won't keep me late. But I may have to meet Scott at the office on Saturday for a few hours to go over some numbers."

She was used to his long hours and weekend absences. She never thought for a moment that he had a girlfriend or anything like that. First of all, it wasn't Brent's style. He was physically and mentally checked out oftentimes but he had never been a "player." Before Campbell, there had been two girlfriends, one in high school and one in college, both to whom he had stayed faithful. The "other woman" was his job. Brent had been a computer engineer for Lockheed Martin since he graduated college, almost 20 years ago. Now his position as a senior analyst afforded his family a comfortable upper middle class lifestyle. It was his "ordinariness," his predictability, and his stability that had attracted Campbell when they started dating 11 years ago.

She leaned over to kiss him gently and said, "Good night, I love you," as was their bedtime ritual. It crossed her mind that she wasn't sure if she loved this man she had married and had children with anymore. But as he clicked out the light and rolled over she forced herself to review all the things she was grateful for, and she fell asleep before she could finish counting.

CHAPTER FIVE

Baltimore, 1976

The New Beginnings shelter for the homeless had become the focus of many people wishing to help others "in need." It was the darling project of Mayor William Shaefer and received a great deal of publicity in the local news. Mrs. Cote's initial anxiety faded as she and Campbell entered the kitchen where they encountered a dozen other suburban housewives donning colorful aprons to protect their holiday dresses and skirts. From all appearances they might have been attending a ladies' hospital auxiliary or a church fundraiser. Once surrounded by the ease of each other's presence, it was if they forgot where they were and chattered on easily about their children and the upcoming holidays. They moved in chaotic harmony, passing dishes from the stove to the kitchen pass-through, stacking paper plates, and arranging forks and knives with precision. Campbell noticed that her mother's dour mood now became light. In a high pitched tone, Elizabeth greeted her friends.

"Why hello, Margerie!" Elizabeth rushed over to give a hug to a plush woman draped in a silk red wrap dress. The woman's large earrings shaped liked Christmas trees dangled as she reached to embrace her Elizabeth. She turned to Campbell and beamed. "My goodness, Elizabeth! How she's grown! How are you Campbell?"

Campbell replied in a meek voice, "Fine, ma'am."

This shift in mood irritated Campbell. This was a tone of voice Elizabeth reserved for her friends when they were out in public, and Campbell wondered why her mother didn't sound this happy when they were at home. She longed to hear her mother use that bubbly tone with her. Campbell also realized that at this moment her mother was fully absorbed in her social agenda so she was free to explore. Campbell softly unwrapped herself from her mother's protective grasp.

"Campbell, honey," Elizabeth said looking behind her. *There was that honey sweet tone again* Campbell thought. "Stay in the kitchen where I can see you, please."

Campbell nodded in agreement, and when her mother turned away she began walking toward the large community room. The mood and the tempo seemed much calmer out there and she felt a small wave of relief. The room was crowded with people, mostly men who were old by Campbell's standards. By varying degrees, they all had grey hair, long beards, and "funny" clothes. Most of them sat without speaking, watching the black and white TV as it flickered images of a cowboy riding a horse. Others stared at nothing. A tall dark skinned man with short greying hair and silver spectacles holding a clip board surveyed the room from the corner. Campbell looked across the room hoping to find the kindly faced man with no teeth, but he was gone. She wrinkled her forehead in sadness.

Then, she saw the man she had seen right before her mother dragged her into the kitchen. Campbell thought this man seemed a little different than the others. He was younger, and Campbell sensed a warmth about him. He seemed nice, just like the man with no teeth. He was perched on the edge of the couch talking with no one in particular. There was sadness and anxiousness in his brown eyes, a look she had seen in her mother's face when her mother didn't know she was watching.

Finn was missing his sister at this moment and cursing Jesse for having brought the subject up while they were walking here. Finn felt a pair of eyes on him. He looked over and saw Campbell gazing at him with friendly curiosity. This young girl seemed to be peering right through him. No liquor was allowed in New Beginnings so Finn knew there was no way to drown out the pangs of nostalgia. Jenna was not much older than this little girl when he said good bye to her. Finn didn't dwell too much in the realm of remorse or regret—knowing that such thoughts were almost a suicidal luxury for alcoholics. But Campbell's presence seemed to ask, "Why did you leave her?"

Finn saw the image of Jenna, a mere eight years old, standing before him with hands on her hips, and her long brown hair twisted in thick unbridled strands down her back. Her bare feet planted on the pavement as if she would block him if he tried to run. Her wide almond eyes had a look of pain and anger. "Daddy says you cain't come home 'till ya clean up," she said trying to sound adult and official. Finn sat there on the ground grateful that his back was supported by the cement girders under the bridge or he would have fallen over in a drunken stupor. He pulled the bottle of Jack Daniels to his mouth and took a deep drink, wiped his mouth with the side of his flannel shirt sleeve, and studied Jenna carefully.

Thank God she won't end up like me, he thought. *Better I'm gone.* Being known as Finn's sister provoked stares and whispers from the townspeople. They looked on Jenna with a pity that enraged Finn.

Once he had been known as a promising athlete and student. In a small coal mining town it was hard to escape the notice of just about everyone. Playing football and keeping straight A's, he was a rising star in a town desperate to see the next generation climb out of poverty and make it in the "real world." But before he turned 18 Finn had discovered moonshine and later whiskey, and since then every event in life had become a blur of sharp threats and beatings from his father, and heart wrenching pleading from his mother to "just stop." But he couldn't. And after a while he stopped trying. The keg parties with the football team which had once been fun turned into moments of rage and humiliation. As the months passed his friends became alienated from him and potential girlfriends grew too disgusted to want to be with him. Before long he found himself alone most of the time, and like many alcoholics, he preferred it that way.

"Jenna, honey, go home," he pleaded with gentle resignation. "You can tell Daddy I ain't comin' home anyway." He looked away from her. She stood, unflinching.

"Ya got a letter in the mail too, from the United States government. Daddy says ya need ta open it. Says it's important ya fulfill your ... patriotic duty." She said the last part slowly trying to pronounce the words. Then she paused and wrinkled her face, "Whatever that means. Finn, what does that mean?" The words hit Finn hard like someone had dropped a 10 ton rock across his spine. He couldn't move. The pain was too great to even register in his body. His draft number had been called.

Rising to his feet with help from the wall he slurred, "It means, Jenna, that it's time for me to go."

He stumbled over to his sister and rumpled her hair between his fingers. He bent down and kissed her on the forehead and fought the tears welling up in his eyes. Leaving town was easy. He hated his father. His mother had simply resigned from trying to save him. And now the army was coming for him. Leaving Jenna was the one thing that tore at his heart. Since her birth she had been the bright spot in his life. Independent, stubborn, smart, feisty, warm-hearted Jenna.

She stared at him, her expression twisted by sorrow. She knew that she would never see him again and that thought ripped through her. Sure, he had been a real mess the last few years, but underneath the pile of problems he had created, she knew he was still the brother she had always looked up to. She started to whimper. "Come on now, Jenna," he said softly. "It's for the best. You know that."

Then assuring her, he said, "I'll be back. I promise. Let me go and clean up and then I'll be back in time to take you to next year's fall festival. okay? And we'll ride the Ferris wheel together, huh? Like we always do?"

She nodded and looked at her feet, sensing this would never happen. Then the corner of her eye, blurred with tears, caught the shimmer of the necklace she had just gotten for her First Communion. She unclasped it from the back of her neck. Finn watched with curiosity.

What the hell is she doing? he wondered.

The gold chain dangled with small gold charms and a crucifix at the center. She pulled one loose with care not to break it. Holding the palm of her dirty hand open, she extended it in front of Finn's face, an odd looking oval shaped image of a person, raised in relief-form. It was the face of someone who looked "religious" to Finn. The man had a ring of flames around his head and he was holding a carpenter's ruler.

"What is that?" Finn whispered.

"It's Saint Jude of Galilee," she said recalling her Sunday school lessons.

She paused with an intent expression. "Where is Galilee, Finn?"

"Jerusalem... I think." The whole conversation baffled him.

"Well, when we had our Sunday school classes we all had to pick a favorite saint before we did our First Communion and I picked him. So Mom ordered this charm for me from some catalog and gave it to me as a present. You know, to add to my charm necklace? I liked him 'cause he's supposed to protect people against lost causes. Someone who helps others who are totally lost, you know?"

"Like me." Finn grimaced, noting the accuracy of her observation.

"So, I want you to have it," she announced without compromise. She had it frozen still in front of his face. He knew there was no arguing with her when she got like this. Better to take it and say thank you. He knew he was going to need all the help he could get, and the reality that he was indeed a lost cause was beginning to weigh on him. His fingers reached down into the palm of her hand. His whole hand was shaking. This was becoming more common lately when he needed more to drink. And at that moment he wanted to flee from her sight and wipe out any consciousness he might have left. The thirst started in his feet and caused his legs to itch with the urge to run. He grabbed Jenna and hugged her to his chest, the charm wound in his fingers behind her small and frail back. She hugged him with

8 year-old ferocity. After standing like that a minute, he pulled away with reluc-
tance, closed his eyes, and reached down to kiss her forehead again. He took in her
smell one last time—a blend of fresh grass, Mom's biscuits, smoke from his father's
pipe, and citrus shampoo.

"Take care, kiddo," he said as lightly as he could, still pressing his cheek to her
hair. "Be good. Ya'll listen to Mom, now. Okay?"

"Okay," she sobbed.

He let her go. And then he was gone. His back was now facing Forest Junction, the only place he had been in 23 years. Jenna stood and stared as Finn disappeared over the horizon of dirt road into the unknown.

CHAPTER SIX

Baltimore, 2011

Campbell pulled her beige Explorer up to the turn-around in front of the elementary school. The front of the building had the contemporary brick façade of most suburban schools. She fell into line behind a caravan of SUV's and minivans loaded with mothers and small children. It all seemed so predictable, secure, and benign.

Each child was handed a book bag, lunch bag or some other object to carry into school. They were kissed on the cheeks and sent on their ways, while the mothers clambered back into their vehicles to move on to whatever it was that the day held for them. Whether it was off to a job, or the gym, or the grocery store, one thought struck Campbell and she chuckled to herself. People who have never raised small children would be shocked to find suburban middle-class women, who have young families, simultaneously think the most frightening and disturbing thoughts—the mother who kneels in her sweatpants to pick up toy blocks is also reminiscing about an erotic romp with a former lover, while the woman who is setting the table for dinner also fantasizes about killing her boss or leaving her husband.

"Mommy, can I play with Ceci this afternoon?" Caroline asked in her sweetest voice. She had learned how to get what she wanted from her mother. Campbell turned toward the back seat and smiled.

"I don't know, baby. I won't be home until after dinner. Why don't you let me call Ceci's mom and see if we can do it tomorrow."

Caroline's face briefly clouded over but then she nodded, accepting this compromise as fair. Ellis was doodling on the car window with saliva on his forefinger. Campbell added, "Make sure you wear your coat if you go outside Ellis. It's cold." The car pressed forward about a foot and the line stopped again. Campbell noted a parent chatting with one of the teachers at the curb, as if a slew of cars was not behind them waiting to move.

"But Mom, I always get so hot!" He popped his finger out of his mouth and drew a heart. Campbell winced. While the drawing was sweet, the germ issue made her insides twitch.

"Ellis, I really like the heart you made but could you please stop rubbing spit on the window?"

"Eeewwww!" Caroline shouted as if she had not been witness to this unsavory artwork the entire trip. It was, Campbell thought, Caroline's way of forming a bond with her mother. *Will she be like me?* Campbell pondered. Ellis made a face at her in response and poked his forefinger in her direction.

"Please, just wear it, Ellis. I don't want you getting a cold, especially with Thanksgiving coming. And Mommy needs to take a trip soon and I don't think Daddy's going to be up for taking care of you home sick all by himself." She chuckled at the thought. The line edged up and Campbell could see the drop off spot 10 feet ahead.

The children took turns giving her a quick kiss before they scrambled out of the car. "Love you both!" she called out after them. "Be good for Kim today and I'll see you tonight." Caroline dashed up the walkway. Ellis paused and turned around and waved before running off behind Caroline.

As the car snaked its way toward the front of the drop off line, she reached for the crumpled pad of Post-it notes she kept in her purse. She rifled beneath a stick of gum, her Camels and lip gloss to unearth a pen. She wrote: "Is stability a trap?" Then she peeled the Post-It off the pad and stuck the question to the dashboard. She wasn't sure why she had written that or what the answer might be. But the weight of the question, and of possible answers was growing inside her.

By 2:00 p.m. she was showered and ready to leave for campus. As she was loading the few plates from this morning's pancake breakfast into the dishwasher, she heard Kim open the front door. "Hi! I'm in the kitchen!" she called.

Kim breezed in smiling as usual. "How are you today?"

"Oh, okay, I suppose," Campbell replied drying her hands on a dish towel. She walked toward the foyer. "I had the weirdest dream last night, though. Afterwards I woke up and couldn't fall back asleep! So I've had about four hours of sleep."

Kim gave a sympathetic frown. She carried the half empty cups of milk from the dining room to the sink. "What was the dream about?"

Campbell was piling books and papers into her wheeled carry-all and she paused to stand up. She looked at Kim. "Did I ever tell you that I was almost killed when I was a little kid?"

Kim's eyes widened. "No! What happened?"

"One year my Dad's dental practice and their families served Thanksgiving dinner to a group of homeless men. My mom hated it!" She paused thinking of her mom for a minute, winced with sadness and went on. "My father gave me a little rubber ball to play with because he could see I was bored. As we were leaving I bounced the ball into the street by mistake and being six I didn't think, and I rushed to get it. Three inches of snow had fallen. I looked up and there was this car headed right for me. Before I could move, out of nowhere came this guy."

Kim's eyes fixated on Campbell as if to say, *Then what?*

"He scooped me up and turned so his back was facing the car," Campbell explained demonstrating this with her body. "He couldn't move fast enough. The car slammed on its brakes, skidded a few feet, and struck him in the back. We both flew forward and landed on the street. He kept his arms around me so I wouldn't hit the pavement, but I heard his elbows crush when they hit the street."

"Was he okay?"

"Yeah, I guess so," Campbell said as she moved back into the kitchen. "I mean, it all happened so fast and I was so young. I remember my mom screaming and my dad running into the street and pulling me up. After he knew I was safe, he reached his hand down to lift this poor guy up and make sure he wasn't hurt. The guy stood up with a small groan." Campbell sipped some leftover coffee in the mug before dumping it into the sink.

"I knew my mom blamed my dad for the whole thing, saying something about 'this never would have happened if you hadn't dragged us here.' I don't think they spoke for the rest of the ride home. We never went back there after that."

Kim's eyes locked on Campbell. "You know", she continued, "I think that incident impacted the way I see things as an adult. I mean, here was this homeless guy, the same type of person most of us avoid or look down on. And he risked his life to save mine when he didn't know me from a hole in the wall."

"Okay, so what does this all have to do with your dream last night?" Kim asked. Campbell laughed at the fact that she had gotten so far off topic.

"Well, ever since that Thanksgiving Day I have had a recurring dream about the guy who saved me. I barely remember what he looked like, so I can't say that he looked like the same guy. But, you know how in dreams you just know things? On and off, usually around stressful times in my life I will dream about him. Sometimes it's just a replay of almost getting hit by the car and I'll wake up right before it hits us. But other times we're just sitting there talking, I don't even know about what. Sometimes I am me now, you know, grown up and so is he, which is strange, huh?"

Kim didn't move. She was a person who believed that much of what made the world turn had little to do with the reality that we could see and measure in daily life. Campbell would laugh the whole thing off. But last night, the dream had borne an impression deep inside her that she couldn't shake.

"And then we were talking… I don't remember where we were… Just that it felt cold out, and I was shivering. And, I think I was in pain—I was hurt, maybe. He hands me this little gold charm. I think it was the one that he had showed me when I was at New Beginnings as a child. In the dream he said something I don't remember, then wrapped my fingers around it real tight, like I needed to hold onto it for some reason. And he says 'It's not time yet,' and then I woke up."

Unable to say anything else Kim whispered, "Wow."

Campbell needed to get moving so she changed the subject. "Speaking of cute guys, there was this handsome guy in the parking lot last night and he was checking me out!" Campbell beamed with middle aged female pride. Kim smiled back. "Of course he was. You still got it." They giggled and moved to finish cleaning the kitchen.

"Anyway, I won't be home until around 8:00 p.m. Brent should be back around 6:00 so you'll have to start dinner. There's a frozen pizza you can put in the oven. Steam some broccoli or something to go with it."

"Sure!" said Kim as she opened the door to help Campbell get her stuff out.

"Maybe we'll stay after school and go to the park. It's supposed to warm up a little later on."

"Sounds great! The kids could use it," Campbell called over her shoulder. She loaded her heavy bag into the back seat, started the car and headed toward the beltway. She couldn't get the conversation with Kim or the dream out of her mind. She realized that she had never involved her own kids in any sort of service work the way her father had with her even though she recognized the lasting impact it had on her. A wave of hypocrisy rose in her chest. Here she was living life in the ivory tower, preaching about the ills of racism and sexism and poverty, but she hadn't gotten her hands dirty since she was in graduate school over 10 years ago. Had she risen above all that? Questions of severe self-examination had kept Campbell from living fully. She needed to unblock this sick feeling inside.

I need to make arrangements to find a place like a shelter and volunteer myself and the kids, she resolved. *Later on this week I'll see if that place I went to as a kid is still open. It would be nice to return to where my life changed.* Having made this resolution she let the thought go, and the wave of guilt dissolved. She lit a cigarette and turned on the radio.

CHAPTER SEVEN

Baltimore, 1976

The compulsion to drink was so great it snapped Finn back into the present moment, where he found Campbell still gazing on him with a puzzled sadness. He forced a weak smile in an effort to cheer her. She took this gesture as an invitation to say hi. Weaving her small body through the crowd of people, she would disappear behind someone and then suddenly re-appear. She kept her eyes fixed on him. Finn's legs started to shake and he forced himself to not run from the room. Then she was standing in front of him, silent and obediently. Her eyes seemed to ask, "Is there anything I can do to help?" For a brief second Finn's urge to drink was transposed into stillness. He hadn't possessed a shred of peace since the day he had said goodbye to Jenna, his last source of solace. They stared at each other. Around them was a cacophony of voices, clattering china and shuffling metal chairs. The meal was almost ready to serve.

Not knowing what to say but afraid she might run away and take the serenity with her, Finn pulled the charm that Jenna had given him from his pocket. Campbell gazed at the small gold object with curiosity.

"Can I hold it?" she whispered.

Finn nodded and smiled. She lifted the charm delicately from his worn blue glove and dangled it in front of her. This sparkling object might as well have been the Hope diamond. She studied it with awe. Finn noted her soft features; the almost indeterminable way her eyes narrowed to see the image of St. Jude, and the slow way she shifted her weight from one foot to the other, as if she were about to pronounce a judgment of some sort. She looked into his eyes and he froze.

"Where did you get this?" she asked with a sudden authority. Finn felt an inexplicable guilt.

"My sister gave it to me when she just about your age." His face brightened as he said this.

"Is she here now?" Campbell asked looking around hoping to find another young girl to play with. Looking back at him she saw his face seemed dark and heavy again. "No."

Before she could think of what to say next, Campbell heard her mother's shrill voice. "Campbell Lee Cote! Get over here right now!" Her body stiffened. Her mother stood, hands on her hips, like an army sergeant barking orders from the kitchen doorway. Campbell thrust the charm into Finn's hands, turned on her heels and dashed back into the kitchen. As she ran she twisted her head over her shoulder, raised her arm up, and waved.

"Bye!" she sang.

Finn offered a small wave of his hand in return. And the noise in his head returned louder than it was before.

He knew alcohol at New Beginnings was not permissible, so he made his way toward the door hoping to find someone who might have a bottle on him that he could take outside. He found Jesse resting on the arm of a green chair next to the admittance desk. Jesse looked up when he saw Finn coming.

"Hey buddy," he exclaimed. "Didn't I tell you this place was great? And a full dinner comin'! I got us two beds to sleep in tonight, too! They were the last ones available."

Finn didn't respond. He leaned in so no one but Jesse could hear him. "Ya' got anything to drink?" His voice cut with a sharp edge.

"Hell no," he retorted. Always eager to please he added, "But Todd and Blue Dot just went outside. I bet they got something."

Without saying thanks or looking at Jesse, Finn hurried out. The cold air hit him. Snow was building along the streets and sidewalks. He pulled his coat around him scanning from side to side. After a moment he heard voices and laughter echoing from the alcove two buildings down. He strode with purpose in that direction until he spied Todd and Blue Dot passing a bottle of Old Crow whiskey back and forth, away from the view of the sidewalk. They startled, afraid they were busted and then relaxed when they saw it was Finn.

"Hey man," Blue Dot argued, pulling the whisky back out from the inside of his jacket.

Finn felt awkward calling this man Blue Dot when his name was Charlie. He felt badly that Charlie should forever be named after a schooling incident in which he was stabbed by another child with a lead pencil leaving a blue permanent dot on his left cheek. After forty years, people still called him Blue Dot.

"Gimme a hit," Finn insisted, trying to hide the desperation in his voice. His hands began to shake. He raised the bottle to his lips, and the smell of the alcohol increased the anticipation in his body. He took four gulps before he could lower the bottle again.

"Hey man, save some for the rest of us," Todd demanded.

He quickly raised the bottle and took three large swigs, then passed it back to Todd. The numbness and relief finally started to wash over him, dulling the pain and noise that had been scratching their way out.

"Thanks." Finn wiped his mouth with the sleeve of his jacket.

Now tethered to her mother's side, Campbell spent the rest of the afternoon mourning her loss of freedom. After being reprimanded with an uncertain but dire punishment for wandering off, they had set the long tables with paper tablecloths, plastic forks, spoons, knives, and plastic plates. Campbell and her mother stood on the other side of the kitchen pass-through while endless lines of hungry, cold, and exhausted individuals shambled down the line receiving small scoops of stuffing, turkey, turnips, mashed potatoes, sweet potatoes, and macaroni and cheese. All the while, Campbell searched for Finn.

Where is he? she worried. *Why hasn't he come to get his food?*

She wanted to see the beautiful sparkling charm again. But the meal ended and the volunteers divided up the tasks of clearing the plates, sweeping, and washing the tables.

"Campbell!" her mother ordered. She could sense her mother was still angry from her tone of voice. "Go give this to your father."

She handed Campbell the now empty silver platter they had brought with them. Campbell realized she hadn't seen her father all afternoon. The men were clustered in the back of the kitchen away from the bustle of the meal serving. It was an unspoken rule that the women should serve the food while the men remained in the background, standing on the ready should anyone be in need of their services. For hours now they had been pushing boxes and lifting folding chairs and tables, and then disappearing again so they could resume their conversations about work and money.

Campbell's mood improved when she saw her father, leaning against the door frame of a storage closet, one hand holding a folding chair and the other gesturing something of importance to the man next to him. William Cote's demeanor was gentle and easy. Everyone loved to stop and talk with "Bill". He would go on for hours about the smallest things. It was these qualities more than anything that made him the successful dentist he had become. He was naturally able to put others at ease.

He stopped talking when he saw Campbell. "Hey, sweetie!" he called, happy to see her. "Are you having a good time?" There was no point in telling the truth so she nodded and handed him the large silver platter. She slumped her shoulders.

"You must be bored by all this," he concluded. She shrugged indifferently.

"Your mom giving you a hard time, huh?"

He seemed to know everything. Not having to always communicate to him with words was part of their special bond.

"Where's the man with the pretty charm?" she wanted to ask him, but didn't.

"Hey, I have something for all your hard work," he teased reaching into the closet. He rummaged his arm around in a large cardboard box sitting on the bottom shelf and pulled out a small purple super ball. Campbell beamed. "I'm sure no one here will mind if you have it," he added.

"Thanks!" she exclaimed, running into the kitchen, treasure in hand, to try it out.

She bounced the ball with caution, afraid that if it bounced too hard it might get lost from view. Then she wrapped it into her fist and skipped back to where her mother was waiting for her. The secret toy left her feeling better. She smiled as she approached her mother.

"Get your coat, Campbell," Elizabeth insisted, now with more kindness in her voice. She hated herself for being so cross with her daughter, and yet the weight of her growing unhappiness seeped into every moment of her consciousness. Being angry had become habit; something she believed couldn't be helped. Elizabeth had come to accept it, as did her husband and daughter.

Campbell stood patiently by her parents' side as they said goodbye to their friends. She rolled the super ball around in her coat pocket like a worry stone. The sensation was soothing. Bill nudged his daughter's shoulders toward the door and told her and Elizabeth to wait while he got the car. Snow now padded a layer of white crystals across the urban landscape.

Finn was still standing under the awning with Todd and Blue Dot, draining the last few drops of whisky out of the bottle and wondering where he would get his next drink. Time had passed quickly. He hadn't realized that he had missed the whole meal, but now with a belly full of booze he didn't much care. The band of three heard voices emerging from New Beginnings and Todd tossed the bottle with a small clank into the farthest corner of the alcove. Finn peered out and saw the small girl with blond braids standing close to her mother. Although he longed to say goodbye, he didn't want her to see him like this, stumbling about and reeking of whisky. He preferred that she remember him, if she did at all, from their previous encounter rather than drunk and useless. He was also afraid of the girl's mother who stood masking her impatience by chatting with the other women. He hung in the shadows and watched.

The sensation of the super ball's amazing bouncing powers was too great to resist. Campbell pulled it from her pocket careful not to alert her mother. *I'll just look at it,* she convinced herself.

Elizabeth was distracted by a conversation with a friend, while also waiting for her husband to come around with their car. When a gust of cold air blew past them, Elizabeth released Campbell's hand to toss her scarf over her neck. As if acting on its own accord, Campbell's hand bounced the ball onto the icy pavement and rather than coming straight back up as it had in the kitchen, it veered with a sharp turn off the curb. Instinctively Campbell panicked and darted and into the street to snatch the ball. Her eyes were on the ball rather than looking to see what was in front of her.

Too late she heard the low rumbling of an engine and she froze. Without warning she felt a violent tug and her body was hurled into the air and then landed hard. She heard a scream that sounded like it was coming from her mother but all she could see was the hood of a yellow car rolling beneath her. She felt a weight holding her down but didn't know why. The car was so close she could smell the exhaust and feel the small drops of ice repelling themselves off the tires.

The force of the car jolted her head backwards. Campbell saw only the grey sky. Then she felt the thud of pavement beneath her. Pain shot up her legs and spine. Her face was pressed into something that stunk of smoke and alcohol. Screams echoed from every direction. Suddenly she realized a man was holding her, shielding her from the force of the car's impact. He groaned in pain. She looked around and saw a tire inches from her nose. The snow stung her cheeks. The almost suffocating grasp released her as the man's arms went limp. She started to cry. Fear crept in as she realized what had just happened.

A laser like pain seared through Finn's eye sockets and he squeezed his eyes shut. He felt the weight of her body being lifted from him. "Don't let me go," she cried.

A set of thick arms Campbell recognized as her father's reached down and her shaking body was passed into her mother's waiting embrace. She saw Finn, lying on the ground. His eyes were closed, and he was not moving. She started to cry again, not just from the pain of the car's impact but because she thought he might be dead.

Hearing Campbell cry, Finn opened his eyes. He was unable to move. Seeing her safely in her mother's arms, he uttered a sigh of relief which came out as more of a painful grunt. This was followed by spasmodic coughing. Campbell craned her neck around her mother's tight embrace to see him.

Please don't die, she screamed inside her head.

"Are you all right, sir?" a voice called from above. Finn slowly twisted his neck to meet William's face, contorted into the greatest look of concern anyone had ever granted him.

"Can you stand? Should we call an ambulance?"

"Yes… No," Finn replied. He tried to laugh, which caused another wave of coughing.

Campbell clung to her mother's neck. She looked down at Finn, calmer now, tears staining her soft cheeks. She sniffled once.

I'm okay. Really, he tried to imply just by looking at her.

William reached down, clasped Finn around the wrist, and pulled him up with care. Finn teetered for a moment unsure if the imbalance and dizziness were from the car hitting him or from the whisky. He mused that being so drunk might have made his body more flexible when he was thrown backward into the windshield.

"My god," William said shaking his hand fervently. "How can I ever thank you? You saved my daughter's life."

Finn said nothing. The whisky buzz was wearing off. He realized that his left knee wasn't moving so well. He shifted his weight to his right leg. He didn't want the girl's father to see he was in pain. "It was nothing. Really."

People from New Beginnings and curious onlookers had begun to crowd around them. Finn felt himself becoming anxious over human closeness. People were leaning over and whispering to each other. The tall man with the clip board, who Finn had learned earlier that day was named Travis and who served as the program director, eyed Finn intently from the building entrance way. Too intently it felt like to Finn.

"Please, let me at least give you something. A reward of sorts. It's the least I can do," William insisted still gripping Finn's hand and looking at him in earnest.

If I refuse, this guy's gonna feel even worse, Finn thought.

Finn loathed being on display and was willing to do or say anything to get the focus off himself. Before he could speak he felt William push a thick wad of bills into his hand. William stammered, "Look, it's only fifty dollars. I wish I could give you more. But it's all I have. The least I can do is offer you some money to help pay for any hospital bills, or a decent meal."

Or a couple of bottles of Jack Daniels, Finn added silently.

"Really, man. I'm fine. Honest. But thanks for the money. I appreciate it."

Finn glanced over at Campbell to make sure she was safe. The throng of people was so thick all he could see was the slight edge of her face, stained with tears, nodding in response to questions the women were hurling at her. Now that they knew she wasn't hurt the maternal instinct had kicked in and concern was replaced with gentle scolding.

"What on earth were you thinking, dearie?" he heard one woman ask.

Campbell was ushered into the waiting station wagon before Finn could hear her response. Once in the back seat she turned to look out the rear window. She saw Finn standing in the street. Snow had begun falling again and she could see his matted hair glistening with white specks. He smiled and raised his hand to wave goodbye. She waved back. Then the car sped off toward Roland Park.

CHAPTER EIGHT

Baltimore, 2011

Everything annoyed Campbell at this late hour. She wanted to go home. Instead she had to go find this Dr. McGinnis guy and discuss the upcoming conference. Dean Robarts had said he was in room 417, the room usually reserved for graduate assistants.

"Why me?" she muttered. "Why couldn't Sandy do this? What short straw did I draw?" Sandy was far more gracious and social than Campbell.

It was already 6:00 p.m. Kim had been understanding about staying until Brent got home, but for Campbell that wasn't the point. Friends, trying to be comforting, always said, "It'll get easier." It never did. The guilt and the anxiety of never being where she thought she should be compounded itself, layer upon layer growing heavier with each day.

When she reached room 417 the door was ajar, and the light sound of music indicated that someone was in there. She reached up to knock and paused to read a poster quote in large bold type:

The vampire may be an escape—an escape of all the limitations of human reality. In our own minds, we can make the vampire whatever we wish it to be.... (Martin V. Riccardo, *Liquid Dreams of Vampires*, 1996)

Beneath the quote was a poster from the movie Twilight and an older one from Buffy the Vampire Slayer. Two youthful, beautiful characters, Buffy and Angel, were in a dark embrace, their soulful gazes peering at their audience.

"Oh geez," she groaned. "He's mister hipster. He's going to be one of those egocentric guys that the undergraduate girls go crazy over because he's so brooding and misunderstood." It wasn't like Campbell to be wrong.

She gave a soft tap at the door and braced herself for a long-winded conversation. When he heard the knock, Finn swiveled his office chair away from the computer, looked up at her and radiated a smile.

Oh my god, I want to eat him, was Campbell's first thought.

His molasses-colored eyes gave the appearance of someone who would never grow old. He was in his mid-thirties perhaps. Behind his lips was a row of gleaming white teeth.

"Hi, I'm Finn McGinnis. Nice to meet you." He reached out to shake her hand. A second more terrifying thought came to her: the right look from this man might cause Campbell to question every belief about her own existence she had ever had. Her insides lurched and she tried to compose herself. Extending a hand and remaining casual, she replied, "Hey, I'm Campbell. Nice to meet you, too!"

It was then she noticed the thick honey colored hair tethered at the nape of his neck in a ponytail. He was chatting about how happy he was to be working at Eastern University in the Cultural Studies Department but his voice was drowned out of Campbell's mind by the realization that this was the same man she had checked out in the parking lot the night before. This speculation was confirmed by the Carhartt jacket she saw draped across his filing cabinet. Her gaze moved toward the plate glass window where she caught her reflection contrasted between darkness outside and the warm light in his office. She winced when she saw her hair flat against her head. Without thinking she pulled her hair back with the sweep of her right hand and forced a smiled.

"So, You are Mike's replacement. Welcome. We're so glad you're able to fill in at such a moment's notice!"

Her voice sounded stupid in her ears. Her mind had gone blank and she forgot why she was standing in his office. "Um..." she started. Finn sensed she needed help and interjected, "Yes, I am sure you're here to talk about the conference, right?"

I'll stand here and talk about anything you want, was her first instinct. She bit her lip.

Campbell shifted her weight and glanced around his office for clues about who he was. "Yes! I wanted to confirm that you'll take Mike's place on the panel and I want to get a sense of what your paper will be about so we're all in sync with one another."

Campbell knew she was babbling. "Barbara Caldwell and Jeremy Lewis will also be on the panel but Barbara's on sabbatical right now and Jeremy is just… luggage, I guess." She rolled her eyes. "He lets everyone else do all the work." Breathing a sigh, she concluded, "So I drew the short straw in terms of planning and organizing this thing." Around the room were dozens of CDs stacked against every wall or shelf: Rolling Stones, Bob Dylan, Jefferson Airplane, Led Zeppelin, Pink Floyd, and Grateful Dead.

"Wow, you like old music, huh?" she commented, a little lost in thought.

"Yeah," he replied with melancholy. "I guess you could say I'm stuck in the 70s" He chuckled like he shared a secret joke with himself. She peered at the teetering piles of books that took up every square surface, but no family photos.

Then again, he just got here. Maybe he hasn't finished unpacking, she figured.

Finn became acutely aware of a static noise filling his thoughts. The usual filters between his keen senses were blurred. Sounds, voices, and thoughts began to ricochet off one another. The lines between what he thought he was saying and thinking were unclear. He began to panic. But the scent of her body , her hair, her essence … all of it was overtaking him. "So…" he interrupted in a sharp tone to get her attention. She did not respond to this prompt, lost somewhere in her own head.

What is she looking for? he asked himself.

She turned away from his desk materials. A shade of guilt washed over the lines on her face. He grew uncomfortable with her silent assessment of his office. Finn suggested, "Why don't we go to Sammy's Roadhouse and grab something to drink. Do you have time?"

"Yes. I called home already and told them I'd be late."

"Great!" He reached for his coat and slung it over his broad shoulder. *Why do I feel so eager to spend time with a woman I don't even know?*

Finn took in her image as if he were feeding on her body. He wanted her. Every cell in his body told him so. This thought was quickly becoming a concern. He had avoided close relations with any humans outside the shelter for so long he wasn't sure if he knew how to have a normal conversation. And he had this strange sense that she was hearing his thoughts, or at least it seemed that her thoughts were inside his head. How would he know? He hadn't sought an intimate relationship with anyone besides Travis in 30 years. But even the bond he felt with Travis had begun to pale in the mere 10 minutes he had spent with Campbell.

"Is your car close by?" she asked.

"No. I had to park a ways from my office. Parking seems to be a high premium around here."

"Yes," she agreed. "Indeed. But I got lucky today." *In more ways than one. I found you*, she added silently.

Here was this beautiful relief from life's tensions—this person standing before her. Campbell felt weightless. He met her eyes and she looked away. "Why don't we take my car and I can drop you off at your car afterwards? We can talk on the way."

"Sounds good," he said. "But I am actually parked closer to the Roadhouse so I can walk to my car when we're done."

As they rode through the side streets across campus Finn and Campbell used the time to play the get-to-know-you game. Finn started, "So …who is 'them'?"

Trying to keep her hands from shaking she gripped the steering wheel tightly and kept her eyes on the road. He smelled of citrus and leather. She felt drunk sitting this close to him. "Huh?" she uttered.

A tug of familiarity pulled at his soul. *Was she married or single? Straight or gay?* He was baffled by his urge to know these things. Embarrassed, he tried to correct himself, "You said in my office that you let 'them' know at home you would be late." He held his breath waiting for her answer. She fixed her gaze on him and almost missed their turn. Campbell had to make a sudden sharp right which sent both of them reeling to the side.

With a somber tone, she said, "Yeah, I'm married. I have two kids. Ellis and Caroline. Ellis is six and Caroline is nine. "

He feigned the best "happy" tone he could muster, "Oh, that's great. A boy and a girl. One of each." He knew enough from socializing with people to recognize this as a standard response in such a conversation. But he thought, *Damn it, that figures.*

Looking at her profile illuminated by the city lights, fading in and out as they passed down the street, he saw that she had something about her features he could not pinpoint. How could he possibly know her before today?

"Did you grow up around here?" he inquired, fishing for clues.

"Born and raised. I lived in Roland Park until I was about 12. Then, when my mom left us, my dad and I moved to the suburbs. She died when I was adult. But I was in college by then."

She hadn't thought of her mom much at all since her death to breast cancer almost two decades earlier.

"I'm sorry to hear that."

He could almost smell the sadness coming off her now. The static in his head was growing louder. His mind was cluttered. Un-namable memories whispered, *I know that face. That sad expression.*

"Yeah, I guess she was pretty unhappy so she left us to run off with another man." Campbell accelerated hard cutting off the oncoming car. Changing the subject she asked, "Have you lived in Baltimore long?" He paused for a long moment, doing the math in his head to offer a "normal" answer. They slowed at the red light.

"Um…yeah, I guess you could say so. Most of my life. I was born in Kentucky, though. I left home when I was about 17 years old and came here."

"Wow…you were so young." She wondered, "How personal can I get at this point?" Trying to keep it polite she simply added, "That must have been hard."

"Yeah." They slowed as they reached Sammy's.

"Do you live in the city?"

"Do you live alone?" was the question she wanted to ask.

"Yep," was all he offered. *What else was there to say?* he argued with himself, *That I live in the basement of a homeless shelter for men? That I was pulled from a drunken stupor into a state of immortality?*

Campbell realized he wasn't going to say anymore. *Talk about his work.* She thought. *All men love that.* They searched the crowded lot looking for a parking spot.

"So where did you do your doctorate?" she asked, trying to stay upbeat.

"Here, at University of Baltimore. I just defended last May."

"Oh. That's nice." With the same perky tone, she continued, "So what on earth compelled you take a job here at Eastern?"

"Something to do, I guess. I was finishing my dissertation last spring but hadn't really pushed myself to find a job. This seemed like a nice breaking-in position."

"What kind of research did you do for your dissertation? Vampires?" She laughed, turned off the ignition and smiled at him again.

"How did you know what I study?"

She grinned. *Her smile was radiant,* he thought. He felt his insides collapse for a brief second. He smiled back. "Yes, as a matter of fact, it was on vampires. Would you like to know more?"

Would you like to become one? he thought.

Their elbows touched as they reached for their book bags lying in the console between their seats. A surge rushed through Campbell's arm like a jolt. She pulled away.

"Yes, do tell," Campbell insisted.

For the first time since leaving Forest Junction, and leaving Jenna, a sense of belonging to another sprang up. He placed his hand gently on the small of her back to usher her through the door of Sammy's Roadhouse. She caught their reflection in the glass. In a flash, she saw herself naked in his arms. The sight caused her to reel back and he caught her. "Sorry," she blurted, flushing. "My heel must have caught on the trim here." She pointed, relieved that there was in fact a raised metal weather stripping in the doorway. "Lead the way."

CHAPTER NINE

Baltimore, 2011

"Let's start with what you think you know about vampires," he offered using a professorial voice he must have rehearsed a dozen times on his undergraduates. The words "think you know" stung Campbell's intellectual ego. She pulled her body back from the table. Sensing he had offended her, he sighed. He smoothed his hair back from his face, a gesture Campbell presumed he used when frustrated or nervous.

After hesitating Finn tried again, "What I mean is, vampires are mythic figures, and everyone has their own take on who...I mean what...they are...what they mean...so it's easier for me to start from what you know than bore you with a recitation of what you may have already deduced through film and literature."

Campbell's mind raced. *What the holy hell do I know about vampires? Anything I say is going to sound stupid.* And stupid was something Campbell did not want to project. She didn't know why his opinion of her should matter so much, especially regarding such a silly subject, but it did. "Explain this to me as if I'm one of your freshman students," she suggested.

"You're a smart educated woman, Campbell." She flushed at the compliment. He added, "You have everything you need to know inside of you already." She grasped for the first thing that came to mind.

"Okay," she began. He smiled and she had to squelch the nervous giggle rising in her throat. "Vampires eat humans. They drink their blood."

Finn didn't respond but allowed her the space to think further. She added, "Um…they're immortal, right? I mean they can't be killed. They have no soul, they're evil or something." The corners of Finn's mouth twisted into a half grin. Or grimace. Campbell couldn't decide. She conjured the image of Finn sinking his luscious teeth deep into her neck. Her body tingled. Finn mistook her facial expression as a sign of confusion.

"Good let's start with that. Now, are vampires the sole creature that feeds on human blood?"

She guffawed without thinking first. "Vampires aren't real, though!"

He looked into her eyes in a way both solemn and playful. The dark brown of his iris reflected the ceiling lights and glimmered just a little. He leaned halfway across the table, and countered, "That remains to be seen. We'll get to that in a moment."

What else in my life, she wondered, *could possibly compare to this*? He leaned back in his chair again.

"Humor me," he said, "Real or mythically speaking, are vampires the only creatures that feed on human blood?"

"No," she retorted, sounding like a well-trained student. "Mosquitoes for one. And other predators do, or would, eat humans if they could. You know, lions and tigers and bears," and then as a humorous afterthought she exclaimed, "Oh my!" and chuckled.

The joke seemed to go right over his head. Keeping his face serious, his hands working the paper napkin into a square smaller than the nail on his pinky finger he continued. "So in that sense vampires are not really different than other creatures. So what is it that makes them unique?"

She wondered, *What makes you so unique that you are able to make me forget everything that I have?* Love at first sight was such a bullshit concept she reminded herself. But the draw was undeniable. Campbell's mind went blank for a moment. Then she replied, "Um….they can't die. They're immortal!" His eyes brightened. She could tell he agreed. A small rush of joy waved over her.

"Right! So there's the conundrum. Think. What other 'things' for lack of a better word, have a beginning but no ending?"

Us? she mused to herself.

This was going way beyond Count Dracula. Realizing she was perplexed, he tried to provoke the conversation further and fed her the answer.

"The soul. Should you believe that humans have one, that is. And that vampires do not. The jury is still out on that."

"There's a great quote by feminist author bell hooks" (hooks, 1995), Campbell said tilting her head in an effort to look attractive and smart. She raised her eyes coyly. Finn gazed at her and waited. "She wrote about the soul. About how it's not what we assume or expect at all. I cannot remember it exactly but she said… something to the effect of," she paused and looked across the room feeling the effects of Finn's eyes upon her, "Um…she said that …" She slowed her speech to assist her memory, "Paradox and contradiction are the mysteries of the soul. The weird, the uncanny are sources of knowledge. To know the self … one must open the heart wide and search every part. This requires facing the unacceptable, the perverse, the strange, even the sick." The truth was Campbell had memorized this quote years ago as an undergraduate because she had liked it so much.

It's just now that I'm coming to appreciate its full meaning, she added to herself.

Finn chuckled again. "Clearly the idea or belief in the human soul is profound and deep. It's an example of something that no one can prove exists in the scientific sense of the word, right? But people's belief in it is one of the most powerful forces that shape human behavior. Faith trumps science. It's real because we say it is."

She noticed her hand was resting just a few inches from his. If she moved it now it would appear too obvious and be read as a rejection of some sort. But to leave it was an acknowledgement of her desire for him. Holding her hand steady, she picked up her water glass and took a sip.

Is this, you and me, real because we say it is? she wanted to ask him.

With a cautious look on his face he paused. He knew with his next move he would be entering dangerous territory. With a clear tone he said, "And, the soul has a beginning but no end. In theory a person's soul begins when they're born and continues after they die."

"You're drawing similarities between vampires and the soul?" she asked.

"The soul is weird and uncanny, right? Isn't that what you just said?"

He flashed his teeth for a moment, making her feel dizzy. This was the most intriguing conversation she'd had in years. She felt alive. He shrugged his shoulders with a mock expression as if to say, "Oops. Is that wrong?" They both laughed out loud. Two older women sitting at the next table stared with annoyance. One of them looked at Finn and whispered something to the other. Their attention gave Campbell a pang of self-consciousness.

What am I doing here, practically flirting with this young guy when I should be at home putting my kids to bed? she asked herself.

Finn and Campbell stared at each other like the two final players at a poker match, with all their chips on the table. Then she shut her mind to the vapor of guilt seeping into an otherwise enchanting evening. Ignoring the glares from the two women, Finn spoke. "Let me segue here for a minute back to your original comment because it ties in to my next point. You said that vampires aren't real. I contend they are as real as the soul. Whether the handicraft of God or from the primordial ooze, we are made of real substances: chemical components, H_2O, CO_2, atoms, molecules, muscle…" He paused. "But, when you wake up in the morning, what do you think about? What weighs heavy on your thoughts when you think of what matters? Is it the nature of our existence? No, of course not. We are thinking about getting to work, maybe about our failing health, or about our families."

Campbell sat in silence. In truth she didn't know anymore what it was that propelled her life forward or where it was going. It was busying herself with the endless tasks of day to day life: school, work and family that had given Campbell's life the appearance of being smooth as polished glass. Campbell avoided giving an answer.

"I thought we were talking about vampires?"

We're talking about us, he wanted to confess. The unspoken flow of words and chemistry poured in a stream between them across the table.

"We are," Finn said taking no notice of Campbell's growing anxiety. "What is real is simply because we make it so."

Campbell took a last sip of her coffee, now cold. She was beginning to feel tired. But she didn't want this conversation to end. Grasping for a way back into the dialogue she said, "Well, I know that! All this circular logic just to arrive at the obvious?" The small folded paper napkin was now in minuscule shreds scattered across his side of the table.

"No. It's more than that," he argued. "Humans created vampires for real. I believe that they became a physical manifestation that began in our collective unconsciousness at the dawn of creation. Imagine that vampires are a branch of the human race that split off, millions of years ago as our evolution from the primates was just beginning. What if, through the manifestation of all human hopes and fears, practiced through myth and ritual, physical changes began to take place? The loop of mind and body into a parallel species that feeds off its progenitor. It's not that far-fetched. Humans have a history of becoming monsters, by losing their humanity." She couldn't disagree, imagining the laundry list of slave ships, concentration camps, and human sacrifices littering human history. He continued, "All species evolved in one way or another, correct? That's not exactly new since Darwin, although I suppose you could argue against evolutionary theory all together. But for my thesis to make any sense you have to at least be on board with evolutionary theory in general." He waited for a response.

"Sure," she said. "I'm with you on that."

"Good. So what if… Just as all other species were evolving, and many others did split into various types of sub-species, humans too split into another sub type …human, but not human?"

"What are you going to tell me next, that vampires are responsible for crop circles???" she retorted.

This was getting a little "out there" but she was transfixed by Finn's energy as he roused his mind and body with such passion as he spoke. Campbell imagined a throng of undergraduates, male and female alike, completely seduced by one of his lectures. The way he gestured his hands in front of his face, the way his lips moved over his teeth, the way his eyes glowed in the tavern light. He could have been reciting the dictionary and she would have been enthralled. She imagined his touch moving up her spine.

After a moment he added, "No. That would be silly." He grinned with ease at her, willing to make fun of himself for a moment. "I think that vampires evolved much like all other animal traits, out of necessity."

"But humans are at the top of the food chain? We're like, the winners. Aren't we? We are surviving, well grossly over populating and polluting to be exact, but, you know, we seem to be doing fine without help from vampires. And besides, don't vampires eat people?"

"Well, yes and no. This is where it gets tricky."

"This is where it gets tricky?" she scoffed. But to herself she added, *Who IS this guy?*

He couldn't shake the idea that he knew her somehow. He could feel it.

"Vampires feed on human blood. Yes. But they also have the power to change people into vampires. I think that it was an evolutionary trait that was built in millions of years ago as a safe guard against extinction. Look at where we are right now. Global warming. The threat of nuclear war always looming. Mutations of deadly diseases that can wipe out whole populations. Maybe all along we were preparing for a moment which hasn't happened yet, but is coming. No species has the capacity to survive global threats more than the vampire. So as imminent extinction nears, the vampires begin changing more and more humans as a way to save the human race. Maybe the mutation from human to vampire was some deep collective instinctual reaction to a fear of knowing our own mortality. That fear, that knowledge of our own death, has manifested itself in this particular 'strain' of human that could somehow supersede death. A trait of survival."

"Well, what about feeding off humans? Doesn't that contradict everything?"

Here was someone who wanted to ask the crazy questions she battled internally every day, in isolation. Little doors inside of her were opening up, and Finn seemed to be the key.

"Think about it," he offered, "As you said earlier, humans are at the top of the food chain. Wouldn't it make sense to feed off of a life form that has a high capacity for survival to ensure you have a continuous food source? From an evolutionary perspective doesn't that make sense?" The tone in his voice was defensive, like he was taking all of this personally.

Oh, Dr. McGinnis, she imagined herself cooing, *Can a human save a vampire? Have you been sent to save me from myself?* Then more soberly she noted, *He actually believes this shit. For him, vampires aren't just a metaphor of pop culture. He believes they're real.*

She noticed that he was beginning to speak of humans as if "they" were the "other" species, as if he himself were not human. She tried to restore her critical mind, her logical self, before she fell down the rabbit hole too deep.

Is he just gorgeous and crazy? Is it possible? Her heart sank a little.

The waitress appeared and interrupted Finn. "Can I get you anything else?" she asked politely.

"No, thank you," Campbell replied. She started digging through her purse to find a five dollar bill for the coffee. Finn didn't seem to have plans to leave the table anytime soon. He gave a polite nod to the waitress as if to dismiss her. Finn didn't want anyone else in their space. This private atmosphere, here with Campbell was its own universe. Then getting back on track, he continued.

"Look, I know this sounds crazy but think about it. What matters most isn't the science of it, it's what we believe, not what we can prove. And it's what we believe about vampires that has also evolved over time in various cultures. The evolutionary move wasn't just a biological one. It was also moral and spiritual, for lack of a better word. Vampires don't define what is right and wrong. You and I are both in Cultural Studies and can appreciate how ideas of good and bad, right and wrong, are relative to time and location. The moral code 200 years ago in America alone was vastly different than it is today. Whether or not vampires are good or evil is a matter of perspective. There is no universality in that sense. Just context. We evolve in tandem with human physical and cultural evolution."

"We?" Campbell said out loud.

Finn reached back with both arms and smoothed his hair away from his face. "Sorry…lost in the moment I guess," he murmured with a sheepish expression. "I mean … *they*, evolve in tandem with humans."

The waitress moved in to clear their cups and they paused the discussion.

Are you happy? he wanted to know.

Were they talking about vampires anymore? She shook her head, as much to clear it as to say, *I don't know.*

"I realize it's late. You probably have to get home. Let me just add one thing, a thought to leave you with. What is most real is how we react to the existence of vampires. What do they represent about us, about our desires? Our fears? Vampires can live for hundreds of years beyond humans. They have extraordinary powers of survival—extra strength, endurance, sensory input. Very difficult to kill, though not entirely impossible."

"The good ol' stake through the heart!" Campbell joked. Feeling drunk she raised her arm to imitate stabbing the air with a stake. But Finn remained serious.

"The vampire is human but not human. The difference is that humans are created …by God? Maybe… but then they die. And humans die fairly easily because of physical injury or illness, or the body's gradual deterioration through old age. But the vampire does not. Remember they have a beginning but no certain end. So the contrast is that the vampire can make infinite choices where humans cannot. When you're 18 you're thinking, 'What do I want to do with my life?' And you make a choice. And you hope it's a good one. Any choice a human makes is ultimately about mortality. Whether or not you've made good choices is often a matter of perspective."

Did I make the right choices? she worried.

Seeing the faces of her children in her mind she believed the answer was yes. *But what if you could have two lives?* she argued with herself, *What if you didn't have to sacrifice one for the other?*

He said, as if to summarize a lecture, "The vampire doesn't exist like that. The vampire existence doesn't have the consequences that a human's does. Vampires are the shape and substance of that reminder. Remember, looking at a vampire is like looking in a mirror—yes reflection and all. A cheetah might sneak up in the jungle and have you for lunch but it's not going to look you in the face while doing so, reflecting your own frailty, your humanity."

The notion of human frailty brought to her mind the smell of burning tires, car exhaust, and alcohol. Her mother's horrified cry and the man lying in the snow. She heard herself saying: *Please don't die.*

Finn went on. "To be alive is to realize that for every choice we make, we also make a sacrifice of something else—the results of which we can rarely predict at the outset, and oftentimes produces outcomes we never could have anticipated. The simplest and smallest, the least noticed acts, gestures, turn-of-the-wrist can lead to life-changing, or life-ending occurrences. For the vampire, since there is no death, choice is irrelevant, and sacrifice is non-existent."

A silence rested between them for a long moment. Campbell didn't have any reply. It was too much to digest. The frailty of her existence was wearing on her. His appearance, his voice, his presence were so all consuming she thought she might cry. But the drowning person does not question the source of the life jacket when it appears. They are simply grateful they can swim again.

She looked at him. She almost uttered the words *I love you*, but instead, trying to be glib, asked, "Can you prove it?"

Looking right through her he breathed in deeply. Then he leaned back in his chair and stretched both arms behind his head. "Of course not." He beamed a smile at her, insinuating that this was all mere speculation. Somehow this was a triumph, some secret he had and held back from the rest of the world.

"You know," she began, finally retrieving five singles from her wallet to leave for the waitress. She had just now glanced at her watch and realized with a panic how unbelievably late she was. How had the time gone so quickly?

"You know," she said again, "A wise person once told me, 'write what you know.' For example, I research and teach on practices and perspectives of motherhood in academia. That's a pretty obvious connection for me. So, I guess this makes you a vampire."

She raised her eyes with caution and met his stare. She shivered momentarily. Then as if he had recovered himself, Finn grinned and said, "Maybe I am, but if I tell you, then I'd have to kill you."

In her mind she reached out to him and caressed her lips along the nape of his neck beneath his hairline.

"So, what exactly are you going to present on our panel, Dr. Finn McGinnis?" she demanded.

She delighted in the way his name rolled from her mouth, like syrup. She wanted to say it a million times.

"Ahhh," he whispered slowly, taking in the image of her. All of a sudden she felt like prey. "That's the topic for our next meeting."

Finn was surprised with himself at this moment. He thought, "Am I asking her out? What am I doing?" But the urge to see her again was too great. He sauntered like a big cat over to her side of the table.

What's he doing? she wondered.

He leaned down behind her to where she could feel the fringes of his hair brush the sides of her ears and neck. His breath pricked the nape of her neck. He reached over her shoulder and scooped her car keys off the table. They lay in a pile clumped by the sugar bowl.

"Don't forget these," he said with Boy Scout charm. "You won't get very far without them."

Her hand was shaking. She pulled the keys from his fingertips.

"Thanks," she murmured.

Then he lifted her coat from the back of the chair. He held it out for her as she rose. She accepted his gesture with a feeling of defiance and he wrapped the coat around her shoulders.

Finn let the static in his head take over. He escorted her to her car. While their voices remained silent she listened to the crunch of gravel and dirt beneath their feet.

Campbell considered that there was nothing to say now that would not defy all logic and social protocol. She imagined what it would be like to kiss him. This strange man she felt she had known a lifetime. This man who seemed to imagine himself a vampire. This man who offered endless possibilities she had never considered. Sensing her approach, he reached his hands down deep into his pockets.

The words, *It's not time yet,* rang in her brain.

Finn stood a few feet from her and wished her good night. Then he walked into the darkness across campus to where he had parked his car. The farther away from her he moved, the more her heart beat resumed a normal pattern. She waited until his tall figure faded into the evening dimness before she turned the key in the ignition.

Reference

hooks, b. (1995). *Art on my mind: Visual politics.* New York, NY: The New Press.

CHAPTER TEN

Baltimore, 1976

The car holding the young child with blond braids sped away from New Beginnings. Finn stood motionless in the snow-filled street gripping a knot of bills tightly in his bruised and wet hand. "I should have died," he muttered. It would have been a good death, better than the one he had always imagined. The program director, Travis, who had been watching intently just moments before, had disappeared. Throngs of people flocked to his side asking if he was okay and patting him on the back. Jesse was sidling his way toward the center and that meant that whatever Finn chose to do with this fifty dollars would have to be shared. And right now he wasn't in the mood for conversation. Jesse's head bobbed over the heads of the people who were standing between him and Finn. Finn could see it in Jesse's eyes. The question, *What'd he give you? What'd he give you?* Finn wanted nothing more than to disappear, so he shrugged off the hands of the well-wishers and twisted his body away from the direction of Jesse's approach.

Finn hopped the Route 13 bus for a while and then meandered down Baltimore Street toward the abandoned warehouses lining the harbor. The area around the harbor was a playground for people who didn't want to be found. Building after building was sewn together by boarded-up windows and crumbling foundations; a labyrinth of hiding places fraught with dangers in the form of collapsing ceilings and predatory humans. In spite of their dangers, Finn found the abandoned factories and stores to be what he liked best—places out of time, devoid of any of the connections to a reality which alcohol had worked so well to erase from his memory. On his way across Fayette Street, Finn stopped in the liquor store, one where he would not be recognized for his usual shoplifting and loitering. Brushing the cold and snow off his shoulders he strolled the aisles of glistening red, gold, brown, clear, and green liquids shining like a Genie's treasure in his eyes.

He ignored the stares from the people he passed, the shoppers stretching their heads over the aisles to catch a glimpse of the drunk desperately grasping for his fix. It was almost an act of voyeurism; observing someone at their most vulnerable, the raw craving bared for everyone to see. He wondered if they saw him as a person, or merely an object made apparent for their speculation.

Finn could feel himself shaking. He was taking too long. *Just grab anything*, screamed a voice inside his head. It was the voice he always obeyed. He reached out for a large bottle of Jack Daniels. Then securing that one under his left arm he reached out for a bottle of Boones Farm wine. His breath was coming faster now with anticipation.

He tried not to run as he headed for the register. Finn had just enough money left over for five shorties of vodka which he stashed in each of his four inside coat pockets. He mumbled to the store clerk for a pack of Camel filter less cigarettes. The store clerk tried not to stare at Finn's ragged expression. They said little during the transaction. Scooping up his paper bag, Finn nodded a thank you and scurried out. He couldn't run fast enough to the old building he called home. He was eager to twist open the top.

The snowy hues in plum and blue dimly lit the sky surrounding Baltimore harbor. Sitting on the broad jagged edge of a large hole made by an incomplete demolition of the building, Finn lifted the bottle of Boones Farm and finished the last of it. His legs hung off the edge and he leaned his head out to get a cold breeze. He studied the orange neon lights of the Domino Sugar Factory that appeared across from him on the other side of the dark still waters of the harbor. The chilled cries of the seagulls echoed as they floated motionless above the water's ripples hoping for a fish. He heard the occasional sound of a horn; a boat warning that it was either entering or exiting the docks, headed for some other destination.

The noise in his head was stilled by the drink. He played back the day's events in his mind. As Finn saw the car speeding toward the young girl unaware of what was happening, it was Jenna's face he had seen and he moved on instinct. But in this quiet moment of reflection, if he was honest with himself, he had to admit he wished that when the car struck him he would have lost consciousness and died on the spot. It would be an easier way to go than death by alcohol withdrawal or whatever other fate awaited his miserable future.

Then he heard a distinct noise. It was different from the din of the harbor noises which had all but lulled him to sleep. It was the sound of footsteps. They seemed to be moving in a pack, scurrying like rats over the littered aluminum cans and glass bottles carpeting the inside of his building. His body froze. He strained his ear to track the direction the footsteps might be headed. Then as abruptly as the noise had started, it stopped. It was as if the persons (or things) making the sounds had vanished. The back of his neck prickled with the keen awareness that someone (or something) was standing directly behind him. He jerked his whole body around and sat facing a ragged group of teens. They were dressed in punk rock attire. Closing one eye to reduce the effects of double vision he thought he counted four kids together. Maybe five. Even through a drunken haze, he was baffled. *How did they simply just appear?* he wondered. Perhaps he had blacked out for a brief moment or two. He gave them a blank stare, hesitating to see if they were going to jump him just for fun as was common with certain gangs in the area. Beating up homeless people had become a rite of passage for gangs lately.

To avoid any provocation he extended his bottle of Jack Daniels which still had about a third of it left and offered it to the teens as a peace offering. The tall male in the middle, who Finn presumed to be their leader, smiled. A chill ran down Finn's neck. Finn had been kicked around before but something about this pack of kids was different. There was no sense of hostility in their positioning. There was no fear or insecurity about their presence in this bombed out shell of a place. There was no self-doubt in their eyes the way there usually was in the others who would come and taunt him or steal from him. These weren't scared, desperate kids out to prove themselves. Yet, they did have a purpose. That much he could discern. Although they showed no signs of aggression, he couldn't help but feel afraid.

The two on the left had fair skin, one with blond hair shaved into a Mohawk and dyed blue at the fringes. He was lanky but strong. Finn could make out the definitions of his arm muscles through the torn T-shirt. A large A in a circle for anarchy blazoned across his front.

A little cold to be wearing just a T-shirt, Finn noted.

His eyes moved to the kid next to him, a shorter dark haired boy donning an ankle-length leather jacket. On the leaders' other flank stood a skinny girl with blazing blue eyes and long brown hair that dangled down to her tiny waist. She leaned casually against her friend, an African American male with a shaved head and three large bright gold hoops hanging from one ear. He had dark circles of eye makeup that made him look almost feline. The layers of flannel shirts and T-shirts didn't hide his taught body. He looked at Finn as if he might pounce on him at any moment. They waited patiently as if they understood that Finn needed a moment to take all this in. Then after another minute the blond boy spoke.

"Hey, man," he said as if they had been friends for years. His voice, soft like velvet, was not what Finn expected. Finn glanced protectively toward his stash of booze, and then looked back at the kids. As if he knew what Finn was thinking, the leader softly added, "Don't worry, we're not here for your stash."

He paused as if a new thought had just occurred to him. He looked at the others who grinned at some private joke that Finn had missed. "Actually we're here to invite you to a party." Gesturing with his head he added with mock innocence, "Just a block up. You seem so alone here. We thought we might cheer you up, man." The others nodded in agreement. The words sounded genuine to Finn. But sizing up the situation, as drunk as he was, he knew the plausibility of this ending badly.

Finn sat motionless, debating what his next move should be. The choices were severely limited. Sensing his unease, like a predator trying to coax its prey from its hiding space, the girl spoke, her voice smooth and lyrical, "What's your name? My name is Seneca."

Finn coughed loose the rubble lodged in his throat and heard himself say, "Finn." His focus was on the leader.

"Well, Finn," she continued, "It appears to me that it's pretty cold out here. We were just passing by and we saw you." Somehow he knew this last part was a lie. "We thought you might want to go somewhere warm, where you can party with us." Then she went in for the kill. "We have more booze. Lots of it. Your supply seems to be running out here."

Finn knew that the whole invitation was a trap to lure him somewhere, for what reason he couldn't imagine. But the bait worked. It always did. He couldn't refuse.

Finn gazed for one last moment at the four youth poised so triumphantly in front of him. Then he rose to a feeble standing position, never letting go of the bottle in his right hand. "Okay, let's go," he conceded, shaking the fear from his voice as best he could. From that moment, time became irrelevant.

CHAPTER ELEVEN

Baltimore, 1976

The next thing Finn remembered was lying on the floor of an abandoned warehouse. *Am I still at the harbor?* His sense of smell and sight told him that something about the aura of this warehouse was different. But he felt warm and happy, a sensation he hadn't felt since he was very young. Small bits of sawdust and gravel attached themselves to his hands and clothing. He brushed them off, annoyed by the distraction from his euphoria.

The young people he had met at the harbor were seated across from him. Looking on and whispering to each other. The room was dim and he could barely make out the traces of their facial expressions. *Were they smiling? Or sneering?* Their eyes seemed to glow and their teeth seemed immensely large. He heard other hushed whispers but was too paralyzed to discern who else might be there.

The girl called Seneca was seated next to him. She handed him a heavy dark green bottle with shimmering liquid inside. He didn't know what was in it. He didn't ask. He lifted it to his lips. All he could see was her face which was glowing, radiant and alluring. She smelled of sandalwood and patchouli. Then she slowly reached out for him, leaned her face into the base of his neck and sunk her teeth in deeply. He felt as if he were being stabbed and experiencing an orgasm simultaneously. He screamed and then blacked out.

Finn was unsure how much time passed after that. But it must have been a while because he was shaking. "*I am having the DT's*," he assured himself. Strange shapes and shadows crawled through the barren blood spattered walls. Images of monsters with fangs and human faces melted and disappeared before his eyes. Every cell in his body felt as if it was being set on fire. He blacked out again.

The first thing Finn was aware of when he resurfaced to a conscious state was the presence of a small black fly dumbly thudding into the cracked window far across the desolate warehouse. *How much time had passed?* he asked himself. Strangely, although the fly must have been at least twenty feet from where his body lay writhing with a surge of pain and tremendous energy, it appeared to his eye as if it were only one foot from his face. *How is that possible*, he wondered? His vision was blurred and the crust made from tears and sleep kept the corners of his eyes glued together. He raised his hand, wiped his face and blinked. The fly, still punishing itself in a vain attempt to escape its confines now appeared farther away. The frustrated buzzing resonated in Finn's ears so loudly his head throbbed. *This is one hell of a hangover*, he concluded.

The second realization that came to him was that for the first time in over fifteen years, he did not have the immediate craving to drink alcohol. But somewhere deep within his bones he felt a new strange craving, for something else he couldn't quite name. This new craving compelled the muscles in his body to get up and begin the search for its object of desire. This sensation was familiar. He had learned to force his body, whatever condition it was in, to push forward in the quest to satiate the compulsion to drink. As he uncurled his feet from the fetal position and into a full stretch it was as if every bone in his body had been reformed. He clenched his teeth together to fight off the shooting pains. Even his teeth felt strangely different. They ached and seemed to protrude from his gums.

What drug did I take? He was growing worried.

Whatever it was, his body was still feeling the effects. His vision, hearing, and movements were disjointed. He could hear the shuffle of feet as they moved across the city streets three stories below him. His vision shifted in and out as if one moment he were looking through a microscope and the next a telescope. As he took a step forward, he lurched and stumbled. How far it was from one step to the next was distorted, as if the floor shifted between being 1 foot to 100 feet below his step. His body instinctively righted itself. Tremendous power surged through his hands. He clutched for the windowsill to keep from falling. As he clutched the wooden frame it cracked under the pressure from his fingers.

This building must be ready to crumble, he rationalized as he watched the splinters float to the floor. This new craving scratched at the corners of his thoughts. Having finally corrected his vision, which by now he realized he could control at will, he made his way slowly toward the stairwell. He could hear the emptiness of the building ring in his ears.

Nobody's here. He could just sense it. That thought gave way to another. He felt compelled to go find people, because it was people that were somehow linked to this unfamiliar urge. This desire to find, rather to than to hide from, people was the strangest new sensation of all.

Finn pushed his way through toward the front of the abandoned space out into the cool night air and the vacant street. Every house in this row had been boarded up years ago. Only the criminal and the insane dared to walk down this street at night. Some new voice in his head whispered, *I need people. I need....* He couldn't find the words to complete the thought, but he moved down the street in search of whatever it was.

Around the corner was the loading dock in the back of the hematology wing of Maryland General Hospital. Although it was still at least 100 yards away and hidden from view, he could hear the shuffle of feet loading and unloading heavy boxes. The smell of human sweat motivated his body to spring forward. Before he could blink he was at the end of the block and crouched at the corner. The lapse of time, moving 100 feet in two seconds felt like a blackout to Finn. He felt time and space intersect in unsynchronized fashion, where a day felt like a minute and a minute could move like eternity.

Like an animal about to pounce, he crouched silently and peered around the corner to find a grey haired man breathing heavily as he reached into the back of a truck. He carried large cardboard boxes marked "Fragile. Move with care" and labeled "Maryland General Hospital Blood Bank." He brought the boxes to the edge of the loading dock. As Finn watched the man move back and forth, he was jolted into the stark realization that what his body craved was this man, to kill him, and to drink his insides empty, as easily as if he were a bottle of tequila. Finn had gone to dangerous and humiliating lengths in his past to do anything to get his hands on a bottle of booze. He knew what urgency and desperation felt like. They were a dangerous combination. And now they were deadly. Without another thought he found himself on top of the man, pinning him down onto the cold pavement, his mind and body pulsing with anticipation.

Terrified, the old man cried out, "Please, please, I beg you, take whatever it is that you want! My wallet is in my back pocket. I don't have much but it's yours."

As he stammered out a plea for his life, Finn could barely hear. His ears rang with power and desire. He glared down at the man, now his prey. Examining his eyes he saw awe and horror staring back. Exactly how bad did he look? Finn hadn't bothered to check his appearance since he awoke. Whatever it was, this man had stopped pleading and now gazed up at Finn, dumbstruck. The whispering in the back of Finn's head urged him to kill the man and to consume what he most craved. But another voice broke in, equally powerful, warning him not to. Within the span of a heartbeat, as the voice of reason was losing out and Finn was closing in on the paralyzed man's throat, he smelled something rich and warm. Blood. Finn froze an inch from the pulsing vein, the tap root he wanted so much to spike.

Finn quickly turned away from the man's throat, and followed the scent. It was coming from the boxes. One had fallen from the loading platform and crushed on the pavement, with a thin stream of blood leaking from its crumpled corner. Whatever amount of blood this man had in his body Finn knew there was even more within those cardboard packages. And what does an addict of any sort want, but more? He left his limp victim lying on the pavement and leaped with the strength of a lion onto the loading dock and tore open the boxes as easily as if they were made of tissue paper. Dozens of shiny plastic bags, labeled A, B and O rolled out and wobbled like beached jellyfish. The old man was now on his feet and gazed paralyzed with fear at Finn who was atop the loading dock with one shiny plastic bag of dark red liquid, labeled B negative raised in a fist above his head. Finn craned his neck, opened his mouth and felt the thrust of two sharp punctures sear through the heavy plastic lining. The warmth ran into his mouth and down his throat.

His whole body sang with relief and pleasure. In seconds he had drained the bag dry. The craving lessoned somewhat and the predatory instinct was now slightly subdued. He glanced around for the man he had almost killed but he was nowhere to be seen. Finn sensed a small feeling of relief that the old man had escaped. He then turned his attention back to the dozen or so bags of delicious liquid the man had left behind, now free for the taking.

CHAPTER TWELVE

Baltimore, 2011

Monday 11/05/2011   11:13 p.m.

To: fmigginis@esu.edu

From: ccotephill@esu.edu

Hello Finn!

Well, thanks to you I am seeing vampires everywhere! Thank you again for a riveting if unusual conversation.

Her fingers paused over the keyboard. She wanted to be very careful with her words here. *Nothing that sounds too flirty*, she reminded herself. He would probably be appalled by that. But nothing too formal either. She typed:

Now I have so many more questions!

When can I see you again? was what she wanted to write. *No, don't write that! I want to bite you! No. I can't write that, either.*

She sighed and twirled her wrists around in small circles to reduce the stress. Craning her neck backward she could glance into the TV room, and noted the tips of Brent's Docksider shoes resting on the coffee table. He hadn't bothered to ask her what she had done that evening or why she had gotten home so late. She couldn't decide if it was because of an ease of living together for so long, or if it was a growing indifference between them. A small voice of guilt whispered in her ear.

Above her computer hung a framed 8×10 photo of Brent and her on the day of Caroline's birth. In the grainy image Campbell could make out the semblance of happiness. In the picture she gazed at Caroline as Brent looked upon them both in the hospital bed, huddled together as a new family. The memory rose from her insides and squeezed her chest. The photo had been hanging there for years, a layer of thin dust resting on the glass. Yet she had never really seen the look in Brent's eyes. The pride and adoration he had for Campbell right then. Up until this evening with Finn, as an alternative point of reference, the picture was a stark reminder of what could be. She had not been conscious of how lonely she had become. She buried the feeling and drew her attention back to the email. She typed:

> Due to your compelling (re) defense of your dissertation-haha-we never had time to walk through the upcoming panel presentation in San Diego. Do you have time next week to meet?
>
> Cheers,
>
> C-

She worried, *can urgency bleed through email? Would he sense what a lame excuse to be near him this was?* She hit send anyway. The rush of hitting "send"—the rush of him—made her feel alive.

Campbell rose from the computer and entered into the family room. "So," she started, "I was thinking of taking the kids to the New Beginnings shelter sometime soon to help out, you know, volunteering at the soup kitchen or something." She waited for a response.

Brent shifted his weight on the couch and scratched the side of his nose as if he was thinking for a moment. Without looking up from the TV with a tinge of disgust, he asked, "Isn't that the place for drunks? Are you sure it's safe?"

Oh my god, he's just like my mother, she observed.

Defensively she retorted, "It's a recovery house. There's a difference. I used to go there with my family when I was a kid when it first opened. Yes, it's safe!" The memory of her experience there had become more pronounced the whole drive home from Sammy's Roadhouse. Then, to make her case she said, "Don't you want our children to be exposed to different people? To learn how to make societal contributions? I mean, they live in this little bubble world of suburbia—their school, their friends, their social lives. It's all so insular."

At this last comment Brent took notice. He was annoyed. "I work 60 hours a week to provide them with that 'bubble' life as you call it!" he remarked sharply. He then gave a low sigh for effect.

Campbell hadn't meant to insult him. In spite of their growing absence from each other's lives, she admired his dedication to providing his family with everything he could. "I know," she reassured him, softening a bit. She sat on the couch next to him, curled her feet under her legs, and touched his shoulder with her hand.

"I am not saying our life is bad the way it is. The kids are happy." She avoided saying "I'm happy." She didn't like to lie if she didn't have to. "I just think it's good for our children to appreciate what they have. To give back. You know?"

The TV announcer exhorted in a velvety voice the powers of some new skin care line that could erase years of aging from your face.

"Well, I am going to bring them this Saturday for a tour at least and see if there are any volunteer positions available. Do you want to come?" She already knew what his answer would be but it was a gesture of politeness to ask anyway.

"I'm playing golf with Bernie. We have a 10:00 a.m. tee time. I won't be back until around dinner time," he explained. The voice was flat.

"All right then. I am going upstairs to read for a few minutes," she said and moved toward the stairs.

"I'll be up soon. Good night."

"I love you," he added, almost as an afterthought. She didn't reply.

An hour later, while Brent was settling into bed next to his wife who was reading the most recent issue of the Journal of Culture and Feminism Finn was making his way toward Maryland General Hospital. After the evening with Campbell he felt a growing urge to make his usual "stop." He had made his usual stop there only two days ago but the urge was strong tonight. He decided it was better to go before heading back to New Beginnings for the night. He would feel more "settled" if he did. The desire to feed had taken him by surprise after leaving Campbell. Something about her had made him thirsty.

Something about her…, he kept thinking to himself, rolling a vision of her face around in his mind like a delicate puzzle. He could not riddle why he was fixated on her. It was disconcerting to him that his desire for her was emerging in tandem with a desire to feed. *Do I want to eat her, or kiss her?* he pondered.

Finn hoped that Harry was working the loading dock tonight at Maryland General. While University of Maryland and Mercy hospitals were much closer to New Beginnings, Maryland General Hospital took him away from being seen by men who might know him and ask questions for which he had no real answer.

Other than Travis, he had kept his "nature" a secret to the men there. More than a reflex or an instinct, he flowed like light and water along the walls of the building.

Harry was lifting a box off a Red Cross truck. He turned his head and stopped. Finn walked quietly toward Harry looking around to see if anyone else was in view. "Evening, Mr. Finn," Harry announced in his usual friendly tone but without smiling.

"Evening to you too, Harry. Kinda warm out for this time of year don't ya think?"

Small talk like this struck Finn as absurd when he was committing a crime, but Harry and Finn had developed a relationship over the years. Harry's aging body, Finn guessed him to be about 65, didn't slow him from his duties delivering and moving box loads of blood donations from the Red Cross to the Maryland General Hospital every Thursday night. Harry wiped his hands on his jeans and walked toward Finn.

"Didn't expect you for another week," he noted causally.

"Yeah. My apologies for coming unexpectedly," Finn replied.

He reached into the inside pocket of his Carhartt coat and pulled out a roll of bills.

"Any way you could spare some tonight?"

Harry looked around and grimaced as he stretched his back, "Well, I suppose. The paper work hasn't been submitted yet so I could still make a few changes to the delivery order form. How much ya need?"

"Just four pints. I hate to inconvenience you too much. I don't want you to get in any trouble."

Finn wasn't completely altruistic. He knew that if Harry was fired he would lose the connection to the food source he had developed and nurtured over the last 35 years. Fortunately for Finn, Harry didn't like change and was happy to stay at the same job, day in and day out all these years. It could also be the large extra sums of money Finn had been giving him every few weeks in exchange for bags of blood, which Harry would claim had "never arrived" at their destination. They both knew that the paper trail in the medical world was so intricate that by the time anyone bothered to deduce where the blood had been lost, they would have forgotten what they were looking for. All Harry had to do was fill in the triplicate form indicating that the number of bags supposed to be delivered was larger than the number that arrived.

Let those fellas in administration track it down, Harry would think to himself. *Aint' never gonna trace it back to me.* Harry didn't care what it was that this strange man wanted to do with bags of blood. Growing up on Baltimore's East side had taught him not to ask questions. What he knew was that the money Finn offered him for this service was enough to send his daughter to college. That was good enough for him. The delivery man before him, back 35 years ago had quit unexpectedly, claiming to have had a nervous breakdown of some sort. Something had happened to him one night at the loading dock, and although he had appeared unharmed, he claimed he was psychologically unwell to continue performing his duties. Harry was grateful for the break. Back in those days his wife was expecting their first child and he was desperate for any job he could find.

Finn handed Harry $600 dollars. "I added an extra hundred for the inconvenience tonight." Treat your food source well, was Finn's motto.

"Thanks, Mr. Finn," Harry muttered placing the roll of bills in his back pocket. "Let me just get you your stuff."

Back in his basement room at New Beginnings Finn drained the last few ounces of blood left in the bag and sat back in his chair to rest. Then he turned on the computer. His whole body trembled with excitement when he saw her name in his email box. Ignoring the dozens of other emails he was bombarded with as a new faculty member, he clicked as fast as he could on her name. He feared that the message would disappear before he could get to it. After reading her email three or four times, he hesitated with a bizarre erotic delight in knowing it was her hands that had typed each and every letter. He sat back and tried to read between the lines.

What else was she trying to say? Was there some hidden message in her words? What else was she thinking when she was typing this? Where was her husband? He cleared his mind of the rampant thoughts and wrote back:

Monday 11/05/2011   11:13 p.m.

From: fmiginnis@esu.edu

To: ccotephill@esu.edu

Ahhh, so glad you've been bitten by curiosity about the vampire. Yes, would love to answer any questions you have. And I promise this time no lectures. We will have time to go over my paper for the presentation. How does next Monday after the faculty meeting sound?

Peace,

finn–

After hitting send, he closed his eyes and rendered an image of Campbell, how her eyes dared him to bare his soul, how her smile cracked him wide open down the middle.

CHAPTER THIRTEEN

Baltimore, 2011

"Why are we going here again, Mom?" Caroline asked as Campbell zipped the back of her jumper dress. Usually Saturday mornings were reserved for cartoons and late breakfasts. Caroline and Ellis were mildly annoyed at having to rush and muddle this Saturday as if they were going to school.

"We are going to speak with the program supervisor to see if we can participate in some sort of Thanksgiving volunteer program in two weeks." The statement was only half the truth. For reasons she could not articulate to herself, there was a gnawing need to just go there, to see it again. She gently pushed both kids toward the door handing them their shoes.

"Ellis, put your shoes on!" she said with as much kindness as she could muster.

What was bothering her so much lately? Her patience with the kids was thin the last few days. Her stomach thrilled at the thought of seeing Finn again on Monday night. It was all she had thought about since he had replied to her email.

"I don't want to spend Thanksgiving somewhere else!" Ellis whined as he pressed the Velcro flaps across the top of his shoe. "I want to spend it with Mee Maw and Paw Paw!"

He stomped his foot in frustration and looked at Campbell for her reaction. But she hadn't noticed the gesture of protest. Campbell rummaged for the keys in her purse. She was a little nervous going to New Beginnings unannounced. She didn't know what to expect. But after several failed attempts to get through the voicemail to speak to a person called "Outreach Supervisor" on their website, she decided to just show up. Campbell was never one to give in to stumbling blocks.

"We're not going to miss Thanksgiving with Mee Maw and Paw Paw," she said as she leaned down to kiss his rumpled hair. Smoothing it out she added, "They'll still come for dinner. We will probably help out at the mission that morning and then be back in time for our own dinner."

Campbell hadn't worked out the logistics of preparing a dinner for her in-laws while also serving meals at the Mission. She decided to worry about that later. She spent a great deal of energy every year trying to avoid thinking about Thanksgiving. Although she got along well enough with Brent's parents, Millie and Josh Phillips, the holiday felt like little more than a dog and pony show where she could wave her "Look at me, my life is secure and happy" flag, thus proving to them that their son hadn't made a mistake in marrying her. Since her own father's death, Brent's parents were the only family she had. One of the many reasons she resented her mother for leaving her and her father was that she had left Campbell an only child. The isolation of her childhood was still a biting narrative. Having Brent's whole family there for the holidays filled her with a warmth she relished and a pain she couldn't name. It occurred to her as she walked to the car with Ellis and Caroline that perhaps this push to help out at New Beginnings had more to do with filling the void in her unhappy life than her desire to promote altruism in her children.

Pulling up along the curb at New Beginnings Mission, Campbell couldn't believe how much it had changed. Or maybe she was now seeing the place through the eyes of an adult rather than those of a child. The facility felt smaller and more worn than it had back then. The shiny gold lettering on the sign she had remembered was faded and chipped. She recalled her conversation with Finn the other night where they had contemplated how much experiences were a matter of perception. Could you change a life by looking at it differently? By seeing different opportunities and making other choices that might have been invisible if you were simply looking another way, would everything else change? Could vampires be real?

Parking was easy since it was an early Saturday morning. Holding a hand of each child, they walked together through the front door.

"It smells funny in here," Ellis whispered to Caroline, who giggled nervously.

"Shhh!" Campbell searched around for someone in charge.

They reached the high-ceilinged foyer. "Can I help you?" someone asked from behind the front desk. It was a light skinned man, maybe 20 years old. "I'm Sid. I'm a client here. But I also work as the front desk manager."

Campbell couldn't imagine what could happen in someone's life to bring them to this point at such a young age. She imagined Ellis sitting behind the desk and shuddered.

"Hi Sid," she said. "Is there someone we could speak with about becoming volunteers for your Thanksgiving program?"

"Well, ma'am. We are self-run for the most part. Since our funding was cut back in the 80's we lost most of our professional paid personnel. But we stayed open by self-organizing. Those of us who have gotten clean and sober stay on to help run the place. It's one way of giving back."

"Wow, well I'm glad to hear you've been able to keep your doors open."

"Yes ma'am," he said. "Anyway, we have two staff members who run things from the top. I guess you would have to speak with one of them. They manage the outreach. Old Travis is a little senile though these days." He nodded his head in the direction of a tall African American gentleman who appeared to be the farther side of 90 years old, sitting in a worn red leather chair in the next room.

Campbell wasn't sure but he looked a great deal like the man who had managed the Thanksgiving program when she was a child. She remembered him: tall and thin with round glasses, checking his sign-in sheet as the men shuffled into the center on its opening day. Now he seemed smaller and frailer, but with that same wise and focused look about his face. It could be him, she thought. He didn't seem to notice that anyone was staring or talking about him.

"He's been here forever, I think," Sid chuckled with affection. "Better to call the other manager to speak with you."

"Sure, sounds good."

Sid picked up the phone and punched a few numbers and started speaking in a low tone. Campbell turned away. She walked a few steps toward the sitting room. Caroline and Ellis were taking it all in. "Don't wander off," she reminded them. The walls were the same oatmeal color she had remembered. It appeared as if they hadn't been repainted in decades. There was new couch, a larger, newer TV and table and chairs in the seating area. She noticed the few men randomly seated around the room. They seemed to take no notice of her presence. The memory of the man who had saved her life punched its way into Campbell's thoughts. Her breathing started coming fast. She hadn't braced herself for this. Campbell thought, *I wonder whatever happened to that guy who pushed me out of the way of the car? Is he dead, or alive?*

Just then a familiar voice rang clear across from the other side of the room.

"Can I help you?"

Campbell spun around toward the voice. It was Finn. She stood, stunned for a few moments. He did too. An aura of guilt, as if they were being found somewhere they shouldn't be, hung thick in the silence.

"Finn?" she uttered in disbelief.

"Campbell?" he said back, moving with hesitation across the room toward her. A few of the men raised their heads to watch.

"What are you doing here?" she demanded, trying to laugh to relieve the stress and anxiety mounting in her chest.

"Mommy?" Ellis inquired, "Who is that?"

Throwing the focus onto her children to deflect how flustered she felt, she introduced them as normally as if she were standing at the grocery store.

"Ellis, Caroline? This is Mr. Finn. He works with Mommy at school."

He smiled warmly at the children and shook their hands.

"Nice to meet you," he replied. She peered into his eyes curiously. "What are you doing here?"

From the corner of her eye Campbell observed that the man Sid had referred to as Old Travis was watching the exchange with keen curiosity. *Is he glaring at Finn?* she wondered. He didn't take his eyes off him for a long time.

"I work here," said Finn. What else could he say?

They stood a moment staring into each other's eyes, neither one saying a word. Caroline turned from one adult to the other, and noticed an expression on her mother's face that she had never seen before.

"This is where I live. I serve as the outreach coordinator and house supervisor in exchange for a small salary and free board."

Her disbelief over this chance meeting, and the sheer excitement of being in Finn's presence paralyzed her mind from thinking of other logical questions to ask. The intersection between the present and the past—fleeting images she could not name, seeing Finn here and now, all collided.

She said, "Wow! Why didn't you say something about it when we were together the other night?"

"I don't know. It didn't seem important at the time."

"How long have you been here?"

"Oh, seems like forever," he conceded, laughing.

Finn didn't blink for a solid minute and gazed at Campbell a minute longer. Caroline broke the silence.

"Mommy," she pleaded, jerking at Campbell's arm, "Let's go!"

"You have a mini-me it seems," Finn said.

"Sorry," Campbell apologized, still looking at Finn. "They get bored easily. We came to see if we could volunteer for the Thanksgiving dinner program. You know, help out in some way."

"Sure! That would be great!" Finn's mind was already calculating the joys of having yet another time at which he could look forward to being with Campbell. "Let me give you the tour."

They entered the sitting room. Ellis broke free from his mother's grip and galloped toward a man seated at the table drinking coffee from a small white ceramic mug. "Hi!" Ellis shouted. The man looked up, offered a broad smile, and waved back. Caroline stood back seeming tentative.

Campbell could feel Old Travis' eyes boring into her back. She reeled around and smiled. "Hi, how are you?" she asked.

Travis didn't reply. He seemed to look right through her and stared directly at Finn. "You know this will never work," he said.

Campbell was confused. The sound of his voice froze Ellis and Caroline in their tracks. His voice boomed with a tone of accusation. She felt as if she had been caught doing something wrong, which in her core she knew she was. She was inexplicably falling in love with Finn. Was it that obvious, even to an old stranger like this?

"Don't you see what he is?" Travis shouted, reaching a high pitch which cracked his voice and left him coughing spasmodically. Dementia had been setting in the last year. Finn forced a nervous laugh and rolled his eyes as if he were apologizing for a crazy elderly relative. Campbell opened her mouth to pacify the old man. Before she could utter a sound he jerked his head in her direction and shouted, "I'd stay away from him if I was you, young lady. Ain't nothing good gonna come from this!"

His glare kept her eyes locked on his. Yet he had a slight grin like he was teasing her. But this joke made her feel ill.

"Now, now, Mr. Travis. Please don't scare off our volunteers," Finn said like a kindly son.

Travis mumbled something else under his breath that Campbell couldn't make out. She wasn't sure if he was at all lucid. A minute later, as if he were now more mentally present, Travis winked at Finn who responded with a glare.

Finn gestured to Campbell and the kids to move into the kitchen. He wanted her out of Travis' presence as fast as possible without seeming suspicious or alarmed. *God damn it old man*, he thought to himself, *Close that mouth of yours!* Travis gave a tiny grin at the corner of his mouth as they moved away. *Ha ha, old man*, Finn thought. There was nothing he could begrudge Travis especially now that his mind had been unraveling thread by thread as old age progressed. He led Campbell by the elbow toward the door. Glancing over his shoulder once, Finn made a gentle warning. Travis was still mumbling words that Campbell couldn't make out. Caroline and Ellis rushed ahead, grateful to be away from this scary old man.

"Sorry about that," Finn sighed, "He's old. In the last year he has really gone downhill and carries on all the time about things that happened decades ago. He's harmless, though. Sweet old guy. He was the director here for years until I took over. He still works here because we are the only family he's got left. I mean, he has a son supposedly but none of us have ever met him."

"I thought he looked familiar," Campbell exclaimed.

The children were leaning over the pass through, their knees teetering on stools staring out at the TV in the sitting room. This TV was in color, not black and white like the one Campbell remembered. To Campbell's relief, they were entertained for the time being. She could focus her attention on her conversation with Finn.

"I remember him from when I came here as a kid!" Campbell continued. "Wow…amazing. After all these years. How crazy is that?"

"What?" Finn blurted. Campbell thought he seemed agitated.

The noise in his mind grew louder. Sounds and colors swirled together making a mosaic of chaos fall into place like pieces to a puzzle.

"Yeah. When I was six years old we came here. Me, and my mom, and my dad. That's why I picked this place to bring my kids. This guy, I assume he was homeless, because he was staying here, he saved my life. I ran into the road like an idiot and this guy out of nowhere jumped in front of the car and saved my life. Even after all these years I still think about it."

She paused waiting for his end of the witty banter she had grown used to. He seemed pale and sick. She continued, "Seemed like it was time to pay back a little by helping out here."

Campbell kept rambling because the look on Finn's face resembled terror. Seeing Caroline here in this room, like a young Campbell, caused his face to feel hot. Tears pushed their way to the surface. He turned away and shoved a few chairs back under the card table.

How could it be? he asked himself.

In an attempt to make him laugh she tilted her head in mock curiosity and joked, "You know…you look a lot like him now that I think about it." She laughed again. "Sure your dad didn't stay here back in the day?"

The truth was Campbell couldn't remember much about what the man who had saved her looked like except that he was in child's terms, "scraggily." He had kind eyes she recalled, and a cool gold charm that he had shown her.

Her smile faded as Finn stared at her. He seemed to be lost in his thoughts. The warm and playful rapport they had developed had disappeared. A fearful knot formed in her stomach.

What did I say? Maybe the comment about his dad was in poor taste, she worried.

In an effort to recover, she said, "Hey, I'm sorry about that joke. That was inappropriate. I didn't mean to offend…"

Finn broke her sentence off. "No. It's okay. Really. Um…." He looked around with alarm. But no one else was in the room. "But um…you need to go. I forgot there's some business I must attend to now. I'm sorry. I have to go. Can you let yourselves out?"

Before she could answer he turned and dashed down the stairs to the basement closing the door behind him. She could hear his footsteps echoing down the wooden steps as fast as they could go. Then Campbell could hear nothing except the sound of the TV coming from the other room. She stood there, baffled, with her mouth hanging open. She reached out and stroked Ellis on his back. "C'mon kids. Let's go."

"Not yet, Mom. Tom and Jerry isn't over! Please?"

"Let's go. Now!"

Ellis and Caroline knew what this tone meant. They untangled themselves from the kitchen stools and moved toward the sitting room. Campbell glanced at Travis. He was staring at her, expressionless.

"You know what he is, don't you? Don't you?" he growled.

She tried a make a weak smile, and nodded. She stopped at the front desk where Sid was still seated, quietly doing a crossword puzzle.

"Um, excuse me," she asked, clearing her throat. Sid placed the pen down and looked at her intently. "How long has Mr. McGinnis worked here?" She didn't know why this mattered but she sensed the answer was important. He paused to reflect.

"Uh, gee. Lemme think here. Well, he's been here ever since I've been here, 'bout two years ago. See, all the other men who stay here and those who work here don't stay long. Either they can't stay sober and they have to leave, or they get clean, help out for a while and then return themselves back into their old lives. Or start new ones, you know? So there ain't nobody here 'cept Old Travis and Mr. McGinnis who's been here more than a few years. Maybe the business folks who run it. But the nonprofit big wigs who manage the financial stuff, the grants and money, they don't ever come down here. So I can't tell you exactly." He smiled as if to apologize.

"Thank you, Sid," she replied and turned to leave. Her mind was reeling now. *What just happened?*

"So are ya'll coming back for Thanksgiving?" Sid hollered out after them.

"Yes. We look forward to it," she said, calling back over her shoulder.

CHAPTER FOURTEEN

Baltimore, 2011

Campbell and her children drove the entire way from Baltimore City in silence. Something gnawed at the thin strands that wove her sense of reality. She didn't know it; it wasn't something she could put into words. But she could feel it. Somewhere in her bones. Her entire life Campbell had been a realist. She didn't believe in things like horoscopes, fate, ESP, aliens, or true love. She didn't take anything on faith that didn't have hard evidence. It was a cold winter day in 1973 when, she gave her first intellectual speech, using logic to prove to her parents that Santa didn't exist. The smell of her mother's floral perfume wafting up from all of the wrapped presents as she opened them that Christmas day had been her first clue. Her parents didn't dispute her allegations. After her mother moved out, Campbell spent years convinced that her need to prove and challenge everything from such a young age had been the cause of her mother's unhappiness.

She consented later that night to Brent's romantic overtures, performing in a perfunctory fashion the series of sexual moves that had become habit absent of passion. It had been about eight days since they had last made love and she knew he would come looking for her tonight. They were if nothing else routine and consistent. As she lay there in bed with him it was Finn's face that she kept seeing. Guilt forced her to open her eyes and focus on Brent. Campbell had never been one to fantasize, yet tonight it seemed as if the only way she could feel anything as Brent moved his hands and lips across her body was to close her eyes and imagine Finn's deep brown eyes gazing down at her, and his soft blond hair brushing the sides of her cheeks and her breasts. At those moments she could feel the blood pulsing from her brain down into her extremities with a rush of electricity. But when the guilt became too much for her she opened her eyes. The appearance of Brent's face, contorted, as it did when he was at the height of his climax, caused a deep revulsion in her. She wanted to push him off and run screaming from the room. But she didn't. She waited until it was over, kissed him and then moved to the bathroom to wash up.

Later that night, Campbell lay in stillness watching the sheer moss green curtains next to her bed move in small nearly imperceptible waves as the heater turned on and off, bringing warm air up from the floor vents into her bedroom. She was unable to sleep. Rather than think any more about Finn, who or what he might be, she focused on the tiniest sounds and movements that surrounded her. She realized that these occurrences went on nightly but until now they had never seemed to exist.

How many other things in life have I taken for granted or ignored that are right in front of my face? She knew she was thinking about Finn again. Down the darkened hallway she could hear the soft muffle of Ellis coughing. *I wonder if I should go and check the vaporizer?* His asthma had been acting up tonight, most likely because they had turned on the heater just two days ago, and in spite of the air filters they had installed, Ellis had trouble breathing every autumn.

How often has he done this when I wasn't aware because I was asleep? she wondered. *Have I been asleep my whole life?* The thought of waking up perhaps for the first time in her life filled her with dread because she didn't know how much she might have to give up or lose as a result.

Campbell rose without a sound and tiptoed down the hall. She settled into her usual spot in Ellis's room, and pulled the comforter stashed underneath his bed. She spread it out like an animal nest on the rug and curled herself in. This was where she slept on many evenings. The spot was familiar and comforting. She rested her head on the belly of his giant stuffed Elmo and tried to imagine Finn wandering with her in a deep dark forest. She searched for him there behind the thickets of trees, in the shaded glens where the mists settled in low. She imagined him watching her, watching her look for him.

Is he a…? Her words trailed off before she finished the sentence. But even the facts couldn't be ignored. Granted her last visit to New Beginnings was over 30 years ago. And granted she was a small child when that man with the shiny charm had leapt out of nowhere to save her from the oncoming car. But she remembered enough. Seeing Finn in that same place 35 years later—clean shaven and healthy, he was a dead ringer for that man. *But how? Unless he never aged. The signals to logical reasoning were jammed with the noise of Finn's vampire theory. Maybe it wasn't a theory. Maybe….*

Deep rhythmic breathing from Ellis brought Campbell back to a conscious state and Finn slipped farther into the woods where she couldn't follow. Not tonight at least. She sat upright, gazed at her son's quiet body, and sighed with relief that his asthma had calmed down. She would be able to sleep knowing that tonight he would not wake up in a suffocating panic.

The next morning precisely at 10:30 a.m., Gillian Macey heard the phone ring; she smiled to herself and mused, *Right on time.* By the second ring Gillian had turned off the faucet in the kitchen sink, searched for a non-existent hand towel, and resigned herself to drying her hands on her jeans, then reached for the cordless. "Sanity check," she said cheerfully.

It had been Gillian and Campbell's routine for many years now to call each other just about every morning at 10:30, except on the days that Campbell worked on campus, just to "check in." The routine had become normal, and no matter what was going on, good day or bad, they always found something to talk about. She glanced at the girls busy at their computer, fighting over a computer game. She reprimanded them. "I'm on the phone…work it out!"

"I am officially insane now," Campbell pronounced with mock resignation.

"I always knew that about you," Gillian said. "What's the crisis today?"

Over the years they had fallen into a comfortable balance. Gillian's no non-sense grounded-ness was a lightning rod to Campbell's mercurial distractibility. Gillian was the stabilizing force in Campbell's world. But today was different, and Campbell knew it. She knew bringing up the question, "Hey, do you suppose that hot guy I work with is a vampire?" would be just too much for Gillian's practical sensibilities to bear.

Before continuing she tried to make her voice sound as normal as usual, as if she were merely throwing out today's witty riddle. "So what do you think about the choices you've made in life?" she asked with the same off handedness she used with any of her unanswerable questions.

"Too much coffee already today my dear?" Gillian shot back. "Or have you been surfing the Internet too much?"

"Well, let's see," Gillian mused with mock introspection, adding, "If Jack comes home from work acting like a dick again, and I choose to kill him while he sleeps, is that a choice? Or do I get a pass?"

"Of course you get a pass, my dear," Campbell replied. "I don't blame you. It feels like I haven't see Brent for weeks. By the time the kids go to bed I am so tired. We barely speak anymore, if he's even home. It's like being a single parent."

Speaking with Gillian also remind Campbell that she had to make extra babysitting time to go get her mammogram done. Another joy of impending middle-age.

"I get to go get my boobs flattened next month, too. I haven't even made the appointment yet!"

"Don't forget to do that, Cam. It could take forever to get an appointment!" Gillian insisted.

"Yeah, yeah," Campbell said, playing the dutiful role of the disobedient adolescent. Campbell continued "Caroline, take that out of your mouth before I take it! I mean it! Okay, I may choose to kill my kids today." She could hear Gillian on the other end. Her voice was now muffled saying something about a keyboard and moving the girls' chairs.

"What's that?" Gillian said in a louder tone, coming back to the phone. "Sorry, I had to do an intervention there…what were you saying?"

"Do you ever wonder if you made the right choices?" Campbell knew Gillian well and knew what her response would be.

"I don't see much point in a question like that. I mean, why make myself crazy over things I can't change? Who is to say that any other choice would have been better or worse?"

Always the pragmatist, Campbell observed. It was why she loved her.

"I know. It's not like we can live forever and make every conceivable choice possible … right?" It was a baited question, with her little secret hanging on the end of the hook.

"Hey," said Gillian excitedly. "Do you know something I don't know? Did you find the secret elixir to life? Can I get some?"

"No, not yet."

Campbell's right hand spun the car into the Super Fresh grocery store parking lot while her left hand held the phone by her ear.

"But hey, listen," Campbell said breaking free from the conversation. "I am at the store now. If I see magic elixir on sale can I get you some?"

They both laughed. "Yeah, get me the cherry flavored."

Gillian pressed the "off" button on her phone and studied it before setting it down on the cradle. *Something is wrong,* she thought. She couldn't put her finger on it … it was something in Campbell's tone. *No. Something in the tone of what was not said. But that makes no sense,* she convinced herself. Gillian and Campbell had long passed the stage of keeping secrets from each other. *If something was going on she would have said so, right?* But in spite of their intimacy, Gillian was not the type to pry. *If something is wrong, she'll tell me when the time is right.*

Campbell needed to start thinking through her vampire theory with someone who knew her better than anyone. Someone who saw the world through a more absurd lens. Lilly. Lilly would know what to say. But that would have to wait until they met for their walking date. First, she had to get her mind centered enough to prep for her lecture tomorrow. She also knew there was a good chance she would run into Finn after her class. She knew she wouldn't rest until she confronted him.

The children were walking down the cereal aisle, Caroline dutifully by her side. Ellis in full stride a few feet ahead of the cart, when Caroline flatly queried, "Mom?"

"Yeah?"

"Are you alright?" Her face was tight.

Campbell stopped in her tracks. The canned beans rolled up and back in the metal cart. She looked at Caroline. "What do you mean honey?" The lines on Caroline's forehead wrinkled.

"You seem," she paused searching for the right word, "Pre-occupied."

Ellis raced back to the cart sensing he was missing something important, and hurled his feet with a slam onto the base of the metal rim of the cart. The tip of Ellis' sneaker made a "thud" of impact. "Ow!" he wailed. Campbell fixed her eyes on Caroline.

She laughed a little, nervously. "Where did you learn that word?" she asked Caroline. Caroline shrugged. She would not give up without an answer to her question. She would not be deterred.

"Well, yeah, I guess I have been …pre-occupied." Campbell had never lied to her children. "There's a lot of stuff going on at Mommy's work."

"With Mr. Finn?" Caroline asked. Campbell's face rushed with a pulse of blood. Her hands shook on the handles of the cart.

How could she tell? Campbell was surprised and impressed by Caroline's intuition.

Caroline fidgeted with her fingers. "'Cause when you saw him yesterday you got all funny looking like you were sad and happy at the same time. But when you're with Miss Gillian you're always happy."

"Mr. Finn and I have a presentation we have to put together before Mommy goes on her trip in a few weeks. I guess it has me, as you said, preoccupied."

The truth, even if not the whole truth. This seemed to satisfy Caroline and they moved on to more pressing discussions over the merits of sugar cereals with prizes inside.

CHAPTER FIFTEEN

Baltimore, 2011

The air was crisp, as if the sun had wiped away the summer's humidity once and for all and erased the city smog. If one looked at the robin's egg blue of the sky that morning rather than the trucks and cars on the Route 83 overpass, attendees of the Baltimore Sunday Farmers Market would have thought themselves to be on a farm, rather than pushing through throngs of the new urban chic. Gillian had a burlap bag slung over her shoulder weighted down with a head of cabbage and 10 apples. They had gone around the entire loop once already. Campbell sucked the last remains of her iced coffee and adjusted the two bags in her left hand. "So, have the carrots, the cheese, and one dozen eggs."

"What about some bread?" Gillian asked.

"Yeah, but Brent just brought some home from the grocery store yesterday because we were out and I needed to make sandwiches for the kids' lunches. Worried it'll go bad before I can use it."

"Just freeze it!" Gillian suggested.

"Always the wise one, aren't you?" Campbell laughed.

After buying a loaf of three-seed multigrain from the local bakery table, Campbell and Gillian walked the three blocks to where they had parked Campbell's car. Campbell began to draw a mental map of where she was now in proximity to New

Beginnings and how to casually suggest to Gillian that they "drive by." Campbell pulled the car away from the curb and headed down Baltimore Avenue.

"Why are you going this way?" Gillian asked. "Isn't it easier to get back on 95 if we go left?"

"I just want to drive by somewhere." The tone in her voice had already changed.

"Where?"

"New Beginnings. It's a shelter for the homeless. I went there as a kid and I am thinking about bringing Ellis and Caroline there to help on Thanksgiving."

"Sounds noble," Gillian said flatly. "But, if you already know where it is, then why are we going by there now?"

Mustering all the casualness she could, Campbell said, "Oh, well, one of my new co-workers also works there."

Gillian could make epic leaps in logic.

"So he's that good looking, huh?" she replied with a tinge of bitterness.

The car swung down St Paul's Street. Campbell's heart had already begun to race. *What if he's outside? What if he sees me? Maybe this is a bad idea.*

So Campbell conceded the truth. "I don't know, Gill." She regretted not telling Gillian more. But the words wouldn't come. Lying would be easiest but Gillian could always detect a lie—ever since 9th grade when they became best friends. Campbell could remember the night at the school dance where she kissed Johnny Slater. She was walking out of the girls' bathroom, the hallways darker than during their usual school day, and there was Johnny leaning against one of the lockers, waiting for her. While Campbell had secretly liked Johnny, she would never reveal this crush to even her closest confidants, including Gillian. Johnny; dark eyes and hair, long and lank in his bad boy appearance, was always in trouble with the teachers.

Campbell, still naïve and innocent, hung with a clique of good girls who prided themselves on their good grades and avoiding raucous parties. Admitting to her affection for Johnny would be like defecting from her own clan. As she exited the bathroom he sauntered over to her with his puppy dog eyes, and after a brief exchange of flirtatious words he leaned in and kissed her hard on the lips. She gasped, and pulled away. Her face turned bright red, and underneath the dimly lit hall lights Johnny could detect her shock. He laughed, in a way that was both mean and pleased at the same time. She turned on her heels and ran back into the gymnasium to find Gillian waiting at the front entrance by the refreshment table looking worried. "Where were you?" she asked with concern. "Um...I..." Campbell stammered. "I was just talking with someone." It only took a few moments for Gillian to wrest the truth from Campbell. She had never even attempted to keep the truth about anything from Gillian since then.

Campbell searched the sidewalk furtively for any sign of Finn. She needed to see him. Maybe he could explain to her his strange behavior at their last encounter. Maybe not. Maybe there was no explanation. Gillian sighed loudly. The sigh that indicated she was becoming frustrated with Campbell's antics.

"Campbell, sometimes I don't get you." Her tone was serious now. "You have achieved everything you set out to obtain. You have your Ph.D. for Christ's sake. And two healthy kids. And a husband. What more do you want?"

It was the emphasis on the word *more* that stung Campbell. She remained silent.

Gillian said, "Nothing has ever been enough for you. In a way that was good, you know? It kept motivating you to achieve things. But Cam, come on. When will you be happy with what you have?"

"Are you happy?" Campbell retorted. She had pulled the car into an empty space along the sidewalk. She glanced around for any sign of Finn.

"Yes," Gillian pronounced emphatically. "Yes, basically I am. But this isn't about having 'things'—this is about a restlessness in your soul. You've had it since you were a kid. I just worry about you. That before you know it you will have burned everything you have built down to the ground." The words *don't become your mother* hung in the silence.

"What if that's what I want to do?" she whispered. But where did her children fit into all of that? There had been sacrifice for them. Was Finn the object of desire or was he merely a reflection of what mattered more; that she could see her life anew through him in ways she never could alone?

Campbell had forgotten about her concerns of running into Finn and focused on Gillian. She lit a cigarette and rolled down the window.

"Aren't we always in the slow process of killing ourselves, Gillian?" She pretended to find herself amusing.

"Don't use your smoking as a distraction, Campbell. You know it's a disgusting habit and I love you anyway."

"I have been settled, Gillian. I have been settled for almost ten years! I haven't cheated on Brent. I work my ass off every day to make my life run smoothly and to provide for my family. I love my children and I fight off the fear that I am little better of a parent to them than my mom was to me. But I haven't run off screaming from my house no matter how many times I have wanted to." She tossed the cigarette out the window and it rolled aimlessly down the curb toward the storm drain.

"We all do sometimes," Gillian agreed sympathetically.

"I'm not just some bored lonely housewife," Campbell continued with a sharp tone. "You know that wasn't a stab at housewives either, Gillian. I am a little old in my life to chase romance. But …what's left once you have everything? What's left waiting for you but death?"

"That's a little over dramatic, don't you think?" Gillian argued.

Campbell needed to downplay her inexplicable connection with Finn. Without knowing what it was herself, she had no words that would satisfy her lifelong friend.

"What's wrong with a harmless flirtation, Gillian?" Having only spent a brief amount of time with him, and a fervent sceptic of "love at first sight," she told herself that while it was not "love" perhaps, the feeling between them was undeniably powerful and near intoxicating. Besides, she had no way of knowing how he felt about her.

"Nothing, Campbell. I know that. But there's something deeper than runs within you. Something that has been lying in wait, waiting for something to up-end the whole cart of apples. I just hope you don't mistake some crush for a sort of 'destiny'." It was easier to fool herself than it was to fool Gillian.

Campbell promised herself as they pulled away from the curb that she would back away from this pursuit of Finn. *Where could it go anyway?* She would repeat this as necessary to remain on the track she had laid out for herself. It was a good one. It was happiness on life's terms. So Campbell pressed her foot on the gas and accelerated smoothly past New Beginnings, forcing her eyes and head to stay forward.

CHAPTER SIXTEEN

Baltimore, 1992

Maryland General Hospital

Elizabeth Cote raised her head from the hospital pillows and glimpsed out the window to see the dawn easing in grey and wet. No longer able to fight the nausea and pressure building in her stomach she vomited into the metal container next to her bed. The chemo was doing everything except making the cancer disappear. When they thought she was asleep she could hear the doctors whisper the words, "late stage" to each other. She coughed, and spit and caught a glimpse of Campbell's head slouched to one side of the bedside chair. Her eyes were closed in partial sleep but Campbell jerked herself upright as she heard her mother struggling to adjust the pillows.

When Campbell first came to the hospital a few weeks ago at Elizabeth's behest, she was shocked to see mother's worn down physical state. She had adjusted to her mother's pitiful appearance but it still made Campbell feel uneasy to see the few sparse patches of hair fall from her head and onto her pillow as easily as the white wisps off a dying dandelion. She dredged up an image of the last time she had seen her mom. She was 8 years old, and walking to the school bus stop. Her mother stood at the street curb in her blue dress and chunky heels. Elizabeth feigned a smile and waved goodbye as her only daughter climbed onto the bus and drove off. Then Elizabeth hurried home to pack her bags. She left a note on the kitchen table next to a defrosting casserole.

Campbell found her father sitting in the kitchen with all the lights off when she walked through the door from school. "Hi, Dad! I'm home!" she shouted. Usually on the days when he was home early she was met with a warm welcome. He would run to her and swing her around in the air, asking, "And how was school today Sweet Pea?" But today he didn't turn around to greet her. Campbell dropped her book bag by the front door and moved cautiously into the kitchen. "What's wrong, Daddy?" she asked, fear welling in her chest. She noticed her mother was nowhere to be seen and the usual hum of housework had been replaced with a vacant silence.

"Where's Mom?" she asked. Her stomach twisted. Her father made no movement.

She sidled up behind his slumped figure at the kitchen table. After a pause, he murmured, "She's gone." The word "gone" didn't register in Campbell's childish vocabulary.

"Is she shopping? When will she be back?"

"No, honey. I mean, she's gone." He gave a thoughtful pause and added, "She's left us."

Campbell had never read the actual note. After gazing on it for several hours at the kitchen table as the defrosting casserole turned from solid ice into water, William Cote crumpled it tightly in his left fist and crushed it into the soft heart of defrosted noodles and cheese. Then it went into the trash with the casserole, glass dish and all.

Campbell had not seen her mother since that day. Now 15 years later she was saying goodbye again.

"Tough night?" she asked, trying to muster as much sympathy as she could. As an added gesture she poured a cup of cold water from the plastic pitcher and handed the small cup to her mother. Elizabeth didn't reply but sipped the water. Careful not to spill, she sighed, and rested her head back with her eyes closed. As the weeks had passed, Campbell had fantasized about the heart to heart chat they would have, where her mother would plead for Campbell's forgiveness. She would utter through sobs that she regretted the day she left her and that it had been the biggest mistake of her life. She would look deeply into Campbell's eyes and tell her what she wanted to hear most of all: It wasn't her fault. Campbell wasn't seeking redemption from her mother; she was seeking redemption for herself. But day after day silence and small talk passed between them. Campbell whittled away the long hours by telling her mother about her university studies and her plans to work in Africa with women's rights in the sub Saharan villages.

"Do you have a boyfriend?" her mother asked one rainy afternoon as they nibbled on saltine crackers. Campbell blushed. It seemed silly, to blush, but the question seemed like it should belong to a close mother-daughter relationship, the kind Campbell had seen in movies, sitcoms and tampon ads. Not here with her estranged mother lying on her death bed. But she humored the question with a reply. "Yeah. His name is Todd. He is who I am going to travel to Africa with." Elizabeth nodded with taciturn approval.

"Are you going to marry him?" Elizabeth asked. Her voice was cold and flat. Campbell didn't try to hide the shock and disgust on her face. Her mother read the expression plainly. "Look, Campbell. I know I hurt you when I left."

Campbell froze. Here it was. The moment she had been waiting for. But the moment wasn't what she had anticipated after all. Elizabeth continued, "I had to leave. I was trapped. Day after day rolling around that empty house while you were at school and Bob was at work."

Through clenched teeth Campbell said, "Why didn't you just get a job if you were so bored?"

Elizabeth sighed and glanced out the hospital window at the raindrops starting to beat against the glass. "You're old enough now to understand this. I was empty inside. That life, married with kids in suburbia. That was chosen for me. Not literally. I wasn't forced into it. What I mean is, that's what you did in those days. There weren't the opportunities women like you have today. Look at you, an amazing job and future ahead of you."

"My job is not that amazing," Campbell retorted. "I work for a non-profit agency, for peanuts. That's not exactly going to make Newsweek's Woman of the Year, Elizabeth." Campbell hadn't called Elizabeth "mom" since she turned twelve and had no plans to start now.

"It's different these days though, Campbell. I didn't have the chance to consider all of the possibilities for what life could be. Your father was nice enough. And marrying him seemed to make sense at the time. Even with my teaching degree I would have been paid next to nothing and would have died a spinster."

I wish you had, Campbell thought.

"When I met Scottie, well, suddenly everything changed for me."

Scottie. That was the name that was never uttered in her house when her father was around.

"I didn't mean for it to happen the way it did," Elizabeth continued with a tone of sadness. "But I had to make a choice, and I did."

Campbell knew next to nothing about what had happened to her mother after she left, or what had happened to Scottie. All Campbell knew growing up came from postcards that arrived in sparse intervals from various places. They said little more than: "Miss you. Be a good girl for your daddy. Work hard in school. Love, Mom." The letters shared little about what her mom was doing. Or where she was. On her birthday and at Christmas she would get a long distance phone call from her mother wishing her a "happy whatever." When she was too young to know better she would ask in a pleading voice, "When are you coming home, Mom?" Then there would be dead silence on the other end. "I don't know, honey. It's difficult to explain. Be good for your daddy, okay? Gotta run now."

Maybe her mom wanted to keep any information about Scottie, or where she was, from her husband. They had never filed for divorce. Campbell had never asked her father why. But Scottie's name was rarely mentioned in the postcards or phone calls. The communications between Campbell and her mother had all but ceased by the time Campbell graduated high school. She had taught herself how to not miss her mother, and her father had done everything he could over the years to make up for her absence.

But why wasn't Scottie here, now? Was he dead? Or did he leave her the way she had left Campbell and her father? *Divine retribution,* she mused. Campbell didn't ask. She didn't care.

"Don't make the same mistakes I made," Elizabeth insisted, emotion tightening her voice.

"You mean leaving us?" Campbell asked, willing to meet her mother halfway for the apology she deserved.

"No. Getting married in the first place."

Campbell's stomach lurched and her head felt fuzzy. She lost all control. "What are you saying!?" she sputtered, "That you wish I had never been born?"

"Come on, Campbell. You know that's not what I mean." Elizabeth seemed cold and distant.

"That is exactly what you're saying!" she shouted back. Campbell stood up and turned to flee the room.

"Wait and sit down, young lady," her mother commanded. She coughed and spit up a few drops of blood into the plastic cup she was still holding. The sight of the blood forced Campbell into a state of reasonableness and she sat back in her chair.

"You are not a child anymore, Campbell," Elizabeth said with indignation.

"You're right. You stole that childhood from me the day you left."

Campbell rose again from her chair. She stared into her mother's watery eyes, old and tired. "Good bye, Elizabeth." She walked away without looking back.

Two days later the hospital called. They were giving Elizabeth her last rites. Campbell sped to the hospital but she couldn't reason with herself exactly why. Something was still unfinished. Her mother appeared in the bed more withered and deflated than before. She was a fragment of a person, motionless under the cold sheets. The doctors made room for Campbell at Elizabeth's bedside. "Say your goodbyes now," they offered. Campbell scanned the room, not sure what she was trying to locate. She turned back to her mother.

"Is she conscious?" Campbell asked.

"Well, she's been heavily sedated with morphine for the pain," one older grey haired doctor explained. "But," he added, "She can most likely still hear you."

After 15 years, Campbell thought, it has come to this. This moment right here and now. She thought about all the things she had rehearsed saying to her mother over the years. She had rehearsed them in her mind over and over. And after storming out two days ago, Campbell had felt nothing but a pure rage of emptiness, and a resentment that all these years of pain weren't going to ever be healed, at least if she waited for her mother to heal them. Her mother hadn't changed. With mere days left to her life, rendered unconscious by the morphine, Campbell would never know what her dying thoughts might be.

Campbell placed her fingers with care upon her mother's forehead. As she did she was sure she saw her mother's eyes flutter in recognition. Her slight breathing seemed to quicken. Campbell closed her eyes and bent down to kiss her mother's cheek. She leaned in to her ear and whispered, "I love you, Mom." Then she stood up and walked away. Campbell wasn't sure if she had even meant it. She didn't feel anything but numb. But she knew she had only one chance to decide what to do in that moment. So she had said, "I love you, Mom." What other choice did she have?

CHAPTER SEVENTEEN

Baltimore, 1992

"Ma'am…Is there someone we need to contact? Ma'am?" The attending nurse looked upon Campbell's stunned expression with a genuine sympathy. She was young, probably new in her position and not yet hardened by the experience of seeing death on a frequent basis. Her brown eyes creased at the sides with a sort of sympathetic smile. Campbell, in a daze, saw her lips moving but had not heard a word she said.

"I'm sorry," she apologized. "What were you asking me?" She was still staring down at the withered motionless body that until just minutes ago had been her mother.

Gently the nurse asked again, "Is there anyone you need to call? You know, to inform them that your mother has passed? Is there any other family we need to notify?"

Campbell pulled herself out of the stupor. "Um…yeah. I suppose my dad." She swallowed hard at this prospect. After a brief few weeks spending time together in the hospital, her time with Elizabeth was done. It was the second time Campbell had lost her.

"There's a phone over at the nurses' station you can use."

"Thank you." Campbell forced a smile and moved slowly out of the room.

As Campbell wandered the fifth floor of the oncology unit, only halfheartedly trying to find her way out of the maze, she played the conversation with her father over in her mind. Calling him wasn't unusual. She called him without fail about once a week just to "check in." She was in full support of his decision to sell the house and to leave Baltimore, moving to Florida where he had hoped the ghosts of his former life couldn't follow him. Though he had a few female friends on and off over the years, he had never become serious with any of them.

"Hi ya, sweet pea!" he said casually as he answered the phone.

"Hi Dad." She paused.

"What's wrong, Campbell? Are you okay?"

She sensed the panic in his voice. Always the over protective father, even from five states away.

"It's Mom."

The word "mom" felt alien, like she was speaking in an unfamiliar language. "She's dead. It just happened."

"Oh." The phone was silent.

She continued. "Yeah. She had breast cancer. It was too far gone by the time they found it."

"Well," he sighed, "Libby was never one to go to the doctors, even when she should have."

"I'll take care of all the arrangements," Campbell assured him.

The rest of their conversation was going over the morbid details that Campbell's memory erased as she searched for the "Exit" sign. She turned right at one corridor that seemed familiar, and then turned right at the copy of an oil painting of a majestic snowcapped mountain dotted with spruce trees.

"Damn it," she said out loud. Campbell reflected on how hospital hallways seemed identical except for the small bronze plaques listing the room names and occasional pieces of faux artwork consisting of trees and snowcapped mountains intended, she supposed, to be soothing.

She got on the elevator down two floors and when the doors slipped open she saw a sign that read "Loading Dock Exit" with an arrow pointing to the left. She vaguely recalled parking along Howard Street where the loading dock was located. So she moved down the brightly lit hall toward the pair of large metal doors marked "Loading and Unloading Only."

It was 7:30 p.m. when Finn arrived at the loading dock in the back of Maryland General Hospital. The summer daylight hours made movement difficult until later in the day. He had grown restless and hungry hours earlier but kept himself cordoned off from the others at New Beginnings, preferring to pace his small room in the basement until the bright glow of the hot August day had subsided. It was his day of the week to arrive and he anticipated that the blood donor truck driver would be expecting him. Cash exchanges made everything so much easier.

Howard Street was quiet; most of the businessmen had gone home already from their day's work. Finn waited with patience leaning against the brick wall of the hospital beside a dumpster when he heard the heavy metal loading doors click open. But when he looked up it wasn't the blood donor delivery personnel he saw but a young woman.

What the hell? he thought as he lowered himself quickly down behind the dumpster. He dropped his head hoping not to be seen. But she had seen him. He could hear her footsteps quicken as she passed by him, nervous no doubt by his presence. Finn didn't necessarily appear out of place, wearing jeans and a solid black T-shirt. He didn't seem odd or dangerous. Yet, lurking about behind a hospital isn't normal either. He kept his head bent toward the pavement so as not to make her more nervous. But before she turned the corner he lifted his head to one side and caught a glimpse of a petite female with long blond hair fluttering back behind her shoulders carried by the breeze and the quickness of her movements. And he knew her scent from somewhere deep within his human memories. Before he could remember who she might be, she was gone. And the urge for his blood delivery was greater at that moment than his desire to follow her.

Finn completed his transaction with the blood bank delivery man and furtively stuffed his back pack with five pints of blood. When he no longer sensed the young woman was around he slung the weighty pack over his shoulder and emerged from the loading area and headed down Eutaw Street toward New Beginnings. He could feel the hunger rising in his throat and was eager to get back to his room where he could feed in private.

A block down at the corner of Franklin and Howard he spotted Travis strolling out of a corner market with a small brown paper shopping bag. Finn stopped and waited for Travis to make it a block away before he proceeded. He didn't want to be spotted. Though Finn hadn't drank a drop of alcohol since "his change," he quickly surmised that carrying a backpack with a heavy load of something, the contents of which he had no desire to explain, might lead to suspicion. He had returned to New Beginnings ten years ago and Travis had accepted him on as a helper, no questions asked. Finn thought about Travis as he walked a block behind, staying out of sight but keeping Travis on his radar.

The neighborhood became more abandoned as they moved away from the shopping areas and closer to the shelter. Fewer people passed by on the sidewalks. As Travis passed by a block of vacant stores Finn sensed the predators that had picked up Travis' scent. Finn's shoulders tensed and the hairs on his neck rose like a dog's in a high state of alarm. "It's them," he growled. "And they're after Travis."

He picked up his pace until he could see the pack of them; he estimated about three total, as their shadows played like dark water running along the sides of the brick row houses. They weren't seen directly by humans when they moved quickly. Only their shadowy movements could be detected. Finn moved mostly at a slower human pace, visible to people. Except when he was on the trail of others like himself, as he was now. Travis adjusted his bag onto to his other arm and kept walking, not sensing that death was following close behind. Finn's jaw tensed. His muscles ached and surged under his blue cotton shirt. *They're moving quickly*, he considered with a rising panic. *I can take three. I've done it before.*

Finn made one quick lunge pushing his body halfway down the block and found himself suddenly face to face with three hungry vampires. They could hear Travis's footsteps nearing the corner. Soon he would stumble upon this vampire brood, including Finn. If he stopped moving in order to confront them, he would be seen. While he knew he couldn't be discovered he couldn't leave Travis to become their prey. It was a chance he would have to take.

They stopped abruptly, surprised by Finn's presence which had come out of nowhere. Busy tracking their prey they had failed to notice Finn's approach. He stood firm in the center of the sidewalk, blocking them in their tracks. Finn sized them up instantly. One was tall and lanky with razor short blond hair. He wore black pants and a long sleeve black shirt. The other two were younger, maybe twenty years old. The first was stocky and muscular, wearing a sleeveless white tank and jeans with a large chain slung low around the waist. The other with short curly brown hair was also in black pants and a faded red tee shirt with Led Zeppelin across the front in an ornate print style. The oldest spoke first.

"Move on. This is our kill," he warned.

"This ain't nobody's kill," Finn replied keeping his eyes steady on the other two in case they made a move.

The one with curly hair lifted his eyes around Finn's left shoulder, tracking Travis. Finn turned his head around and saw Travis turning the corner three blocks up. He seemed not to notice them. The older one made a move to push past Finn. Finn blocked him again. They stood chest to chest in a face off.

"What gives you the right to stop us? Huh? Who the hell do you think you are, loner?"

Travis was now just a block away from where they stood. They leaned in closely beside the narrow alleyway cluttered with empty boxes and a tall garbage can.

"That old man belongs to me," Finn replied. "That's all you need to know. Go find your food elsewhere."

They paused in silence for a few seconds. The two younger ones seemed too distracted and hungry for a fight.

"C'mon Chester," protested the one with the white tank top. "Let's just go. There's plenty more around tonight to pick from. I'm too hungry to deal with this mess."

The others nodded in agreement. Chester backed away from Finn keeping his eyes on him. He emitted a loud growl and was gone. Their shadows flew swiftly across the building facades. Finn breathed deep with relief. Then he leapt forward into his shadow form and rushed toward New Beginnings fearful that others might also be waiting by the shelter for easy targets.

The kitchen lights were low and Travis was facing the counter, motionless with his back to the entrance door and Finn tried to quietly glide past him. "Hold up, Finn," Travis said with his voice low.

Uh-oh, thought Finn.

"I need to speak with you if you have a minute."

Finn shifted his weight holding the backpack clenched in his left hand.

"Um…sure…but I need to start getting set up for the evening pretty soon."

"Yeah, I know. But come, sit down for a few minutes."

Travis turned with a cup of tea in his hand. He pulled two chairs out from the small linoleum table in the center of the room. Finn sat down like an obedient son and tried to keep the tone light.

"Hey. What's up?" He forced his hunger down deep and tried not to think about the contents of his backpack.

Travis paused as if choosing his words carefully. "I was grateful when you showed up here ten years ago. I knew you'd return." His lips curled upward at the edges.

Finn was confused. "What do you mean…'return'?"

"It's time, I guess," Travis began. "That day, back in 1976, you showed up here for a Thanksgiving dinner. It was snowing. Then, you all but disappeared for seven years. Not that I found that odd of course. Men come and go all the time. Most never come back." He paused. "But you did … all sobered up and looking healthy. Most folks in my line of work would agree that's pretty miraculous. You came back. Changed." He placed a strange emphasis on the last word. Travis sipped his tea and raised his eyes to meet Finn's. Finn felt his stomach lurch.

"I guess you could say I changed," Finn said with a weak smile.

"Yeah. I guess you could say that," Travis conceded.

"I'm grateful that you've let me stay and help out. I didn't have anywhere else to go," Finn said with all earnestness. *Where would I have gone anyway?* he wondered. *Home? To join a vampire coven? To wander aimlessly?*

"Well then, I guess you could say that we need each other."

Travis paused and sipped his tea. "So if we are to continue our working relationship I think it's time we put all our cards on the table."

Finn's mind went blank. He had no idea how to put all his cards on the table. Travis sensed this and stated with slow deliberation, "I know what you are." He waited for Finn's reaction.

Trying to keep the innocent act going, Finn replied, "I am sorry. I don't know what you mean."

"Yes, you do," Travis said. Finn waited.

"Let me tell you a little story, Finn. I grew up in Louisiana. Back in the 1930's and 1940's. Not a stellar time to be a Black man in America, much less down south, if you know what I mean. My family lived just outside of Lafayette near the Atchafalaya swamp. Black folk were still segregated back then and we had our own neighborhood right on the edge of the waters. Great fishing and hunting. We made much of our livelihoods that way. But I remember being no more than about five years of age, sitting on the front porch shelling peas with Mama. My older brother Samuel had been out in the woods past dark, and I remember my mother pacing back and forth on the front porch waiting for him. That expression on her face I knew was pure fear. It was a rule amongst all of us to be indoors before dark. He must have lost track of time or something. Rule number one was that none of us was to go into the swamp alone, and never after dark."

Travis strolled over to the stove and set the teapot. The gas burner clicked on, and he walked back to the table, and eased his body into the chair. "There was one thing that scared us more than White folk coming round our homes after dark wearing white sheets, carrying nooses and crosses. Do you know what that thing was?" Finn shook his head but he knew instinctively where this was going.

"There was this other group of … people," he said, pronouncing the words with exaggeration, "Well, sort of human I guess. At least that's how they appeared. They were both brown and white folk. They came alive in the swamps after dark. I never saw one as a child, but my grandfather sat us down that night. That night when Samuel came home after dark, Grand Pop told us. He told us about the things that fed on humans. 'Course back in those days no White police force was going to spend a whole lot of time worrying about Black folk that had gone missing, so I guess we were easy targets for them. My great grandfather was a slave, freed after the war. He taught my grandfather that during the war these things came out in droves taking advantage of the killing and carnage and all. Dead bodies were lying everywhere and people by the thousands gone missing. After the war these things retreated to the swamp. But he also said that while he was a slave he heard stories. Stories about these things that resembled humans, helping escaped slaves pass to freedom. These creatures had incredible force. They could see their way in the dark and move like jungle cats. These weren't your average abolitionist. No average White person trying to help out The Cause. No. These were something more. My grandfather heard of a group of escaped slaves who made it all the way up across the Pennsylvania line under the protection of a band of White people who disappeared during the day but then came out at night to help the runaway slaves to move safely through the darkness."

Finn had never given much thought to vampires in history. The idea was fascinating to him but he kept a somber and straight face. Glancing around he noticed that crowds of men were beginning to fill the halls and the dining room. The clock on the wall read 8:30 p.m. Travis read this cue and said, "Don't worry. Johnny's got it covered. I won't take too much of your time." Then he continued his story.

"My point is this. Growing up I heard all kinds of tales about vampires. They weren't just myth to us. They were real. As real as all the other forces that helped or terrorized my people." He stared straight into Finn's eyes. "And I know you're one of them. Thing is, from what I can tell these many years now, that you are one of them who wants to help. My grandfather figured it this way: The man you were becomes the vampire you will become. There are folk as mortal as me who kill and feed off one another just as much, if not more, than vampires. A murderous man finds killing easy no matter what he is. Evil isn't what you are. It's what you do."

His face softened. "That's why I sent those vampires after you that snowy night in 1976. To change you."

"What?" Finn whispered. *What was he saying?* It was as if he was seeing Travis for the first time.

"The day I saw you save that little girl from being hit by that car, I knew that you had something deep inside you worth saving. Had never much given thought to whether or not, or how, someone could be 'turned' but the experiment seemed worth it. I needed to know if my grandfather had been right. And I needed help. So these young lookin' teens, vampires they were, had been lurking around the center for weeks. Acted harmless enough. I guess they got their food somewhere else. I offered them a safe hiding space during the day in our basement in exchange for tracking you down and changing you. So they did. And finally, you returned."

Finn wasn't sure if the avalanche of emotion rising in his core was betrayal or gratitude.

"I figure it this way. There are things we need for survival and then there's the things we think are necessities that aren't, but we justify our desire to have them by saying they're a necessity. For you, blood is survival, but killing isn't necessary." Finn glanced downward to his backpack. Travis, if he noticed gave no indication, but continued, "You don't need to kill or murder to get blood. That's the difference."

Travis rose to take the whistling tea kettle off the burner. He sighed. "Look. I don't know how you survive. Don't know and don't care how it is you find your ... um ... sustenance. But I do know that on more than one occasion you have saved these men." He gestured with a nod of his head toward the pass through into the living room. "These men, homeless, sick, intoxicated, disabled...they are all the easy prey nowadays. No one is going to care if they go missing. No one 'cept you and me."

Finn uttered the only words he could. "Thank you." His voice cracked. He coughed and moved to get up. He didn't want Travis to see the tears in the corners of his eyes.

"One last thing," Travis added with his face still pointed down toward his tea mug.

Finn stopped short in the doorway.

"As long as you're going to live forever, why don't you go back to school or something for God's sake? Might as well educate yourself. Got free rent and food here. Go sign up for some night classes." He laughed, amused with himself as he said this last part.

"Okay," replied Finn as obedient as a son listening to his father. Travis was the father Finn had never had. Finn hurried downstairs to empty the contents of his backpack and satiate the craving before he could busy himself with sleeping arrangements for the seventy-five weary men who were waiting for him.

CHAPTER EIGHTEEN

Baltimore, 2011

On her way through the bustling hallways the following late afternoon on campus, Campbell felt herself going through the motions: "Good afternoon … Yes, I'll have that to you by Wednesday … Why don't you schedule an advising appointment …Email me that." Before Campbell had a chance to wander onto the third floor listening for Finn's voice giving what she was sure was a compelling discussion on the merits of vampires in modern culture, he found her.

She turned her back to lock her office door, arms loaded with notebooks and papers from the students' assignments they turned in tonight. *How the hell am I going to get these all read and graded before next week?* she was desperately wondering. The lingering panic of preparing for her conference presentation now less than a week away, falling right before the Thanksgiving holiday was already provoking anxiety in her. Keeping up with the expectations of academic life and raising two young children had been a dubious tightrope walk at best. When she was with the kids, she thought about the writing she ought to be doing and when she was working, she felt horrible for not being home with the kids.

She didn't sense the person moving up behind her. But the static in her mind was moving in like fog. She swung her body around with a rush of urgency. Her face crashed hard into Finn's chest. She screamed. The stack of books in her arms crashed to the ground. *Was he here in anger? To confront her about the other day?* She couldn't read his facial expression. He had been quick to kneel down and gather the mess of papers up in his arms. He stood back up and handed them to her wearing a sheepish grin. *How could this possibly be the face of a vampire?* she wondered.

Finn stammered. "I am sooooo sorry, Campbell! I didn't know you were going to rush up on me like a whirling dervish. I was about to speak when you crashed into me. I promise I wasn't trying to stalk you." *Not tonight at least*, he confessed inwardly. He laughed nervously. "What a jackass I am," he muttered.

She stared at him in disbelief. Finn wondered if her stand-offishness was a rejection because of how he treated her the other day. "Look," he said in an attempt to sooth the tension, "I am also really sorry about the other day. I was rude. You didn't deserve that. Your presence at New Beginnings did catch me off guard." She smiled back but waited.

Oh, I need to hear the explanation for this, she told herself. *What explanation can there possibly be?* She looked directly at him, trying to appear indignant. She wanted him to feel her discontent.

"Um…" He reached up and ran his fingers through his thick amber hair, pulling it away from his face as if he were nervous. The fact that she should be racing up the beltway by now to get home to relieve Kim and to say good night to her kids had vaporized. She didn't want to feel the intrusion. He smiled again and took a deep breath.

"Look, I can't offer a reasonable explanation for you." He didn't want to lie. He was a crappy liar anyway. But the truth wasn't an option, either. "Let me buy you a cup of coffee, okay? I mean," he paused and looked into her eyes, "That is, if you don't need to get home right this second. I promised you the other half of my vampire theory anyway." She couldn't refuse this peace offering. She went with him, calling Kim along the way to let her know she wouldn't be home until late.

They entered the diner together, side by side trying not to stare at each other. It was a polite dance Campbell had decided to name the "Come here, go away" game. She sought proximity to Finn, even the slight brush of their shoulders, yet she understood that too much of this would be dangerous, if not unwelcome.

Finn eagerly played the gentleman to make up for his rash actions at New Beginnings. He began with light conversation to take the focus off of that unfortunate event, and to get Campbell to avoid asking questions about it.

"So, Dr. Cote, we spent all last time talking about me. Let's talk about you." She gave him a blank expression.

Oh no, she thought.

"You haven't told me much about your work or the presentation you plan to do at our panel," he said. The waitress was at their table and Campbell ordered a glass of wine. She wanted to order the whole bottle. Finn ordered a cup of coffee.

"I do research and teaching on women's studies. In particular, I focus on how women are represented through media and pop culture in American society."

"Hmmmm," Finn replied, "So how did you decide to get into this particular field of study?"

"Well, my mom died of breast cancer back when I was in my early 20s. I think I told you last time that she left me and my dad for another man when I was eight years old. I was raised by my dad. He never remarried. I never really saw her the whole time I was growing up. There was the occasional postcard or phone call from where she was. "

You don't have to die, he imagined whispering in her ear as he pictured his teeth tasting her life flowing from her warm body into his mouth.

Her face was sad, with a far-away look. Finn had a vague recollection of the woman who held Campbell so tightly in her arms—the little girl whose coat was crusted over with dirt, ice, and snow. He could not equate that same woman, holding on to her daughter for dear life, ever turning her back on her. What would lead someone to leave the people they loved the most? What could be missing that makes our greatest life's fulfillment become life's greatest burdens?

He fought the urge to ask, *What would you give up to have everything else?*

Campbell sipped her wine and continued, "Mom never stayed in the same place long. I don't know whatever happened to the guy she ran off with. All I know is that years later I got this phone call. It was her, and she said I needed to come and see her because she was dying. So I went. I stayed with her for two weeks and cared for her in the hospital until she died."

I know. I was there, he admitted to himself, now that the other memories were forming a larger cosmic picture. He had been with Campbell her whole life, somewhere, somehow. Because of her, he had almost died, and because of her, he lived.

Campbell shut out her thoughts about that last night with her mother. She wasn't ready to go back there. She took another deep sip of wine. She noticed that Finn had barely touched his coffee. She was feeling a little lightheaded.

Finn's thoughts wandered chaotically. *We convince ourselves it is fate to relieve ourselves of the burden of admitting it's a choice. It's what we believe that's most real, isn't that what I wrote in my own theory about vampires? Would I exist if Campbell didn't believe in me?* He returned his attention to her. She looked as if she might faint.

Finn slid his chair around the corner of the table so that he was no longer facing her directly but rather sitting by her side. Their chairs did not touch but he could sense every emotion, and the thoughts inside of her pouring out like spilled blood. He knew the smell of the soul being released from the body. Her scent, her energy, her sorrow, her doubts all being lifted out of her body. He placed his arm across the back of her chair. She leaned back to feel the full weight of his arm on her shoulders. She felt safe.

"Are you okay?" he asked.

I am now, she thought. She looked at him solemnly. "I was just wondering if we have control over our decisions when in fact we really don't. I mean, did my mom have choice? It's easier for me to believe she didn't. It hurts too much to think I didn't matter enough to her to stay." She knew she wasn't talking about her mother anymore.

The words, *I did not just choose you Campbell. We found each other. And we've been bound together ever since that moment*, formed but didn't leave his lips. There was no way he could tell her all that.

She sighed a bit overdramatically and ceded a smiled to him. His face was warm and open. She wanted to cry right then and there. "Anyway, so I think it was spending that time with my mom, you know, in the oncology unit, seeing women weighed down by the fear of death, by the fact that their bodies had somehow betrayed them. It got me thinking about what the female body really symbolizes in our society. It represents so much about our values and beliefs. Plus, I had quit my job and needed a new path, so applying to a doctoral program seemed like a good option."

A great place to hide, too, she admitted to herself. She focused on her glass of wine and twirled it around lightly in her fingers. She watched the beams of light refract as they passed through the glass.

Finn had the urge to reach out and brush her cheek, to wipe the pain away if only he could. She seemed like a child and he saw in that instant the small uncertain girl standing before him at New Beginnings. Her face hadn't changed in all these years. *How had it come to pass,* he marveled, *that I should cross paths with her again? How could that possibly be a coincidence? There must be some reason.*

"And now here you are!" he proclaimed with zeal. "A professor! Married with two kids! Speaking of, is your husband, what is his name?"

"Brent." She looked away as she uttered this. Her voice was flat. In truth she had to admit he did not deserve such an unwelcome introduction. Brent had done nothing wrong. It was she who was committing acts of transgression.

"Brent. Is he okay with you being out so late?"

"Yeah, he's fine. And we have a great baby sitter who helps out and stays late when I need it."

She turned the conversation away from home and family. Talking about Brent with Finn was like uttering a curse word in the middle of a church mass. She felt loopy from the wine and wanted another glass to wipe away the last few moments. She raised her arm gesturing to the waitress who was standing and waiting, looking bored at the corner of the room. The waitress nodded, understanding the universal language for "Hit me again. God, I need another drink."

CHAPTER NINETEEN

Baltimore, 2011

The diner was growing more crowded with the late night shift of students flowing in for drinks. Finn had shifted his seat back to the other side of the table to accommodate the influx of people. Campbell had rehearsed this conversation with Finn a hundred times since seeing him at New Beginnings. Being a good researcher, she had taken the facts, the few that she had, and arranged and rearranged them every which way she knew how, trying to find some answer that might explain all that had happened. But she needed more information. *Or perhaps*, her unconscious voice would whisper, *You need more faith to accept what is real.*

Campbell leaned forward across the table, hoping to catch the scent of him. "So now it's your turn, Dr. McGinnis."

Did Finn know that it wasn't learning more about vampires that now interested her? She was on a fact-finding mission to know more about him. And if the two happened to intersect, then so be it. She knew she was playing on his intellectual ego to get what she needed. Once he started talking about his research maybe he would slip up and share a little too much. She saw him put on his lecture face.

"Now, where did we leave off?" he asked. Finn knew he wasn't ready to tell Campbell everything. How could he? The vampire theory stuff was great as theory, he knew that. But how many humans would believe him? And if they did, what then? He wasn't ready to out himself to the world, and in that world no one was coming to mean more to him than Campbell. So he would keep this conversation as objective as possible. Better not to implicate himself.

"We left off with how the existence of vampires as a parallel race to humans can be evidenced through myth." Campbell hadn't missed a single word of what Finn had shared the last time. She was ready.

"Human beings have used mythology to explain natural phenomena for centuries. Many myths are replaced by scientific theories that come along later, but don't for a minute be foolish enough to presume that we are so advanced we don't still create myths to explain things. Remember, at the time that the other myths were created, they were not considered fiction. They were used as real explanations and laws that governed the rules of the natural world. Early cultures had creation myths to explain the origins of the earth for example. It's how we explained the unexplained and attributed moral value to life's events."

He eyed his coffee, and lifted his hand to stir it a bit but didn't drink it. The coffee swirled silently around the rim.

"The vampire has always been explained through myth. If you read vampire literature you can also see how the vampire parallels moral dilemmas of the time. In the span of 250 years the vampire has transformed from a dark, monstrous and evil figure such as Nosferateu, to today, in our Western culture where we have vampires who are young and sexy."

Like you? Campbell wanted to ask.

She buried her lips in the wine glass instead and inhaled a deep gulp, and realized she was going to need to order a coffee and sober up before she drove home. Finn continued, "We no longer live in a world of absolute right and wrong. In the postmodern era ambiguity and uncertainty reign, and the vampire reflects this change. The vampire is not evil. He is likeable. He is the character we are rooting for, not against. The vampire has come to represent everything from fear of AIDS, female sexual liberation, to teenage angst."

Campbell only had a vague notion of some of these references. Maybe she had watched some of those shows or movies but hadn't paid much attention to them at the time. Finn repositioned himself in his seat, placed his hands behind his head and pulled his hair away from his face. He was going in for the kill.

Finn said, "So why do we believe that the vampire has no soul? That he is at odds with God? Well, humans lack perspective and memory of history—God and evolution/scientific progress have always been at odds with one another. If you follow the news about stem cell research, you have two opposing sides: science and religion. There are those who would argue that stem cell research is a sin against God. Because we have no scientific explanation for how and why the vampire cannot die (at least in the same sense that a human does), humans interpreted this as being un-natural or super natural and therefore against God. But in truth, we don't know. Is the vampire really damned? Is he really soul-less? I suppose it is a matter of perspective."

Without planning to, Campbell blurted out, "So which are you, Dr. McGinnis?" She kept her eyes steady, never wavering from her lock on his face, waiting for the answer. And she had the liquid courage now to not back down. His face revealed nothing. It had turned to stone for a brief second. But then the sides of his mouth softened and he smiled. He reached across the table for her hand. Her heart leapt into her mouth as she felt his fingers intertwine with her own. She didn't pull away.

"I think, Dr. Cote," he said affectionately, "that you have had too much to drink. Let's get you a coffee."

"I'm fine," she lied. Finn gestured to the waitress. As she drew near to the table he said politely, "Can we get a black coffee please, to go?"

"I have to go, Finn." Campbell's thoughts rushed back to her children. She pictured them sleeping at home. Pangs of guilt wore on her buzz. The realization *I have to leave before I decide never to return*, crossed her mind.

"How about I drive you home?" he offered. She shot a look at him.

"Yeah right, that'll fly!" she blurted out sarcastically. She tried to picture it in her head. Walking through the door, to find Brent waiting up for her. "Brent, this is Finn. I think he's a vampire and I want him so bad I can taste it. Hope you don't mind."

Finn, too, realized the absurdity of this idea. He wanted to help her, to get her home safely, but bringing her there himself wasn't an option. *Reason number 212*, he thought, *that I can't reveal to her who I am.*

"Hmmm. New idea," he countered, "How about I follow you home?"

"You are going to stalk me?" Campbell teased. Finn blushed for a short beat, and looked down at the table.

"No," he said emphatically. "I will have my car follow yours to make sure you get home safe. And to protect all those other poor people out there on the roads. The first sign, Campbell, that I see you are not driving safely, I will pull you over. This is not up for debate."

Campbell was amazed at how her mind cleared when they left the restaurant. Perhaps it was the assault of the cold night air on her face, or maybe it was the coffee she had chugged. Finn gently led her out of the building, guiding her by one elbow through the maze of tables and people. Once outside she realized that it hadn't been the wine alone. She was also delirious at the thought of what might happen when she was with Finn. She had imagined the reaction she might have when he threw his arms around her and looked deeply into her eyes and confessed,

My darling, I am a vampire. But that hadn't happened. She would go home not knowing much more than she had before this evening. He was reticent and anxious. She fell back into a dark contemplative and serious mood.

He kept himself formal and at a respectful distance as she got into her car. His standoffish mood surprised her. "Is everything cool?" she asked him. "I mean, did I say something?" Her insecurity made her feel ridiculous. He closed his face just slightly.

"Yeah, Campbell," he stated coldly, "Everything's fine."

It's not time yet. The phrase was screaming inside his consciousness.

Campbell believed that with each encounter the proximity between them would grow closer. While she had no idea exactly what she would do if he stepped in to kiss her or utter words of passion, part of her was expecting that.

"Remember, I'll be right behind you," he assured her.

"Sounds like a plan," she replied sarcastically. "I'll be fine. You don't need to do this!" she argued. In her mind she was screaming the opposite, *Just leave then. Fuck you!* The inexplicable desire for someone so badly that you wish them to be as far away as possible, was a thorny contradiction that tore at Campbell's consciousness.

"I'm not leaving you," he insisted.

Finn follow her down Route 83 into the quiet, tree-lined streets of her neighborhood. As he glanced at the homogenous rows of brick homes, with kids' plastic slides and bicycles scattered across their manicured lawns, Finn felt a strong sense of loss he hadn't felt since he was human.

I can have everything I want—except her, he thought. Not that he had been on the fast track to middle class bliss in his human form. This recollection was strangely a comfort to him now. He'd had nothing to lose, anyway, back then in 1976. But Campbell had everything to lose and he couldn't imagine bringing that on her. Not telling her the truth had been the right decision. He watched her as she moved from the car onto the front walkway. She turned and waved at him just to be courteous, and then placed the key inside the lock to the front door.

Campbell discovered the children's clothes strewn across the bathroom floor, and piles of dishes lingered in the sink. The anger she felt toward Brent began rising in her chest. "Why the hell does he leave this for me to do?" she mumbled. Rather than confronting Brent, she found it easier to wash her anger away by remembering tonight's flirtation with Finn.

Eros and intellect. She realized that's exactly what it was.

A pile of clothes she tossed down the stairs landed with a soft thump. Did she hate her life so much? No. What was it, then? Why Finn? Why now?

She began stacking a pile of wooden blocks into the plastic toy box in the middle of the living room. The noise clanked and echoed in her ears as each block fell. Campbell could hear Brent's footsteps creaking upstairs. He shuffled out of the bedroom toward the bathroom. She heard him drinking and then putting the cup down hard on the counter. The footsteps moved toward the living room. He fumbled down the stairs, his hair rumpled. He gave her a tired boyish grin. "How was your late meeting?" he asked. She scanned the floor for more errant blocks.

"Oh, fine," she sighed.

"You've been working late a lot," he noted with a yawn. "You have tenure now, Cam. Time to relax, right?"

"Yeah, maybe."

She stood and stretched. In the stillness she could see him as the young man she once knew, the man who seemed so nervous and sweet on their first date. It was a dinner party hosted by mutual friends, and later the look of admiration on his face when he announced, "My fiancé is getting her doctorate." She could sense the intensity of his touch when they first made love.

"How was your day?" she asked. *Yes*, she noted to herself, *There is still some affection there.*

"Good." He yawned. "Long."

Without turning her head from box of toys she said, "Don't forget, we have the party at Sandy and Charles' house."

He leaned over and kissed her on the forehead and ran his hand down her arm. "Yes, I remember. I'm going back to bed now. Don't stay up late. This crap can wait until tomorrow."

His lank body, clad only in a pair of plaid boxer shorts moved into their bedroom.

CHAPTER TWENTY

Baltimore, 2011

Sandy's house resembled a fairy tale illustration. Flowers of every hue and height clustered on the edges of a cobble stone walkway that wandered through the center of their vast green front lawn. Campbell watched the sun starting its gradual dip below the tree lined hills and the brilliant residue of yellow melded into the soft blue of the coming evening. Even this late in the season as the sun was setting, the cool bright green of their grass shone in contrast to the brilliant speckles of autumn's warm palette of orange, yellow and red flowers that could withstand the first frost. Caroline hastily stopped and picked as many as she could before they arrived at the front door. Brent corrected her briskly.

"Caroline. Those are not yours! Campbell, tell your daughter to stop picking the flowers!"

This was Brent's usual behavior management system for controlling his children—get Campbell to do it. She ignored his request. The door swung open. They were greeted by Sandy's husband Charles—a dark skinned, plump man with short black curly hair and eyes flecked with brown and green depending on the light.

"Hello!" Charles exclaimed embracing Campbell in a gentle bear hug. "I'm so glad you're here. We would have had to cancel it if you hadn't come."

"Charles," Campbell replied, "We haven't missed this for eight years. Why would we start now? So is the usual cast of characters here again?"

"Of course! Plus a few new additions."

Campbell immediately thought of Finn. Would he be here? Sandy always invited colleagues as a courtesy, though few to Campbell's relief, ever made it.

"Where are the brownies, Miss Sandy?" Ellis asked. Campbell laughed and rumpled his hair. "Say hello first at least, Ellis!"

"Hello, Miss Sandy. Where are the brownies?"

Sandy bent down and gave both children a warm embrace. "My, my! You keep getting bigger now don't you?" Sandy's children were grown and in college by the time they formed a close friendship. Campbell had met them a few times.

The two men disappeared into the study where the Raven's announcer could be heard on the large screen TV. As Campbell watched Caroline and Ellis turn the corner into the dining room where there was an enormous spread of treats for them, a familiar face appeared. It was Finn. Campbell's heart raced.

Sandy paused and made note of Campbell's uncomfortable reaction. "I invited Finn so that he could get to know everyone a little better. Since he's new."

With his eyes glued on Campbell he sauntered over and said, "Hello, Campbell. Good to see you again." The smile was warm but formal. Neither his face nor his body language revealed anything of their last encounter or sensual familiarity.

Beautiful as always, she thought.

She followed his lead. "Hello, Finn." She reached out to shake his hand, as if they were meeting formally for the first time. "Good to see you!" As their hands touched she felt an electric shock run up her arm. She had to force herself to let go. *People are watching*, she reminded herself. Brent was talking in the next room. Campbell looked down the hall as if she might get caught shoplifting lipstick from a drugstore. Sandy strode over and politely took Finn's arm.

"Finn, what can I get you to drink?"

He turned to Campbell and grinned.

"Um, well, what do you have?" he inquired with a bit too much enthusiasm.

A commensurate hostess, Sandy escorted him into the kitchen leaving Campbell in the living room with her thoughts. She could hear Sandy's voice trailing off below the whistles and cheers blaring from the television. "Coffee, wine, beer, juice?"

"Just water, thank you." His voice oozed as smooth as liquid velvet.

Campbell stepped onto the back porch and sucked in a deep pocket of cool air—trying to swallow the bubble of anxiety that lodged inside her throat. The evening porch lights revealed a lawn which sloped gently toward the tree-line. Shrubs and young saplings were surrounded by fresh mulch. Campbell had never had time to work in her yard. She marveled how Sandy could be so brilliant in her scholarship and teaching and still have time to perfect her domestic self. She sipped her tepid cup of coffee puzzling out what she could do to deal with Finn's presence. Avoiding him was on her list.

Behind her, the sliding door moved. "Hey."

She spun around. Wisps of hair grazed across Finn's face with the soft breeze.

"Hey back." Her voice cracked as she tried to speak, so she coughed and sipped the bitter liquid in her mug.

"Sandy's house is very nice isn't it?" he offered.

Campbell glanced around not paying attention to anything in particular. "Yeah. It is."

He moved like a cat toward her and her heart raced. She gazed at her feet, and then more boldly looked up. His body was inches from her. His arm brushed her shoulder as he moved to the edge of the deck. Campbell let her breath out. The light of the sun left only scant traces of rays pushing up with effort, as if they were resisting the force of the earth's rotation to bend them below the horizon. Finn searched the fading hilltops and winced. Campbell pulled her arms around her waist and shivered.

"Do you need a jacket?" he asked. Finn was wearing a white button down collar shirt and a pair of dark blue jeans. Having no coat himself he had little to offer in the way of a solution.

"Sandy can lend me something if I need it," she said. They stood in silence for a few seconds, considering each other. *Say something, please,* she thought.

The urgency to tell her the truth overtook him. It was impulsive. He had no plan. But he started anyway. "Listen, Campbell. I need to tell you something…" Finn's sentence was interrupted. The sliding door whooshed open.

"Hey, Cam?" It was Brent. She noticed that Finn's demeanor turned from plush to a hardened shell. He turned away and gazed over the back lawn.

"Hey, Brent," she said quietly.

Brent walked toward her. "Are you okay?" he asked. "Are you cold?" He rubbed her arms with a brisk warming motion. She stepped back and he paused. He looked at Finn standing at the railing and then back at Campbell who turned her head away from them both and toward the shrubs below.

"Brent," she motioned, "This is Dr. Finn McGinnis. He is our new faculty member."

Brent stepped across the deck and reached out his hand. "Hey man, nice to meet you."

"Finn will be presenting with us on our panel. He's taking Dr. Hugh's place."

Finn grasped his hand firmly. "Pleasure to meet you. Campbell's told me a lot about you."

"Really?" Brent replied, his face twisting for a brief second.

"Finn and I have spent a little time on campus going over the panel presentations" she interjected.

Brent was not stupid. He was just moments away from asking the logical question, "So this is why my wife has been working late the past two weeks?"

"Yeah," said Finn, "I think we're all set too. Thank you for helping me catch up to speed, Campbell. It helps me a lot." He turned his attention back to Brent. His eyes sparkled in the dim light. "So I hear you're a golfer!"

How the hell did he know that? Campbell wondered. Assessing the personality of someone like Brent struck Finn as an easy task. The man was clearly unencumbered by deceit or complexities. It was a good guess.

Brent's complexion lightened a bit. "Yes. Well not a very good one." He gave a self-deprecating laugh.

"You'll have to recommend some courses around here for me."

I could eat you for lunch. And then take your wife. Finn's thought was wicked. But true. He just grinned.

Campbell slipped herself between them and pretended to check for the time on Brent's watch. She wasn't sure where this impulse came from. They stood staring at her, oddly.

"You golf?" Brent asked. Campbell's body relaxed a bit.

"Um," Finn said distracted by Campbell's sudden move. Somehow Finn had known exactly how to take the heat off the situation. He craned his neck over her head and added, "Not yet. It's one of those things I always say I'm going to take up. You know, to get away from sitting in front of the desk grading papers all the time."

Please don't tell Brent you work at New Beginnings, she pleaded in her head.

"I don't get out enough," he added.

Brent nodded in a statement of male camaraderie and said, "Yeah I sit in an office all day. The grind gets to you after a while." Brent rubbed Campbell's side arm again. Finn's back straightened just a bit and she watched his eyes shift in color like a kaleidoscope from brown to green and then back again.

"Cam, why don't you go inside? You're shivering," Brent said. She looked at Finn with a side glance and then moved inside without saying a word.

Two hours later the children's shoes clattered on Campbell's foyer floor and they dashed upstairs. After leaving the scene on the back deck with Brent and Finn, Campbell had relegated herself to helping Sandy in the kitchen. She kept herself away from both men. At home the children ran up to Caroline's room chattering excitedly between themselves about the recent events at the party. "Molly said she has a real pool table in her living room!"

Brent hung his fleece jacket on the peg by the door and tossed the car keys onto the marble foyer table. Campbell sat in the living room chair and pulled her boots off. Her feet ached. Her whole being ached.

"Dad?" Ellis called from the top of the stairs, pulling his shirt off over his head.

"Yes?" Brent's voice sounded weary.

"Dad?" Ellis pleaded again. "How come we don't have a pool table? Can we get a pool table?" This question was met with rounds of approval from Caroline who was calling out from her bedroom.

"I don't know, buddy," Brent said with exhausted resignation, as if he knew this was not a debate worth trying to win, when there was no logical response to satisfy his children. Campbell looked at Brent feeling sad for him and far away from him at the same time.

"Maybe we'll get one for Christmas this year," he grumbled.

Peels of whooping calls and "Oh yeas!" rolled down from the upstairs, followed by a stampede of running feet and laughter. Campbell moved slowly toward the staircase. "Come on guys. It's late! Brush your teeth and get into your pajamas. I'll be up there in five minutes!"

Brent sorted through a stack of bills piled on the dining room table. "Sandy seems like she's doing well," he noted with a hint of exhaustion.

"Yes, she's great. Nice to see her," Campbell responded. Standing up, she was unsure of where her body should move next. Her mind was reeling from her earlier proximity to Finn, with thoughts of Brent as almost some vile interruption of her imaginary world with Finn. Her fantasy was redirected to the sounds of events upstairs. The annoyed tone of Caroline's voice told her that she would need to go and intervene soon. But she did not want to walk away from Brent. So she stood in place. Placing the bills back on the table as if he had satisfied his curiosity, Brent continued, "We should try and see them more."

"When could we?" she blurted out. It sounded harsher than she had intended. "You and I are hardly ever home at the same time!"

Brent pushed air through his throat the way he did when he was annoyed. "Campbell, what the hell is your problem? You've been acting weird all night. Are you and Sandy having a fight or something?"

There was a loud scuffling sound from upstairs. "Noooooo Caroline! That's mine!"

"Everything's fine, Brent. Sorry. I didn't mean to sound snippy. I just meant that..." She paused. What did she mean anymore? She wasn't sure what had any meaning.

"What, Campbell! It's just what? You know our lives are not what they were ten years ago. Okay? You're the one who wanted kids." The comment stung and she could feel her face burning. But she'd promised herself she wouldn't fight with Brent in front of the kids and she had always been good about keeping that promise. "This is the life we chose, Campbell. I'm happy. Maybe I don't show it all the time the way I should but I am. Really."

The fighting upstairs was escalating. She heard a loud banging noise. "No, Caroline! I want that one!"

"Hey!" Brent shouted turning his attention toward the stairway. Campbell felt the walls shake his voice was so loud. Then there was complete silence. "You better knock it off!"

Campbell pushed forward. "What, since I wanted kids, any time our lives aren't perfect it's my fault?"

"No," Brent replied with less aggression this time. The sound of his own voice echoing back at him caused him to feel a pang of self-consciousness. He checked his temper. "I am saying that our lives have just changed. That's all. I thought this was what you wanted, but you seem so unhappy lately. Or tense. Or something. So I was just suggesting that maybe you take some more time to spend with your friends, like Sandy. You know, away from the kids and away from work. I have never tried to stop you from taking time for yourself."

She hung her head. She knew this was true. "He may be absent too often and distracted even when he is here," she admitted, "but when push comes to shove he's always been there for me."

When Ellis was in the NICU after his birth, and Campbell camped out at the hospital day and night, Brent had taken family medical leave to stay home and care for Caroline. And when she went up for tenure, whittling away the late night hours in an exhausted haze completing her dossier, she could hear him in the other rooms pulling laundry out of the dryer, unloading the dishwasher, and picking up the toys. When she had really needed him, he was there.

"Campbell, go take a hot bath or something," he suggested walking over and kissing her lightly on the forehead. "I'll put the kids to bed tonight. Go take a break."

Here it was. A good life. Not perfect. But good. She wanted for nothing. But more than a bath or a good book, all Campbell could think of was getting on her computer to email Finn or to see if he had emailed her. *What's wrong with me?* she screamed silently. *Why is all of this not enough when I am with Finn?*

CHAPTER TWENTY-ONE

Baltimore, 2011

After dropping Ellis and Caroline off at school, Campbell was eager to get home and put on her running shoes to meet Lilly at the corner of her street. It was their weekly ritual. Every Tuesday morning Campbell and Lilly walked the mile that looped up the steep tree-lined hill, left at the corner of Highmount and Devere and finally sloped down the winding footpath between the local park and middle school. Lilly and Campbell had been friends since Campbell had moved into this neighborhood right after Caroline was born. It was after a seeing each other several times along the same jogging route that they realized they were both university professors.

There was nothing that Campbell was going through that Lilly couldn't genuinely identify with. Lilly had been divorced for six years. Her oldest, Suzanne, was in high school at the time and her second daughter, Rose, was in middle school. She had raised her daughters as a single working mother. She was also a theoretical mathematician at large state university about twenty-five minutes away. Campbell knew she was secretly brilliant but appreciated that she never acted that way during their weekly strolls. As she walked toward the corner Campbell mentally rehearsed what she might say to Lilly about Finn.

Lilly looked fabulous as usual. She was wearing a pair of light blue Juicy Couture running pants that hugged her tiny frame and a matching light blue zip up sweatshirt. Campbell glanced self-consciously at her oversized yellow T-shirt that had a big spot of maple syrup right on top of her left nipple, from serving pancakes this morning. "That figures," she sighed.

"So what's it like to be smart and sexy, my dear?" Campbell called out as Lilly neared her house.

"Ha-ha ...why don't you tell me?" Lilly shot back.

They laughed and hugged each other. As they stood back from their embrace Lilly immediately honed in on Campbell's unease.

"Okay, tell me everything," Lilly said eagerly.

They started walking in sync, side by side. "Is it Brent?" Lilly offered. Campbell knew Lilly had little affection toward Brent. Some of it justified she supposed, but it was also a reflexive reaction from surviving a painful marriage herself. Lilly had a tendency toward over defensiveness for all women, everywhere.

"No, Brent's fine. Brent's..." She paused. "Brent. You know. It's not that."

They walked together in silence past three or four houses. "It's just that ..." Campbell felt her face get hot. In an instant, the fear, the rage, and the confusion were rising to the surface. She could feel the tears start to brim from beneath her eyelashes.

"How do I explain this?" she sobbed. "I'll just say it. There's someone else."

This news didn't catch Lilly off guard. Events such as infidelity didn't surprise her, especially in women of a "certain age" who though vibrant and intelligent found themselves suddenly trapped in mediocre marriages with nothing to look forward to except old age and death. Lilly started thinking of what to say next; something wise and witty, when Campbell dropped the unexpected bomb. "And I think he might be a vampire." She added this last bit as more of a question than a statement. Lilly fell silent.

Along their one-mile trek Campbell did her best to bring Lilly up to speed with the latest developments. It had been difficult, summarizing the patchwork of illogical suppositions that were based on little more than the memory of a six-year-old girl, and the emotions of a confused middle-aged woman. But such happenings were well suited to Lilly, whose professional life was devoted to theoretically proving things that were mostly beyond the scope of the human language. How did one explain, much less prove, the notion of infinity for example?

Rather than feeling a sense of shock or horror, Lilly was intrigued by the whole thing. They sat, catching their breath on Campbell's front steps. Campbell lit up a cigarette. There was no fighting the urge now. She knew how ridiculous she felt sitting there on her front stoop, in jogging clothes, with a butt hanging out of her mouth but she didn't care.

"Fascinating," Lilly mused. "So a creature who can experience both eternity and infinity? Wow."

Campbell chuckled. Only Lilly could think about the world this way. She felt a tremendous relief that Lilly not only knew everything but that, just as she had hoped, was offering up no judgment for how she was feeling.

"You know, now that I think about it, it makes a lot of sense," Lilly added triumphantly.

"Huh???" Campbell replied.

"Think about it, if what Finn is telling you is possible, then by evolving into a parallel species, humans have genetically tapped into a source that is much closer to the mind of the cosmos." Lilly deliberately omitted the word god. A die hard agnostic, Lilly preferred to believe in a creative intelligence rather than the image of a white man with a beard sitting on a cloud passing judgment on everyone. Faith in science and faith in god were not so far apart as people might think.

"Great, glad to hear you have the idea for your next paper, Lilly. But what do I do? This isn't your average crush!"

"Well, you know what they say?" Lilly replied.

"Who is they, Lilly," Campbell asked in exasperation.

"You know—They!" Lilly laughed. She pronounced, "When in doubt, don't do anything."

"What the hell does that mean? How do I not do anything?"

"Well, it means my dear," Lilly said while reaching for Campbell's cigarette and pulling a drag off of it and handing it back. She paused and blew a gentle puff of smoke from between her lips. "It means, waiting to see how things unfold. You haven't exactly been steering the ship on this so far, right? Why not wait and see where the universe takes you. And decide what to do when the right moment arrives."

Campbell stamped the cigarette out in the dirt of the flower bed strewn with dying mums. "Sounds like a plan", she called out. As Lilly sauntered off leaving Campbell alone to her thoughts, she mused at the absurdity of walking two miles every week and then lighting up a cigarette. These were obviously two very contradictory actions. It occurred to her that most of life was pretty contradictory when you were honest about it. Lilly's words "infinity and eternity" rolled around her imagination.

There are no limits to what is possible, she decided.

As Campbell considered this she walked back in the house, stripping off her sweaty workout clothes as she went. She walked to the bathroom to start the shower and paused to study herself in the mirror. For an instant she saw the glare of her mother looking back at her. The image was jarring.

If you had told me when I was a little girl that my mother was capable of leaving me and my father I would have told you that was impossible. And yet, it happened. Things that seem impossible, events that revolutionize our perception of what is real, are happening daily.

On the mirror rested a Post-it which read, "BUY TOILET PAPER" in her scribbled capital letters. Whenever she travelled, a litany of "to-do" reminder Post-its for Brent would litter the house. With the trip mere days away, she had begun the ritual.

Steam from the hot water rose from behind the plastic shower curtain. *What we consider possible is a matter of perception. Reality is constructed out of a series of habits, things we do over and over again. And we forget that other ways of living are equally possible. Would my life have been better off if my mother had never broken free from the constraints of her prescribed reality and left? How would my life today be different if she had stayed?* This last thought hurt too much to consider so she stepped into the hot water and washed any lingering pain away along with the day's residue.

Campbell tossed the wet towel onto the bed and searched for a pair of underwear. On her bedroom dresser she found the Post-it she had left for herself. "Call Quest Diagnostics for mammogram." She winced. Campbell knew she couldn't put off making this appointment. Dr. Katz continuously nagged her to keep up her annual exams because of her mother's history.

Thanks, Mom. Leave me with nothing except the likelihood of getting breast cancer. Way to go. Bitch.

CHAPTER TWENTY-TWO

San Diego, 2011

The conference hotel in San Diego was exactly what Campbell had expected. Here was the frenzied clank and rattle of academics pulling wheeled suitcases and briefcases weighted down with important knowledge across the grand marble floor of the lobby. People were moving into small cliques, colleagues who saw each other once or maybe twice a year calling in friendly high pitched voices, "Hi! How are you?" across the large space that then echoed against the high ceilings.

Where is he? she asked herself as she searched the room for any sign of Finn. Saying goodbye to her children and Brent, making sure she had packed everything and that Kim had all her necessary contact information had kept her happily distracted. But once she settled on to the airplane, her mind began wandering back to Finn. He had mentioned in an earlier email that he would be arriving some time that evening. She checked her watch. It was only 4 p.m. She decided to seek out her friends and colleagues to avert feeling the knots lodged in her chest. Before locating her colleagues she stepped outside to smoke and announce her safe arrival to Brent.

She texted Brent: "Arrived safe and sound. How are you? Kiss the kids for me." She hit send and pulled another drag off the cigarette looking around furtively, in case she spotted anyone she knew. And to search for Finn. She stubbed out the cigarette with the toe of her boot and went back inside. She settled into a friendly conversation with some friends from her doctoral studies, almost forgetting the nervousness she had developed inside.

Thirty minutes later the double glass doors whooshed open with a push of air as Finn entered the hotel lobby. He slugged his duffle bag over his shoulder and sauntered to the front desk. A petite brunette at the front desk smiled broadly when she saw him coming. "Welcome to San Diego Business Suites. Are you checking in?"

"Yes, I'm Dr. McGinnis," Finn replied. He dropped his bag by his feet. Finn had packed lightly. Aside from a few books, a change of clothes, and his paper presentation, there was little else he needed to bring. Slugging along several bags of blood would have aroused alarm at the airport security so he had made sure to double his visits to the loading docks at Maryland General Hospital to satiate his hunger before leaving. *It's only three days,* he reminded himself as he fumbled for his wallet. I *have gone more than three days without feeding before.*

"Your room is on the 14th floor, sir. Is that okay?" She offered him a key card and stared intently.

Finn's handsome appearance had a compelling effect on almost everyone he encountered. He took his key card and turned for the elevators when he saw Campbell seated at the bar at the far end of the open lobby. He could smell her even at this distance. Since their first evening in the restaurant only a few weeks ago, her scent had become a homing device for him. Even from several floors down in their building while he was holding class he would sense when she was in her office and when she was leaving the building. Then, as if she could feel his eyes upon her, Campbell's head turned and met his face and they both froze for an instant. She beamed at him. "There you are!" she shouted. Everyone at her table paused in their conversation and looked up at Finn.

Oh crap, he thought. Campbell stood and gestured for him to come and join them. Two of her colleagues stared at each other and raised their eyebrows. "Who is that delightful morsel of eye candy?" her friend Tasha asked. Campbell played it cool.

"That's one of our new colleagues," Campbell pronounced matter-of-factly, trying to sound unimpressed.

She never took her eyes off Finn as he made his way across the broad marbled hall. "He was hired to replace Dr. Hughes while he's on medical leave. He is presenting on our panel."

"He can sit on me anytime," Kyle jested, who never missed an opportunity to make openly gay jokes when in the presence of a welcoming audience. Two other friends chuckled and playfully reprimanded him. "Shhhh, he's coming. He might hear you. Quit it you guys!" Finn tried to hide a smile since he had heard it all anyway.

Campbell felt a small confidence in being surrounded by friends. They had "grown up" together, watching each other go through the growing pains of school, landing their first jobs, and helping each other through the first few years in the academic jungle. Tasha and Robin also had young children so they spent most of the annual conference commiserating on the trials of being mamas in academia. Campbell felt that she was on her own turf here with Finn, and that gave her confidence she had lacked in his presence at their prior meetings. "Don't worry. They won't bite, I promise," she announced to the others as he pulled up a chair to the table.

"Yes, but I might," he quipped back.

Everyone laughed and Campbell was impressed by his ability to join in so seamlessly. Tasha was the first to jump in. "So tell us new guy. What brings you here to this wasteland of a conference?"

Campbell could tell that Tasha was on the brink of being drunk and knew that she had a history of blatant flirting when she was in that state. Tasha reached over and grabbed his left arm. "You look too young to be a professor. How old are you?" Finn felt a slight discomfort at being caught on the spot, and being touched by someone he barely knew. Campbell noticed a small jealousy rouse within her.

"Um… well, I'm thirty-one."

"You had to think about that one for a minute?" Kyle said, laughing.

"My god, Campbell!" Tasha said, "He's just a baby!"

Campbell blushed and turned away to hide it.

Kyle leaned in across the table. "So tell us, where did you study?"

Finn was easing into the scene. He expounded to no one in particular, "I did my work at University of Baltimore. I worked my way through my studies, a little bit at a time. I completed classes part-time in the evenings and worked during the day."

He didn't add that work during the day meant staying in the basement of a homeless shelter feeding and caring for alcoholics. Such work lent itself to avoiding the bright light that daytime brought with it.

Campbell was running the math in her head. That would mean that he went to school non-stop from the age of 23 in order to qualify for his Ph.D. by 31. That is, unless he had an eternity to do it in. She was grateful that everyone else at the table was too intoxicated or too busy trying to be the center of attention to think this fact through.

"Yeah, it felt like an eternity," Finn concluded, and glanced at Campbell.

"Give this man something to drink!" Kyle insisted, pouring a glass for Finn and sliding it across the table.

"Thank you. But I am really tired. I think I'd better pass for tonight."

"Finn studies vampires!" Campbell announced, trying to stall him from leaving the table. Everyone at the table "oohed" and "ahhed."

"Studying vampires!" Ellen said, who had been quiet up until now. In her usually serious low tone she added, "So how does one go about doing that?"

Tasha leaned close to Finn's face. "Can you make me one?" she teased.

Finn leaned back, almost tipping his chair over. Campbell heard a low growl in her throat. She felt protective and possessive. Tasha's over sexualized humor had always been funny to Campbell, but now Finn was the object in her sights, and Campbell's blood surged with a new aggression toward Tasha. Pushing his chair away a few inches Finn said with hearty friendliness, "Well, I guess you'll have to come to our panel and see for yourself."

Then, seeming almost apologetic Finn leaned in toward Campbell and said in a hushed tone, "I'm going to go to my room. It's been a very long day. And we have the first session at 8 a.m. tomorrow so I still need to prepare."

Campbell's hopes that her friends would glean information from Finn had backfired. She cursed Tasha under her breath.

"Yeah, okay. I think I'll head up too."

As she arose and gathered her purse, Campbell's friends gave furtive glances to one another, all thinking the same thing: What's going on here? Kyle stood up and shook Finn's hand. "Nice to meet you, man," he said and then leaned in to hug Campbell. "You—be good," he whispered in her ear. She examined his face with mock indignation.

"Who, me?" she giggled.

"We'll be there tomorrow, sweetie," said Tasha.

"She might be hung over, but we'll show up, coffee in hand!" Ellen added.

"Okay guys, see you then. Thanks."

There was an awkward silence between them as they waited in front of the elevator doors, watching the dial crawl slowly from the 30th floor down toward the lobby. "So what floor are you?" Campbell asked. What she wanted to ask was *So what are you?*

"Fourteenth," Finn replied. "And you?"

"Ummm, I'm not sure. Let me check." She pulled the key card out of her purse. "Eighth."

The elevator doors opened and Finn gestured to Campbell to step in first. He reached over to press the button that read 8. The elevator was paneled with mirrors and small advertisements for surrounding restaurants. Campbell looked at Finn in the mirror.

"I thought vampires didn't have reflections," she said, her eyes fixed on his.

The question was bold and absurd. *But why the hell not?* she told herself. *Gloves are off. Let's just rip this open.*

He stared at her with a gentle expression. "Well, I guess I would have to see one to know for sure."

She stared at him as the floor jolted upward. Finn stared back. The button made a "ding" sound as it reached the 8th floor.

"This is your stop," he announced. "Here, let me help." He lifted Campbell's bags and moved out of the elevator with her. He didn't want to leave her any more than she wanted to leave him. They reached for reasons to keep the conversation going.

You feel it too, don't you? she nearly asked him out loud but then thought better of it.

Her whole body was shaking. She felt her teeth chattering, making it hard to get out the words that she couldn't believe she was now uttering. Being away from home somehow made it easier to say what needed to be said.

"I don't know what to do Finn," Campbell finally confessed. "What do I do? What do I do with this?" She gestured to the space between them. He lowered his head.

"I don't know, Campbell."

Hearing him say her name made her want him even more. "I feel it too." He paused and then added, "It's complicated." She laughed with disbelief. "No shit." He lifted his head and gazed at her longingly. He wondered, *Is this the moment where I am supposed to lean in and kiss you?*

The wry smile on his face suggested she knew what he was thinking but she couldn't move from her spot. The wall held her up, a physical force for which she was grateful.

"Campbell," he asked again with pleading in his voice, "I...." He didn't know how to finish the sentence. "There's so much I need to explain. I just don't have the words yet. I feel something for you too. And I know it's wrong of me to feel this way."

"I know." She felt sympathy towards him. "I'm married. With kids." She added internally, *Which was the bigger impasse? Being a vampire or being married?*

"Can we just agree that this is something? That we're not crazy? And we'll know what to do when the time is right?" he asked. "We don't have to know what to do right this instant."

"Agreed," she replied, nodding slightly. He reached over and brushed her check with the tips of his fingers. She trembled, but kept her focus on her shoes. If she looked at him now there would be no going back. He recoiled his fingers slowly and shoved both hands into his coat pockets.

But this isn't over, she insisted privately.

"Okay," she sighed out loud, "I'll see you in the morning. We are meeting in the Mariners Room I think."

"Good night," Finn said as he pressed the up button on the elevator.

She pivoted away. "Good night."

Then she turned down the hallway while he stepped inside and the elevator doors closed. Finn was gone. She took a deep breath. Her hands were still shaking and she had to struggle to slide the key into the slot to open her room door.

CHAPTER TWENTY-THREE

San Diego, 2011

Campbell slammed the thick metal door with a thud and pressed her back against it. She breathed deep several times and forced herself to not open the door and run after him. Her mind reeled with words unspoken. Her face was flush and hot and it took her a few beats to notice the hot stream of tears rolling down her cheeks. After washing her face with cool water she began unpacking. "Don't do anything...." That had been Lilly's advice. The two queen beds were draped in thick maroon and olive green flowered comforters. The perfectly matching wallpaper, curtains and furniture made her feel nauseous. The space was silent except for the slight hum of the mini refrigerator. After she hung up her dress, she pulled on a pair of sweat pants and an oversized T-shirt. Her breathing had finally returned to normal.

What now? she wondered after sitting for ten minutes. Sleep was out of the question. Her mind was racing. The alarm clock on the nightstand registered 8:00 p.m. Between tonight's drama and the time change, Campbell knew she wouldn't be sleepy any time soon. *I need a cigarette,* she decided. Glancing at herself in the mirror, draped in the dumpy sweat clothes she debated about going back out looking like that.

There are probably people still drinking at the bar. But I can take the elevator down and slip out the back entrance without being noticed.

More than concern about her appearances, Campbell couldn't face idle chit-chat with people, not after her last conversation with Finn. She needed to process what had just transpired. The evening was warm and she didn't need a coat, so she grabbed a cigarette and a lighter with one hand and her room key card in the other.

I just have to make it down the elevator without running into anyone, she thought. It was a chance she was willing to take.

Her feet, hushed with the rustling sound of walking shoes, slipped down the carpeted hall and toward the elevator. She could hear people in one of the rooms laughing and chatting loudly. The elevator doors opened and she stepped inside grateful to be its only passenger.

Once in the lobby she found she was correct. She could hear Kyle's booming voice, drunk from the brandy. From his tenor and tempo she discerned that he was "holding court," a term they used when one of them decided in their inebriated state to demand the attention of everyone else at the table, espousing what they believed to be the most important theory or research of the day. It was friendly intellectual jousting. Usually she enjoyed watching, but tonight she was on a mission to remain unseen. She scurried down the hallway to the metal door which led outside; it clicked open and then shut again. From where she stood, all that anyone could see were the rows of cars filling the parking lot, and a few pedestrians making their way past the hotel's back entrance. Campbell lit the cigarette and settled into a low crouch to relax her body. She replayed her and Finn's entire conversation, chiding herself.

Crap. I screwed that up. You should have kissed him. What's wrong with you? She lowered her cigarette and tried to make herself inanimate as a young couple glided arm in arm past the hotel rear entrance toward one of the cars parked in the row closest to Campbell.

Totally engrossed in each other they didn't notice her. She returned to her thoughts. *What would I have done anyway? Gone home and told Brent? Seriously. What could come of this? I still don't know for sure who or even what Finn is. You're being ridiculous, Campbell.* When she talked to herself in this way the voice in her head always sounded like her mother's. She remembered the day that she had wanted to wear her newest party shoes given to her by one of her mother's friends for her birthday just days before. Being six, it didn't occur to her that wearing patent leather shoes in the rain was a bad idea. All she knew was that she wanted to wear them to school to show her friends. Her mother insisted on the brown rain boots, which Campbell detested. The two of them stood in a standoff for ten minutes.

"You're being ridiculous, Campbell Cote!" her mother shouted in total exasperation. Campbell gave in and placed the hated brown rain boots on her feet. "Really, Campbell, a vampire?" She could hear her mother's voice ringing in her head. She knew the whole idea was absurd. Campbell had taken the fantasy of another man to a whole new level. But he had become the other man, vampire or not. There was still that issue to deal with. She took the last draw off her cigarette and crushed it deep into the dirt and pine straw beneath the shrubs.

As she stood up she saw Finn coming toward her. He was wearing what appeared to be jogging clothes, and breathing hard. She ducked behind a thin pine tree that lined the corner of the hotel wall, the one farthest from the floodlights.

Damn it. He's coming this way! What do I do? Pop out and yell 'Surprise?!' I just happen to be standing on this corner in the middle of the night and ....' Yeah, dressed like this. There is no way I can let him see me, standing in the dark like a freak! She held in her breath as he neared the entrance pulling out his hotel key card from the slim pocket of his running shorts. *Who the hell goes running at this hour anyway?* she wondered. His shirt was slung low around his neck, probably stretched out from being pulled up onto his forehead to wipe off sweat. Finn's muscular shape glimmered as it reflected off of the floodlights.

"He is beautiful," she murmured. Then as her eyes moved from his sinewy thighs, up across his broad chest, and onto his neck, she saw it; nestled within the small recess right below his throat hung a gold charm dangling from a thin gold chain. It was clear as daylight as his whole body moved under the bright floodlights. Without moving her crouch, she peeked her head around the slim tree trunk to get a better look. She had seen that charm once before and she had never forgotten it, not a single detail of the shiny charm that the nice man in the homeless shelter had shared with her all those years ago.

"It is him," she whispered. Finn paused for a moment at the door. Campbell froze. Then he slid the key card into the slot and the door clicked open and he went inside.

Finn had a strange feeling that caused him to stop in his tracks in the empty hallway. He sensed Campbell but didn't see her anywhere. He couldn't smell her either as he usually could. All he could smell as he came toward the building was cigarette smoke, and that had clouded his sensory input. The barrage of noises coming from the four lane promenade of cars had made it harder to hear, but he could have sworn he heard someone standing in the bushes.

So what of it? he argued with himself. Probably two people in an illicit embrace, hiding from view. He had heard of this sort of thing going on at conferences and had no desire to stumble upon such a scene. His mind was still buzzing from the incident with Campbell beside the elevator. *I should have just kissed her,* he said to himself. He had hoped that going out for a jog would burn off the energy that had been building up inside of him. Despite his fill of blood from Maryland General Hospital he still couldn't shake the urge to prowl, something he did regularly at home. Then after being so close to Campbell, desire paired with innate hunger drove him out for a long run. Of course in public he had to control his speed, so he ran at what he thought was a normal human jogging pace.

Why didn't I tell her? he had asked himself as he ran through the crowded streets of San Diego's main thoroughfare. *Tell her what? Guess what, by the way, I am a vampire. Sure Finn, that will win her over. She's married, you dumb ass. What is the point in telling her anything? It's not going to go anywhere. It can't. If I care about her at all I need to just stay away and let her carry on with her life, not ruin it.* He had felt a new sense of resolve as he slowed down toward the hotel entrance. So why, now, as he pressed the up button on the elevator did he feel her presence so close he could taste it? She was under his skin, no matter what he convinced himself of otherwise.

Campbell could feel hot tears running down her cheeks. She didn't wipe them away. She was sure he was gone by now and that she had gone undetected. But she couldn't move. To move, to make any gesture whatsoever at this moment meant that time would pulse forward and propel her toward whatever was next. She wished she could freeze time to wrap her head fully around the new realization. She wasn't just wrangling with the moral dilemma of being attracted to another man anymore. Now, her entire conception of what was real or even possible in the universe, in her universe, had been utterly shattered.

CHAPTER TWENTY-FOUR

San Diego, 2011

The chandelier lights in the Mariner room early the next morning did nothing to hide the exhaustion on Campbell's face or the ache her eyes felt under their gleaming gaze. After a sleepless night, lying sprawled across that elegant duvet Campbell had tried in vain to put her mind at ease. As the red digital numbers on the alarm clock ticked away minute after minute she wrestled with herself trying to find a reasonable explanation for what she had seen that night. For every minute that went by, she developed another logical or rational explanation. But 240 minutes, and 240 explanations later she couldn't shake herself of the truth she knew deep down in her core.

The ballroom felt vast in its emptiness. Pacing the small hotel bedroom fed her anxiety so she had decided to arrive early and prepare her PowerPoint and paper. But her mind wasn't on her presentation. Instead, she was rehearsing what she would say to Finn when she saw him. Would she confront him about what she now knew? Was it even possible to keep it from him? Campbell had never been that good at lying, and at some point the matter would have to be addressed.

The projector bled soft blue light onto the large white screen, and she plugged in her thumb drive to make sure that the slides for her presentation would come up.

It's only fifteen minutes, she reminded herself. *I can talk without having to think for 15 minutes. Wouldn't be the first time. Hopefully no one will come since our session is so early.*

Moments later she heard voices outside the room. She recognized Tasha's laughter, and Kyle's chipper voice. *Well, at least they showed up,* she smiled to herself.

"Good morning," she heard Tasha say from the hallway.

"Good morning!" It was Finn's good-natured voice that replied to Tasha.

Campbell's insides imploded and she held back the urge to vomit; grateful she hadn't eaten since early yesterday evening. The small crowd shuffled into the room carrying folders, laptops and book bags. Looking up with a forced smile she called out to no one in particular, "Good morning!" She was careful to avoid eye contact with Finn, afraid she might come completely unglued right then and there. But she could feel his attention like a warm lamp pressing against her skin.

"Good morning," he replied as he walked toward the front of the room. "I see you sure got an early start."

"I couldn't sleep", she said. She wanted to tell him, *I was up thinking about who and what you are.*

He rested his laptop on the chair next to her and started to unpack his materials, eyeing her cautiously.

"Ready for some more vampire theory?" he asked trying to force a smile out of her.

"Theory my ass," she muttered

Finn winced. "Are you okay?" he asked.

"Yep. Just fine." Her agitation was palpable.

"I love you," he whispered beyond hearing range.

Campbell could not control her nerves. Her hand jerked, knocking over a glass of water which spread in a flood toward her stack of papers. Fortunately the buffet table at the far wall was stacked with paper napkins and a water pitcher. She clutched the napkins. Rushing back to her papers she tried frantically to wipe up the mess.

"Can I help?" Finn offered. Before she could reply Tasha announced, "Kyle was in rare form last night!" Kyle added with a low throttle laugh, "You missed quite a scene at the after-hours club. I don't think we even slept!"

Campbell wasn't listening as they retold their humorously sordid tale. She stomped over to the garbage can with dripping cold napkins, careful not to get any on her clean slacks. Two more presenters arrived. Campbell was grateful to see one of them was Sandy. She walked around the other side of the table and hugged her.

"Hi! How was your flight, Sandy?"

Campbell could feel Finn as his eyes followed her every move. *What is he thinking right now?* she wondered.

"Oh, we had a delay in Toledo. Technical difficulties with the engine. That always scares me," Sandy added.

Oh good. Idle chit chat. I can do this, Campbell thought. Sandy was elegant and graceful as usual. She felt a newfound appreciation for Sandy; who she was, the work she did, and how she seemed to carry herself through life so effortlessly.

"I would have called you, but it was so late when I arrived I thought you might be asleep," she apologized, unwrapping a delicately woven scarf from around her neck.

With her black hair pulled up in a soft bun, and the turquoise and black silk top that draped across the slope of her neck bone Campbell thought her the most beautiful woman in the world. She wanted to cry.

Sandy looked at Campbell whose face had turned a dull grey. She was curious that Campbell, usually at ease in any social situation, was barely glancing up from the computer to acknowledge Finn. She noted the way Finn beamed at Campbell and the way Campbell avoided him in return, and she could sense the thick haze of tension emerging between them.

Oh dear, Sandy thought, *This spells trouble.* Campbell grabbed the first seat behind the long table in the front of the room. The other panelists slid in behind her and found seats, with Finn on the far end. Campbell was relieved to have the distance between them. She shook hands with Dr. Sorrel, a benign and intelligent scholar from UCLA whom she remembered meeting last year, who was sitting next to her.

The presentation chair announced the beginning of the session. "We'll just go in order of seating," he explained gesturing to the panelists. "Dr. Cote, that means you'll go first. Is that okay?" Everyone nodded in agreement. As she stood at the podium, clicking away at the slides behind her, Campbell couldn't recognize her own voice but she knew the words. She read slowly:

"The notion that there is a distinctive and gendered perception, the male 'gaze' if you will, is supported by the feminist standpoint theorists such as Harding (1986), who in her 1986 text, challenged rationality and universalism in the social sciences as both being fabricated constructs."

She could discuss the research in her sleep. The male gaze at hand right now just happened to be Finn's. Whatever else she read on those pages was a blur.

"In conclusion," she heard herself say after 13 minutes of dutiful attention by her audience, "My research findings suggest that feminist challenges to main-stream social science are diverse and influential. Whether consciously or unconsciously we cannot escape the idea that all science is affected by gender-based ideologies, which affect who and what we believe about ourselves." She sighed with relief and thought, *Over*.

She heard the calm applause from the few dozen people who had turned out for their presentation. She glanced at Finn as she moved back toward her seat. He had a look of pride on his face, clearly impressed by the work she was doing. She held tightly onto her paper to keep her hands from trembling. Her throat was dry but she feared that if she lifted her water glass it would spill across the entire table.

Twenty minutes later, it was Finn's turn. As he rose toward the podium Campbell took in every movement of his tall sleek and ripped body. Sandy watched Campbell with the acute skills of an ethnographic researcher, one dedicated for two decades to the study of human actions and reactions. She could weave together the unspoken language of a love between them. Campbell tried not to seem like a lovelorn puppy. She felt self-conscious. She knew that being seated directly in front of an audience someone might be watching her rather than Finn. Campbell looked down and scribbled something on the paper as if she were taking notes on Finn's presentation. She listened to his voice, her desire for him mounting, and felt every sound and syllable wash over her like a symphony. Finally, toward the end of his 15 minute presentation she sucked up the courage to look at him. His hair was loosely tied at the base of his neck. She could see his stance behind the podium, his light blue button down shirt, brown tie, and jeans radiating off his muscular form. She stared, but tried to make it appear as if she were adjusting her seat. He raised his head above the crowd, turning toward the doors at the back of the room and in a bold voice pronounced his conclusion.

"The issues of identity and meaning construction, between self and other, between survival and death as presented within the walls of the academe, suggest why, as Hollinger (1997) explains 'some vampire texts mirror aspects of that peculiar human condition which has come to be termed 'postmodern.' Postmodernism, she argues, 'is one of the more productive and challenging paradigms through which contemporary Western reality is currently being conceptualized.' Allacquere Rosanne Stone contends this need for a new vision can be achieved in two ways. One is by becoming aware that the control of the apparatus of meaning has slipped out from under us. The other means to survival Stone writes is 'to accept the vampire's kiss'."

After saying those words he turned his head to the right and stared without shame into Campbell's eyes. *Kiss me,* they seemed to say.

Campbell flushed and turned her eyes away. *Did anyone else see that?* Sandy was staring a little too intently at her. Following the panel discussion the audience was given time to ask questions. Campbell was brought back to reality by the sound of her name. A clever graduate student in the front row was addressing her. "Dr. Cote, I found it interesting how your findings and Dr. McGinnis' theory intersect each other." She pushed her tortoise shell glasses up the bridge of her nose. "I was wondering if the two of you had done any collaborative work bridging the connections between feminist theories and vampires."

Finn glanced over at Campbell, playfully raising one eyebrow. The young student looked on with earnest curiosity, oblivious to the subtext between Finn and Campbell. She went on, "Um … According to Griffiths (2002), traditional women's work including the work of motherhood, is cyclic, it must be done over and over again, characterized by repetitive chores, fetching water, or washing clothes. By contrast, men's work which is linear, lasting over time, massive developments, isolated rather than repetitive, is considered much more valuable."

Campbell nodded slightly with a wry grin. She felt a rush of pride that some part of her work was being acknowledged. The graduate student kept an earnest gaze and jumped in, saying, "So, what I think is that this notion of feminine time, repetitive and circular, is much more like the existence of the vampire as Dr. McGinnis is describing. The vampire exists through blood ties. It creates more of its own through blood transfers and sustains its life by feeding off the blood of humans. Women, you know, human women, also are linked more closely to life through blood. It is how we are able to create new life."

Finn watched this young woman intently. She was locked and loaded, he could tell, because she had not even paused to take a breath and her hands were shaking. She went on, "And, the vampire's trump card over the human, even as a parallel species, is that... it ..." She paused and turned to Finn for silent assistance, "He? She? I don't know…"

The crowd laughed a little. "He or she," Finn replied smiling.

"Well, I mean, the vampire's whole existence is for an eternity, so like, she faces an existence where even if certain events are finite, her whole worldview would be much more circular, because she would have no real ending. Right?"

At this last question she searched around, hoping for some eye contact or nods that would suggest she had expounded something brilliant. But the clock was working against them. The chairperson abruptly moved on to announce, "Thank you to our panel for today's presentation. We are out of time and we need to clear the room for the next session."

References

Griffiths, J. (2002). *A sideways look at time*. New York, NY: Tarcher Publishing.

Harding, S. (1986). *The science question in feminism*. Cornell, NY: Cornell University Press.

Hollinger, V. (1997). Fantasies of absence: The postmodern vampire. In J. Gordon & V. Hollinger (Eds.), *Blood read: The vampire as metaphor in contemporary culture* (pp. 199–212). Philadelphia, PA: University of Pennsylvania Press.

CHAPTER TWENTY-FIVE

San Diego, 2011

The presentation now completed, Campbell tried as best she could to evade the well-wishers who would commend their research and exchange emails or business cards. The young graduate student who had spoken at the end made a beeline for Finn. Since Campbell was in the line of her trajectory she stopped to talk with Campbell who smiled and mumbled something to no one in particular about needing to use the restroom. *Of course she is going to make sure she speaks with him rather than to me. Even the feminists can't resist a dashing intellectual. None of us is immune to that,* Campbell noted with gentle admonition toward the young woman.

Finn was shaking hands and chatting while keeping a fixed focus on Campbell as she dashed out of the room with her papers stuffed underneath her arm. She hadn't taken the time to pack her things properly. *Something's wrong,* he knew. The graduate student had reached his side by now and was going to hold his attention as long as she could.

Campbell pushed her way through the wooden door to the women's restroom. It made a loud bang as it slapped against the back wall. Looking around and under the stall doors she found the bathroom empty and then heaved a sigh. The tears came without notice. "God damn it!!! Shit, shit, shit!!!!!!" she cried. Her voice reverberated against the walls. The universe had officially split apart.

He knew, too! He knew who I was and he didn't say anything! This explains his strange behavior at New Beginnings a few weeks ago. That must have been when he realized who I was.

For a moment she felt a wave of sympathy for him and thought about the shock of all this, that he must be experiencing as well. Anger gave way to rational questions. *If he really is a vampire, how is it he can be around in daylight? It's only 9:30 a.m.? I must be wrong, or crazy.* Then her heart sank again. *He's been indoors all morning. Probably hasn't left this hotel room since last night.* She had to concede to her original theory. This was happening. He was that same person she had met thirty-five years prior. She would have to figure this out. She let herself sob briefly, and then went to the sink to splash cool water on her face. She had to find some way to avoid Finn until she could think of what to do next.

Throughout the day Finn searched the hotel in vain for Campbell. He phoned her room several times and left messages at the front desk. He wandered many of the other conference sessions hoping to run into her but she was nowhere to be found. *Maybe she flew home early. Maybe there was an emergency with one of her kids,* he told himself.

By 6:00 p.m. there was still no sight of Campbell. Finn had put on his running clothes and gone out for a long run to burn off the excess energy and anxiety that was creeping up his spine. He found Campbell's friends, the ones he had met the night before, sitting at the bar as if they had never left. Tasha had her legs propped up on a cushioned lounge chair. Her velvet blue Gypsy skirt draped toward the floor. Kyle was seated across the other side of the small round café table. His bright red Polo shirt off set his stark blond hair.

"Hey!" shouted Kyle eagerly. "It's Finn, right?" Finn nodded stoically, wiping sweat from his brow.

"Why don't you go change, and then come on down and join us for a night on the town?" Kyle's expression was genuine and open. Tasha studied Finn up and down with desire. Finn wasn't used to feeling like someone else's dinner. He stammered, "Um. Sure. Here? In about 20 minutes?" He knew that if Campbell was still in San Diego it was only a matter of time before she met up with her friends. They would serve as his tracking device.

The evening marina lights glimmered on the water's surface like twinkling stars. Finn sat at a wrought iron outdoor table in a chicly designed Americana-themed restaurant, nestled in the heart of the harbor district with Tasha, Kyle, and a few other people he didn't know. He tried to sit at the very edge, away from being the center of attention. He had grown bored with their bawdy humor and self-absorbed analysis of their work hours ago. He scanned the room, trying to make out Campbell's face in the crowded club. The table was littered with empty bar glasses and two half emptied bottles of Merlot.

Just minutes earlier Campbell had received a text from Tasha. It read: "We are at Duvall's on 28th Street. Have your cutie pie with us. Come retrieve him before I take him! Ha-ha."

So ... this is it, Campbell told herself reading the message. She had done nothing but ride the trolleys all day going as far from the conference center as she could. As if she could sense Campbell's stress from all the way across the country, Gillian had called her earlier in the afternoon. Over the roar of the trolley Campbell answered the phone and shouted with joy, "How did you know I needed you? You always know, don't you?"

"Well, I did the math and adjusted my phone calling time for Pacific Time. That's the kind of person I am. Is it 5:00 p.m. there? And where the hell are you right now? It sounds like a train or something."

Campbell started crying a little. "I can't really talk now though," Campbell shouted over the roar of the engine. "I am riding the San Diego trolley trying to decide whether or not to jump from it while it's moving."

A white-haired elderly Asian woman with a heavy canvas bag overflowing with groceries eyed Campbell nervously. Campbell returned her glare and explained, "I'm not really going to jump." The women glared and turned away. Campbell could hear Gillian saying something about her daughter's recent incident at the craft store. "Sorry. It's hard to hear, Gill."

"Are you alright, Campbell?" she asked, loud and clear.

"No. I'm not. But I can't explain it right now. I am having the mother of all mid-life crises. Let's just leave it at that for now."

Gillian tried to reply but their cell phone connection was lost. Campbell placed the phone back in her purse.

As she rode up and down the streets of San Diego staring blankly out of the open window she pondered what to do about Finn. She hadn't decided to do anything until she received that text message from Tasha.

With an emerging sense of courage and resolve, Campbell returned to her room and rifled through her clothing bag seeking the most flattering pair of jeans she could find and a "sexy yet not trying too hard top" V-neck black cotton shirt. The pickings were slim, but when Campbell stood in front of the full length mirror she radiated the aura of a woman on the prowl. She pulled her hair up into a loose bun and cinched it on top with a clip. A sense of purpose was growing silently from within. It didn't matter that she didn't have the slightest clue what she would do or say. She just knew that she was going somewhere and there was no going back. Finn embodied eternity and possibility, the fresh rush of unfettered unknowing; and she wanted to fall down the rabbit hole as far as she could go.

Between the cacophonous sounds of the band warming up and the smell of barbeque, Finn had no idea that Campbell had entered Duvall's. With no real urgency she made her way through the crowded dark room to the large wooden bar at the far edge of the main area. She scanned the room. In the mood lighting it was difficult to make out the details. But then the stage lights came on and the band that had been warming up introduced themselves. The singer, perhaps in her early thirties with short red hair rang out in a raspy voice, "Welcome and thank you for coming tonight! We are Swamp Slo. Are ya'll ready for some rock and roll?" A few people in the front row table cheered.

"We're going to start with one of our personal faves by Lucinda Williams" (Williams & Gardener, 2001).

There were more hoots and cheers.

As the electric guitars split through the speakers with a sharp twang, Finn and the others at the table on the adjoining patio looked up and over toward the stage. Finn's eyes locked on Campbell's. The singer whose voice sounded like an exact replication of Lucinda Williams' had selected one of Campbell's favorite songs. The moment swept over her. *This was fate*, Campbell decided.

Slowly, she sauntered toward Finn's table. *Well, she's smiling. That's a good sign*, he considered with relief. *But why is she looking at me that way?* Campbell's attention gave Finn a deep thrill and he fought the growl resonating in his throat. He wanted her. Now.

Campbell let the lyrics wash over her. The low growl of the lead singer vibrated off the wooden dance floor; singing about addiction, blood, death, and love. *How fitting*, Campbell thought. Finn was the drug she wanted to shoot into her veins. She, like Finn, was ready to flirt with death.

She reached his table and without acknowledging anyone else looked down at Finn with an expectant gaze and requested, "Dance?" He rose and grabbed her hand and obediently followed her onto the dance floor. She pulled him close and wrapped her hands around the base of his firm muscular waist. He pressed his face into her shoulder. They moved slowly, their bodies locked in sync with each other.

Campbell looked up and he lifted his head from her shoulder. He waited for her to say something. She stretched her neck closer to his ear and whispered loudly, "I know who you are."

He pulled his face back a few inches to gauge her expression.

What does she mean? How did she find out? Or is she referring to something else? What else could she be referring to?

Maybe he hadn't heard her correctly. Finn was puzzled but didn't say anything. Her face was soft but expressionless.

"I choose you," Campbell confided.

She registered the subtle shock on his face and uttered again, "I know who you are."

They stood there not moving in the middle of the dance floor, neither one wanting to let go of the other. Around them a small crowd of people kept time with the slow rhythmic beat.

She added louder to make herself clearly understood over the music, "I know what you are. You saved my life when I was a child. You're him. But here you are, unchanged. Vampire … theory? My ass. I can't explain it. I don't want to. I don't care. I choose you." Then she nestled her face into the nook of his broad shoulder before he could respond.

"How did you know?" he asked.

She looked back up at him. "Somehow I've always known. Since the moment I saw you in that parking lot on campus. I just didn't want to admit it. And here I am now. With you." They stared at each other. The singer's voice moaned. The guitar wailed a long slow note. Before he could react, Campbell leaned in and kissed him. Her knees gave way and a bolt of warm electric current shot through her body. Finn's mouth felt soft and inviting.

How could this be the mouth of a vampire? she asked herself. It seemed absurd to her that in the midst of what felt like the most erotic experience of her life she should be wondering about his fangs. They stared at each other. Then Finn slid his hand around the back of her head tangling his fingers into her hair, leaned down and pressed his mouth hard on her lips, kissing her back with all the force he had been saving up. In the midst of the large mass of people, no one from their table seemed to notice what was happening. Finn and Campbell turned toward their friends who were still busy leaning in toward each other shrieking and laughing over the music. Campbell gave Finn a wily smile.

The smiled implied, "Let's get out of here."

Reference

Williams, S., & Gardener, M. S. (2001). Essence [Recorded by L. Williams]. On *Essence (Album)*. Nashville, TN: Lost Highway Records.

CHAPTER TWENTY-SIX

San Diego, 2011

They sat across from each other on Campbell's hotel bed. For a minute or two they remained still and silent, sizing each other up in disbelief. Then Campbell slowly pulled Finn's face toward her own. She felt a low growl resonate from his throat and it rippled through her, sinking into her blood and bones. To her surprise she found herself crying softly, and as the tears rolled down her face Finn lifted his fingers to wipe them away.

I have no idea why I am crying, she thought, though she suspected it was from relief more than anything else. She looked at him, his dark endless brown eyes, looking straight through hers. His eyes searched her entire face, the pupils unable to remain still, his face was twisted in a position of fear mixed with desire. She wanted to say, "It's okay. You're safe here. I know everything you're thinking and feeling. You don't need to say word. No explanation is needed."

Was he shaking? She could have no more pulled herself away from Finn than she could have elevated herself from the forces of gravity holding to the earth.

"This is what I want. I choose you," she crooned again with confidence.

Campbell raised her right hand and traced the rugged edges of his imperfect nose. As if she were studying a map in Braille she wanted to know the entire landscape of his face by touch. She followed the edges of his high cheek bones and across the scar that rested just at the brow line between his forehead and his hair.

With that same finger she lifted the few long strands that hung by his cheek up over and behind his ear.

Then Finn cautiously raised his right arm and curved the large part of his smooth palm back toward the base of her neck and pulled Campbell's face toward his. She didn't pause. As he leaned in to brush his lips across hers, a slight chill crossed between them, followed by a bright hot electric shock that ran down the base of her spine. It wasn't the vampire in Finn that craved Campbell. It was what remained of his human self that desired her. Finn wished she could make him human again—to bring him back to life. Yet, the irony was that Campbell was now certain she wanted nothing more than to become like Finn, and have life immortal.

His lips grazed the space between her ear and neck. She heard him growl again. There was no fear. What she felt was total stillness. Whatever it was that she was experiencing, it filled her with an intense rush of ecstasy she hadn't realized was missing from her life. She didn't want it to ever go away. At that moment she could rationalize anything.

"I want you so much Finn," she cried.

It was a plea of insatiable hunger. "I want you too," he admitted, his voice low and bold. Then he paused and examined her with small wrinkles of doubt around his eyes, "But, are you sure Campbell?"

She placed her fingers to his lips to silence him. "Unless you are going to bite me or kiss me, I suggest you stop moving those lips."

She grinned, and Finn felt something welling up inside of him—a desire more powerful than the desire to feed; a desire greater than any he had for alcohol while he was human. It was the desire for her, completely.

The smooth tips of his fingers ran along the side of her right arm, arced inward, and ever so lightly passed over her erect nipple, a sensation that rippled through the layers of her clothing. She lifted both arms and without needing instructions, he pulled her shirt up over her head and aimlessly dropped it to the floor with a soft thud. Then he brushed the hair away from her shoulders and leaned in. The deep pressure of his mouth upon her neck caused her to arch her whole body backwards, and he ran his mouth, open with teeth bared, down toward her breasts. Dizzy, she fell backwards onto the soft pillows. More aware now of his own weight and power, combined with a passion he had never known before, Finn became conscious of his massive size. Not wanting to hurt or alarm her, he raised himself up slightly with his elbows and then he slid his body atop of hers, leaving just a breath of space between the two of them. She raised her hips up to his torso, wrapped her legs around him, and pulled his lower body down tightly to soothe the aching heat that was burning between her thighs. The urge was nearly unbearable. She wished she could magically cause her pants to dissolve without effort. Using the force of her right shoulder to guide him, she nudged him over to his side and then onto his back. His eyes glowed a deep amber.

"Yes. It's time," she said.

Though her hands trembled, with all the control she could muster she undid the buttons on her jeans and slid them, along with her underpants, down past her ankles and kicked them off. She took some time to look at him—this beautiful creature, his hair lying so still on the pillows behind his face. With the traces of old scars along one side of his face, and a nose that had perhaps been broken in a life before this one, he had the appearance more of an outcast damaged angel than that of a vampire. That was, until he opened his mouth to smile, and she could see his desire for her in the gleaming whites of his elongated teeth. But there was no threat. There was no fear. Her eyes locked on his, she placed the fullness of her desire on top of him, and then for the first time perhaps in her entire life, Campbell let herself go. For once, she was free.

How much time had passed?

Campbell could feel her breathing subside into a slow series of ebullient waves. The endorphin rush was waning and she gradually opened her eyes and turned her head toward the alarm clock on the bedside table. It was almost 4:00 a.m.

She turned her head slowly to feast upon Finn resting beside her. His eyes were closed. She noted their breathing was now in perfect sync. Suddenly, Campbell felt her body rise from the bed, even as it appeared to still be lying there, and float silently toward the bathroom. She turned on the light switch. The dull yellow light flickered a few times and then glowed steady with a soft hum that ran up her spine. The shuffle of her bare feet echoed on the cold tile floor.

She studied her image in the mirror, staring unblinkingly at the face that once resembled her own but that she longer recognized. It was as if it were a stranger gaping back at her for the first time; the first encounter with someone, where you notice the infinitesimal details of that individual. These are the same minute details which, after time as familiarity grows, become blurred and non-distinct.

Campbell carefully noted the sharp arched lines of her dark brows. Now they seemed incongruent with the paleness of her skin. She noted the smooth curve of her shoulders as they sloped downward to become sleek forearms. Her breasts were small but full, perceptibly different having nursed two infants. Campbell reached up and pulled the scattered stray bangs way from her forehead and leaned in closer toward the image in the mirror. Staring into the glassy blue eyes, she was demanding an answer, waiting for this person in the mirror to speak ... for the eyes to reveal some unspoken secret.

It was in this moment that Campbell realized she had successfully accomplished what she had set out to do. Making love to Finn wasn't an act of rebellion, or a way to punish Brent for their wavering marriage. It wasn't the act of a woman desperately seeking love and attention. It wasn't motivated out of a fascination for who, or what Finn was. It wasn't even out of an ordinary affection, or desire for Finn himself. Peering now at this woman in the mirror whom she did not recognize, it occurred to Campbell as hard as a rush of wind punching her in the chest, that she had successfully made herself disappear. It was like suicide without the messy evidence of a dead body. Someone else was born in her stead.

CHAPTER TWENTY-SEVEN

San Diego, 2011

Three hours later, the room transformed from a cool blue into a warm translucent ochre yellow as the sunlight forced its way through the sheer window treatments. Finn winced and leapt from the bed to draw the thick floral curtains closed, ensconcing the room in an artificial night time. Campbell awoke and flipped on the lamp fixed to the wall above the bed.

Finn smiled and regarded her expectantly. Then he leaned over and kissed her on the check. She felt her face flush. He could paint a warm glow on her body with his fingers and lips.

"Okay," she stated with a slow determination. "I only have about three hours before I need to leave for the airport and go back to the grim reality of our daily lives. So while I have you captive in this delightful parallel universe I'd like to ask you a few questions. Well, maybe a million, but I will try and narrow it down."

Finn's insides ached at the thought of having to return to Baltimore where Campbell might vanish back into her previous existence, away from him. It was one thing to live for an eternity but unfortunate that he did not have total control over where that eternity might be spent, like right here lying in bed next to Campbell.

"I need coffee for this," she announced, rising from the bed and padding across the carpet. The bed sheet slid to the ground revealing her middle-aged figure. Her self-confidence winced. Two pregnancies had certainly left their mark. But Finn's gaze was as if he were looking upon the Sistine Chapel. With renewed confidence, she stood naked and poured water into the top of the tiny one serving coffee pot.

"So, Dr. McGinnis, what's with the daylight myth? Will you explode into a puff of smoke if you go outside before dusk?" He chuckled.

"You watch too many movies, Dr. Cote. Actually, for the first few days, I still had no idea what had happened to me but I was developing some theories. The idea of vampires being real was as absurd to me as it is to most people. But when something is happening to you personally you can become convinced on the impossible pretty quickly. Anyway, so I had holed up in this old warehouse for about a week I guess, time was so blurred then, but one day I stepped out of the doorway and I was struck with this terrific pain all over my body. I guess the best way to describe it is what people feel like when they're having a stroke. It's incredibly painful to be outside in the light and if I stood out in it long enough I would probably be killed by stroke like symptoms. I can withstand it for brief periods of time like moving from a subway and down a few blocks to a building if I move fast, and as long as it's not a bright summer time noonday sun. But even in overcast weather, it is extremely unpleasant, and a little frightening, so I try to avoid it."

He lifted his body from the bed and stood to pull on his pants. Campbell tried not to ogle like a school girl.

"Hmmm. I see," Campbell replied nonchalantly, keeping her eyes fixed on him. The next question hit her suddenly with a new sense of panic.

"When did you um… change?" she asked, unsure how one phrases such a question.

It had occurred to her that Finn was the same age as he'd been when she met him when she was six, and that he must have changed right around that same time. Something inside her knew she was linked to this chain of events. Sensing her unease, Finn tried to be selective with his words when answering this question.

"Well … it happened after the car accident. That night when you were a little girl?"

She nodded.

"Your father gave me a fistful of money, you know, for saving you."

Campbell interjected while looking up at him, "I never thanked you by the way. For saving my life."

Finn wasn't sure what to say in response, so he continued. "So you know, I bought as much booze as I could with it. Went on a massive bender. And sometime that evening I was visited by a pack of what I now know were vampires. But at the time, they just seemed like some strange kids. They asked me to go party with them. I didn't learn the reason why until about ten years later."

This last comment he made more to himself than to Campbell. She poured a cup of coffee into the plastic coffee mug, added creamer, and stirred, without speaking. Her face darkened.

"So, it's my fault this happened? If you hadn't run into the road and if my father hadn't rewarded you, then none of this would have happened?"

Campbell's mind refracted this chain of events like light bending and moving around the faces of a prism.

"Campbell," he pleaded, trying to reassure her, "You know as well as I that any chain of events is broader than A to B to C. Think of all the other factors that lead to any moment. I could have camped out at another abandoned building where maybe they wouldn't have found me. I could have done something else with the money, like, use to it to pay a doctor to check out my wounds."

He knew this last suggestion was a lie. Buying alcohol with that money hadn't been a choice. "I could have refused to go with them," he said. He knew this last suggestion was a lie as well.

"If I hadn't been there, outside right when you ran out into the road, you probably would be dead right now," Finn argued emphatically moving across the room toward her.

She sipped the coffee. It tasted bitter, even with the powder creamer.

"And if I hadn't saved you that day, then maybe those vampires would not have changed me and I would have died drunk in a ditch within a few years."

He wrapped both his arms around her waist and nestled his face into her hair. He murmured, "And I wouldn't be standing here with you today. The universe never would have brought us together again. I guess we saved each other's lives."

"Maybe you're right," she agreed, convincing him as much as herself. The truth was she didn't know what anything meant. But she knew what she felt. And that was to be with Finn, above all else. At that moment, Campbell was jolted back into reality by the ring of her cell phone. She answered it, knowing who would be on the end.

"Mother," declared Caroline urgently without waiting for Campbell to say hello. "When are you coming home? Ellis is being mean. He took my Barbies and tied them up and attacked them with his army guys yesterday. And Daddy's being crabby. I miss you."

Campbell turned away from Finn, as if she could hide the conversation from him, toward the window for better reception and whispered, "It's alright, honey. I'll be home in just about ten hours. Probably by dinner time. Okay? Tell Daddy I'm going to take a cab home since you'll probably be cooking dinner right around that time."

She knew asking Brent to multitask by making dinner ahead of time, and loading both kids in the car to come and get her at the airport was too daunting for him. Better to keep things simple. She had become accustomed to accommodating him to keep their universe running smooth. Campbell pressed "off" and looked sadly at Finn. Her mind snapped shut. She was back on autopilot, except this time something inside her could no longer swallow this state of being. She buried the resistance out of necessity.

"I need to get ready to go," she sighed coolly. The spell was broken.

"I know," he replied. "I'm flying home tonight," he added. "Can I call you tomorrow?"

"I don't know," Campbell muttered. "I have to think through this. What do we do now?" She started pulling her clothes out of the dresser drawers and tossing them into her small suitcase.

"Can I help?" he asked feeling a strange sense of helplessness.

"No. But keep me company a little while longer, if that's okay."

"Of course," he offered, sitting on the bed.

"So…" She paused pulling her light green sweater over her head. "How did you pull off the PhD, Finn?" Little strands of blond hair flew up with static and she quickly knotted her hair up with a hair band, creating a loose cinch of hair at the nape of her neck.

"Ahhh, that…" he began. They sat side by side on the bed as he retold her everything: About the blood bank, about Travis and his knowledge of vampires, and how he returned to New Beginnings to protect the community, about taking what he had learned from Travis to develop a deeper working understanding of vampire evolution and complete his PhD. Time sat suspended in the hotel room. She knew if she only dropped this suitcase and tore up her plane ticket she could lie there with him and the noise in her head would stop. Could she even consider the inconceivable? *What if she was to become … like him?* This question led her to something else that she had been afraid to ask, afraid to know the answer.

"Honestly Finn. I don't know where we go from here. It's all just too much to figure out." The fear of losing Finn, of watching him gradually dissipate before eyes like some sort of magnificent mirage filled her with dread. She needed to give him something.

"Well, does the offer to come and help at New Beginnings on Thanksgiving still stand?" she asked. "I'll have the kids with me of course." The absence of Brent's name hung between them.

"Yes, please, that would be great," he replied emphatically.

He was fully dressed now and leaning against the dresser, waiting intently on her every word. His hair hung softly across his broad shoulders. He smiled coyly and stroked his hands through his hair one time.

"I'll call you. Or email you when I am home and settled in," Campbell added. "Thanksgiving is in four days, right? I have my in-laws coming into town."

Again she had chosen her words carefully to avoid using the words husband or Brent. "I need to go shopping, clean the house. All very exciting, right?" She chuckled and sighed. *How absurd and mundane all this must seem to him in his world.*

"No," he insisted with genuine affection and respect. "It sounds wonderful."

Wonderful and impossible, she realized.

As she passed less than a foot away from where he was leaning she stopped. Campbell dropped her bags with a thud, some of her papers sliding out of the top of her briefcase onto the carpet. She looked at him, and as she opened her mouth to utter something else, with lightning speed, faster than she could see, he had embraced her tightly around the waist with both hands and placed his lips on hers with a fierceness that caused her to gasp.

I don't have limitless time, she thought with a sense of urgency. The span of her brief existence seemed to move even faster when juxtaposed with Finn's eternal existence. Finn could make endless and limitless choices. She couldn't. Unless, she became like him. But then how would she ever see her children again? Campbell could feel the tears collecting. She wouldn't let them.

CHAPTER TWENTY-EIGHT

Baltimore, 2011

Campbell turned the key in the lock of the front door. She could hear plates being tossed into the dishwasher and high pitched voices in the living room. Caroline's laughter reverberated through the house. Brent was talking to Caroline about something that Campbell couldn't quite make out.

With heart racing, Campbell consciously moved her facial muscles to appear as she always had, hoping no one would sense the change in her. Her mind was running like a digital display advertisement in bright red letters that she was sure were visible across her forehead that read: I slept with Finn.

As they heard the door open Ellis and Caroline shouted, "Mommy!!!!" and came rushing to wrap their arms around her.

"Whoa!" she cried, trying to keep her balance by bracing the wall of the foyer. "How are my monkeys?!"

She kissed them and nestled her face into Ellis' hair hoping the smell of his head, a scent that to Campbell was the most amazing of all sensory experiences, would jolt her back into her former self. She breathed deep and felt at home. But the antidote did not work completely. As she asked them, "Were you good for Daddy?" and, "How was school?" a voice in the back of her mind was whispering Finn's name.

Brent smiled and politely extended a "welcome home." Campbell reached out and hugged him. "How was your trip?" he asked.

"Oh, you know," Campbell sighed and tried to keep her tone of voice from reaching a high pitch. "A bunch of egg heads off their leash for three days. Pretty nuts." Then she forced a laugh.

"So how are you all?" she exclaimed and reached to tickle Caroline's belly. Ellis nuzzled up beside her. He gave her his best puppy dog eyes.

"My asthma got real bad, Mommy," he whispered with a tinge of guilt as if he was somehow at fault for this occurrence. Campbell looked at Brent whose reaction gave her the response she halfway expected.

His eyes indicted her, saying, "This wouldn't have happened if you hadn't left." Her whole life came rushing back down upon her like thick mud. Then she recovered, as she always did. She wrapped her arms around Ellis and nuzzled the side of his face.

"But you're okay, right? Did Daddy take good care of you?"

"Yes. I used the inhaler. Even though it tastes really yucky."

Brent insisted "It wasn't a big deal. We handled it, didn't we, bud? Everything went fine, Campbell. It's just that we missed you. All of us."

Before knowing Finn, this last statement would have left Campbell feeling as if the world was all right and that the chasms between her and her husband were little more than what any married couple might experience. And she would go on reminding herself that her life really was perfect. But tonight, Brent's well-meaning attempts to play his role in righting the world left her feeling more off kilter than ever. A chilling tide of resentment washed over her.

If Brent had in fact simply been an abusive husband and negligent father she could have more easily justified her relationship with Finn. Few would have disapproved of her actions. "Of course she found another man," she imagined people saying. "What other choice did she have? He drove her away." But life, Campbell knew, both the truth and reality of it, were rarely ever that simple, or easy. Instead, she would have to live with the greyish in-between of the moral terrain she was now traversing, precariously poised to fall at any moment.

The next morning she watched the clock ticking minute by minute until it displayed the 10:00 a.m. hour. The children were at school and she was dressed and ready for her weekly walk with Lilly. Her need to talk was so full it gave her heartburn and a nauseous feeling. She stepped outside her front door to greet Lilly at the sidewalk. The air was crisp. A last trace of Indian summer refused to let winter arrive in its slow slide toward December. A few bright red and orange maple leaves dangled from the tree at the edge of her front yard. She was surprised every year by the number of autumn leaves that would hang on until the weight of a heavy snowfall finally pulled them down. She noticed their brilliance; red as neon stop lights and rich deep yellows, each made brighter by their contrast with the blue sky. *No clouds at all today*, she noted.

Campbell imagined Finn, working down in the basement back at New Beginnings. *What is he doing right now? She wondered. Does he even look out the window to marvel at this beauty? In spite of his beautiful immortality, what did he have to give up in this strange existence? Did living forever make him feel lighter than air with an absolute freedom? Or did eternity, the majority of which might be spent in the basement of a homeless shelter helping dying alcoholics, weigh as heavily on him as her fleeting existence weighed upon her? Would becoming like him make any difference in how she felt about herself?*

Before she could answer those questions, Lilly turned the corner and sped up to a trot when she saw Campbell waiting. Lilly was wearing Campbell's favorite outfit—the light pink sweatshirt that hugged her slim waist so well, and her black cotton sweats that felt as soft as worn sheets. As Lilly neared she read Campbell's twisted expression immediately.

"Oh boy! You slept with him, didn't you?" she shrieked.

"Yeah, and now all my neighbors know it too. Thanks, Lil," she replied searching around, hoping no one was standing in their front yards raking leaves or unloading groceries. To her relief they were the only two people visible on the block.

They started walking quickly in sync, side by side up the street. Lilly insisted, "So, my dear. Tell all."

"Uh. Lilly. It was…." She couldn't fight the grin that was spreading across her face, "Amazing!"

"Are you still human? Or did he turn you? What is the word for it when they change into a vampire? Is he really a vampire? Can you tell when they're standing naked?"

"One question at a time! Yes. No. Not sure what the word is. Yes. No."

Lilly laughed—partly at herself for behaving like a schoolgirl, and also at Campbell for the answers she provided. "So how did you finally conclude that your fair young lad is indeed among the um…other worldly?"

The possibility that such a thing could be a reality was not a far reach for Lilly. She held on to the potential of cosmic possibilities beyond the scope of most people. To Lilly, it was as matter of fact as finding out if he was gay or married.

"Ah…." Campbell sighed. She swung her arms over her head to stretch them, struggling to find the shorthand version to describe the series of events which had spanned across the reach of her life starting with her childhood. "It was his charm," she finally teased, pleased with herself for producing this spontaneous double entendre.

By the time they headed back down the cobblestone trail that lead through a copse of slim trees to the back ball field of the middle school, Campbell had given Lilly every last detail: how she and Finn had met when she was a child, the gold charm necklace, their confrontation on the dance floor, their night together.

"I haven't slept for days, Lilly." Campbell's tone had taken a serious, almost sad turn. The rush of erotic details had worn off and reality was pressing upon her. "All I keep thinking about is the 'what if's.' The 'what if's' we all face. The smallest of things that had to happen to create this set of events. We spend so much of our lives worrying about the big things, you know? Like which job to take, which person to commit to for the rest of our lives, what state or country to live in. But it's the small things, isn't it? The super ball that hits the small grain of gravel on a snowy sidewalk and makes a sideways trajectory. Isn't that just like the universe?"

"Yes, it is," Lilly replied somberly. "I'm glad to see you've been reading some of my published papers!"

They both cracked up at this, knowing that Campbell didn't understand much about Lilly's work in theoretical mathematics.

"It's like this, Cam," she started, "Either everything we do matters, or nothing matters. What is 'big' and what is 'small' in terms of life events is a matter of perception and subjectively defined. Let's say I leave the house and forget my cell phone. So I go back. Maybe that extra one minute causes or saves me from a horrible car accident. But we can never really know."

Campbell broke the silence as they passed the blue colonial that had been advertising a For Sale sign for the last nine months. It lay neatly trimmed and happy, but empty on the inside.

"I just don't know what to do now. I can't imagine not seeing Finn anymore. I don't know that I love him … yet, at least. I'm not even sure I know what that means anymore. I could love him. Easily. We are grown-ups, Lilly. I know it takes more than pheromones and great sex to develop real love. But I know what simply good sex feels like, too. And this … this is just so much more. It's like …" She paused searching for the word, "Like, it's this whole other parallel existence I am supposed to be part of. With Finn. I'm in the wrong lane of traffic. I walked on the wrong play stage…" Her voice trailed off.

"Enough with the bad metaphors, Cam! I think I get what you mean."

The simple thought that she was meant for something different which would take her away from the life she had chosen left Campbell with a rush of panic and grief. "But…what can really come from it? And what if Brent finds out? Or, do I leave Brent? Do I even want to do that?" Her voice rose in pitch with each question. Lilly placed her arm gently around her friend. Though they were sweating, Lilly's body shivered slightly from the cold breeze that passed between the houses. Both women were temporarily lost in their own secret thoughts.

Lilly remembered her defining moment: the one where she knew that if she didn't leave, she never would. Even six years later she could still taste the salty blood dripping from her ruptured lip, the sting on her face and in her psyche; that she had become one of those women; the kind whose husband hit her. It had happened so fast. The origin of the argument so minor as to be forgotten—something about money she had spent on a pair of new gloves. Or, was it the new rug for the playroom purchased without his consent? But she remembered with crystal clarity the rage that rang out from his every pore. His eyes were wide black discs. His mouth a distorted gaping cavern spewing hot breath and spit which caught her on the face like a light rain. The defining moment always meets you half way. Her whole face reeled from the impact of his knuckles. She instinctively reached up to her lip and held her fingers there, pressed against the rising swelling.

Her first thought was, *What do I tell the girls about how I got this?* Her eyes filled with tears. She hated her body for betraying her in this way. She didn't want to show any emotion in front of Chris. His handsome face, with large blue eyes and boyish curly brown hair, looked at her with more softness now, his rage expelled with his fist. She could see the remorse running across his face. He was out of breath and searching for what to say next.

You don't have to check your calendar to know when the defining moment is coming. You just need to know what to do when it arrives. Standing there in their pastel green kitchen, casually disarrayed with recent dinner preparations: chopped onions, a colander full of lettuce greens, a stick of butter softening with every minute of exposure to the kitchen warmth, she said with as much calm as she could unearth from her core, "I need to take Amanda and Kylie to the store for some assigned readings that are due tomorrow. Forgot to do it earlier, so we have to get to Barnes and Nobles before it closes at 8:00 p.m."

Her voice came as more of a declaration than a request. Over the ten years of their marriage her voice had gradually trained itself toward compliance and acquiescence. But tonight was the first time she had ever felt the force of his fist. Ice hides the bruising but not the memory. He must have been convinced by the tone of her voice. Or maybe this was his way of apologizing. He nodded silently and allowed her to pass through into the living room.

The girls were downstairs in the playroom. She was grateful that the room was out of earshot from her fight with Chris. They were playing quietly not sensing any disturbances upstairs. As she moved with the surety of one evacuating a sinking ship or a burning building she didn't hesitate to think. As she stepped quickly down the stairs to the basement playroom she used the side of her brown knit sweater to wipe away the blood from her lip. She re arranged her face to something that resembled a motherly expression familiar to her children.

"Hey guys!" she said cheerfully, "Let's go!"

"What?" said Amanda plaintively "We are in the middle of our Monopoly game!"

"I know," Lilly replied apologetically as she bent down to begin cleaning up the toys, "But we have to go. Now."

The girls must have sensed something in their mother's voice as she uttered the word *now*. Without arguing further they stood up from their game board and moved like a silent school of fish toward the front door. Now meant a myriad of things. It meant that if they didn't leave now, if Lilly forgave him now, if she spoke the words, "He didn't mean it. It won't happen again." That mantra would become easier to say with each incident. And slowly, Lilly would succumb as so many women did, to the rip tide of resignation and despair that took so many battered women down into the undertow.

Maybe it was a one-time incident. Maybe it wouldn't happen again. She had no way of telling. But the decision had to be now. In the other room she heard Chris on the phone, most likely talking about something to do with work. She heard him shouting angrily into the phone at who she supposed to be Andrew, his business partner in their painting business. She had to leave before he had a chance to get off the phone and change his mind. So pulling their shoes on and coats over their small confused shoulders, she loaded the girls into the car, taking only her purse and her cell phone with her. She left everything else behind and entered the free fall.

"Cam, maybe we're not meant to figure it all out. Once you've done that, what's left?"

She hugged her friend tightly as they stopped in front of Campbell's house. Lilly added, "And once you think you've figured it all out, you discover you're probably wrong anyway." They each gave a forced laugh.

"Frigging fabulous. Thanks. Good thing you never went into therapy for a living, Lil. Your patients would be locked up by the dozens." Over her shoulder Lilly called back, "Love you too!"

She walked up the steps to the front door. Nothing in Campbell's house was out of place, except her. With a shock, as if someone had splashed cold water on her face, Campbell remembered she would most likely see Finn tonight when she went to work. Her mind began reeling with the possibilities and she jogged quickly upstairs to shower and dress.

CHAPTER TWENTY-NINE

Baltimore, 2011

Her desire to imagine Finn watching her as she moved through the motions of her daily life was increasing at a slow fevered pitch. Earlier that day, as she made breakfast for the children she pictured Finn standing there, resting his broad lean torso against the kitchen entry way as she flipped pancakes.

What would he think me now, standing here in my sweat pants, hair shoved up in a knotty pony tail discussing cartoon characters with the same intensity as if I were debating who to nominate as the Great American author? she mused. *Would he laugh and join in? Or would he find me suddenly absurd and ordinary?*

In her mind, Finn had also come along with her to the kids school drop off and the gas station as well. He was everywhere with her like a ghost whose presence pervaded her entire consciousness. Campbell anxiously looked for him everywhere as she made her way up the hill from the parking lot. Her heart pounded in her chest as the elevator rose up to the third floor. By the time she was mid-way through her lecture for her Intro to Cultural Studies class, she had forgotten to think of him. Now she was more involved in trying to explain for what felt like the twentieth time, the expectations for their final paper. *Students,* she thought with disgust. *Even if they read the syllabus they claim you didn't verbally explain the outline.*

And even when you verbally give line by line item details about what they need to do, they won't be listening. You couldn't win with students.

"Now," she said with determination, "Let's go over this again." She waited until all 40 pairs of eyes were on her. They seemed so young all of a sudden. And Campbell felt older than she ever had before. Slowly as she could she said, "The paper needs to be between ten and twelve pages in length. Make sure your references are in APA style. Spelling and grammar do matter. I suggest going through the questions, one by one, and answer them bullet style so that you don't forget anything."

It was then that she sensed him standing there at the double doors at the top end of the lecture hall. She looked up from her syllabus. He wasn't a ghost of her imagination this time. Her stomach knotted and she couldn't hide the broad smile that stretched across her face. Her changed expression must have been apparent to the students who had been paying attention because several of them twisted their heads around to see what, or who, could inspire such a response from their professor. Finn casually lifted his arm to wave and gave her a small wink. Then he sauntered off, no doubt to his office. He was still wearing his Carheartt jacket and holding his backpack. He must have just arrived on to campus. The students turned back around and stared at Campbell expectantly. "Um…" she stammered trying to make a quick recovery. "I also recommend that you have someone peer edit your paper before you turn it in. It's hardest to find your own flaws."

Finn knew that she was teaching at this time down in Lecture Hall 112. He had to see her. He had fought the urge to go by her house last night. But later that evening he relaxed a bit when he opened his emails, and saw her name there. In the middle, buried beneath the string of dozens of other emails, was her name. He clicked it open with anticipation. He wondered, *What would she write now that she was home? I miss you? Or would it be, I realize that this weekend was a horrible mistake. It's over?* He fidgeted in his chair waiting for the file to open. It read:

Home safely. Hope you are, too. See you tomorrow.
C-

That was hopeful at least. After shutting off his computer, he rushed straight away to Maryland General Hospital for his weekly delivery. He would see her tomorrow. The word *tomorrow* threaded itself into his skin, and he wore the anticipation of it all night, waiting. Seeing her now, down at the steep end of the lecture hall, using her lecture tone, his desire grew even more. When he caught her return his blushing furtive gaze, in front of forty students, he knew she was still his.

She rushed to her office to drop off her large pile of books and papers, before speeding off to the faculty meeting. *Would she sit next to him? What would she say? Would others notice?* Her stream of questions was answered when she felt a pair of bold hands reach around her waist from behind as she was unlocking her office door. No one else was around in the office suite except her. All the other office doors were shut with darkened windows. She felt a strand of familiar blondish hair, smelling of citrus and leather, fall over the curve of her shoulder. "Who iiisss it?" she asked with a mock curiosity. The heavy bag dropped from her left hand, which fell with a thud onto the laminated tile floor. Her eyes rolled into the back of her head and her mind went blank. She arched her neck backwards to meet the gently graze of teeth and his wet lips.

"Mmmmmm…" he moaned. "I missed you."

Her knees gave way underneath her and her soul flew upwards from her body. He held the weight of her body which was now fully ensconced by the length of his arms, hands clasped at the lower edge of her torso. With her eyes still closed, she mustered the strength and clarity to unlock her office door. They moved as one large amorphous body into the room and she kicked the door shut behind them.

Only Sandy noticed when both Campbell and Finn slid like children sneaking in past curfew into the back table, fifteen minutes late to the faculty meeting. She caught the knowing glance that passed between them. And Campbell's smile. *Oh dear*, Sandy thought to herself. *This is not good. I will need to talk with her.*

Sandy noted Campbell's laser like intensity fixed upon Finn, a physical affect that emanated from her head to toe. Most likely it was indiscernible to anyone else in the meeting. But Sandy knew Campbell better than anyone else in their department. It was a whole-body response she hadn't seen in Campbell since her committee announced her dissertation defense had passed—that sensation of immense satisfaction from conquering something larger than yourself. Sandy knew that Finn was Campbell's latest conquest.

Meanwhile Finn and Campbell, oblivious to everyone around them, and to the announcements being delivered by Dean Robarts, passed notes back and forth in Finn's yellow legal pad.

Finn: I can taste you.

Campbell: I missed you last night. I watched for you in the stars above like a wanderer seeking their way on a long journey.

Finn: I will always be there. I want to lick your spine. When can I see you again?

Campbell scanned the room. Everyone was taking notes on the Power Point being delivered about the changes in courses that would take place next fall. Then she caught Sandy staring at her, hard. She returned the cold stare for a quick second and then looked down at the notepad.

Finn: When can I see you????????

Campbell: Don't know. Thanksgiving this week. We will still be there Thanksgiving
            Day! Is that still okay?

Finn: Of course. Would love to see your kids again. And you. Always.

She pretended to be listening to one of her colleagues rambling on about the latest course revisions. Finn was scribbling something. He put the pen down and waited. A second later, she pulled the pad toward her. It read:

Nothing will ever take us away. Not even us. (does that make sense?) We are beyond amazing.

Campbell could feel her heart racing and she could not hide the smile. *How could anything that had come before her relationship with Finn ever compete with this?* But reality still loomed. How would she justify her trip to New Beginnings to Brent? Her in-laws would be arriving that day and she had so much to do at home for her own dinner. It didn't matter she decided. She would figure out a way.

CHAPTER THIRTY

Baltimore, 2011

Dr. Campbell Cote Phillips locked the front door to her comfortable split-level brick ranch in the suburban corner just southwest of Baltimore and loaded her two children into the car. The air had moved from chilly to a biting freeze over the last two days. She felt the cold wind seep in through the threads of her long wool coat, chilling her skin. She wrapped one arm around her waist to close off the unbuttoned front of the coat while pulling the car keys out from the pocket with her other gloved hand. The kids seemed eager to go to New Beginnings. It was someplace new and in their eyes, a place where adventure and mischief might occur.

As Campbell started the car, Caroline asked, for the fifth time it seemed, "Why isn't Daddy coming?" There was a lilt in her voice, suggesting to Campbell that her children had not spent enough time with her and Brent together.

"He has to go to the airport to pick up Mee Maw and Paw Paw, honey. They are arriving in less than an hour. We don't want them to have to take a cab and arrive here to an empty house do we?"

She had little difficulty finding parking, pulling up curbside along Lafayette Street, just a block away from the center. The steps of the row houses spilled out along the sidewalk.

"Stay with me, you two," Campbell demanded. "Don't get too close to the street."

Caroline followed obediently, counting the bricks as she hopped from one to the next with her right foot. Ellis swung his body around a lamppost, locking his elbow around it and hurling himself forward with all his weight. Better, she thought, to keep a calm, relaxed, and upbeat attitude. Agitation with Ellis would only heighten his anxiety by the time they got there.

Finn immediately stood out among the rest. He wasn't hard to spot—the tall youthful glow of immortality, made even starker in his contrast to the frail and tired bodies of the men who sought refuge at New Beginnings.

"So, how are you?" he asked her, breathlessly.

She couldn't avoid blushing as he lowered his face right next to hers and whispered, "Happy Thanksgiving. Did you bring me anything good to eat?" She chuckled and then remembered the bag of rolls and breads she had brought.

"Oh, um, yeah. Here," she said, sticking the bag out in front of her.

"That's it?" he teased.

She searched around the room and gestured her head toward her children, both bearing fistfuls of cookies.

"For now it is."

She held his gaze for a long while. He sighed with feigned disappointment. Caroline and Ellis studied him expectantly.

"You remember Mr. Finn don't you kids? We met him here about a few weeks ago? This is where he works to help the men who need a place to stay."

"Because they're homeless," said Ellis, proud of his keen eye for observation. The children ambled off when they saw an incoming tray of buns and rolls being placed across the brown, orange, and yellow table cloth.

"You better get back to work, Dr. McGinnis. I will go into the kitchen and see what I can do to help." He reached over and touched her fingers, and squeezed tightly.

"Don't go too far," he called.

A long line of men filed in slowly through the front door. They were a string of mottled jackets, shirts and blankets, of various heights and sizes, linked together by their desire to be inside. Travis was seated in a metal folding chair in front of the double wood doors with a clipboard. As individual men shuffled in, he scribbled something down, and made a check with his pencil. His administrative tasks however did not prevent him from eyeing Campbell cautiously. In the decades they worked side by side, it had never concerned Travis that Finn might one day need something more than his service to the men at New Beginnings was providing for him. What advice would he give his own son, if he was here—if Travis hadn't lost him to the streets of Baltimore. His paternal love and care for Finn had eased his own loss. This love Finn showed for Campbell was something not even Travis could offer.

Finn strolled into the storage room nestled behind the stairwell and heaved out four folding chairs. As he moved into the main dining area he heard a familiar voice and his body stiffened. Peering carefully toward the cluster of people at the front door he saw Jesse. Jesse, who he had presumed after all these years to be dead, in prison, or institutionalized. There were few other options for alcoholics as serious as they had been. Following the lost days in the warehouse, while undergoing his change, Jesse had seemed to simply disappear. Although Finn avoided his old haunts and drinking buddies, he was able to keep a pulse on what happened on the streets. He prowled silently behind groups of homeless people as they moved from safe spaces to the park seeking refuge from the likes of Chester and other predatory opportunists. He overheard their conversations and silently tracked the places where Jesse would normally be found. Not that Finn was prepared for what he might say or do if he ever ran into Jesse.

Jesse strode with confidence into the dining room lined neatly with five rows of long tables, decorated brightly with paper plates, Thanksgiving tablecloths, and Horns of Plenty centerpieces. He was dressed in a crisp white button down shirt and clean khaki pants. He appeared less like the Jesse that Finn remembered and more like a healthy happy twin brother he might have never mentioned. But Jesse had also aged. His once long hair was trimmed short above the ears and he was balding across the front. He wore gold rimmed glasses, and had a clean shaven face. Finn's fleeting thought that somehow the vampires had gotten to him too dissolved immediately. He wasn't sure if what he felt was relief or disappointment.

He must be what, sixty-something by now? Finn pondered. He kept the side of his face concealed behind the door trim. Jesse was followed by a group of four men whose hope and despair suggested they were from the nearby halfway house for men in recovery from alcohol addiction. Their faces were etched with lines deep and dark, scars, and broken blood vessels. Yet, their eyes shone hopefully and their smiles were armor against the tide of demons that stood at bay at least temporarily. He overheard Jesse say, "Okay guys. Let's grab a seat here. After dinner we'll go into the backroom for our meeting."

Ahhh. Finn made a private smile. *He's sober.*

Then Finn felt a pang of something he had not felt in a very long time: envy. Could that have been him if he had stayed human long enough? Could he have gotten sober? Or would he have died frozen in a ditch? He was grateful that becoming a vampire had relieved him of all physical and mental cravings for alcohol, a feat he never could imagine on his own. His lack of conviction toward

12-step recovery programs back in his twenties left him feeling alienated from any notion that god would help him. He realized now that he had given up on himself long before god could have given thought to the matter.

Jesse laughed loudly and assured the man next to him, "One day at a time, Ben. You can't worry about getting your wife back until you've made a commitment to this program." Ben gave a grateful nod of agreement.

Finn looked over to the kitchen pass through where Campbell and her children stood scooping piles of mashed potatoes, sweet potatoes and stuffing into the paper plates being moved down the packed line of hungry men. Her face was soft and warm, hair pulled loosely into a ponytail that made her look at least 10 years younger than she was. She nodded and chatted easily with everyone. She was beauty itself. And her children who resembled her so much in every delicate feature, attended eagerly to their assigned duties, occasionally nudging each other's elbows out of their shared space. He knew that he could no longer imagine Campbell without imaging Ellis and Caroline.

Finn quietly slipped downstairs under the auspices of needing to pull some dried goods out of basement storage. He sensed Travis' presence behind him and turned around quickly with eyes blazing defensively.

"You can't have her. You know that, don't you?" His voice was gentle and empathetic, but convincing.

"I know," replied Finn. "But without her I can't imagine anything else. An eternity of feeling this way? Of feeling alone? Of being without her? I can't imagine that either." He pushed some empty card board boxes around with unnecessary force.

"Sounds like you're at the alcoholic's jumping off point, where you can't imagine life with or without alcohol. With or without her."

"The irony though is that even if I jumped off some high building I won't be able to kill myself." He grimaced somewhere between finding this humorous and grimly accurate.

"Want me to stake you?"

They both chuckled.

"Back off old man," Finn teased. He reached over and lovingly patted Travis on the back, and then went to find Campbell.

By now the meal was coming to a close. Groups of men convened at tables, sipping coffee quietly, while others rested contentedly by the television to watch the football game. Jesse had moved his small team of men into the meeting room. Ellis and Caroline had found a collection of other young children and were playing at the foosball table. Campbell was in the kitchen shuffling plates and dishes between the pass through and the sink. Every few minutes she craned her neck to check on her children. She saw Finn watching her from the doorway by the stairs and blushed. She wiped her wet hands on the legs of her jeans and moved deftly through the bustling crowd of volunteers to reach him, never taking her eyes off of Finn as she went. When she was less than one foot away she said, nodding toward her children, "That's new."

"What, the kids? They look kinda old to me." They laughed.

"No. The foosball table. It wasn't here when I came as a little girl."

He paused and nodded. "Yeah, we got that a few years back with a donation from the Ravens football team. It's a nice addition."

Campbell's eyes wandered through the room. "I wonder what was going through my mother's mind the day she came here with me and my dad."

Finn searched around trying to re-imagine the scene through her eyes. He waited for her to say more. She whispered, "What makes a woman, who by global standards seems to have everything she could want—a roof over her head, a partner to support her, food on the table, healthy children. What could make that person burn her life to the ground?" Her voice began to crack. "Why did she leave us?"

"I don't know, Campbell," he replied softly. He reached for her hand. Their fingers intertwined and she squeezed tightly.

Campbell continued, "Maybe survival and happiness are sometimes at odds with one another. I'm looking around here at men who are struggling to survive. They get through each day as it comes, hoping to see the next. And my mom, she didn't have to worry about that. When you don't need to work so hard at surviving you would think that happiness would be an inevitable result, wouldn't you?"

"Happiness is a luxury, Campbell. People who don't have to worry each day about their basic survival have the luxury of analyzing their options and have the freedom to choose what they want to do. They have time and space to think, maybe over think, their quality of life." He was convincing himself. This way he could convince himself he didn't need her. Standing here with Campbell he felt what he considered must be happiness.

"No, I think it's necessary for survival," she replied adamantly. In the subtext of her judgment about her mother, she knew she was really wondering about herself. *Would I burn everything I have to the ground to keep Finn? Would I survive it?*

Ellis and Caroline were playing cards with a collection of other children in the far corner. Finn pulled Campbell gently by the hand into the hallway and opened the storage closet beneath the stairwell. He closed the door part-way and grabbed her waist with both arms. They held each other tight for a long moment. He brushed his lips across her ear and down her neck. Campbell's knees buckled. She let out an involuntary groan.

"We don't have to decide anything right now, Campbell," he assured her.

"I can't decide anything right now!" She started crying. "I have to take my kids home and prepare a Thanksgiving dinner for my in-laws."

Trying to lighten the situation she added, "Thinking is the greatest luxury of all to mothers everywhere. If you don't have time and energy to think, you can't ruminate too much on whether or not you're happy. And *that*, is the key to survival." She gently cupped the side of his face with her palm. Then she lifted herself onto her toes and kissed him deeply on the mouth. His eyes glowed just a little like embers in the darkened space. "I need to go," she said.

"I know. Let me walk you to the front entrance." He pushed the door open a crack.

They slipped furtively from the closet, grateful that nobody had seen them. "Come on, kids. Time to go," she shouted softly to Ellis and Caroline who were still stationed comfortably at the folding table, holding cards. They ran obediently to her side and she slid their coats on.

"Say thank you to Mr. Finn," she said.

"I'm the one who should be thanking you," he replied, helping to zip up Ellis' coat. "In fact, I just happen to have a little thank you present here for the two of you for being such good helpers."

Caroline gasped with joy. "Candy???" she asked eagerly. Campbell laughed.

Finn's face lit up. "No. Something better." He reached into his inside coat pocket and pulled out four tickets. "I just happen to have four tickets for the new exhibit at the aquarium! Sea horses!!"

Ellis and Caroline jumped up and down excitedly. "I love seahorses!" Caroline shrieked clapping her hands together in rapid motion. Campbell gave Finn a knowing smirk. "Thank you."

He shrugged casually. "It's nothing."

Leaning in toward Campbell so the children couldn't hear he added, "They were a gift to the center. We get 'em all the time from the Aquarium. Figured they'd enjoy it."

"And um ….who is the fourth ticket for?" she asked playfully. He shrugged again innocently.

"Thank you, Finn. I guess we could go one day during Thanksgiving break, in the late afternoon of course," she suggested, but then added, "When it's getting dark."

Finn could hear Jesse speaking in the next room to an audience of about twenty men all seated in a circle. "Today, I am happy, joyous, and free," he was saying. *I'm glad one of us survived*, thought Finn.

CHAPTER THIRTY-ONE

Baltimore, 2011

Brent had returned to the house with his parents in tow, too busy to ask any serious questions about his family's outing to New Beginnings. Campbell was grateful that Brent was man of few questions, although the flip side to this freedom was the painful acknowledgement that maybe her life and the lives of her children just weren't of great enough interest to provoke deep curiosity.

Campbell immersed her arms up to her elbows in a deep pot of water for the potatoes while also trying to think her way through her emotions. There was not just a merging of bodies between herself and Finn she mused, but also a merging of the mental sphere. It was why Campbell had been so drawn to Finn from the very beginning. The entire immersion of one's physiological being with another's. It gave new meaning to the term "physical attraction." They were bound by blood and bone. And in a world where either/or no longer existed, she could also see justifying to herself the possibility of living in two parallel universes; both here with her family and one with Finn. Her thought was suddenly interrupted.

"Mom!!! Tell Ellis to stop kicking me!" Caroline wailed from the living room. Last she checked they had been sprawled out on the soft blue rug happily working on jigsaw puzzles together.

Campbell wondered, *where is Brent right now?* Didn't he hear the escalating scuffle between the children? She could hear the TV on downstairs with the drone of the football announcer's voice declaring some significant play. Brent's voice rose to a moderate shout, cursing somebody or something that had just happened, followed by the sound of her father-in-law's voice echoing in agreement. Ice cubes clattered as the men brought their glasses of scotch down on the table. Brent wasn't a big drinker but something in him compelled him to drink scotch whenever he was with his father. Within a few hours he would be teetering between overly and annoyingly jovial and just plain loud. Campbell heard Ellis whine. Her hands were wet and slimy from the potatoes.

Millie, Campbell's mother-in-law had announced her exhaustion after their long delay in Charlotte, and promptly went upstairs to the master bedroom to nap upon her arrival.

"Brent!" Campbell shouted, "Can you deal with that, please?" She tried to be as polite as possible, masking the last nerve rising in her throat that wanted to erupt into a liquid rage.

"Huh? Yeah," was all she heard back, followed by the slow heavy sound of his steps moving up the stairs from the TV room toward the children. Then the shrieking and scuffling subsided and she went back to her work. The water was boiling now and she slowly dropped the cut potatoes into it and tried to replay her morning with Finn.

Back at New Beginnings Finn couldn't dislodge the thoughts of Jesse from his mind. The afternoon had worn on quickly into the evening, and with dinner now over, tables folded and dishes cleaned up, he was alone with his thoughts again. Some of the regular volunteers had come in to relieve Finn and Travis who were in need of a break after the long day. Travis patted Finn on the back, his body weary and appearing a little more hunched and withered each day. "Good work. I'm going to go lie down for a while. Wake me up if you need anything."

"Will do, Travis," Finn replied. The sight of Jesse brought Finn back to a storage of memories that had buried themselves like archeological artifacts under his skin, in his bones somewhere, presumably he thought, forever. But they resurfaced, screaming and clawing their way out. Jesse was a reminder of what Finn could have been if he hadn't been changed. Jesse hadn't died or been committed to the asylum or the prison. It was clear even from where Finn was standing, that Jesse had gotten sober. And he was still human. His eyes gleamed with clarity and new purpose. His skin no longer emanated the saturated smell of alcohol. His skin color was almost rosy, not grey. And his body held a healthy weight. He was showered and dressed. And, he seemed happy. But approaching Jesse and receiving him with open arms wasn't an option. Finn receded into the shadows as the small cluster of men walked past the kitchen into the meeting room. There were so many things he wanted to say and questions he wanted to ask: *How long have you been sober? What happened to you all these years? You disappeared for decades it seems and here you are. How are you?*

Instead, after given the approval from Travis to take off, Finn slipped out of the center, and moved like a shadow along the brownstone walls through the city and out into the suburbs in search of Campbell. He sensed the air was becoming cooler as he moved off the city streets and along Jones Falls Parkway into the trees where he was less likely to be spotted. There were a few joggers or dog walkers along the way. Finn kept himself to the parks and small wooded areas all the way to Stevenson Avenue and slowed down only when he was a block from Campbell's street.

The well-manicured lawns and the two story colonials made a stark contrast to the brick and cement towers of the cityscape to which he was so accustomed. Here, swing sets grew together like vines connecting the backyards. *A jungle-gym jungle,* he noted with amusement. The curbs alongside many of the homes were lined with cars, no doubt from extended families coming in for the holiday. He could hear a cacophony of voices inside the brightly lit warm houses, emanating a sense of cohesiveness and security. He pushed his hands deep inside the pockets of his Carhartt jacket and looked at the trees. Against the streetlight he observed the empty branches except for a few maple leaves that refused to die. He heard a voice pierce the air from down the street. It was a woman's voice he did not recognize—but before he could see who it was, he knew the voice was directed at him.

"Hey! I know who you are."

He shot his stare like a laser through the dimly lit night, to see an attractive petit middle aged woman with brown hair sporting a pink jogging suit. He stopped on the sidewalk, his toe kicking a cement rupture formed by last winter's freeze which had caused an immense raised crack in the pavement. He waited. She took a few cautious steps toward him.

"You're Finn," she said with slight accusation in her voice.

"How do you know who I am?" he asked, not willing to openly admit to the accuracy of her statement.

"I get paid to be smart," she joked more easily, making assertive strides toward him.

But, do you know what I am? he wanted to ask, noting her lack of fear and caution as she headed boldly in his direction. She wasn't afraid, that was for sure. He noticed they were only three houses away from Campbell's and if he walked halfway to meet this woman they would be standing directly in front of her house, and he became agitated and nervous at the thought of being caught here. He waited for the woman to come to him.

"I'm Lilly," she offered with more friendliness in her tone this time.

Finn recollected Campbell mentioning something about a friend named Lilly. She stopped a foot away from him, wrapped her arms across her waist and tilted her stance to one side, leaning casually on the weight of her left hip. She stared at him. "Wow. So you're Finn." It was as if she was marveling at the Grand Canyon for the first time. He gathered from her expression that indeed, Campbell had told Lilly everything.

"Yep. That's me."

She paused, sizing him up. "Wow, a real vampire." He stood silently allowing her to digest this fact. "So, do you have any friends you could hook me up with? Do you know what it's like trying to find a single, mentally stable, employed man over the age of forty in this town?"

A small smile crept out of the corner of his mouth. "Sorry. I kind of keep to myself. I don't hang out with my own kind."

She didn't press for an explanation. "Don't you have a sire? Or whatever it's called?" Finn's eyes creased a little around the edges, bemused.

"I suppose I do, but I don't know who he or she is." It was true. After that night, he never saw any of the roving teenage band that had changed him at Travis' behest, ever again.

"Huh. So everything I learn on TV is wrong," she said with mock seriousness. "But why …you? Why did they choose you when you could have just as easily been their meal? How do vampires choose who to kill and to who create? What makes you so fucking special?"

With all earnestness he confided sheepishly, "It's a long story." After considering the question, he added, "I suppose it's a lot like human life and death. Why does an innocent infant die in a plane crash while a man who smokes two packs of unfiltered Camels a day live to be ninety-two? Maybe it's destiny. Maybe there is a plan and we just don't see it. More likely, it's just random luck of the draw with no meaning or plan attached to it. It just is."

He was growing tired of this philosophical debate. His whole body trembled with an urge to see Campbell. She was a mere few feet away. He could smell her. He arched his neck past Lilly and tried to catch a glimpse of Campbell through the window.

"So, Finn, what exactly are you doing here?" She sounded like one of those cops on the crime shows asking the perpetrator seated at a barren metal table in lock down, "So where did you hide the body? Tell us."

CHAPTER THIRTY-ONE | 181

Thinking quickly he replied, "Campbell and her kids came to the New Beginnings center today to volunteer. I just wanted to check that they made it home safe." He gave his best poker face. He even tried to appear a little scary by straightening his tall posture and baring his teeth, just slightly.

"Oh, bull," she said, with a slight laugh. "Look, you may be super strong and immortal and all that but you're a crappy liar." She smiled again and Finn eased his stance.

He sighed. "I just …" He searched for words. "I just wanted to see her. I don't know." She nodded as if she was willing to consider this as an acceptable answer.

"Do ya really think this is a good time for that? What, were you going to knock on the door, offer a pumpkin pie and announce Happy Thanksgiving everybody!" She opened her arms and bounced a little on her toes mimicking the imaginary scenario.

"No." He couldn't finish his sentence. Finn looked at the trees and the car that was passing by on its way to somewhere. She waited until the car had turned the corner, as if the passengers might overhear their conversation, and divulged, "Her husband's family is in town, you know. Normally she and I walk together at this time but she's a little busy today."

She pulled her left leg up behind her and reached around to stretch the hamstring. "Let's go take a peek," she insisted lowering her leg and turning on her heels toward Campbell's house.

Unsure what to do or say, Finn simply followed. *I pity the vampires who would ever try to take this woman down*, he speculated. He imagined Dozer, the imposing long-haired vampire known to stalk around New Beginnings trying to corner Lilly. He could picture her, glaring at Dozer, fangs bared and eyes gleaming, and saying as calmly as if she were arguing over a mistake on a grocery receipt, "Really Dozer, who are you kidding. Go home." And if he launched an attack, she would probably pull a lead pencil out from some secret region of that pink jogging suit and simply stake him.

They reached the brick walkway that led to Campbell's door. Finn's heart raced. The window was lit warmly from within. Peach colored sheer curtains hung softly on either side of it with a clear view into what appeared to be the dining room. He could hear Campbell's voice.

"It's dark out here. If we sneak up to the window I don't think anyone will see us," Lilly said. Finn gave Lilly a look that said, "No way" but he didn't argue with her. She lowered her body into a crouch and waddled side to side until she was underneath window. "Come on," she insisted with a parental sternness. "You want to see her. Don't you?"

Campbell moved for what felt like the 100th time back from the kitchen to deliver more food to her husband, children and in-laws, now seated at the dining table. The only empty seat was the one saved for her. She wondered if she would have a chance to eat before everyone was done. She reached over Caroline's head with a bowl of mashed turnips.

"Everything smells great," Campbell's mother-in-law Susan said. There was a murmur of agreement around the table. She smiled compliantly. "Thank you, Susan."

"Mom, I need more milk," Ellis implored. Campbell grabbed his cup and walked back toward the kitchen.

She counted. *Trip number 101.*

Finn focused keenly on Campbell's face as she fluttered around the dining room. Her eyes looked sad. But she was smiling, especially when she talked to one of her children. "Brent tells us he is up for a promotion at work," Davis, Brent's father said proudly.

"Yes, we're very excited," Campbell said.

"Well, Pop, the papers haven't been signed yet," Brent added. "But Joe says it's promising. We just need to crunch the numbers from the last fiscal report to decide how much of a raise will come with this promotion." He took a large bite of turkey. "Otherwise," he said, with a mouthful of turkey, "this supposed promotion will simply mean more work for same pay."

Campbell sat down and pulled her napkin onto her lap. "That's not true Brent. You deserve more credit than that. You've worked hard to establish that new division and I know Joe is going to recognize that." She scooped a mound of stuffing onto her fork and opened her mouth.

"Honey, do we have any salt?" Brent asked. She put down the fork, still full, and pushed her chair back from the table, and went slowly into the kitchen. Finn could tell from her body's subtle movements that she was tired, but he remarked out loud, forgetting that Lilly was crouched beside him, how beautiful she was.

"Yes, she is," Lilly agreed in a low whisper. Then she stressed, "If you hurt her. If you break her heart. If you turn her into a frigging vampire. I will kill you. It might take a lot of time and effort to figure out how to do that, but mark my words mister, I will find you and take you down." There was no humor in her voice.

He turned his head and looked directly into her eyes. Lilly jerked back instinctively when she saw his eyes glowing in the dark like a cat's. With sadness and earnestness in his voice he said, "I know you will." They turned their attention back to the scene inside.

Brent stood beside his chair with his glass raised. Campbell stood with a dish of butter in her hand in the doorway between the dining room and the kitchen.

"I'd like to make a toast!" Brent proclaimed. Everyone raised their glasses. Ellis kicked Caroline quickly as they moved out of their seats to stand up, and splatters of milk fell from her pink princess cup. Finn's lips curled into a small grin.

Brent gazed at Campbell expectantly. "A toast to my wife, Campbell. For making this amazing dinner. For working hard every day to raise our beautiful children. For making our life possible. I love you." Finn felt a nauseous wave of panic fill his body.

Campbell blushed and smiled softly, lowering her head in modesty. *Or, is she hiding another emotion?* Finn wondered. Everyone clanked their glasses together, and chimed in "Here, here!" Brent moved around from the far side of the dining room table and reached out for Campbell's hand. He kissed her affectionately on the cheek. The children clapped. Finn clenched his fists.

"Thank you, Brent." The fantasy had been met with reality, and the latter had trumped the former. Here was what he hadn't seen before, the night in San Diego he held Campbell in his arms and breathed in the sweet smell of her presence.

Brent wasn't doing this for show. He meant what he said. At that precise moment Campbell noted that anyone else in her shoes might have asked themselves, *Should I feel guilty? Should I feel remorse? Should I break free of this obsession for Finn and return to my senses?* But she didn't ask herself any of these questions. She leaned in and hugged with genuine affection and appreciation, but absent of longing.

"Go. Sit down. Eat your dinner," he insisted affectionately.

Finn turned to Lilly and said, "I'm leaving now."

Lilly appeared sheepish for having been privy to this small family portrait, guilty of a conspiracy to thwart Finn, which she sadly noted now, may have worked. "Come on. Let's go," she whispered sympathetically. Before she could stretch her aching knees to a standing position, Finn had dissolved into the night air.

CHAPTER THIRTY-TWO

Baltimore, 2011

Finn paced in front of the looming triangular frame of the Baltimore Aquarium, keeping his vision and hearing keen on the slightest sign of Campbell and her children.

Where are they? he worried as he panned the rising skyline of buildings. They loomed like stoic giants, shuddering in the cold November wind.

The changes in the Inner Harbor were almost as remarkable as the changes one went through from being human to becoming vampire. Finn saw the city as resembling himself. Thirty-five years ago both he and the harbor he inhabited, and that inhabited him, were in shambles. And now they had both risen above their misery and poverty, to attain a veneer of impenetrable success. At least to all outside appearances. Where his old abandoned factory warehouse had been crumbling was now a four story faux-antique brick building with the words Hard Rock Café emboldened in neon across the top. The harbor waters were crowded with "pirate ships" and paddle boats for the tourists. This new transformation in Finn, like the Harbor, made people want to be like them. To desire to attain what they had.

Campbell appeared from around the corner of Gay Street, with Caroline, dressed in a bright red wool coat walking dutifully by her side, and Ellis, jacket unzipped and left shoe lace untied, skipping two feet in front. He could hear Campbell's voice raise with annoyance, "Ellis! Come back here and stand by the curb. The cars won't stop because they can't see you, honey!"

Finn's memory recalled with a violent rush, the sensation of being struck with moving tons of metal and glass, with a young and frail Campbell tucked safely in his arms. What if he hadn't been there? His left knee still ached on occasion, but he concluded that it was more the memory of the pain than the actual physical damage since the change had rendered his body completely anew with no trace of human fragility.

They crossed the cold and windy street at the crosswalk, and scurried through the holiday crowds toward the visitor's entrance to the aquarium. When Ellis spotted Finn standing by the entrance, he broke free of his mother's yoke and dashed across the stone pedestrian area shouting, "Hi, Mr. Finn!"

Campbell's heart surged with a mix of joy and confusion to see her son embrace Finn so readily. But who wouldn't? She had, so why not her son? Finn knelt down with his forearm across one knee.

"Hey, buddy! How's it going?" he replied with genuine eagerness. Finn smiled broadly at Caroline and softly greeted her with, "Hello."

Always polite, Caroline responded "Hello" back, but Campbell could tell from the look in her eyes that she was wary of Finn. Caroline looked intently at her mother's face, able somehow, Campbell worried, to read her thoughts.

Campbell's throat closed for a brief second. Does she see me the same way I saw my mother? This whole thing is ludicrous. *What am I doing?* But the alternative—to not have Finn in her life—was a cosmic impossibility for her if her world were to continue spinning.

Deflecting the situation Campbell said, "Sorry. There was an accident on the beltway and we got stuck behind it. That's why we're late."

"Better late than never. I'm not getting any older."

Campbell gave a playful snort.

Finn said cheerfully, "You guys ready to go see some seahorses?"

Ellis pleaded with Finn until Finn lifted him deftly onto his shoulders and the four strode through the ticket line and into the aquarium. As they moved around the coatroom, lockers, and bathrooms and down the elevator into the various exhibits the lights grew dark. The aim was to create an effect where the lighting within the tanks in contrast to the darkened rooms made for spectacular viewing of the colorful fish and other marine life.

At the long spiral walkway that followed the shark exhibit, Ellis clambered down from Finn's shoulders and darted along the descending ramp which moved in large circles down and around the shark tanks. Campbell panicked when she lost sight of him in the crowds.

"Ellis!" she shouted.

The panic in her voice must have registered. Several people turned their heads instinctively and stared at her. She sped up her pace, gently shoving crowds to one side to make her way down the ramp. Finn followed close behind. Caroline dutifully followed weaving through bodies with determination. Caroline stayed close on her heels.

"Don't worry. I'll find him," Finn assured her.

He disappeared into the throng of people, somehow able to move them out of his way with barely a polite nudge. Thirty feet farther down the winding ramp Campbell could make out the top of Finn's head. Her chest tightened for a moment until she saw Ellis, his forehead plastered to a thick glass-plated wall that stood between him and a great white shark.

"We're right here," Finn called to Campbell. She breathed a sigh of relief followed by a quick spate of anger surging in her throat.

"Don't you ever run off like that!" she snapped. Ellis gazed at the tank. "Look at me, young man," she said again to get his attention. He looked at her with his deep blue puppy dog eyes, and her anger dissolved.

"Sorry, Mommy. But I wanted to find this shark. See? He's looking at me." Indeed the shark had been swimming close by the tank wall, giving Ellis the much desired close up view of the killer beast.

Finn knelt down beside Ellis to watch the shark with him. Campbell was struck with what appeared, in her limited understanding of animal behavior, to be a strange reaction of the shark. Just moments ago it was calmly swimming back and forth alongside the thick plate glass, no doubt used to being surrounded by thousands of human faces. The shark neared Ellis and Finn, and in a spasmodic jerking motion flailed its body backwards away from the glass and turned swiftly in the other direction as if it were being chased by something.

"Something scared it away, Mommy!" Ellis said.

Finn stood up quickly and without looking at Campbell, he offered, "Come on! Let's keep moving. There is so much more to see!" But in that darkened space Campbell was sure she caught Finn's eyes glowing, if only for a brief second. The edge of his predatory animal side was finally showing itself. Here was a love she had waited for: Impossible and necessary, lifesaving and dangerous.

The time was nearing 6:30 p.m. when they finally left the aquarium. The streets had emptied.

"Where are you parked?" asked Finn. "Let me walk you to your car."

"That would be great!" Campbell replied. *Anything to buy more time with him*, she thought. She pictured an alternative world where Finn was the father of her children instead of Brent.

"Don't run ahead!" she warned both children who skipped at a pace or two ahead of them up Gay Street. She felt Finn's fingers slowly wind around her own and they silently held hands down the block. Twenty feet farther up Gay Street Finn stopped in his is tracks. His expression hardened.

"What?" Campbell asked peering carefully at his face.

"Quiet." There was agitation in his voice.

She was both annoyed and worried at his sudden rudeness. "Listen to me," he whispered leaning in toward her face, "You're only one more block from the car, right? Grab the kids and go as fast as you can. Now! And then get in and lock the doors. I'll meet you there in a minute."

Annoyance dissolved now, Campbell simply panicked. "Why? What's wrong?"

"I'm not sure yet. Please, Cam. Just go."

She could sense the tension in his body growing. She dashed ahead grabbing the children's hands and proposed cheerfully, "Come on! We're going to race Mr. Finn to the car!"

When he saw they were down the block, Finn moved as a shadow along the wall of the Bank of America building and into an alley at the corner. He could smell him and hear him. "Jesse," he muttered. Jesse was not alone either. "Chester," Finn murmured again, his teeth growing sharp in his mouth. His muscles tightened. In the darkness of the alleyway, between a stack of broken wooden crates and a rusty metal dumpster Finn found Chester leaning toward Jesse who was pinned against the wall.

"Back off!" Finn demanded. Without the slightest shift in his body or facial expression, Chester leered his head around to face Finn.

"Oh man, you again? What the fuck? This ain't your concern." Jesse focused his eyes intently as he could to make out Finn in the darkness.

"I said let him go," Finn demanded again. He was ready for a fight. He'd had many encounters with Chester over the past few decades.

"Finn?" Jesse sputtered in disbelief. "Is that … you? How could it be possible?"

Chester looked from Finn to Jesse and back again. He sized up Finn and growled. "I don't have time for this," he fumed, looking back at Jesse. Chester shrugged his shoulders and added, "Sorry man, deal is off." Then he disappeared, dissolving his corporeal presence into a shadow in the night air.

Jesse and Finn stood alone in disbelief for another few seconds. He slid his body off the wall and ambled slowly toward Finn.

"Where the hell have you been for over thirty years?" Jesse asked, bewildered.

"Around." Finn hesitated. "Sort of."

"Not that I ain't glad to see you, but you just really screwed up an important deal for me."

"You don't know what Chester was going to do to you, man," Finn replied protectively. "Did he promise you drugs or something?"

"Naw, man. I know exactly what that dude was. I don't need drugs. I need immortality. I was going to pay him to change me." He pulled a pack of cigarettes from his shirt pocket and lit one.

Finn was stunned and speechless.

"I'm guessing from the way you faced off with this dude that you could do me this same honor. Since you blew that chance for me, I suppose you owe me one now."

Finn smiled sadly. "You haven't changed that much, have you?"

"I'm sober," Jesse proclaimed defensively. "Have been for a few years. Felt a new life appearing before me. Felt some hope for the first time." He blew a ring of smoke through his nostrils that wound around his face like a serpent. "And now, I'm dying. Found out a few months ago I have cirrhosis of the liver. It's killing me. Too late to cure. And now, you blew my one chance to change that."

"But how did you know about Chester?"

"Come on, man. We homeless guys—we know. We see them. I mean you" He Sneered. "As you move across the city. How you prey on us. You think we don't got eyes to see? We see what everyone else don't."

Finn considered this. He hadn't ever noticed vampires when he was drunk and homeless. Or did he? His mind whirled, trying to recall. Jesse walked a few steps toward Finn.

"It is great to see you though. Thought you were dead after that Thanksgiving Day when you got hit by that car. You just disappeared." He smiled looking Finn up and down. "And now look at ya. So um…what do ya say ol' buddy. Care to help an old friend in dire straits?"

Finn's mind had already wandered back to Campbell and the kids, and he was eager to find them before perhaps Chester, now in a foul and hungry mood, did.

"I don't know, Jesse. I need to think about it. What you're asking is…" He paused and wondered to himself, *What is so wrong with what he's asking*? But something in him couldn't simply say "yes." He felt sick all of a sudden. "I'm sorry. I need to go. I will think about it."

Jesse's face fell. "Yeah," he muttered with disappointment. "Whatever. It's easy for you. A privilege to decide whether or not to kill or create the life of someone else. All I can do is wait. Or die waiting." He glared hard at Finn.

"I'm sorry man, I gotta go now. Meet me at Loudon Cemetery next week, okay? Monday after midnight."

Then he turned toward Campbell's car.

Finn found Campbell, Caroline, and Ellis waiting in the car with the engine running for heat and the radio on. He could hear the children arguing over which radio station to listen to. He sidled up to the driver's window and tapped on it lightly. Campbell jumped. When she did, Caroline shrieked. Then they all laughed with relief when they saw it was Finn. But Campbell's face was tight. She rolled down the window. Her face was creased with worry.

"Are you alright?" she asked. "What happened?"

"I can't explain it right now. Ran into an old friend."

Fear was slowly being replaced with anger. She needed to know.

"Finn. Tell me. What happened?"

He leaned in closer to limit what the children might overhear. "Safe to say it's good to remember that I am not the only one like me in Baltimore."

She froze. For some reason the thought of other vampires surrounding her in their invisibility all these years had never occurred to her. But why not? Of course Finn wouldn't be the only one. He was simply the center of her universe, not the universe. He smelled her fear and some deep part of him honed in on it. *It smells good,* he confessed to himself. He buried the instinct, but not quickly enough. Campbell noted what he must have been thinking and pulled away slowly, not taking her eyes off of him. She opened her mouth to ask another question, but before she could he reached into the car, patted Ellis on the head, and said, "Get home safe guys! Good night!"

"Thanks, Mr. Finn! Bye!" they both shouted. He pressed the side of her shoulder with his hand.

"Please, go now. I'll feel better knowing you're not in this area tonight. I'll email you later to make sure you got home in one piece."

"Fine," Campbell said, remaining cool. For the first time in his presence she felt fear and doubt. This emotion was compounded by the safety she felt with him just an hour ago in the aquarium.

Sensing her doubt he looked at her sadly and murmured, "I'm sorry."

She nodded, forced a smile and responded flatly, "I'll talk with you soon." She closed the window, and headed back toward the safety of the suburbs.

CHAPTER THIRTY-THREE

Baltimore, 2011

Campbell had no difficulty making love to Brent later that evening. Years of internal debate over the reasons and outcomes of her mother's choices left Campbell to conclude that life was simply what you perceived it to be, and believed that all things, barring the laws of physics, were doable if allowed to be so. Her mind lingered over the evenings frightening events at the aquarium, but somehow she was able to turn it off when time came to turn her attention toward Brent. At 1:00 a.m. still unable to fall asleep, Campbell tossed on a pair of sweatpants and a T-shirt that were folded on top of her bedroom dresser and made her way quietly down into the TV room.

On the screen Campbell watched a peroxide blond vampire with a British accent named Spike exchanging witty repartee with a petite young blond woman who, from the scene before in which she single-handedly leveled a pack of zombies, appeared to have super powers. Campbell presumed this to be Buffy, the heroine of the show *Buffy the Vampire Slayer* (Whedon, 1998). From what Campbell could glean pf this episode, the young woman was in love with another vampire called Angel who apparently had re-obtained his human soul.

Now that's just silly, Campbell chuckled knowingly to herself and wedged a guilty fist-full of Cheetos into her mouth. Buffy was convincing Spike that she and her other vampire-lover, named Angel, were "just friends."

Spike spoke: "You're not friends. You'll never be friends. You'll be in love till it kills you both. You'll fight, and you'll shag, and you'll hate each other till it makes you quiver, but you will never be friends. Love isn't brains, children, it is blood. Blood screaming inside you to work its will." Spike took a long drag off his cigarette, and announced, "I may be love's bitch, but at least I'm man enough to admit it."

What Spike had surmised was the truth. Campbell swallowed hard on the salty sharp taste in her mouth. It dawned on her at that moment that vampires, even the fictitious ones, had it right. They knew what humans didn't, or couldn't admit: That love is the mysterious pull of the moon on the tide. And water is just like blood. The vampire seeks out blood, reaching for something greater than itself. The compulsion draws down both the seeker and its victim. And in the end, love either sucked one or two lovers dry and left for dead, or the exchange made their love immortal. No one just shakes hands and walks away unchanged.

Campbell shut off the TV and logged on to the computer. She needed to reconcile her last encounter with Finn. Sure, she had insisted she had to "go," but in her core she knew she could never really leave him. In a panic, she needed to reconnect herself somehow. The turbulence of her feelings roared over the logic of her reality.

What if he has changed his mind about me? she worried. She decided to send him a message to be sure. It said:

November 26, 2011

From: ccotephill@esu.edu

To: fmiginnis@esu.edu

You're in my blood now. You know. You may be the vampire, but you are coursing through my veins. I need to taste you again. I'm sorry about tonight. We're okay, right?

Love,

C-

For weeks since San Diego, their trysts had flowed seamlessly into their work together. She found herself meeting him in the late afternoons, before her classes, at an inn tucked away off of Greenspring Avenue, in an area of Baltimore that catered to up and coming business people. Part of its million dollar charm was the neighborhood's country feel, just miles from the city, where it's historic buildings including the Red Rooster Inn, a small expensive inn that received few visitors.

She and Finn had arranged to meet there four times now, lingering for a few hours in the slumber of suburbia before making their way to Eastern University to teach their evening classes. There were also the brief intoxicating instances of intimacy in her office, but like a drug, she wanted more.

One week left in the semester, she thought with relief, impressed at how she had survived the flurry of balancing her job and the appearance of a normal home life, with Finn deliciously folded into the mix. Somehow it had become "natural." Then she would have a winter break, and Campbell had already begun to chart in her mind how and when she might spend time with Finn.

Now, Campbell was conspiring to make time during winter break. As they walked together through the campus parking lot she insisted he come Christmas shopping with her. This time they would not spend their brief hours in intense love making and idle lover chatter, but out in public, at a mall, shopping for gifts for her children. *Why not?* she argued with herself, *It's not like anyone can tell just by looking at us that we are doing anything wrong.* Another deeper part of her knew she was simply tempting reality with a match and lighter fluid.

While picking Caroline and Ellis up from school, Campbell relished the thought of strolling through the mall with Finn. She wondered, as she inched through the car rider pick-up circle, how many other mothers would be going out tonight with mysterious vampire-lovers. Campbell tried to ease her guilt with the justification that she would have been going out shopping anyway. She was willing to sacrifice a lot to see Finn but had been careful not to take time away from her children.

All doubt was erased a week later when she saw Finn standing in front of the Macey's entrance, dressed unassumingly in his Carhartt jacket and jeans. His honey colored hair and angular face were illuminated softly by the string of large Christmas bulbs that had been arranged meticulously around each of the store-front windows. She slowed the car and rolled down her window.

"Hey, sexy," she growled slowly in a low voice.

His face lit up even more at the sight of her. She looked him up and down mockingly. "Do you ever wear anything else Dr. McGinnis? This is a date you know."

He leaned his head into the car window and strands of his hair fell down across his face. Her senses reeled. He brought his lips just to the edge of her ear. She shivered delightfully. "You look good enough to eat, Dr. Cote."

A car behind her honked impatiently. She glanced in her rearview mirror and sighed. "Let me go find parking. I'll be right there."

They walked side by side quietly, people-watching as they went. Their presence, though appearing to themselves to be the center of the universe, was completely unnoticed by the throngs of shoppers rushing past each other, caught up in their own worlds, too busy to note the giddy couple that walked alongside them. Campbell could have worried that people who knew Brent might see her. But she decided instead that, like being a vampire, they could appear as one thing (friends) while actually being another.

"What was your childhood like?" Campbell asked softly. She had never dared to tread on this territory. All Campbell really knew of Finn was his life after becoming a vampire. In the privacy of their afternoons at the inn, or over coffee in the Cultural Studies building, Finn would ramble on about his theory about vampires, using his own life as a detailed example. But he never spoke of his life as a human. All she knew was that he had struggled with alcoholism, had left home at a young age, and arrived in Baltimore while she was still a child.

Finn's body tensed slightly, and she knew maybe this was too sensitive a subject. "It's fine. You don't have to talk about it if you don't want to." *But I want him to*, she thought.

"Not much to tell," he replied. "We grew up pretty poor in Kentucky. My dad worked a bunch of different jobs. Wasn't around much. Wasn't happy when he was around. My mom, well I guess she tried to make up for that somehow. She was always taking us fishing and to the park when she could. She worked a lot too to pay for food and stuff. She cleaned houses mostly. But she was usually happy, you know? Just that kind of person, I guess." The image of his father sprung to memory. Every Saturday he and his father would load up the old Ford pick-up truck with rifles and gear and go off deer hunting. The look of pride on his father's face, after Finn's first successful kill at the age of 12, was the last memory of fondness he had for his father. Funny, he thought of it now, how love and death are so often intermingled.

They stopped in front of an electronics store, and watched as a young boy about the age of ten, pleaded with his mother to buy the video game displayed on the center wall. She couldn't hear what they were saying, but Campbell smiled with familiarity at the mother's plight. She could hear the soft high pitch of the son's voice followed by the hushed but sharp tone of the mother's.

"She says if he doesn't stop making a fuss right now, she'll take him home," Finn reported to Campbell.

"Yeah. That never works." Campbell smirked. She peered at Finn intently. "What's it like? You know, being able to hear everything like that? To be able to smell and see so much more than humans?"

"I've gotten used to it I guess, so it doesn't feel so strange anymore."

"So how come you never went home after you changed? You could have gone back to see your family."

Finn had a pained expression on his face. Campbell was brought back to the vague memory of her childhood and the time when he had given her that same look as they stood together in New Beginnings with a shiny gold charm in her hand.

"I couldn't," he replied. "The person I was had changed. I didn't know how to face my family. And now it's too late. Too much time has passed. Once people think you're dead, it's better to stay dead." He paused, thinking of his encounter with Jesse and of Jesse's request. "Besides, Travis needs me here."

"I need you here" she said. The thought of him leaving hadn't occurred to her until now. She added, "You've done a lot for them. The men at New Beginnings, I mean."

Finn moved away from the storefront and sat down on a bench on the side of the electronic store. "There's something I haven't told you."

Campbell's mind reeled. Good lord, how much more could there be?

"The night we went to the aquarium with your kids. Remember how I ran down the street and told you to wait at the car?"

"Yeah. I remember. What happened?"

"I found an old friend in the alleyway, with an enemy of sorts. A vampire who stalks the drunks and old men around New Beginnings looking for easy targets. I've had more than a few scrapes with him, trying to protect these guys. Jesse, my old friend, and I used to hang out together. So here we were in this alleyway with Chester. I convinced him to move on without a fight. I thought I was saving Jesse, but he got real angry with me. Guess he had a plan for Chester to change him. He says he's dying of cirrhosis of the liver. What he doesn't know is that Chester would sooner have him for dinner than make him his buddy."

"So, even if Jesse doesn't know it, you did save him."

Campbell had never given much consideration to the responsibility of being a vampire as way to grant immortal life to others.

"For now I saved him. But he wants me to change him."

The thought that Finn could do that to her, that they could be together forever, rushed through her like a strong sudden wind.

"What did you tell him?"

"That I'd have to think about it. What would I have to sacrifice in order to change him?"

Campbell was mildly bemused by how perplexed men, even this immortal one, can become. She chuckled. "What's so funny?" he asked scornfully.

"How confounded you men are by life's choices," she answered. "Women don't see their choices so much in the language of sacrifice. Rather, these are just life events from which something was always given and from which something was lost. The balance in the universe is always struck. Somehow."

Trying to shift the conversation from the inevitable decision he would have to make regarding Jesse, he reflected, "I think working with people, people who need so much, helps to keep my instincts in check. Travis believes that the choices we make in our human lives shape the nature of the vampire we become. He watched me jump in front of that car for you and assumed that I would make a good candidate for his experiment."

"You mean, to see if you'd be good or evil?"

"Yeah. I guess that's what I mean. There is some trace of my humanness that I hang on to working to help addicts survive, when they do everything to destroy themselves. My close contact gives me empathy. A reminder too, that I was there once. So I don't forget. Once you have no memory, no connections, then killing is easy."

Little doors inside of Campbell were opening up, places she had long ago buried or locked away. Finn could so easily enter these hollow spaces and fill them with a sense of peace and anticipation she didn't know possible. Brent had been an "easy" choice. He fit the role for what she thought she had wanted back then. Never had she had to evaluate what she might lose in order to acquire something else so compelling and significant that she would be willing to give up other things. Not until now. Finn was a stark reminder of how everything else she had done until now somehow belonged to someone else. Another "her." A person she did not recognize anymore. Finn embodied eternity and possibility.

Campbell and Finn stood up and began moving again; Campbell glanced in store windows, trying to keep her focus on buying gifts for her children. But her mind was elsewhere. She looked up at him and he smiled—the smile that no one else in the world, even her children, could give only to her.

As they moved toward the elevator, Campbell made eye contact with another parent who she frequently saw at PTA meetings and the pickup circle at school. She tried to bury herself behind a crowd on the escalator, but it was too late. She had caught Alice's eye. As Alice moved up the escalator, and Campbell and Finn moved down, Alice shouted cheerily, "Last minute shopping!" Her short blond hair was pulled into a stump of a ponytail, her classic features stood out with minimal makeup. She was, in Campbell's terms, the "queen bee," of Upper Fairmount Elementary School. She was always in the center of school activity and gossip.

Oh, hell. She's going to tell everyone, Campbell thought. But another part of just didn't care.

Campbell gave her best social face and replied, "Yeah, a bit crowded tonight too! Guess we're not the only ones." Alice nodded to Finn politely and raised an eyebrow to Campbell in a way that seemed to suggest, "Nice pick!" Finn gave her a pleasant nod. Campbell looked at her shoes to hide her blushing. Without looking up she exclaimed, "See you Monday at the drop off circle!"

If these two worlds, she realized, *continued in tandem with each other long enough, they would crash or converge*. But she didn't want to think about it just then. An hour later they departed the mall with three bags full of computer games, clothing, and toys for Caroline and Ellis. Campbell had deliberately avoided any shopping she might do for Brent. Finn had purchased small toys for both children.

"Please bring the kids by New Beginnings sometime so I can give them their presents," he said as they strolled through the cluttered parking lot.

"Yes, I will. They keep asking when we can go back to the aquarium with you."

Even Caroline had warmed up to Finn, and it pleased Campbell that her affair had traces of an ordinary side to it, an ironic balance of extremes. She was wary that Alice might be somewhere in the parking lot, so she gave Finn a slow kiss on the cheek and held his hand tightly, rather than pin him against a car the way she wanted to. "How will I see you now that we're not on campus teaching until January?" he asked.

"We always find a way, right? We were brought back together like this for a reason. We can't be separated again so easily."

At this moment, Campbell couldn't imagine a future without Finn. But fate and chance are intimate partners who often trade places when you least expect it.

Reference

Whedon, J. (Writer), & Whedon, J. (Director). (1998). *Lover's walk*. Buffy the vampire slayer. Mutant Enemy Productions. Los Angeles, CA: 20th Century Fox.

CHAPTER THIRTY-FOUR

Baltimore, 2011

The phone rang Monday morning as Campbell was rifling through heavy stacks of bills and papers, hoping to find her car keys at the bottom of the pile. She cradled the phone under her chin. "Yeah I know. I'm running late," she announced without saying hello. She knew it was Gillian inquiring why, now that it was 10:30 a.m., Campbell had not arrived.

"Come on, my dear," Gillian chided, "You can't put off the inevitable. The mammogram awaits."

"Ugh," Campbell sighed. "I know. I can't find my frigging keys! Couldn't we have put this off until after the New Year? I am so far behind with everything from grading to decorating!" She glanced at the dining room table where the keychain was peeking out from beneath a pile of clothes that belonged in the dirty laundry pile but seemed to have lost its way. "I'm on my way right now. Thanks for coming with me. I don't know why I am being such a sissy about this."

"Because you are a sissy."

"Haha. Will be there in three minutes."

Weeks had passed since Campbell had returned from San Diego. She had seen Gillian twice during that time, once for coffee and once with the kids for a play date. Neither time could she find the words to confess her secret life. She was determined that today was the day. She loved Gillian with a deep passion of friendship, shared fears and joys. This secret felt like a gaping hole that was separating her from her tight bonds with Gillian. She knew it was odd that she felt this guilt for keeping secrets from Gillian but not from Brent, the person she was deceiving most. But the bonds of friendship run deeper than marriage sometimes. It wasn't Brent who came home from work to help when she had to work and the kids were sick, but her friends, Gillian and Lillian. And she reciprocated by watching Gillian's girls on days when Gillian had errands to run or was just in need of a well-deserved break from being "mama." Her loyalty to these women felt greater than it did to any man. She had known Gillian since high school. And their friendship had survived into adulthood.

Gillian slipped into the passenger seat and wrinkled her nose. "You know, smoking isn't going to help avert fears of cancer, Cam."

"Yeah, but it takes the edge of anxiety off."

"Are you okay?" Gillian asked. Her eyes softened and became serious.

"Yes. No. I don't know, Gill."

They pulled onto the main road and made their way through each stoplight toward the Quest Lab clinic. As they inched along Campbell told Gillian everything. By the time they pulled into the parking lot she was up to date, including the strange visit to the aquarium.

Gillian's grace and kindness did not forsake her. She lived by the motto that if you don't have something nice to say, don't say anything at all. She said, "I don't know what to say, Cam." There was a silence between them, but Gillian's face told Campbell that in spite of what her friend might think, their friendship wasn't changed.

"Thanks for not saying anything, Gillian."

As they turned into the doctor's parking lot Campbell thought, *Through our friendships we make determinations about what we want others to see about us. Friendship also shapes what we see in ourselves, not by looking inward but by looking outward at the reflection that our friendships cast back at us. Where do we stand in relationship between ourselves, our friends, and the world around us? What experiences call us to draw upon resources we didn't realize we had? Or the capacity to make moral choices, to risk everything, to sacrifice losing what we have or not getting what we want for the sake of another? We test the mettle of who we are against the experiences of friendship. It's not our lovers who define us—it's our friends.*

Gillian waited in the blue and white waiting room flipping through back issues of People Magazine while Campbell slipped on her paper gown in the dressing room. If nothing else, the talk with Gillian had taken her mind off her fears about the process she was about to endure.

"Dr. Cote?" a voice asked from the other side of the curtain. "Yes I'm ready."

She took a deep breath. The room was dim and littered with all sorts of equipment with numbers and knobs. Having done this once a year for the last four years, he knew the drill.

"Hello," began Abby the technician in a pleasant relaxed tone, "Sorry my hands are cold. Lift your left arm up above your head." She gently reached out and assisted in maneuvering Campbell's breast into position. Campbell moved her body compliantly. "You're going to feel some pressure now," Abby said, as she lowered the clamp down onto Campbell left breast. Campbell winced at the pain, which did not go unnoticed by Abby. "Sorry. Just a little tighter." Then she walked back to the X-ray machine and announced, "Now, hold your breath for me, Campbell."

While her body remained in Abby's capable hands, her mind and soul floated up out of the building and she imagined herself lying beside Finn, curled up in post coital adrenaline rush, relishing the sight of his lithe body, his warm brown eyes gazing upon her as if she were a treasure newly discovered by desiring conquerors of a new land. The way Finn looked upon her made her stomach flutter even as the X-ray machine beeped and blurped, and the heavy plastic clamps sucked her breasts into a pancake. Abby approached her with a serious expression. "Alright, Dr. Cote. You can get dressed and meet Dr. Holmes in his office. He'll be with you shortly after reviewing the slides. We'd like to have a look at these immediately."

Abby walked out of the room leaving a hollow, cold silence behind, her heels echoing down the hall. Campbell stood unsure what to do next. She thought to herself, *Everything women do involves sacrifice, and so acts of sacrifice or choice become indistinguishable as unique occurrences. Every day, everywhere women are sacrificing having children to further careers, or sacrificing careers to have children, or sacrificing sleep to have both. Women living in poverty sacrifice feeding themselves in order to feed their families first. Women sacrifice their personal safety to protect their children, sacrifice personal freedom at the hands of male-dominated regimes, and sacrifice the opportunity to have an education to meet the demands and expectations of their families. They sacrifice their dignity to survive, or sacrifice their lives for their dignity.* She walked across the room toward the dressing station where her clothes lay in a heap like a withered body.

Yes, she decided to herself, sliding her red cotton blouse back over her head. She pulled her slacks off the bench and sat down, sliding one pant leg up and then the other, and then standing up to fasten the button. *But in the circular universe it all comes back somehow, perpetually balancing the equation so loss wasn't loss anymore. Sacrifice was transformation. And the vampires' existence is like this as well. There is no beginning or end, just an endless loop of potential and actual choices. Our lives are intertwined through blood. Isn't blood the source of life? That which connects us, binds us metaphorically and literally? The cycles of a woman's body are connected to the earth through blood. We hold this knowledge not in the abstract through our minds but knowledge in our bodies. Only Descartes could separate the two. I think therefore I am. What bull shit. Did Descartes have a wife?* She wondered ruefully, sliding her purse over her shoulder.

Through the patient check-in window she could see Gillian, waiting in a relaxed posture, flipping through a fashion magazine. Campbell poked her head out through the sliding window and called, "Gillian, I'll be there in a few minutes." Heading down the hall toward the doctor's corner office she concluded, *Through war, conflict, and domination, a masculine world spills blood, whereas a feminine world passes it on. Vampires, as a parallel species, do both—just as humans do. Yet, they create a universe in which eternity in this body becomes possible. Why hadn't she thought of this earlier in her studies? It made perfect sense.*

CHAPTER THIRTY-FIVE

Baltimore, 2011

While pregnant with Caroline, Campbell remembered the soft image of her full body coiled like a satisfied snake among the newly purchased baby things. The sweet smell of perfumes that whispered innocence and possibility emanated from every item. She dreamed of all the ideals that would be manifested in this new relationship with her baby. She would nurse at least a year. She would feed this new life only homemade organic baby food. She would sing to it every night. She would never raise her voice. The list went on and on, until Campbell dozed off buried beneath this reverie. She awoke several months later to reality, where sleep and sanity were a distant memory. Organic home-made baby food became store bought jars of apple sauce. Nursing for a year became nursing for five months. Who can pump in a tiny office on campus between classes and student advising? The promise to never raise her voice was replaced by "time outs" while she snuck onto the back porch for a cigarette and momentary peace of mind.

What is "good enough" suddenly changes when you realize you may be living on borrowed time. What would be good enough to give her children now? Even if she chose not to run off with Finn, the universe seemed to be conspiring to take her out for the count anyway.

The hot water had all but steamed its way out of the bathtub, and Campbell's fingers were pruned: tight little rivulets of skin created canyons in her fingertips.

She noted this blandly. The numbness from today's news had not worn off. She replayed the entire scene over and over again, hoping that maybe she had missed some detail, some facet of the procedure that could be explained, which would make it all disappear. She recalled the nurse calling her into the room with the mammogram machine. She replayed the doctor's words, noting the shadows on the X-ray as "serious" and requiring an immediate follow up appointment right after the New Year. Campbell felt her body lift off the ground and she floated away.

Campbell regretted that she had not called Finn earlier that evening as she had promised. He would have noticed by now she had cancelled class. The words, what she would say, just wouldn't come. Her finely laid schemes and plans had come unraveled, and she had no idea how to pull them back together.

She lay in the tepid bath water, frozen in mind and body, when she heard the key turn in the door and Brent's heavy footsteps on the landing one floor below her. He had arrived home late, after the kids had gone to bed several nights this week already. She heard him lumber his way up the stairs and stop in front of the bathroom door. There was a pause.

"Cam?" he called.

"In here."

He came in seeming weary and sad. "You're home early," he noted.

"Yeah, I sent Kim home."

His tie hung loosely around his neck, his button down shirt pulled up slightly around the belt. She opened her mouth to begin telling him about her visit to the doctor's, but he interrupted her. He sat down on the toilet seat cover next to the bathtub.

"Look. I know I haven't been around much." He sighed and paused, choosing his words carefully. "It's not like I'm running around, Campbell. I'm working. The job is killing me. I know I've been a little distant from you and the kids. I guess I'm not very good at keeping work at the office, so I just tune out the first chance I get."

She opened her mouth to speak.

"Before you say anything, I need to get this off my chest." He sucked in a deep breath and exhaled. "I know you're seeing someone else. Or, at least I am pretty sure that you are."

Her face went ashen. She lifted her fingers carefully above the water's surface—making note of them, avoiding eye contact with Brent. She swirled them around watching miniscule bubbles whirl and dissipate. Beneath the water her hands were shaking.

"You know I respect your privacy. I'm not snooping around. I don't go through your things. Believe it or not, I do pay attention to you, the way you look, your tone of voice, your smell-when you're here, when you're not here. I'm not stupid.

And I don't want you to give me some grand confessions either. The truth is I don't really want to know any details. If I am wrong, so be it, then I apologize. But…" he breathed in deep, "If I am right, all I ask is that you make a decision. If you want to stay in this marriage, then end the affair now, and we will both work to fix things. But if you want to go, if you're that unhappy, then go."

She turned to him with deep sadness. This was a defining moment, and all of eternity might as well have rested in the few seconds that ticked by.

"I think I have breast cancer," was all she could say.

CHAPTER THIRTY-SIX

Baltimore, 2011

Finn had not been in the Irvington neighborhood of Baltimore in at least a decade, and was surprised to find that while certain areas like the Inner Harbor had transformed themselves from impoverished industrialized wastelands into bright beacons of tourism, that other communities like Irvington had changed little since he arrived three decades ago.

Small clusters of men gathered around the front of the local bar, smoking. Young mothers with small children in strollers dotted the sidewalks along store fronts, many of them boarded up or closed. There had been no new buildings constructed, no renovations, few, if any new businesses that Finn could recognize. He noted one of the few trees that had been planted along the city street, bare and scraggly from lack of fresh air and clean soil, had an empty plastic bag waving like a flag in the crisp wind, inflating and deflating in rhythmic fashion.

Hard to imagine, he thought, *that I am only a few miles away from downtown, and I might as well be in another world.* He thought of the men who came through the doors of New Beginnings, so many of them born and raised right here. *What real starting chance in life did they really have in comparison to the people who lived in neighborhoods like Campbell's?*

For the first time since he could remember, he allowed himself to think of Jenna and his own childhood. With industries shutting downs and high unemployment, his father had become an estranged and bitter man, hanging on to a string of jobs, doing everything from mopping floors to working the mines, in order to put food on their table. His mother worked too, cleaning houses for the wealthier families who lived in the steeply hilled roads on the fringes of town, with white pillars in the front and manicured green lawns. Finn had known before he left elementary school, that his chances for success were wrought with more obstacles than those of the few privileged children who were bused to the private school twelve miles away from town. In hindsight, now himself no longer needing to be concerned with such matters, he wondered how humans had survived this long.

Finn landed without a sound onto the moist grass of Loudon Cemetery and put his radar on high, searching for any sign of Jesse. He had arrived home after his freshman lecture at Eastern, feeling exuberant. His class discussion had captured the imaginations and intellect of the forty young minds that were in his class. He expected to see Campbell for their usual Monday evening tryst in her office afterwards, but she had cancelled class today. *Where is she? Why hasn't she called?* The gnawing fear that he might lose her gave way to his focus on the matter at hand. He could sense Jesse before he heard his voice from around the backside of a mausoleum five feet to his left.

"You came."

Finn noted gratitude and relief in his voice.

"Jesse." Finn couldn't mask his reaction to Jesse's gaunt face and thin frame. How had he not seen this in his old friend the other night? Maybe had not been looking closely enough. Even in the relative darkness, Finn could see him clearly now. The city lights cast a faint light over the cemetery.

"I'm dying, man."

Jesse pulled a pack of cigarettes out of his shirt pocket. The air was pointedly cold. Finn couldn't feel it and wondered if Jesse, wearing no jacket, even cared that the frost would be setting in this evening. It was mid-December. They stood there motionless, sizing each other up.

"What can I do to help?" Finn asked. "Do you need money for treatment? I can get you some."

Jesse looked up; the streetlights showed that he was beginning to cry. With a hardened voice he replied, "You know what I need, man." He glared at Finn with an expression of envy and desperation.

"I don't know, Jesse. I don't know if I can…" Finn's voice fell away.

Angered now, and fueled by fear, Jesse sputtered, "You are a god damn hypocrite, you know that?" His breath came fast and hard. "You spend all your time saving these guys from themselves. But half of 'em don't even want your help! I know this for a fact. I'm sober now. And I keep myself sober helping others. And yeah, that's great, but they're dying too and they know it. And their addiction is so great they don't care. The voice in their head tells them they don't need help. I'm sick of it. I am sick of all the death."

He pressed his back against a granite mausoleum for support and slid down to the ground sobbing. Finn sat beside him. Jesse raised his head.

"I don't know much. But I've been watching your kind. I've given this a lot of thought. The difference between humans and vampires is that humans, in spite of their selfishness and supposed progress, are hell bent on self-destruction."

Finn nodded in agreement. He had argued as much in his dissertation thesis. He knew Jesse was right.

"Vampires are designed for self-preservation. Humans killing humans is worse than whatever it is you do. Getting sober gave me the chance to see that there's more to life." He lowered his voice. "I don't want to die, Finn."

"Jesse, you have no idea what it is I do. I don't kill people. That's a choice, not an obligation, of being what I am." Finn felt as if he was reaching for words, utterances, sounds, anything that might get him past this moment, until he could find something honest and meaningful to say.

"I know what I'm getting into," Jesse retorted, "I know what I'm asking."

Finn studied Jesse's weary face, sunken with weathered lines and scars. He had imagined the possibility of making Campbell like himself. If he wanted to be with her forever, which he did, he knew this decision would eventually confront them. He had never thought of changing anyone else. But maybe this was what he was meant to do. Jesse was dying. The morality of this decision hinged on that fact for Finn. A lifetime of acting as a non-interventionist was giving way to a new set of considerations. His philosophy had always been that people must make choices for themselves, since that choice had been taken from him. But what if those vampires had not made that choice for him? He most likely would have ended up dead.

If humans were in fact hell bent on their own destruction, were his efforts in the past few decades really affecting any change? Or had he been whistling in the dark making himself feel better, giving him false sense of purpose. This way he could avoid making the hard decisions to initiate real change. Finn worried, *Have I used my helpfulness all this time merely as a way to avoid facing real decisions and responsibility for the power I hold in my hands? Was it,* he realized, *perhaps more immoral to leave Jesse's life to wither and disappear? But what if Jesse became one of those who stalked and killed the very people I am trying save?* Then he would face the responsibility for that. There was no guarantee that Jesse wouldn't become a killer. But if Finn's theory, and if his own observations up to this point were true, then Jesse would ostensibly remain Jesse. And Finn would just have to watch him carefully. Take him under his wing.

"I am going to give you a New Year's gift," Finn offered with new conviction. He stood up. "The holidays are real busy at New Beginnings. But right after that, on the 31st, come and see me. You can stay with me, undetected, until you've adjusted to the change."

Jesse rose to his feet slowly. He raised his shoulders and chin up straight with the awareness of someone already reborn.

CHAPTER THIRTY-SEVEN

Baltimore, 2011

This time of year had always been dear to Campbell. The evergreens, the twinkling lights, the snow. It all held the promise of renewal. The everyday world somehow magically transformed into a place fit for any snow globe. But now it felt like illusions, all of it false promises. The light that sparkled in Ellis and Caroline's eyes as they tore through their Christmas gifts was her only consolation this year. She and Brent had resolved not to tell the children anything about Campbell's health concerns until they knew more. The radiologist had agreed to fit her in for an emergency appointment January 2nd to take a biopsy. Until then, no one knew what the future would hold. She was grateful that Christmas Day had taken her mind off of the decisions she would have to make. Maybe. Perhaps, the illusion wasn't so bad. It brought temporary relief.

But now, in the evening, as the children were in bed, all the wrapping paper stuffed neatly into bags for recycling, the dishes from dinner cleaned, as Brent slept exhausted from the day's excitement-here in this solitude and silence, the voices came whispering. She had avoided contacting Finn for days now, since her mammogram appointment and Brent's confession, and she knew she could not stave off the inevitable.

She slid on her snow boots and flipped on the lights for the back porch. The flood lights spilled yellow over the brown, green, and white landscape. She reached into the row of wooden planting shelves fixed to the outside wall and pulled out a crumpled pack of cigarettes. *I am going to die or live regardless of whether or not I have this cigarette*, she rationalized. She lit the end and watched as it glowed orange, and she pulled the rich aroma into her body. She blew smoke out with slow deliberation, watching it dissipate into the cold night air. *Who am I fooling?* She stubbed the cigarette into a small patch of snow.

She thought of Finn. *Who am I fooling?* she asserted again. Cigarettes were not the only thing she had to be willing to give up now.

A loud sound rustled in the cypress trees lining the edge of her property. Finn emerged like a jungle cat. As if she were expecting him she casually whispered, "Hey." His face was hardened and jagged. She knew she owed him an explanation. He sauntered over to the porch and looked around. "Is it okay? I mean, for me to be here?"

Without making eye contact she replied, "Yeah, everyone's asleep." Everyone being code for Brent, whose name she refused to utter in Finn's presence. She ran to him instinctively, pulled his encompassing frame around hers, and began sobbing uncontrollably. His anger toward her softened.

"Hey, it's alright. I was just worried when I didn't hear from you. I know you're probably so busy with the kids and Christmas. It's no big deal. Really." He stroked her hair and drank in her smell.

"It's not that," she told him. "I may be sick. Like, really sick. We don't know yet. Remember how I told you my mom died of breast cancer?" She didn't finish the thought. Finn took three steps back and held onto the porch railing to keep himself from falling. He released it when he felt himself so filled with rage that he could lift the wood rails out of their foundations. He reached for her hands.

"What do you need from me?" Finn asked. "I'll do anything you ask." More slowly, he added, "I can change all of this for you." And she knew it, too.

They examined each other for several beats, not a word between them. Since their love affair began he had fantasized about making her like him, about the two of them leaving this place together. But this fantasy was always overtaken by a sense of guilt he had over what that would do to her children. But now, in light of her possible death, he felt adamant about it.

She shook her head. "No. I can't do to my children what my mother did to me and my father," she argued.

"I would have never even given it a thought, Campbell, except that you might be dying. I can't lose you. Not like that."

"Then I'll make it easy for you. We can end it now before I know what the outcome is. All they know so far is it's a 'shadow.' It might be nothing."

She realized now that the distance she had kept between herself and Finn over the last few days was shoring her up for what she had to do. "I've come to realize a few things about my life in the last three days. It's not that I want to lose you Finn. This hurts more than you know. But I have to."

He was desperate for some way to change her mind. He stammered, "Now that we are both the same age. Now that we're adults and I see the remarkable woman you have become, I cannot imagine being apart from you again. I need forgiveness for the fact that I never really lived-not until now. Saving you was the one right thing in my life. That. And leaving town to spare Jenna. The only way I knew to help those I loved was to disappear. Are you asking me to do that now? That the best way I can help you is to not exist in your world? Fate brought us together. If I negate you, us, I negate any life I could have or will have."

His chest was like lead, and he could feel his face throbbing with the push of tears. Campbell wrapped her arms tightly across her chest to fend off the bitter wind. She knew he was right. And she knew that he knew this was exactly what was running through her mind. He surged ahead, pleading.

"You are me, Campbell. You are a part of me. You always have been. All this time. You think it's a coincidence that the universe brought us back together? There has to be a reason."

"Yes," she responded calmly, "But that doesn't mean that we need to know what that reason is."

"Maybe it's so I could save you from this horrible death." He hoped using reason might sway her. Images of her mother, spitting blood into a plastic hospital cup came rushing back to her.

"Maybe." Then, she added, "You know, Finn, watching my mother die of cancer was hard. Very. But what was really painful was all those years I was growing up, waiting and wondering. Where was she? Why did she leave?"

Campbell let out a slow sigh. "Now as an adult I kind of get it. I can understand better what she was feeling. I look at you and I get it completely." She made a sad smile.

"But I can't do to my kids what my mom did to me. Leave them wondering."

"That's bullshit, Campbell." His face was hard but she could see he was holding back tears.

"Either way Finn, this is not what I would choose. Death? Or losing my kids even if I don't die? I don't know. But I guess—why should I have to lose you too?"

Grasping desperately for some way not to lose her he suggested, "Let's make a deal. After your biopsy, when you get the results, if it's benign and you're okay, I'll go out of your life forever. But, if the result comes back with a fatal determination, you have to promise you'll at least come and tell me. That you'll consider my offer."

"Sure. Why not?" she said. The sur-reality of her possible death seemed more impossible to grasp now than the fact that she was negotiating immortality with her vampire-lover. Snow began falling in heavy clumps. The forecasters had called for a winter storm arriving in the next few days, but she had been too distracted to concern herself with this.

"I love you, Finn. But I have to make a choice. Maybe nothing, not even us, is inevitable. It's so easy to rationalize something as morally justified when you call it inevitable. Isn't that what you said about vampires who choose to kill humans?"

Finn wasn't listening. Something in his being seemed to be shutting down. His hair hung low around his face and he forced his eyes upward to hide the pain in his face.

"Leaving you rips out a part of me, too," she sobbed. "But I will not do to my kids what my mom did to me." Her body was shaking now. He wrapped his arms around her as snow began coating his forearms.

"I know, Campbell. But maybe there's another way around all this. One we just haven't thought of, or imagined, yet."

"Please, just promise me," he pleaded gently kissing her cheeks, "That you won't make any decisions tonight. Please?" The sobbing ceased and she lifted her head. "Agreed. Just for tonight. Just for tonight let's remain suspended in the unknown. And have faith."

CHAPTER THIRTY-EIGHT

Baltimore, Dec. 31, 2011

11:20 p.m.

It was getting late and the snow was coming down in a frenzy of heavy white flakes, glittering flakes that flew across the glowing streetlights in chaotic swirls. Campbell closed the curtain in the living room as if to shut out reality. The snow was at least two feet high. She stepped onto the front porch to get her thoughts about her. As she contemplated her next move she could see the soft downy piles of white rising like building additions on the tops of the cars and fence posts which ran along their front yard. She was less concerned with how the snowstorm might cancel her appointment for an emergency biopsy the day after tomorrow than with whether or not she would be able to access emergency services tonight if Ellis's breathing didn't improve.

Ellis's fever was not going down even with the Tylenol. She went back up into his dimly lit room and sat very still next to him. The room felt hot and confining from the steam she had tried to push through his humidifier. His breathing was more labored, and she was convinced she could hear him wheezing. Campbell padded down the hall to Caroline's room and crept softly to her bedside. She realized how strong and beautiful her daughter was. How independent she had become, so unlike Campbell herself at that age. She tucked Caroline's covers around her warm body, and placed her favorite doll by her side.

Then she strode down the carpeted hall to her bedroom. "Brent," she intoned flatly. "It's Ellis. His breathing is getting worse and the fever is still 104."

There was silence for a few seconds. She said, "I think I need to take him to the pediatric center. Or the ER."

Through the dim lit room he asked, "Cam. How can I help?"

Fighting the urge to cry caused her face to ache. Brent never panicked. He never showed loosely held emotions of any kind. It was what made him so good at his job and easy to get along with. But right now Campbell wanted to jump on him and shake him. *Get upset! Freak out!* she wanted to scream. Instead she just said, "I don't know." She walked out of the room instead to gather her thoughts. She paced, and her mind was a frenzy of "what if's?"

If I bring him to the pediatric emergency clinic now how will I get through these roads? But leaving him like this means he could die. And calling 911 or an ambulance on a night like this is insane. It could take them way too long to get here. They're going to be mobbed with emergencies.

She marched back into the room with more resolve. "Look. We can't call an ambulance; there are so many accidents out there right now it will take too long for them to get to us. And sitting here isn't going to cut it. Stay with Caroline. I am going to get him dressed and take him to Howard County General Hospital."

Brent was awake by now. He knew she was right. "Okay," he agreed. "I'll get the car brushed off and warmed up while you get him dressed."

She said nothing but turned on her heels and rushed back to Ellis.

"Where are we going, Mommy?" Ellis asked wearily, exhausted from lack of sleep and the high fever. She pulled his Transformers T-shirt over his forehead, now beaded with sweat.

"We're going to the doctor, baby," she explained with as much calm in her voice as she could muster.

Outside, she heard the car engine revving and then the sound of a shovel pushing the snow away from the car. In a half-conscious state Ellis agreed to have his coat and hat put on him. Campbell hastily grabbed for some socks and unable to find a matching pair in the jumble of items in his top drawer grabbed a blue one and a white one with a shark on it and the words, "National Aquarium." After pulling her long wool coat over her sweat pants she stepped into her snow boots, and carried Ellis to the front door.

Brent was walking back inside, brushing the wet melted flakes off the sleeves and shoulders of his down coat. "Alright," he insisted firmly. "Be safe. Call me when you get there."

"I will."

He handed her the keys. "The car's been brushed off."

She felt Ellis shift in her arms uncomfortably.

"I'm sorry," she admitted, gazing at Brent. He looked at her, puzzled, trying to interpret what she meant, and his eyes closed halfway with curiosity.

"For what?" he asked, although he knew the answer. He knew. But now was not the time to go into it.

"I don't know. Everything, I guess."

He gave a half smile and gently kissed Ellis on the forehead.

"Bye" she said, resting her hand on his forearm. The word sounded heavier than she had intended. Some shadow of a thought was creeping into her mind that she may never come back. Letting go of Brent's arm she caught sight of her cell phone on the table with sets of keys and unopened mail. *Thank god, I didn't forget that*, she noted, reaching out to grab it and closing the front door behind her.

Campbell tried not to panic at the fact that she could see no more than two feet of road ahead of her. Ellis was asleep, or so she hoped. She heard his labored wheezy breathing and this caused her to speed up the car. All she could see in front of her was a moving white wall and blackness behind it. *It's my fault*, she reminded herself. Now that no one was around she could let the tears fall freely down her face. *I am so stupid. What am I doing? If I hadn't been so obsessed with Finn maybe none of this would have happened. I am the worst mother.* She looked in the rearview mirror at Ellis.

"How ya doin', monkey?" she asked.

He sniffled and whimpered, "I'm alright. Are we there yet, Mommy?"

"Almost," she assured him. She allowed herself to relax just a bit and her mind wandered to thoughts of Finn. It helped her panic less about the current situation. She replayed their conversation in her head. *Never come around here again. I can't see you anymore.* She had locked the sliding back door behind her as she went inside. He had stood there blankly, watching her leave.

She interrupted these thoughts long enough to read the road signs, and to wipe the side of her face, now stinging cold and wet. *I wish he were here right now.* The empty space where Finn had been was filled with the icy winds that pushed across the windshield of her car. It was unbearable.

Campbell was brought back to full attention when she saw red blinking lights ahead. She slowed and looked out the driver-side window to see three police cars. She rolled down her window as one policeman approached the car.

"Road's closed, ma'am," he apologized.

"But my son! I have to get him to the emergency room! His breathing is all wrong. He's wheezing! Can't you take me?" Her voice trembled.

"Sorry, ma'am," he replied in earnest. "We have an accident here. I have to stay and wait for the fire trucks."

He wiped the melting snow off his brow and looked at her more sympathetically. "If you take this left here," he offered, raising his arm draped in the fluorescent yellow raincoat, "The roads aren't so good but you can pass through the Patapsco State Park and cut your travel time in half if you're trying to make it to the end of Route 40."

The Explorer usually does really well in the snow, she reminded herself, *I don't really have a choice anyway, do I?*

"Okay, thanks," she replied and rolled up her window. She cut a sharp left and heard the thick crunching of snow under her wheels. As they tread their way toward the state park, the street grew darker and the streetlights faded. Then they fell into total darkness except for the beaming headlights of her car. The way ahead appeared like a tunnel, visible only by the yellow high beams. Trees were weighted down by the amassing snow and thick drifts like ghostly sculptures passed by her view often causing her to slow down even more. The road was completely invisible. No cars or plows had touched this road since the storm began and there were no tire marks. Once she felt the car lurch right, down into a small drainage run and realizing she was off the road pulled quickly left on the wheel to regain the car's equilibrium.

Campbell needed to think of something other than Ellis' shallow breathing. Plowing her way through the maze of trees, stumps, and the occasional sign posts, she considered how she couldn't live with the idea of keeping Finn out of her life. Finn belonged with her. Her universe was all out of sorts, and she couldn't imagine living whatever time she had left on this earth without him. Campbell decided, *It isn't in having everything that I achieve happiness. It isn't in gaining possible immortality that I might feel free.* She listened to the wheels moving smoothly and quietly over the snow. Her muscles relaxed. *It's in finding that one other person, whether a friend or a lover, it does not matter, to whom we feel bound. Some people spend their whole lives actively moving from person to person, looking for that feeling, sometimes leaving behind a wake of dead and broken families and relationships. However, if you're patient enough, those opportunities will find you. The most we can do is choose how to respond to these situations as they appear.*

Yet, looking back at Ellis who was finally asleep, she wondered if she could imagine her life any other way than the path she had chosen before Finn re-entered her world.

It was then that the car began to slide.

CHAPTER THIRTY-NINE

Baltimore, Dec. 31, 2011

11:30 p.m.

There would be no avoiding it. They had been making their way down a gradual incline, but as they crossed by the river she realized that the river had likely overflowed the last few days, and that a huge, and now invisible, sheet of ice was covering what was once pavement. Campbell pulled left on the wheel to right the fishtailing at the back of the car but it did no good. The incline grew steeper and the car was now picking up speed. The breaks were no use and whether she cut right or left Campbell realized she was at the mercy of gravity and ice. As the car silently glided down the hill Campbell discerned the image of a looming oak tree directly in front of them and getting closer. She knew there would be no avoiding it, and at the angle the car was moving it was likely that Ellis' side of the back seat would have the first impact from hitting the tree.

Without thinking, Campbell unlocked her seat belt and scrambled her forearms and shoulders through the two front seats and clutched wildly at Ellis's head, wrapping her limbs as best she could around him while keeping him locked in his car seat. Aroused by the sudden motion he uttered something in confusion. Before she could understand what he saying she heard a loud sound of crushing metal and then felt the bone crushing pain of metal hitting spine. The oak crushed the steering column, pinning her legs beneath it. Ellis was crying softly, his breath warm on her right arm where a large tear in her coat had left her skin exposed. *He's crying. That means he's alive,* she thought with some relief.

Her head throbbed with a rush of pressure and pain. Then, everything went black.

Campbell's mind drifted into a dream-like state of semi-consciousness. In this semi-conscious state, where the immediacy of her current state of emergency didn't exist, a realization fell on Campbell with full force. "Don't be ridiculous, Campbell Cote" she heard her mom saying. She saw her mothers' face peering in through the broken windshield. "Don't make the same mistakes I made," she said. But there was love in her voice, and a softness in her expression that Campbell had never remembered seeing before. Campbell felt a wave of forgiveness wash over her body. And then her mother was gone.

Campbell could change nothing about her life now. But it was then that she changed her mind. She changed her mind about everything she had once believed was possible or impossible. This change of mind sprung from the realization that she had been wrong. She did not have to be destined to become her mother. Nor did she have to choose to say good bye to Finn. Now, in this god forsaken moment of terror, a third option revealed itself to her. And she would fight for the chance to realize the other possibilities now being revealed. *Deep true love*, Campbell told herself while still immersed in this altered state, *requires sacrifice and forgiveness, and I have not experienced either with him, or for him ... yet.* Campbell knew she loved her children. She had loved Brent at one time, too. And Finn loved her. She knew she was bound to him in a way she had yet to find a language to express. She would have a future with him in it, somehow. And while she couldn't change the past, she realized that, *maybe isn't too late to change what might happen next.* Campbell knew that in order to accomplish this she would need more time; and there was only one way now to survive and to make the time that she needed.

The sound of Ellis crying pulled her back from her semi-conscious state and to her immediate crisis. *How long have I been out of it?* Panic returned

"Ellis!" she screamed. Campbell couldn't move her body from the waist down but she could turn her head. She looked around into the darkness, shattered glass hanging from the window and bent frames twisted into a strange sculpture protruding into the night sky gradually becoming covered in a sparkling light bluish white of small ice crystals.

"Mommy!" he whimpered, "What happened?"

She uttered a cry of pain and relief. *He's alive. He's okay,* was her first thought, followed by, *I can't move. We're trapped.*

Although the tree had impacted the driver's side, she noticed that Ellis' car seat had been propelled out of place by about 6 inches. Still seated, he was tilted slightly to one side, and the seat belt was jammed. Her one leg had been crushed by the huge weight of the steering column. A large branch forced its way in through the windshield. She was pinned in, and she could sense that somewhere she was bleeding. *Think, Campbell!* she told herself, her mind blurred by pain and panic. She pulled her left arm out from beneath her unpinned leg and reach toward her purse. Her fingers fumbled for the phone.

"Damn it," she said under hear breath. "Come on …"

Campbell had no sense of where she was at this point. She had followed the police officer's directions, but never having taken that road before, she had no real idea where on Route 306 it came out. She had lost track of how far she had come down through the state park, or if she had taken any right or left turns off the main road because of the lack of visibility on the road. *I could call Brent. But he can't do anything anyway. He has Caroline, and I have the only car that can drive in snow.*

In the grim depth of silence, she realized just exactly how silent it was. There was no sound of the engine. The impact had caused the engine to stop, and with no engine, there was no heat. The cold air suddenly felt even colder, especially now with at least one window smashed open. Both she and Ellis would freeze to death soon if she couldn't get help. Campbell's mind numbed out the pain as she reached for her purse, flung to the far side of the passenger seat, and using her finger tips, clawed for her phone.

All of this had been in her dream; a dream which felt like a lifetime away now. But she knew she had to change this one circumstance. This one. Right now. She made the one choice she could. She took a breath. She looked at Ellis one last time, smiled weakly, and said, "I'll get us out. Someone is coming for us. I promise." And then her fingers dialed the number that had become so familiar to her. The text screen shone bright and the letters of the name appeared: Finn.

CHAPTER FORTY

Baltimore, 2011

Finn wasn't big on faith. He needed to hear her, to see her, to smell her. Even the distance of a few days was taking its toll on him. In spite of all the fantastic events that had come to pass in his existence; the suspension of disbelief he had achieved to acknowledge that reality goes far beyond what one can imagine as one is lying in an abandoned row house writhing in pain, becoming a vampire, he still could not believe Campbell's words. He could not accept that she was dying-perhaps. And worse, that she was ending their relationship.

Now it was time to think about Jesse, and what was to come. The weight of life and death swirled around him and his brain clouded. He opened his email and typed feverishly:

December 31st, 2011

11:45 p.m.

From: fmiginnis@esu.edu

To: ccotephill@esu.edu

My Dearest Campbell,

I want these to be the first words you read when you wake up.

Let them resonate through every inch of that beautiful body and mind of yours

YOU ARE THE ONE

The ONLY one.

You have been more than enough from the moment we met. You have reassembled my life. The lost fragments, I remember being scared. I remember you being there for me. I want to be there for you. That's what I realized tonight. Looking at eternity sometimes makes one feel inadequate. I know that we are eternity. We create it. Everything is more amazing than I ever imagined. Please...reconsider my offer. It stands. Forever.

Love, Finn

Finn looked outside his small basement-level window. The snow was coming down heavily now and all but blocked any view of the sky from his room. Weathermen had predicted this could be the storm "of the decade." He could smell the trouble that was to come in the air.

As Finn closed his laptop for the night he felt a tingling ache along the back of his neck. Where the hell was Jesse? He worried that something, like Chester, had gotten to him before he could fulfill his promise to keep Jesse alive forever. *Was he worried?* He wondered honestly, *or was he relieved?* His mind was muddied, frazzled, and full of noise. Since Campbell had told him it was over, his mind had simply gone numb. Which was worse? That Campbell had told him goodbye? Or the ordeal that faced him next if Jesse showed up? The decision made in Loudon Cemetery was seeping into Finn's body. He imagined what it might taste and feel like to sink his teeth into another being. To feel their life force rush into his. The exhilaration he was feeling at the mere anticipation made him wary. He was beginning to concede in the farthest regions of his conscious mind that sometimes one's instincts can override the power of choice. Had he been fooling himself this whole time, about Campbell, about the nature of his own existence, about everything?

The dread and pleasure evoked at the thought of a human's life-blood rushing from their soft throat made him wonder about Campbell's choice. Finn couldn't hide the rage, either, Rage, not directed toward Campbell, really, but toward the idea that she preferred to die rather than to live her life. He argued with himself, *She would be leaving it either way, right? Why sacrifice this love they had discovered? What good would it do her family?*

He turned and saw Travis standing in the frame of his door. He tapped softly.

"Hey, man," Finn said quietly.

Travis said, "You seem a little shook up friend. Everything okay?"

"Um...sure." Finn stumbled over his thoughts and words. He aimlessly shuffled some papers on his desk, then briskly brushed his long hair out of his face. He looked straight at Travis.

"Campbell doesn't want to see me anymore," he confessed.

Finn held a facial expression that, in over fifty years of working with dying and desperate men, Travis had never seen. But he masked his own reaction with a calm composure.

"Hmm. I see." He nodded his head sympathetically.

"That's it? That's all you've got, old man?" Finn's voice was cracking.

"I love you, Finn, like a son. So I am just gonna say it like it is. What did you think was going to happen? "

He moved slowly into the room and eased himself into a chair. Finn became aware suddenly of Travis' advanced age. *Was everyone he cared about going to die around him, while he carried on?* He didn't feel so lucky. He had the rash thought to just scoop them all up: Campbell, Travis, Jesse, and change them all whether they wanted it or not.

What the hell, and while I'm at it, I'll go find Jenna and change her, too. he thought.

As if he could read Finn's mind, Travis said cautiously, "Be careful what you do next, Finn." Finn nodded absently. Travis pushed his left arm feebly against the back of the chair to stand up and placed his hand on Finn's shoulder. "I'm going to lie down for a while. The snow's been piling up since yesterday. Plows are having a hard time getting through the city streets. Stanley is working the front desk until dawn if you need something. Everyone else is settled in for the night. We got a full house tonight because of the snowstorm and the holidays. Every place that's got half a warm spot is gonna be packed tonight. God help the rest of them." He sighed and walked out.

Resigning himself to Travis' advice, Finn turned off his computer. He would wait for Jesse. Then his hands froze and he searched around his room in a panic. He sensed that something was wrong with Campbell. But he had promised to stay away and so he would.

I can't call her, he told himself. He'd given his word. *But what if something were really wrong? Wouldn't she want me to be there to help her?* In the silence he could hear two men arguing on the floor above him. He could also hear shuffling feet above him in the TV room. "Damn it," he murmured and pushed the large wooden chair back from the desk, "I better go deal with that." Perhaps focusing on a more immediate crisis would take his mind off Campbell. But before he could pass through the doorway, the phone on his desk vibrated. He rushed over. Maybe it was a message from Campbell.

CHAPTER FORTY-ONE

Baltimore, Jan. 1, 2012

1:00 am

The weak yellow reading light on Finn's desk at New Beginnings cast a faint reflection on the scattered stacks of papers, but the rest of the room remained dim at the dark morning hours. The air was silent with the blanket of snow that had transformed the city from a place of noise and action to one of complete stillness. Jesse paced, focusing his ears on the sound of his own footsteps, moving back and forth across the grey linoleum floor. He noted the small grains of dirt or sand that created a small crunching sound as his toes twisted and turned each time he neared one wall and turned back the other way. The clock registered 1:00 a.m.

Where the hell is he? he worried. *He said after midnight. Tonight.*

Jesse scoured his mind over their last conversation at the cemetery to be sure he hadn't missed anything. When he arrived tonight, all the men except the one handling the front desk were asleep. There was a lights-out rule, as he recalled, and so the rec room, kitchen, and hallways were empty, except for Travis who had been sitting quietly in the kitchen reading a book and having tea. He wondered why Travis was still here. Usually he went home at night and left the dawn patrol to the others. Jesse had slipped past him, unnoticed. *Better not to involve him,* Jesse thought.

For days now, this moment was all he had thought about. He tried to imagine what the transformation might feel like. He relished the unanswerable question of what he might now do for an eternity. *Go back to school like Finn, maybe*, he mused. *Or travel the world.*

Just as he rounded his twenty-fifth lap around the small space of Finn's office he heard a noise. Something was creaking in the doorway. He spun around expectantly. "Finn, man. I was getting worried you wouldn't ...." Jesse's voice trailed off before completing his sentence. Chester, poised like a mountain lion in a state of rest, leaned against the frame of the doorway.

"Where's Finn?" Jesse demanded.

"How the hell should I know?" Chester snorted. "I'm not here to see Finn. I'm here to see you." His grin glowed in the dim light of the office. He raised his hand and inspected his finger nails, as if bored already with the way things were going. Jesse's legs quivered uncontrollably. He looked past Chester, wondering if there was enough room to pass by if needed, but he knew his efforts would be in vain. With a mock expression of care and concern, Chester said softly, "I could finish what he promised to start, you know." Jesse gulped hard. His heart was pacing faster. His hopes rose a little. "You ...you could?"

"I could. Or," Chester sighed, "I could just have you for dinner. I am feeling rather piqued. Besides, I am rather selective about who I choose to become one of us. You might wind up like your friend Finn and become a major pain in my ass." He turned his fingers slowly, inspecting the cuticles. Jesse instinctively he let out a small whimper.

In a deriding tone Chester commented, "I'd say you have a fifty-fifty chance here, buddy." He paused, lowered his hand slowly and began walking slowly toward Jesse. "But then again, you've never had very good luck now, have you Jesse?" Jesse backed up until his back was against the far wall.

"How did you know I'd be here?" Jesse could feel his own voice tremble. He swallowed hard to regulate his tone. He tried to sound demanding but his courage was falling short.

"I could tell you." Chester sighed. "But then I'd have to kill you. Oh, wait. That's probably going to happen anyway." He leaned his head in toward Jesse's throat and emitted a low growl.

"Or, I could just kill *you*." A voice rang clear across from the doorway. It was Travis. He was leaning feebly against the frame, supporting himself with one hand, an old pistol held in the other, aimed right at Chester.

Chester spun around, alarmed at first. Then his brain registered the weakened and aged-condition of his challenger, and he relaxed a bit. He let out a cold hollow laugh. "Stick around old man. I might still want dessert when I'm finished here." Chester turned back to face Jesse, whose eyes were now focused on Travis.

"Travis. Run. Get the hell out of here!" Jesse shouted.

"No," Travis said confidently, "I got this, Jesse. I've been saving this bullet here for a long, long time. It's special, you see? My grandfather was a bit of a gun smith. He made bullets. Special bullets." He emphasized the word *special*. Chester slowly turned his head again toward Travis. But he made no move away from Jesse. He was protecting his prey. Travis went on, seeing he now had Chester's attention.

"When I was growing up, we had a full understanding of whom, and a lot of times, what, was after us. There wasn't much we could do to fight the lynchings, or Jim Crow. But finding ways to protect ourselves against vampires was a little bit easier, believe it or not. Turns out, all you need is a little silver mixed in with some mercury. Pour the mixture into a bullet mold …," his voice trailing off as if he were recalling a special memory. Then he carefully made his way over to the desk, and rested his body against it, keeping the gun poised at Chester the entire time. Travis added, "Then, all you need is the right moment." He was breathing hard. But his face registered determination. Chester was unsure of himself, and took a few steps away from Jesse and toward Travis.

"Come one old man. Put that old piece of crap down. You think that's gonna stop me? That … antique?" He forced a laugh.

"Me, and this gun, might be old. But my sharp-shooter's eye is as good as it was when I was twenty. And this here gun? Well, it's taken out more vampires than I can count. Let's see who's going to live longer, Chester. You? Or me?"

A shot rank out, and a blinding blast of gun powder filled the room.

CHAPTER FORTY-TWO

Baltimore, Jan. 1, 2012

12:15 a.m.

Knowing that Finn was on his way, Campbell eased her body back into a resting position where the pain was lessened. She kept vigil over Ellis who was still breathing slowly but regularly in his car seat. She dimly perceived his breath still swirling in cool masses as it met the cold chill of the night air. The rear directional light was still blinking on and off, casting a red glow upon the snow that banked around the car. Light flakes layered themselves across the windows. Campbell felt their cold kiss her face. She embraced the icy water melting down her cheek because it was a reminder that at least she was alive. Ellis' eyes were open but he seemed calm.

"Someone's coming, baby."

"Who?" he whispered.

"Mommy's friend, Mr. Finn is coming to get us."

"How will he get here?" Ellis replied innocently.

"He's special, honey. Like one of your super heroes. He can get here faster than a car."

She tried to smile but her face ached as she did so. Ellis dutifully smiled back.

"I know he's special, Mommy."

"You do?"

So long as I keep him conscious, there's hope, she reminded herself. She would have discussed the benefits of recycling if it kept Ellis calm and awake.

"Yeah" he said softly, "Like at the aquarium. I could tell even the sharks were afraid of him. But I'm not. I think he's nice."

"That's good, baby. Because he is going to get you out of here. I need you to trust him, okay?" She could feel herself losing consciousness. The blood was pooling around her left thigh.

As he raced through the night, Finn played back Campbell's message in his mind. It read: *We are trapped. Help. Ellis might die. We are somewhere in Patapsco Park near Route 40. By a bridge.* He imagined the anxious pain-ridden sounds of Ellis in the background. He fine-tuned all of his senses now, tracking her through Patapsco State Park. Campbell's text had said something about being off Route 40. Entering the park from there he followed the car tracks which were all but buried now by fresh layers of snow. The view in front of him was sheer darkness, and flecks of swirling white. There were no streetlights. It was like being in the foothills of Kentucky again, tracking animals; in the days when, as a human, he actually hunted deer and rabbit. But then he saw it. A beacon in the void. A faint dot of blinking red light. *It must be her rear tail lights,* he concluded. From that point his muscles burst with a strength he hadn't even realized was ever his before now.

Campbell jerked her head forward violently. *Did I pass out? Did I fall asleep? Where's Ellis?* She arched her neck to see him looking at her curiously. The rest of her body was still rendered immobile. She tried once to lift her legs out from under the weight of crushed metal that had pressed in on top of her, but she stopped when she felt the searing pain tear through her leg. Campbell muffled a scream. She couldn't imagine what was going through Ellis' mind. What stunned her most was that he was not crying. Was he staying calm for her? Even at the age of six, Ellis knew what to do.

He announced, "Finn's coming, Mommy. I can hear him."

Campbell could hear snow crunching and the rustling of branches cracking as if a herd of deer was moving across the landscape. Then she saw Finn, suddenly at the broken driver's side window. She sobbed with relief. He raced around to the passenger side where he could reach his hands and neck inside.

"Shhhh. Shhhh. It's okay," he stressed, smoothing her hair, clotted with blood from her forehead. While the scent of her blood was stunning, Finn felt no hunger rousing in him, only fear. He could sense the tremendous blood loss that was rising up around her broken body. He leaned his neck through the window and smiled at Ellis.

"Hey, buddy. You alright?"

"I think so, Mr. Finn. Are you here to save us?"

"Yes, I am, Ellis."

Finn pulled himself to a standing position and assessed the car's damage. The door frame on the driver's side was so warped there was no opening it. While the passenger side remained largely intact, the broad circumference of the tree was thrust squarely between the two front seats. Looking at the driver's side door, closest to Campbell, he knew he would have to pull it off its hinges. He leaned in again. Her breathing was coming hard and infrequent.

"Cam." She didn't move. He could hear her heart beating. "Cam, Wake up. Come on. Stay with me." She opened her eyes. "Can you move at all?"

"I don't think so. It just makes the tear in my leg bigger when I do."

Searching around frantically Finn observed, "I have to try and get this door off the car to get you out."

"Do what you have to do, Finn."

Walking briskly to the other side of the car, he pulled off his coat and tossed it into a drift of snow. He grasped the inside of the door's window with both hands and pulled. The car creaked and groaned under the weight of his arms. It rocked to the left and the top edge of the door started coming away from the frame. Campbell instinctively let out a piercing cry and he let go.

"Are you alright?" he called.

"Yeah, it's just my leg."

She looked at Ellis. His breathing had become a thin trail of steam from his mouth. "Ellis. Honey. Talk to me."

Ellis strained his voice. "Mommy. I can't really breathe too well."

Campbell jolted her attention back to Finn and stared at him. Her voice trembled. "Now listen to me. You have to get him out first. I think the back doors work. All you have to do is lift him out of his car seat." Finn started to say something, but she shouted, "Just do it!"

He looked alarmed. He knew what she was asking. She begged, "He has to go now! He won't make it much longer. Get him. Wrap him in your coat and go! Do you know which way the hospital is from here?"

Finn studied the blackness, making out the slight indentation of the road created by the shrubs lined on either side. "Yeah. If I head north up that way, I can get to Howard County Hospital. Saint Agnes is back that way." He nodded his head left. "But I think Howard County is closer. Especially if I head up that hillcrest and go through the park rather than taking the roads."

"Can you make it going that way?" Her voice was flat and calculated.

"Yeah. I can make it," he replied obediently.

"Get him out now, Finn. We don't have time to mess with my leg. And carrying the two of us will just slow you down. He will die, Finn. Please, don't let my baby die."

She was crying. "You saved my life once, when I was his age. Now it's your chance to save his life too."

He leaned into the car and pressed his face against hers. She could feel him crying, the warmth of the tears melting the cold snowflakes carpeting her cheeks and forehead.

"Please don't make me choose," he pleaded.

"I have to choose. Now, so do you. I realized just now that I was wrong about so many things. But I am right about this. You must take Ellis! I'll stay here. It's not over yet." She laughed weakly at her bad attempt at humor. *Like I could go anywhere if I wanted to*, she thought. But her resolve felt strengthened with her realization. She whispered, "I know where I want to be now. I'll be waiting for you." He nodded and understood.

He kissed her lips softly and murmured, "I love you. I always have. I always will. Don't you die on me, Campbell Cote. After I get him to the hospital I am coming back for you. It doesn't have to be this way."

"Maybe," she agreed, kissing him back. "Promise me, you'll take care of Ellis." With slow deliberation she urged, "If it looks as if he is not going to make it before you to the hospital, I want you to …" She stopped. He fixed his brown eyes on her, knowing with dread what she would say next. She didn't say it out loud, but he knew. "Okay," he conceded.

"Mommy? I can't feel my legs." She sighed with relief. At least he was conscious and able to breathe well enough to speak. That meant there was hope.

"Finn is going to get you out of the car now, Ellis. He's going to take you to the hospital where they can help you."

For the first time since they'd slammed into the tree, she heard his voice begin to weep with anxiety. "What about you, Mommy?"

She swallowed the black knot that sat in her throat and performed the "everything's okay" act she had practiced when he'd fallen out of a tree and cracked his head open on a rock. "You're going to be fine, Ellis."

"Finn is going to come back for me after he takes you. He cannot take both of us at the same time. I am going to wait here." She feigned certainty, and forced herself to add, "And then I will meet you at the hospital." She knew he was perhaps too clever to buy her story, but either out of fear or his own injuries, he accepted it and nodded.

"I love you, baby. Listen to Finn now."

"I will," Ellis responded. He wanted to be brave for her.

Finn reached gently into the car and unclicked the safety straps. "Ready, bud? We're gonna take a fast trip. Like a race car!" Ellis nodded.

"I'm coming back, Campbell," he promised. Finn lifted Ellis and carefully wrapped his coat around him. He fell into Finn's arms like a ragdoll. Finn reached over with one arm and slid a small object into the palm of Campbell's hand. She fingered it gingerly. "It's your sister's charm, isn't it? The one Jenna gave you. The one you have worn ever since."

"Yes. It is" he said. "And you will hold onto it. Hold onto hope. This isn't a lost cause, Campbell."

Here now was the opportunity she had never imagined possible: to simultaneously die for the love of her children, and to live (again) in the hopes of discovering how to love Finn, and to realize the answer to the question that had daunted her; to discover what her destiny was, what it could be. She squeezed the charm tightly into a weak fist. A chasm of possibilities she could now imagine ruptured and exploded like a million stars. A warmth spread through her body. This revelation signified that this was just beginning for her ... if he could make it back in time.

Her core rose and fell with her breathing. "I'll be waiting for you. We have so much to do yet." She let go of his hand, and then Finn and Ellis disappeared into the dark landscape.

The hospital was only a few miles away now. Finn could begin to make out the glow of the artificial light of the town reflecting off the white blanket draping itself among the tall tree line.

"Still with me, Ellis?" he asked.

"Yeah," Ellis whimpered from beneath the coat.

Now, away from his mother's side, all bravery had been drained out of him, but he had a sense of security from being held by Finn, arriving soon to a hospital where they would be able to get his breathing under control.

"Good. We're almost there. You're gonna be fine."

CHAPTER FORTY-THREE

How much time had passed? Campbell's body was numb. At least the searing pain was gone, and a strange sense of relief was washing over her mind. The dark skies, silence of the woods, and falling snow consumed her senses. Her thoughts pivoted immediately toward Ellis. *He's with Finn. No matter what happens to me now at least I know he will be safe.* She hesitated, and the added, *One way or the other.* Then, as if on cue, she made out a figure moving through the darkness. Blinking the snowflakes from her eyelashes she strained her eyes. The figure was moving closer, quickly.

Was it...? Could it be...? she wondered.

Campbell held her breath. Yes. The figure was Finn. She could make out his frame, his coat, now foregrounded by the reflection of the white earth beneath his feet. He was alone.

That must mean Ellis is safe inside a hospital.

Her entire frame shook with joy for a brief second. Then she lost consciousness and started to dream. In her dream she was watching herself; standing before her, wearing her hooding attire from when she had received her PhD. Cloaked in a navy blue hood and robe, she saw herself walking across a stage, at the university she presumed. There was a line of a dozen people walking across the opposite side of stage coming toward her. Their heads were bent, and she could not make out their faces. As she passed by them, they each raised their hands to reveal a golden goblet in one and a lit candle in the other. "This is your journey," they each said ceremoniously to her. She nodded. Her dream-self seemed to know that that meant.

Without hesitating, she reached out and took a sip from each person's goblet, and then blowing out the candle. The taste of the substance in the cup was unfamiliar to her. She could not identify it with anything she had ever had before. It was neither sweet, nor salty; neither alcoholic, nor dairy. It required a familiarity with a taste palette she had never acquired before, like someone trying to conceive of a color they have never seen. It was impossible to locate. *Why am I the only one moving in this direction, while everyone else is going the other way?* she wondered as she watched her dream-self; *Why are they all going in the other direction? Why is there no one else behind me?*

Behind the twelfth person stood Finn, also wearing his Ph.D. attire. Campbell rushed her pace in line a little faster at the sight of Finn, goblet in one hand and candle in the other. He lifted his head and gazed at her. She spoke aloud, "Is Ellis okay? Did you get him to the hospital?"

Finn's eyes glowed as he stood on the dim stage, his face poised above the glimmer of the small white candle. His white teeth glistened. "He's exactly where he needs to be. You don't need to be afraid for him," Finn replied. But Campbell was alarmed by the lack of emotion in Finn's face. *Didn't he remember the accident? Where was Ellis now?*

"Can I see him? Take me to him, please?" She felt a renewed panic and tried to wake herself but could not. He remained silent. "Is this real, Finn? What is happening to me?" she asked with concern.

"Shhh," he said and soothed her hair with his hand. "Yes. It's real. Your mind is creating a way to process the changes happening to you right now by using a familiar memory. For you, that was your hooding ceremony. You will be alright. But you need to keep moving, Campbell. You're stopping up the procession. Here, take the cup."

Not knowing what else to do she followed his instructions and took a sip. This time, a warm rush flowed through her every limb. Her body was telling her mind a secret, whispering through her veins a silent truth beyond words to utter. Her body began to shake.

"It's time to begin again," Finn softly murmured in her ear. She smiled, and Finn smiled back.

"Yes" she cried, "I choose this. Another life. With you. But my soul belongs to my children. I will go back for them, too ... somehow. There is so much more possible."

"We can do anything. So long as I am with you, I will be happy," Finn whispered.

"A world of limitless possibilities" she murmured.

"Yes, my love."

"Now," he said pulling the hood back from her face and leaning down to press his teeth against her soft neck. His hair tousling her neck in the way that never ceased to make her feel so alive, "Now, blow out the candle."

So she did.

Afterword: An Ending About Endings and Some Words About *Currere*, Inquiry, and Fiction

Fictional *Currere*

The purpose of this Afterword is to analyze my purposes for writing a work of speculative fiction as an example of *currere* (ficto-*currere*). I wanted to privilege my scholar-writer's voice only after the story had concluded. It was necessary to read the story first, so that the reader can now analyze the story (and conclusion, in particular), without the ending being revealed while reading the Introduction.

Both Finn and Campbell's life journeys, (re)constructed through the course of the narrative, embody the four stages of *currere*: Regressive, progressive, analytical, and synthetic (Pinar, 1975).

Campbell engages in the regressive step as she recalls her own history as a child, including her first encounters with Finn and the memories of her mother. Meeting Finn as a child directly impacts both their futures, thus, understanding how the past not only affects her, but the people surrounding her (Pinar, 2004). Finn is reminded of his sister Jenna when he first spies Campbell as a child, and because of this connection, he establishes a rapport with her that leads to everything that follows. Campbell's memories of her mother influence the choices she makes as an adult, herself.

The reader also engages with the memories of Campbell's friends: Lilly, Sandy and Gillian, each of whom recount the "defining moments" in which the past affects profound moments of decision in the present. Regarding the regressive state, Pinar writes that, "One's past is shared, each in his or her own way, by us all" (2004, p. 135). This story is not merely about Campbell's subjective experience. It is about multiple subjectivities, and as such attempts to contest and, "irreversibly destabilize the phenomenological quest for essential meanings" (Gough, 1994, p. 554).

After meeting again as adults, by chance (or perhaps fate), Campbell and Finn are engaged in step two (progressive stage) of *currere*. Again, each has an opportunity to (re)think the future. The future they previously believed to be die-cast is shattered in light of re-encountering one another. For Campbell, there is the realization that reality as she thought she knew it has been shattered as well. As the story progresses, she begins asking herself: If vampires could exist, then what else could be re-imagined as well? Discussing the similarities between Pollack's work and the synthetic stage of *currere* (Slattery, 2018) reminds me of when Campbell stands in front of the hotel mirror, and watches as, "someone else is born in her stead," (*Blood's Will*, p. 154). This is a "visceral" experience (Slattery, 2018, p. 191) indicating how, like Pollack's view of the blank canvas devoid of a preconceived still-life, Campbell realizes that her life had become a still-life, while what she wants is to become like one of Pollack's painting, full of possibilities. Campbell's synthetic moment, echoes Slattery's description, in which "the self is no longer a mirror image of reality ... the irony of a person proclaiming not to be a self..." (2018, p. 192).

As they engage in their bourgeoning love relationship, and their ongoing friendships with other characters, Campbell and Finn find their analytical phase intertwined with one another's. What freedoms and possibilities exist? What limitations might be revealed? The choices made by the supporting characters of Lily, Jesse, and Travis, as revealed in their own personal (side) stories, allow the reader to juxtapose the inner thinking and desires of Finn and Campbell against the backdrop of a bigger world of which they're all deeply involved.

The synthetic phase is revealed in the moment of the car crash. Literally and metaphorically, Campbell's past, present, and futures come crashing in upon her in an unexpected way. From this, she is confronted with an alternative reality, and from which the ending is revealed. In Finn's "vampire theory," the reader is brought along through an academic analysis (a moment where research and fiction blend) to consider the most fundamental of human questions. As Finn shares his dissertation and scholarship with Campbell over coffee at the Roadhouse, he expounds:

> To be alive is to realize that for every choice we make, we also make a sacrifice of something else; the results of which we can rarely predict at the outset, and oftentimes produces outcomes we never could have anticipated. The simplest and smallest, the least noticed acts, gestures, turn-of-the-wrist can lead to life-changing, or life-ending occurrences. (*Blood's Will*, p. 57)

Currere and Vampire Theory

Finn's character deeply engages the reader in an exploration of the contingency of existence, and thus the role of emergence and intertextuality in the making of one's *currere*. A full analysis of Finn's vampire thesis serves as an exercise in understanding Rorty's arguments on language construction, meaning-making, irony, and contingency (1989). Finn's elusive suggestion that vampires are real and/or not real, based on the language choices we make (which intersect with our beliefs and consciousness), reminds me of Rorty's statement, "liberal societies … have produced more and more people who are able to recognize the contingency of the vocabulary in which they state their highest hopes—the contingency of their own consciences" (1989, p. 46). Finn, if he had known Rorty, could have easily agreed that, "changing languages and other social practices may produce human beings of a sort that never before existed" (p. 7), such as the evolution of the vampire.

The novel offers a philosophical treatise by virtue of its speculative fiction genre which enables the author and the characters to examine inquiry and existence in imaginative ways not limited by definitive proofs. Finn's existence, the existence of "possibility" itself, depends not on being rationalized, but on being "poeticized," as happens through speculative fiction. The uses of vampire fiction toward this end serves as an opportunity for extending the complicated conversation of *currere*. Given that the vampire "never dies," one might assume the journey across and between the four stages could go on in perpetuity. What possibilities might lie beyond our current finitudes? Identifying vampires as the "monster of choice" (Gordon & Hollinger, 1997) for such inquiry, Hollinger (1997) writes:

> (I)t is the monster that used to be human; it is the undead that used to be alive; it is the monster that looks like us. For this reason, the figure of the vampire always has the potential to jeopardize conventional distinctions between human and monster, between life and death, between others and ourselves. We look into the mirror it provides and we see a version of ourselves. Or, more accurately, keeping in mind the orthodoxy that vampires cast no mirror reflections, we look into the mirror and see nothing but ourselves. (p. 201, emphases in original)

Finn's vampire evolution theory is representative of the "narrative-as-thought-experiment" explored by Gough (2010) who, quoting Donna Haraway, states:

> (H)ow closely fact and fiction can be related in her description of biology as a narrative practice: Biology is the fiction appropriate to objects called organisms; biology fashions the facts 'discovered' from organic beings. Organisms perform for the biologist,

who transforms that performance into a truth attested by disciplined experience; i.e., into a fact, the jointly accomplished deed or feat of the scientist and the organism ... Both the scientist and the organism are actors in a story-telling practice. (p. 4)

Similarly, Finn suggests that the evolution of vampires is something not "proven," but in fact exists (not only by his mere presence), but via the myths and beliefs we create and pass down through generations. He says:

What matters most isn't the science of it, it's what we believe, not what we can prove. And it's what we believe about vampires that has also evolved over time in various cultures. The evolutionary move wasn't just a biological one. It was also moral and spiritual, for lack of a better word. Vampires don't define what is right and wrong. You and I are both in Cultural Studies and can appreciate how ideas of good and bad, right and wrong, are relative to time and location. The moral code 200 years ago in America alone was vastly different than it is today. Whether or not vampires are good or evil is a matter of perspective. There is no universality in that sense. Just context. We evolve in tandem with human physical and cultural evolution. (*Bloods Will*, p. 56)

Campbell's transformations (in the hotel bathroom, and then later in the car crash) exemplify a similar evolution:

Looking now at this woman in the mirror whom she did not recognize, it occurred to Campbell as hard as a rush of wind punching her in the chest, that she had successfully made herself disappear. It was like suicide without the messy evidence of a dead body. Someone else was born in her stead. (*Bloods Will*, p. 154)

Here, characters become the site of our own inquiry into how we make sense of our own theories for living, and for dying (Daspit, 1999), holding us between "murder and suicide" (Daignault, 1983) in the process of knowledge construction.

Un-Death of the Author

A second layer of *currere* is perceived through the role of my own autobiography in shaping the story. Campbell and Finn both explore (process, cycle, examine, and return to) their intertwined life journeys as an example of how fictional characters can exemplify the four *currere* stages. In addition, the question behind all works of fiction is the influence of the authors own experiences in developing character, plot, and setting. How much of my story is "reflected" (despite the vampire motif) in this narrative? How much of my own *currere* journey was, in turn, influenced as a result of the process of writing the story?

A play on the idea of the "death of the author" (Barthes, 1977) for me was in creating a story about the undead; about something beyond death, such as happens with a vampire story. This is the "un-death of the author" (reading my own intentions into it while using a stylistic approach in the ending that frees the reader from anything about myself as the author). I concur with Barthes that, "To give a text an author and assign a single, corresponding interpretation to it 'is to impose a limit on that text'" (p. 142).

Choosing a love-story-in-crisis—between a mortal and supernatural character was intentional, as the options and issues illustrated in their relationship are distinctly different than they would have been had both characters been limited by mortality. The role of un-death provided the trope necessary to examine the more existential questions that confronts us mortals, and me in particular. I was wrestling with the same questions as Campbell not too long before I had the idea for the novel. I too have confronted the difficult question, "What if...?" that Campbell routinely asks herself throughout the story. In that sense, her struggles have been, to some degree, my own.

As I struggled in my own life with circumstance and challenges similar to those confronted by Campbell (and to another degree, Finn), the writing of this novel became a way for me to process a particular phase of my life that I had yet to deeply examine. *Currere* became a process which was necessary and compelling. Fictionalizing the moral dilemmas became a useful psychoanalytic tool. It was also the timing. I began the process of writing this story during the height of the Twilight Saga (2005) craze. I have a long-standing interest in vampires. The characters and story line of *Twilight* agitated both my pragmatic and feminist sensibilities (I found it unrealistic in a bad-story-line sort of way, even for fantasy fiction, and Bella was a feminist's nightmare). Additionally, once informed that the author, Stephanie Meyer, was a "stay at home" mother potty training her kids, I thought, "If she can do it, I can do it." So it became a challenge to myself, as much as it was a means for dealing with my own demons (pun intended).

And yet, Campbell is *not me*. I took the advice of my friend Sue Gilliam who in 2011 said, "Write what you know." This advice enabled me to craft descriptions and scenarios that "worked" because I had a familiarity with them, enabling me to draw from details that supported a compelling narrative arc. I wove into the story many of my own personal experiences. In the writing process, I was able to re-examine my memory of those events, to revise my history, and thus, alter my perception of future choices. The writing of the story became part of my *currere* (a process of examining my past in light of the present), and the reading of it may (I hope) will affect the *currere* of my readers.

As a process for (re)constructing what was, is, and what might be, fiction in the form of *currere*, (ficto-*currere*) brings us toward a process of writing which:

> (S)eparates us from what we know and yet it unites us more closely with what we know … distances us from the lifeworld, yet it also draws us more closely to the life-world … decontextualises thought from practice and yet it returns thought to praxis (or thoughtful action). (van Manen, 1990, pp. 127–128)

Finn's character has a different set of choices he must make. Faced with saving Jesse or saving Campbell, he chooses Campbell. She is alive because of his actions thirty five years before, and he is now what he is, because of that moment. In the form of *currere*, Finn was, "connecting 'present reality' with past and/or future possibilities" (Gough, 2003, p. 51) in his existence. In other words, the narrative is not merely shaped by my own autobiography. Rather, the relationship between fiction and *currere* lies with the fiction writing process itself which shapes my auto-biographic experience and using fiction to experiment with imaginative notions of possibility. The writing is therefore an attempt to, "attend to the historical nature of our experiences and understandings—to attend to the ways in which the past occurs simultaneously in the present, and deeply influences how we imagine the future" (Donald, 2012, p. 40).

Currere (as Campbell mentioned in the Introduction) in this story had become a "theory for living and a theory for dying" (Daspit, 1999); not only for Campbell, or for me … but for the reader, too. In this regard, I would have to agree with Barthes that the idea of reading a text in a singular meaning which is aligned with the intention of the author, has "died"…and "someone (thing) else was born in its stead" (as was Campbell).

The accounts of Campbell, Finn, and the others as a form of ficto-*currere* inter-act not only with my autobiography, but with the autobiographic narratives of my readers. How do the readers feel about Campbell and Finn's choices in light of their own histories/memories? What do we wish to see in literary character we read about? How much of our own lives, and our own values do we insert?

These questions become imperative in particular when analyzing the ending of the story.

On the Ending

The reading of fiction is a matter of interpretation (Barone, 2000; 2007). In earlier versions of the story (going back to 2011), I had written different endings. In the process of working toward publication, many individuals have read and reviewed the manuscript. Everyone has a different opinion of how the story should end. Their diversity of opinions is rendered in part based on one's own set of values or experiences. Therefore, a reviewer's own lived experiences influenced how they feel Campbell and Finn should conclude their fates. One of my readers, a middle-aged friend of mine who is currently benignly disengaged from her own marriage, demanded that Campbell be free to "live again" with Finn. In doing so, she can embody the reader's own wishful thinking. It is far more satisfying, even if perhaps unrealistic.

Likewise, notable writer, news reporter, and vampire scholar Margot Adler reviewed my earliest version of the book, in which the fate of Campbell was more open to reader interpretation. In that version, the final dream sequence left the reader having to decide for themselves if Campbell in fact died, or was being "changed." Adler assumed that Campbell had died before Finn could return. In one email exchange, she told me how, as a feminist, she felt outrage that I would "punish" (her words) Campbell for pursuing her true desires. I responded, "Oh. I see. So you think she died in the end." Adler replied with a long "Ohhhh!" as if she had discovered something she had not realized was possible.

The original ending had been devised to be deliberately vague so that the reader could read into what they wanted to have happen. It was a literary version of the dress (aka "The Dress") that went viral in 2015, in which some people saw it as a silver dress, while others saw it as blue, or pink, or black. It's not the text itself that is postmodern, but the reading/engagement that is a postmodern process. The plot and ending were intended to trouble notions of finitude, or singularity.

But after volumes of reader feedback, I concluded I had to commit to a clear ending. No one who read the book besides myself was satisfied with the idea that the ending was left indefinite. Most people seek finitude in their narratives. The original inspiration for the writing of this novel was in part a reaction to Twilight and other novels of its sort, in which beautiful young people (who, let's face it, really are immortal anyway), have the pretend "choice" between an immortal life with the person they love, or maintaining their "human soul." I'll take what's behind door #1. At that youthful period in one's life, who wouldn't? The predictable ending always concludes with a happy coupling.

But what about when you're half-way through life? What about confronting immortality and a love that involves far greater sacrifices, such as giving up the life (children and career) one has already chosen? In the real world, such troubled love affairs end badly more often than not. In reality, and in middle age, love and choice are far more complex issues. I wanted to tackle the harder questions. To have her "live happily ever after" with Finn belied that entire premise, then. But killing her off just sort of, well…sucked. I was trapped, just as Campbell was in the final car wreckage scene.

As it turns out, the novel wasn't done writing itself, and Campbell still had other options I, the author, hadn't considered. Along the way of editing the novel, one reviewer argued she did not find Campbell's love for Finn "believable." "Lust?" she said, "Desire?? Yes. But love? No."

I thought about re-writing some of my verbiage, to make Campbell's amorous feelings more "believable." It dawned on me that maybe, just maybe, Campbell didn't love Finn. Had I been wrong about my own character this whole time? I couldn't make my characters lie, and perhaps their true feelings were, in fact, being revealed. Campbell was after all, as stated in the Introduction, the subject writing herself. Maybe Campbell, in writing her story, realized she had been lying to herself. It's a rather "un-story-like" plot twist, but it is true-to-life. I know scores of people (myself included) who have thought, in the thralls of excitement and passion, that what they feel was love, only to wake up one day and realize that what they were feeling was something else disguised as love.

The turning point, if I had to name only one as most important, would be this: "It was at that moment that Campbell changed her mind" (*Blood's Will*, p. 224). It was why I foreshadowed what was to come by making that the first line of the story. But it isn't until the conclusion that we fully realize, and she fully realizes, *what* it is she is changing her mind about. In that moment, Campbell has a revelation. It is this moment, when she loses consciousness in the car crash, as in *currere*, where she "brackets" the past, present, and future all in one synthetic moment. The line in the opening and final chapters: "It was at that moment that Campbell changed her mind," echoes the idea that in bracketing, "what is, what was, and what can be, one is loosened from it, potentially more free of it, and hence more free to choose the present" (Pinar & Grumet [1976] in Slattery, 2018, p. 190).

Campbell was now telling me, the author, what to write. She needed more time. And she finally realized what she wanted. Time to be with Finn, time to develop a love for him, time to discover a world of possibilities for herself and her children. She was not giving up her life for love. She wanted time to do so many other things with her life. She did not have to sacrifice one for the other. It was a revelation neither she, nor I, had considered prior to that moment. In the so-called real world, where women every day, everywhere, are faced with sacrifice (and their own mortality) for the sakes of their families, careers, and communities, the dilemma is both deeply personal and one with which other women can identify.

Conclusion

The process of writing a work of auto-fiction, as well as the narrative of this story itself (the life-trajectories, and ultimate intertwined fates, of Finn and Campbell), both serve as *currere*, which embodies, "the middle passage, that passage in which movement is possible from the familiar to the unfamiliar, to estrangement, then to a transformed situation" (Pinar et al., 1995, p. 548). The story of Finn and Campbell is fictional. It is also built on (true) autobiographical experiences. The Introduction was designed to layer in more inter-subjectivity, troubling authorship and identity, by framing the novel as a fictional auto-fiction. Vampires are fictional. But they are also constructed based on truths about humans experience with mortality.

Both the writing process, and narrative product, remind me that, "We are not the stories we tell as much as we are the modes of relations our stories imply, modes of relations implied by what we delete as much as what we include" (Pinar, 1994, p. 218). The characters themselves question what is real and what is true, or morally "right." The role of the novel in inquiry (curriculum, narrative, and many others) is to implode boundaries, to invite possibility, and offer an example of writing our ficto-*currere*. As McDonough (2011) writes:

> Narrative can manipulate time, truth, and power. It enables the writer to define his own terms and to construct a story that reflects his priorities. It is a craft, with its own creative freedoms and limits. (p. 96)

Campbell's ultimate "un-demise" embodies the notion of this possibility beyond "freedoms and limits" … a "transformed situation"; her transformation signifying my own processes of fiction writing process, and *currere*.

The writing-as-process was a journey of *currere* circling itself from past, present, and future via the four-stage spiral process leads the individual toward untapped possibilities. Now, finally, I was able to write an "ending" that worked—for me, for my readers, and most importantly, for my characters. I remain undecided on who matters the most.

References

Barone, T. (2000). *Aesthetics, politics, and educational inquiry: Essays and examples*. New York, NY: Peter Lang.

Barone, T. (2007). A return to the gold standard? Questioning the future of narrative construction as educational research. *Qualitative Inquiry, 13*(4), 454–470.

Barthes, R. (1977). "Death of the author." *Image/Music/Text*. Trans Stephen Heath. New York, NY: Fontana Press. Retrieved from https://rosswolfe.files.wordpress.com/2015/04/roland-barthesimage-music-text.pdf

Daignault, J. (1983). Curriculum and action research: An artistic activity in a perverse way. *Journal of Curriculum Theorizing, 5*(3), 4–18.

Daspit, T. (1999). "Nothing died; it just got buried": Theory as exhumation, as duty dance. In M. Morris, M. Doll, & W. F. Pinar (Eds.), *How we work* (pp. 71–78). New York, NY: Peter Lang.

Donald, D. (2012). Forts, curriculum, and ethical relationality. In J. Rottmann (Ed.), *Reconsidering Canadian curriculum studies* (pp. 39–46). New York, NY: Palgrave Macmillan.

Gordon, J., & Hollinger, V. (1997). *Blood read: The vampire as metaphor in contemporary culture.* Philadelphia, PA: University of Pennsylvania Press.

Gough, N. (1994). Imagining an erroneous order: Understanding curriculum as phenomenological and deconstructed text. *Journal of Curriculum Studies, 26*(5), 553–568.

Gough, N. (2003). Intertextual turns in curriculum inquiry: Fictions, diffractions and deconstructions. Submitted in fulfilment of the requirements for the degree of Doctor of Philosophy, Deakin University, August 2003. Retrieved from https://www.researchgate.net/publication/265046137_Intertextual_turns_in_curriculum_inquiry_fictions_diffractions_and_deconstructions

Gough, N. (2010). Performing imaginative inquiry: Narrative experiments and rhizosemiotic play. In T. W. Nielsen, R. Fitzgerald, & M. Fettes (Eds.), *Imagination in educational theory and practice: A many-sided vision* (pp. 42–60). Newcastle upon Tyne: Cambridge Scholars Publishing.

Hollinger, V. (1997). Fantasies of absence: The postmodern vampire. In J. Gordon & V. Hollinger (Eds.), *Blood read: The vampire as metaphor in contemporary culture* (pp. 199–212). Philadelphia, PA: University of Pennsylvania Press.

McDonough, S. (2011). How to read autofiction. A thesis submitted to the faculty of Wesleyan University in partial fulfillment of the requirements for the Degree of Bachelor of Arts in English and French Studies with Departmental Honors in French Studies, April 2011. Retrieved from https://wesscholar.wesleyan.edu/etd_hon_theses/696/

Meyer, S. (2005). *Twilight.* New York, NY: Little, Brown and Co.

Pinar, W. F. (1975). *The method of currere.* Paper presented at American Educational Research Association, Washington, DC. Retrieved from https://files.eric.ed.gov/fulltext/ED104766.pdf

Pinar, W. F. (1994). *Autobiography, politics and sexuality: Essays in curriculum theory, 1972–1992.* New York, NY: Peter Lang.

Pinar, W. F. (2004). *What is curriculum theory?* New York, NY: Routledge.

Pinar, W. F., Reynolds, W.M., Slattery, P. & Taubman, P.M. (2005). Understanding curriculum as an autobiographical/biographical text. In W. F. Pinar, W. M. Reynolds, P. Slattery, & P. M. Taubman (Eds.) *Understanding curriculum: An introduction to the study of historical and contemporary curriculum discourses* (pp. 515-566). New York, NY: Peter Lang.

Pinar, W. F., & Grumet, M. (1976). *Toward a poor curriculum.* Dubuque, IA: Kendall/Hunt.

Rorty, R. (1989). *Contingency, irony, and solidarity.* Cambridge, MA: Cambridge University Press.

Slattery, P. (2018). "I am nature": Understanding the possibilities of *currere* in curriculum studies and aesthetics. *Journal of Curriculum and Pedagogy, 14*(3), 184–195.

van Manen, M. (1990). *Researching lived experience: Human science for an action sensitive pedagogy.* London, Ontario: SUNY Press.

Subject Index

A

addict, 68, 196
addiction, 12, 148, 173, 209
alcoholic, 28, 29, 131, 163, 173, 174, 238
alcoholism, 12, 14, 194
autobiography, 1–4, 244, 246
autofiction, 2–3

B

Bram Stoker's *Dracula*, 3–4, 52
Buffy the Vampire Slayer, 46, 191–2

C

cancer, 22, 48, 93, 100, 109, 128, 200, 205, 212, 213

choice, 9, 57, 64, 76, 85–86, 95, 97, 109–110, 157, 159, 162, 191, 195–196, 200–2, 209, 214, 218, 221, 224, 241–3, 245–7
conscious, 1–2, 49, 66, 70, 85, 97, 113, 141–2 152, 161, 200, 216, 220, 224, 232, 243
consciousness, 8–10, 30, 40, 53–54, 62, 116, 124, 167, 232, 237, 243, 248
Currere, 1–3, 5, 241–6, 248–9
culture, 11, 22, 56, 71, 107, 109, 114

D

death, 2–4, 24, 48, 55, 57, 61, 63, 76, 92, 95, 99, 102, 110, 126, 142, 148, 180, 194, 209, 212, 213–4, 215, 223, 243–4, 245–6
decollage, 2, 5
desire, 2, 53, 56, 66, 67, 71, 76, 91, 101, 105, 116, 138, 142, 146, 152–154, 167, 168, 172, 185, 242, 247

Name Index

OMPLICATED

A BOOK SERIES OF CURRICULUM STUDIES

Reframing the curricular challenge educators face after a decade of school deform, the books published in Peter Lang's Complicated Conversation Series testify to the ethical demands of our time, our place, our profession. What does it mean for us to teach now, in an era structured by political polarization, economic destabilization, and the prospect of climate catastrophe? Each of the books in the Complicated Conversation Series provides provocative paths, theoretical and practical, to a very different future. In this resounding series of scholarly and pedagogical interventions into the nightmare that is the present, we hear once again the sound of silence breaking, supporting us to rearticulate our pedagogical convictions in this time of terrorism, reframing curriculum as committed to the complicated conversation that is intercultural communication, self-understanding, and global justice.

The series editor is

Dr. William F. Pinar
Department of Curriculum Studies
2125 Main Mall
Faculty of Education
University of British Columbia
Vancouver, British Columbia V6T 1Z4
CANADA

To order other books in this series, please contact our Customer Service Department:

(800) 770-LANG (within the U.S.)
(212) 647-7706 (outside the U.S.)
(212) 647-7707 FAX

Or browse online by series:

www.peterlang.com